'No one owns this corner of the crime genre the way Lisa Gardner does' Lee Child

'Sharply written, tension-filled yarn full of twists readers are unlikely to see coming' *Daily Mail*

'Lisa Gardner's fast-paced novels twist when you expect a turn, and turn when you expect a twist. I couldn't recommend her more' Karin Slaughter

'Lisa Gardner – nerve-shattering suspense' Tami Hoag

'Lisa Gardner has always been one of my favourite writers, and this time she truly hits it out of the park' Tess Gerritsen

'For years, Lisa Gardner has been the best in the business' Harlan Coben

'Plots and characters that won't let you go. Lisa Gardner is at the top of her game!' Kathy Reichs

'Original, chilling and so gripping I had to remind myself to take a breath' Clare Mackintosh

'A first-class crime novel by a master of the thriller genre' David Baldacci

'A rocket-fuel-propelled thriller that will leave you breathless' Gregg Hu

'Tense and immersive, Gardner's latest is a sure bet both for readers drawn to gritty gumshoe fiction and for the growing legion of true-crime podcast fans' *Booklist*

'*Before She Disappeared* introduces what may be the most powerful sleuth of the decade, "ordinary" women driven to uncover the truth at any personal cost. There's only one thing to ask for by the time the book ends: please, please, a sequel and a series!' *New York Journal of Books*

'This book, the bestselling author's first stand-alone novel in twenty years, is a sharply written, tension-filled yarn full of twists readers are unlikely to see coming' *Associated Press*

'To read Lisa Gardner is to put yourself in the hands of a master storyteller. In *Before She Disappeared*, she gives us a crackling mystery, gritty atmosphere and an unforgettable heroine' Riley Sager, *New York Times* bestselling author of *Home Before Dark*

'*Before She Disappeared* is another sophisticated, gritty, unnerving read by Gardner that has all the twists, turns, suspense, in-depth character development and forensic analysis we've come to expect and love from all her previous novels' *What's Better Than Books*

'In this rare stand-alone, the prolific Gardner has come up with one of the most original characters in recent crime fiction, a woman readers can care about even while not being entirely sure of what to make of her' *Washington Post*

'I just read *Before She Disappeared* in a day and a half. It was that gripping. And Frankie is one of my new favourite characters. Highly recommended!' Shari Lapena, author of *The End of Her* and *The Couple Next Door*

BEFORE
SHE
DISAPPEARED

BEFORE
SHE
DISAPPEARED

LISA
GARDNER

PENGUIN BOOKS

PENGUIN BOOKS

UK | USA | Canada | Ireland | Australia
India | New Zealand | South Africa

Penguin Books is part of the Penguin Random House group of
companies whose addresses can be found at
global.penguinrandomhouse.com

First published in the United States of America
by Penguin Random House 2021
First published in the UK by Century 2021
Published in Penguin Books 2021
001

Typeset by Jouve (UK), Milton Keynes
Printed and bound in Great Britain by Clays Ltd, Elcograf S.p.A.

The authorised representative in the EEA is Penguin Random House
Ireland, Morrison Chambers, 32 Nassau Street, Dublin D02 YH68

A CIP catalogue record for this book is available
from the British Library

ISBN: 978–1–787–46437–7
ISBN: 978–1–787–46439–1 (export)

www.greenpenguin.co.uk

Penguin Random House is committed to a
sustainable future for our business, our readers
and our planet. This book is made from Forest
Stewardship Council® certified paper.

To all those who search,

so that others may find

BEFORE
SHE
DISAPPEARED

CHAPTER 1

*T*HE WATER FEELS LIKE A *cold caress against my face. I kick deeper down into the gloom, my long hair trailing behind me like a dark eel. I'm wearing clothes. Jeans, tennis shoes, a T-shirt topped with an open windbreaker that wings out and slows my descent. My clothing grows heavier and heavier till I can barely flutter my legs, work my arms.*

Why am I in clothes?

Wet suit.

Oxygen tank.

Thoughts drift through my mind but I can't quite grab them.

I must reach the bottom of the lake. Where the sunlight no longer penetrates and sinuous creatures lurk. I must find . . . I must do . . .

My lungs are now as heavy as my legs. A feeling of pressure builds in my chest.

An old Chevy truck. Dented, battered, with a cab roof sunbleached the color of a barely lit sky. This image appears in my mind and I seize it tightly. That's why I'm here, that's what I'm looking for. A sliver of silver in the lake's muck.

I started with sonar. Another random thought, but as I sink lower in the watery abyss, I can picture that, too. Me, piloting a small boat that I'd rented with my own money. Conducting long sweeps across the lake for two days straight, which was all I could afford, working a theory everyone else had dismissed. Until . . .

Where is my wet suit? My oxygen tank? Something's wrong. I need . . . I must . . .

I can't hold the thought. My lungs are burning. I feel them collapsing in my chest and the desire to inhale is overwhelming. A single gasp of dark, cloudy water. No longer fighting the lake, but becoming one with it. Then I won't have to swim anymore. I will plummet to the bottom, and if my theory is right, I will join my target as yet another lost soul never to be seen again.

Old truck. Cab roof sun-bleached the color of a barely lit sky. Remember. Focus. Find it.

Is that a glimpse of silver I see over there, partially hidden by a dense wall of waving grasses?

I try to head in that direction but get tangled in my flapping windbreaker. I pause, treading my legs frantically while trying to free my arms from my jacket's clinging grip.

Chest, constricting tighter.

Didn't I have an oxygen tank?

Wasn't I wearing a wet suit?

Something is so very wrong. I need to hold the thought, but the lake is winning and my chest hurts and my limbs have grown tired.

The water is soft against my cheek. It calls to me, and I feel myself answer.

My legs slow. My arms drift up. I succumb to the weight of my clothes, the lead in my chest. I start to sink faster. Down, down, down.

I close my eyes and let go.

Paul always said I fought too much. I made things too hard. Even his love for me. But of course, I didn't listen.

Now, a curious warmth fills my veins. The lake isn't dark and gloomy after all. It's a sanctuary, embracing me like a lover and promising to never let go.

Then . . .

Not a spot of silver. Not the roof of an old, battered truck that was already a hundred thousand miles beyond its best days. Instead, I spy a gouge of black appearing, then disappearing amid a field of murky green. I wait for the lake grasses to ripple left, then I see it again, a dark stripe, then another, and another. Four identical shapes resting at the bottom of the lake.

Tires. I'm looking at four tires. If I weren't so damn tired, I'd giggle hysterically.

The sonar had told the truth. It had sent back a grainy image of an object of approximately the right size and shape resting at the bottom of the deep lake. It just hadn't occurred to me that said object might be upside down.

Pushing through my lethargy now, urgency sparking one last surge of determination. They'd told me I was wrong. They'd scoffed, the locals coming out to watch with rolling eyes as I'd awkwardly unloaded a boat I had no idea how to captain. They called me crazy to my face, probably muttered worse behind my back. But now . . .

Move. Find. Swim. Before the lake wins the battle.

Wet suit. The words flutter through the back of my mind. Oxygen tank. This is wrong. Wrong, wrong, wrong. But in my befuddled state, I can't make it right.

I push myself forward, fighting the water, fighting oxygen deprivation. They're right: I am crazy. And wild and stubborn and reckless.

But I'm not broken. At least, not yet.

I reach the first tire. Grab onto the slimy rubber to get my bearings. Quick now, not much time left. Rear tire. I crab my way along the algae-covered frame till I finally reach the front cab.

Then I simply stare.

Lani Whitehorse. Twenty-two years old. Waitress, daughter, mother of a three-year-old. A woman with an already long history of bad taste in men.

She disappeared eighteen months ago. Runaway, the locals decided. Never, her mother declared.

And now she was found, trapped at the bottom of the lake that loomed next to the hairpin turn she drove each night after the end of her two A.M. bartending shift. Just as I had theorized while poring over months of interviews, maps, and extremely thin police reports.

Had Lani misjudged the corner she'd driven so many times before? Startled at a crossing deer? Or simply nodded off at the wheel, exhausted by a life that took too much out of her?

I can't answer all the questions.

But I can give her mother, her daughter, this.

Lani dangles upside down, her face lost inside the floating halo of her jet-black hair, her body still belted into the cab she'd climbed into eighteen months ago.

My lungs are no longer burning. My clothes are no longer heavy. I feel only reverence as I curl my fingers around the door handle and pull.

The door opens easily.

Except . . . doors can't open underwater. Wet suit. Oxygen tank. What is wrong, what is wrong . . . My brain belatedly sounds the alarm: Danger! Think, think, think! Except I can't, I can't, I can't.

I am inhaling now. Breathing in the lake. Welcoming it inside my lungs. I have become one with it, or it has become one with me.

As Lani Whitehorse turns her head.

She stares at me with her empty eye sockets, gaping mouth, skeletal face.

"Too late," she tells me. "Too late."

Then her bony arm thrusts out, snatches my wrist.

I kick, try to pull back. But I've lost my grip on the door handle. I have no leverage. My air is gone and I'm nothing but lake water and weedy grasses.

She pulls me into the truck cab with unbelievable strength.

One last scream. I watch it emerge as an air bubble that floats up, up, up. All that is left of me.

Lani Whitehorse slams the door shut.

And I join her forever in the gloom.

RUMBLE. SCREECH. A sudden booming announcement: "South Station, next stop!"

I jerk awake as the train lurches to a halt, blinking and looking down at my perfectly dry clothes.

A dream. Nightmare. Something. Not the first or the last in my line of work. It leaves me with a film of dread as I grab my bags and follow the rest of the passengers off the train.

I'd found Lani Whitehorse three weeks ago, locked in her vehicle at the bottom of a lake. After months of intensive research on an Indian reservation where my presence was never welcomed by the locals nor wanted by the tribal police. But I'd stumbled upon the case online and been moved by her mother's steadfast assurance that Lani would never leave her own daughter. Lani might be a screw-up with horrible taste in men, but she was still a mom. Why people assumed those things couldn't go together, I'll never know.

So I'd moved to the area, became a bartender at Lani's former workplace, and started my own investigation.

Lani's mom hugged me the day the police finally dragged the Chevy truck out of the lake in a deluge of muck and horror. Wailing, crying relief as Lani was finally brought home. I waited around for the funeral, standing outside the small crowd of mourners, as proving yourself right almost always means proving someone else wrong and therefore rarely wins you many friends.

I did what I needed to do. Then I headed to the local library, where I booted up the computer and returned to the national chat rooms where family members, concerned neighbors, and crazy people like me compare notes on various missing persons cases. There are so many. Too many, sometimes, for local resources. So, more and more, people like me have been stepping into the vacuum.

I read. I posted a few questions. And in a matter of hours, I knew where I was headed next.

Like I said, so many missing persons cases. Too many.

Which has brought me here, to Boston, a city I've never visited. I have no idea where I am or what I'm doing, but that's hardly new. Now, I follow the mass of humanity hustling across the train platform to the exit signs, all of my worldly possessions packed into a single piece of luggage rolling behind me. Once I had a house, a car, a white picket fence. But time erodes and now . . .

Let's just say I've learned to travel light.

Out on the bright sidewalk, I stop, blink, then shutter my eyes completely. Walking straight out into downtown Boston feels like an assault on the senses. People, shrieking horns, crosswalks. The stench of diesel fuel, fried fish, harbor brine. I've forgotten the crushing feel of the concrete jungle, even one with a glittering waterfront.

I work on taking a deep, shuddering breath. This is my new home until I complete my mission. I exhale slowly. Then I open my eyes and square my shoulders. The last of my nightmare and travel daze falls away. I'm ready to get to it, which is good given the flood of annoyed pedestrians shoving past me.

From my worn leather messenger bag, I withdraw the file filled with papers I printed out days ago. It includes a map of Boston, articles on city demographics, and a photo of a shyly smiling girl with smooth dark skin, gorgeous brown eyes, and deep black hair cascading down in a mass of carefully groomed ringlets. Fifteen at the time of her disappearance. Sixteen now.

Meet Angelique Lovelie Badeau. Angel to her friends. LiLi to her family.

Angelique disappeared eleven months ago from Mattapan, Boston. Walked out of her school on a Friday afternoon in November and then . . . Poof. No sightings. No leads. No breaks in the case. For eleven whole months.

Bostonians will tell you that Mattapan is that kind of neighborhood. Rough. Poor. Filled with hardworking souls, of course, and a rich cultural heritage thanks to having the country's largest Haitian population outside of Florida. But also a hotbed of gang activity and violent crime. If you want to get shot or stabbed, Murderpan, as the locals call it, is the neighborhood for it. Which is where I now plan to rent a place, find a job, and question the neighbors.

And I hope, through sheer guts, determination, and blind luck, I will find a girl the rest of the world seems to have forgotten already.

I'm not a police officer.

I'm not a private investigator.

I have no special skills or training.

I'm only me. An average, middle-aged white woman with more regrets than belongings, more sad stories than happy ones.

My name is Frankie Elkin and finding missing people—particularly minorities—is what I do. When the police have given up, when the public no longer remembers, when the media has never bothered to care, I start looking. For no money, no recognition, and most of the time, no help. Why do I do what I do?

So many of our children have vanished. Too many will never be found, often based solely on the color of their skin. Maybe the question shouldn't be why am I doing this, but why isn't everyone looking?

Angelique Lovelie Badeau deserves to come home.

I consult my map one last time. I need to find the commuter rail to Morton Street. The map of Boston's T system shows it as a purple line, which of course matches nothing that I can see. I spin around here. I spin around there. Then realize: I shouldn't have left South Station. Back I head.

I don't mind being lost. Or confused. Or even scared.

All these years later, I'm used to it.

Paul warned me I would push away everyone I loved, that I would end up putting myself in harm's way, that I didn't do this to save others but to punish myself.

Paul was always a very smart man.

I spot the giant map for the MBTA system, follow the purple line with my finger and spot my target. Once more on track, I head to Murderpan.

CHAPTER 2

IT'S FOUR P.M. BY THE time I reach my first location. *Stoney's*, the sign announces out front. The red backdrop of the two-story building is peeling, with the white lettering more of a suggestion than a statement. In other words, it matches its squat, derelict neighbors jammed shoulder to shoulder down both sides of the block. The sidewalk is broader than I expected and nearly empty this time of day. After some of the articles I've read, I would have expected to see gangs and dealers loitering in every doorway. In fact, I see random people bustling about with their everyday concerns, most of whom eye me, the lone white woman, with curiosity.

I'm grateful to get off the street, pushing open the door and wheeling my bag into the dimly lit interior. For most of my adult life, I've worked as a bartender. Easy job for a transplant to get, and for the past ten years a good way to pick up local intel. Plus, I like the work. Bars are inevitably filled with the lonely and the loners. Feels like home.

Now, I register the stale scent of cigarette smoke sunk deep into the pores of the old building. Before me is a cluster of round wooden tables with mismatched chairs. Four booths line the wall to my right, the red vinyl cushions cracked but still putting up a fight. Three more booths to the left in much the same condition.

I make out half a dozen customers. All Black men. Sitting randomly around the small space, where their attention has been focused on the drinks in front of them. Now each one raises his head long enough to regard me. If the locals on the street regarded me with curiosity, here I get blatant suspicion.

In this neighborhood, I'm the minority. Then again, same with the past year, and the year before that, and the year before that. I'm used to the looks, though that doesn't mean it's always easy to take.

At least midday drunks have more serious matters to tend to. One by one, they return to their individual miseries, which leaves me with the dark wood bar, straight ahead, where a lone Black man stands, drying a tray of beer glasses one by one.

I head for him.

A trim figure, he sports gray hair and a groomed salt-and-pepper beard. His dark eyes are lined heavily and he has about him the air of a man who's seen it all and lived to tell the tale.

"Stoney," I guess.

"You lost?" He sets down one tall glass, picks up another. He wears a white apron tied around his waist and wields the dishtowel with practiced dexterity. Definitely the owner, and a long-term tavern operator at that.

"I'm here about the bartending position."

"No." He grabs the next glass.

I park my suitcase next to the bar, take a seat on a stool. His answer doesn't surprise me. Most of my conversations start this way.

"Twenty years of experience," I tell him. "Plus I have no problems cleaning, brewing coffee, or working a fryolator." Fried food is the natural partner to booze—and this close to the kitchen, the air is thick with grease. Fried chicken, fried potatoes—maybe even fried plantains, given the Haitian community.

"No," he says again.

I nod. There's a second towel. I pick it up, select the wet glass nearest to me, and start drying.

Stoney scowls at me but doesn't stop me. No business owner argues with free labor.

We both dry in silence. I like the work. The rhythmic feel of twisting a glass, buffing it with the towel. Even dry, the top lip of the glasses bears a faint white line. Years of beer foam, human lips. They are clean, though. Which makes me partial to Stoney and his establishment. Plus, he has a room above the bar to let, at a price I can almost afford. I found it posted on a community board.

"I don't drink," I offer. The first tray of glasses is done. Stoney removes it from the bar. Lifts a second tray of wet half glasses.

"Teetotaler?" Stoney asks.

"No."

"Here to save us?"

"You're assuming I've been saved."

He grunts at that. We both resume drying. From what I've dug up, a significant portion of Mattapan's population, being from the Caribbean, speaks French, French Creole, patois, et cetera. But I hear none of that in Stoney's voice. He has the clipped tones of most New Englanders. Maybe he's lived in Boston his entire life or moved here from New York or Philadelphia to open his own place. It's always dangerous to make assumptions, and yet nearly impossible not to.

"Friend of Bill's," I volunteer after we finish the whiskey glasses and that tray is replaced with dozens of shot glasses. We both get back to work. Quick, brisk, thoughtless. The perfect meditative exercise.

Stoney doesn't answer. He dries faster than me, but not by much.

"Water glasses?" I ask when the shot glasses are done.

He raises a brow. So, not an establishment big on nonalcoholic beverages. Good to know.

"You have a room to rent," I continue, folding my arms on the heavily lacquered bar.

"Go home."

"Don't have one. So this is what I'm thinking. I work for you four nights a week, three P.M. to closing, in return for free board."

Stoney is a man who can communicate volumes with a single eyebrow.

"You're worried that I'm white," I fill in for him. "Or that I'm female. Or both. You think I can't handle myself."

"I'm a local business. Frequented by locals. You're not local."

I make a show of twisting around on the barstool. "Funny, because I don't see too many locals lined up for the open position. And you've been advertising for two weeks. Room's been vacant even longer than that, which must mean something given how desperate everyone around here is for housing." I regard him curiously. "Did someone die up there or something?"

He shakes his head. With no more glasses to dry, he crosses his arms over his chest and looks me straight on. He still doesn't say a word.

"I work hard." I tick off a finger. "I'm on time, especially because I'm going to be living upstairs, and I won't siphon your booze. I pour fast, I know how to change out a keg, and I'm an excellent listener. Everyone likes a good listener."

"They won't like you."

"Neither did you, but you're coming around. Give me a month. By then, no one will notice my white skin or superior gender. I'll just be another fixture behind the bar."

He raises another eyebrow but doesn't say no. Finally: "Why are you here? Plenty of other neighborhoods in Boston."

"I have something to do here."

He stares at me again.

I hold his gaze. I like Stoney. A survivor. He's my kind of person—and sooner or later, he'll come to see the same about me.

"Five nights a week," he says. "Three P.M. to close."

"Rent includes utilities," I counter. "One free meal a day. I keep my tips."

He regards me a moment longer, then abruptly extends his hand. We shake. Definitely my kind of person.

"Room comes with a roommate," Stoney informs me.

"That wasn't in the ad."

"Now you know."

"Male or female?"

"Feline."

"The room comes with a cat? And that's why no one will take it?"

For the first time, Stoney smiles. It wrinkles his salt-and-pepper beard, softens his weathered face. "You haven't met the cat yet."

STONEY LEADS ME upstairs. At first glance, the tiny, single-room setup is exactly what I'd expect from an apartment in an over-crowded, economically depressed neighborhood. Double bed shoved against the far wall. Lone nightstand to one side, tightly drawn black curtains on the other. A metal rod bolted to the wall serves as a closet opposite the bed, while next to the front door is a small kitchenette with a European-size fridge and a microwave. No oven, but a coffeemaker and a hot pot, which suits me fine. On the other side of the door is a plain white curtain wrapped around a curved rod attached to the ceiling, much like a hospital room setup. A quick look behind the curtain reveals a bathroom with the world's skinniest standing shower and a minuscule mounted sink. Again, City Living 101. Not much space or privacy, but priced right.

Not to mention, the room is unerringly clean, while the bed is topped with a surprising colorful handmade quilt. Again, there's more to Stoney then meets the eye.

I glance around. "Where's my roommate?"

"She's not social."

"Does she have a name?"

"Piper."

"And this is her room?"

He shrugs. "Suits her."

I'm still not sure what to make of this. In theory I like cats. But Stoney's words of warning have made me cautious. I wheel my bag to the center of the creaking old floor, then pause.

I bend over, carefully lift the quilt, and peer under the bed.

It takes me a moment, then I spy a pair of glowing green eyes regarding me balefully from the far corner. It's too dark to make out her build or coloring. I have more an impression of pure hostility.

"Piper," I acknowledge.

She flattens her ears and growls low in her throat, followed by a distinct hiss. I take the hint, drop the quilt.

"Okay then."

Stoney is already turning back to the hallway.

"Hang on. Cat food, water, litter box, what do I need to know?"

"Nothing. Piper takes care of herself. She's not stupid. Just hates people."

"How long has she lived here?"

Stoney scratches his beard. "Long enough."

"You took her in off the street?"

"She came in off the street." Stoney gestures to the open door, which I now realize has a small pet-sized hole cut out. "Piper heads downstairs at night, patrols for mice. She's got food, water, and litter box in the basement. Nothing for you to worry about."

"Um, we didn't talk start day." I don't know why, but I suddenly feel a bit panicky. Not about being alone with a cat. So then about being alone? Except I'm alone all the time. It's my way of life. No reason to balk at it now.

"Tomorrow," he says. "Oh, door lock isn't so great. Got a computer in that bag, I'd hide it before you leave each day."

I nod.

"Hot water comes and goes. Mostly goes."

"Okay."

"No smoking."

"I don't."

"No guns."

"I don't."

"And in the event of trouble?"

"I rely on my charming personality."

He grunts. "I keep a baseball bat behind the bar. In the event your wit fails."

"Good to know."

Final nod, then he's clearly ready to get back to his customers down below. Leaving me and the feral cat.

He surprises me by turning back at the last minute. "Come on down when you're ready and help yourself to some food. I don't have time to wait on a nonpaying customer, but you can make yourself a sandwich. I keep all the fixings on hand."

It's the most words he's spoken to me. I wonder if Piper received the same offer when she showed up. Maybe Stoney has a thing for strays. Or maybe, like most bartenders, he recognizes a lost soul when he sees one.

I nod my thanks. He leaves. I remain standing in the middle of my new home. For weeks? Months? I have no idea. Beginning is the hardest part. And though I've done this before, I can't help but feel overwhelmed.

Which makes the dark beast of my addiction stir in my belly, opening a single eye to survey the opportunity. While I'm down-stairs making a sandwich, I could pour a beer. Or even better, vodka, tequila, whiskey straight up. Something potent and searing that would turn my muscles into liquid and chase all my fears away.

I think of Paul. I feel the familiar pain squeezing my chest. Deep breath in, deep breath out.

Then, I leave my suitcase to the mercy of a feral cat and, as long as it's still light out, head back to the street, where I consult my printed map again, and the red X that marks Angelique's aunt's house.

I resume walking, aware once more of all the eyes falling upon me, and the deepening chill whispering up my neck. I keep my head up, my shoulders back. I smile in greeting. I tell myself I'm strong enough.

And I pray this time that I really am.

CHAPTER 3

ALL I KNOW ABOUT THIS area is what I looked up prior to arrival. Mattapan is densely populated, more than thirty-five thousand people crammed into apartments, city housing, and so-called triple-deckers. The majority of the people are immigrants, which adds splashes of ethnic food and specialty hair salons. There are small pockets of Latin and Asian Americans, as well as an even smaller cluster of Caucasians.

Google Earth revealed some shocks of green space amid the mass of overcrowded streets—Harambee Park, the Franklin Park Zoo, and the Boston Nature Center. Not being accustomed to city life, I'd probably be more comfortable in those areas, but I can barely afford a single room with a hostile cat over a bar. An apartment with a view is out of the question.

My primary concern is the area's crime stats. Half a dozen stabbings a week, not to mention the monthly shootings and annual homicide rate. Gang activity mostly, but predators are predators, and as a middle-aged woman I'm not particularly intimidating.

The best I can do, as I start navigating the confusing mishmash of city streets, is utilize basic personal safety rules. One, I don't carry anything of value. No smartphone, no electronics, no purse. I have the world's stupidest Tracfone, which is one of the reasons I'm old-school when it comes to research and navigation. In lieu of a purse, I have my driver's license and a couple of bills jammed deep into my front pocket. Some kid wants to demand all my worldly goods, have it. You can't take from someone things she gave up a long time ago.

Tucked into my jacket pocket is a red rape whistle, because there are worse things than muggings. I also wear stainless-steel "tactical clips" in my hair. Each boasts tiny saw teeth, a wrench, a ruler, and a minuscule screwdriver for the low, low price of $3.99. I have no idea if hair clips can really be that effective and hope I never have to find out.

Finally, I have my necklace, a plain gold cross, picked up at a pawn shop years ago and now worn tucked under my shirt. Again, sometimes the simplest things remain the best deterrent.

Another trick—attach myself to others when possible. Predators prefer the lone game, so don't look too lonely.

This time of evening, that strategy is easy to accomplish. Five P.M., buses are screeching to a stop, disgorging piles of weary locals grateful to be heading home. The sun is still out but lower in the sky, a fall breeze starting to kick up, carrying with it the stench of diesel, grime, and human sweat.

I catch the occasional whiff of fried food and savory spices. My stomach rumbles again. I've never eaten Haitian food. Judging by the smell, however, I'm looking forward to trying it.

For now, I keep hoofing it. I don't really understand Boston's mass transit yet and I have at least a mile to cover, from Stoney's place to the side street where Angelique's aunt lives. Everywhere I look are tired buildings and worn faces. Bit by bit, I start to parse it out. The groups of teens with thousand-yard stares, peering out sullenly from beneath their hooded sweatshirts. The wide streets jammed with brake lights and blaring horns. Intermittent booms of music, from reggae to rap, blasting out of various vehicles. A crowd of older Black men, probably returning from a local construction project given the dust on their clothes, laugh and clap one another on the back, grateful for the end of the workday.

Ahead of me, another city bus screeches to a halt. This time a group of Black women in pink hospital scrubs and bright-colored headscarves disembark. Local healthcare workers. I fall in step behind the last member of the line as they stream forward into the night. The woman directly in front of me notices the slowing of my gait as I slide in behind her. She nods once in acknowledgment of my presence. I'm no threat to her, and she clearly recognizes my strategy. Safety in numbers.

I think of this often, drifting from community to community, always being the stranger and never the neighbor. People all over really are the same. They want to fall in love. They're glad to survive each day. They pray their children will have a better life than they did. These truths bind us. At least I like to think so.

The sun sinks lower but the street grows brighter: more car lights, shop lights, streetlamps. My lead companion peels off to the right with a parting nod. I return the gesture, plodding forward on my own.

At the end of the next block, I have to pull out my printed map. I hate doing that in the open, as it marks me as lost, and even now I can feel gazes boring into my back.

I wasn't lying to Stoney when I told him all I had to rely on was my quick wit. Which, interestingly enough, can be very useful when dealing with people above the age of twenty-five, but completely irrelevant to anyone younger.

I didn't grow up in a city. Nor as a young girl did I ever picture myself doing this kind of work. I was raised in a small town in Northern California. My father was a drunk. As an adult looking back, I came to recognize his addiction as I learned to fight my own. But for most of my childhood, I associated my father with silly adventures and sloppy smiles, as well as the smell of beer.

My mother was the intense one. Worked two jobs, the first as a secretary in a law firm, the second doing the books for mom-and-pop businesses. I don't remember her smiling, or playing, or even stopping long enough to give me a hug. She got up early and worked late, and in her brief moments at home, mostly gritted her teeth at the dishes my father hadn't done, the meals that hadn't been cooked, the dirty clothes that hadn't been washed.

I think my father loved my mother for her fierceness, and she loved him for his sense of fun. Until they didn't.

I ran around outside a lot. Through woods and scrub brush and winding streams. In my childhood we didn't have Amber Alerts or stranger danger. Even seven-year-olds felt free to dash out their front doors and ride their bikes for miles. I had friends who were latchkey by nine because why not? We didn't worry. We just were.

I don't think any of us realized that was a magical moment future kids would never get to experience. Certainly, we didn't understand what bad things lurked out there. Until one of my classmates went missing in high school. Then another girl from the town over. And four more girls quickly after that.

The police caught the killer when I was twenty-five. By then I'd moved down to L.A. with no real plan other than to get the hell out of small-town life and party like a rock star. Turned out I was damn good at the partying part. And pretty enough for others to buy my drinks, my meals, maybe even a new dress or two.

I'd like to say those were my free spirit days, but the truth is, I don't really remember them. It was a rush of drugs and booze and sex, and that I'm alive at all . . .

Paul. He saved me. At least until I grew strong enough to save myself.

House, white picket fence, suburban bliss.

Funny, the things you can grow up not wanting, then suddenly crave with single-minded obsession.

Funnier still, the things you can end up having only to realize you'd been right the first time.

But I loved Paul. I still love him. Even now.

I arrive at my targeted block, which peels off the main road in a sharp diagonal. Definitely no grid system here. Instead, the streets come together, then explode in a crazy hub-and-spoke system. This is not going to be one of those places I learn to navigate quickly or easily. My best guess, weeks from now I'll still feel exactly as dazed and confused as I do at this moment. Maybe Boston neighborhoods aren't meant to be understood. You either know where you are, or you don't. I definitely don't.

Now, the rows of squat, brick commercial buildings are replaced by a wall of triple-deckers, wedged shoulder to shoulder like a line of grumpy old men. I make out chain-link fences, dirt patch yards, and sagging front steps that delineate each residence. Some have new vinyl siding in shades of pale blue and butter yellow. Others appear one strong breeze from total collapse. Mattapan has some of the last affordable housing in the city for a reason.

Fifth home down the block, with bay windows and a sturdier-looking front porch. This is it. I double check the house number to be sure, then note the light glowing from the second-floor apartment that is listed as belonging to Angelique Badeau's aunt.

This is the moment it becomes real. Where I go from being well-intentioned to being fully committed. I don't know what will happen next. A tentative welcome, a harsh refusal. A wailing torrent of desperate grief, or steely-eyed suspicion. I've experienced it all, and it never gets any less nerve-racking.

From here on out, my job is to listen, accept, adapt.

And hope, really, truly hope, they don't hate me too much.

Lani Whitehorse's grandmother hugged me in the end, though the tribal council pointedly gave me their backs.

I remind myself I'm good at what I do.

I swear to myself that I will make a difference.

I think, uneasily, that like any addict, lying is what I do best.

I head up the front steps.

ON THE FRONT porch, I encounter six buzzers, meaning the triple-decker hasn't been carved up only by level, but within each floor as well. Beneath the buzzers is a line of black-painted mailboxes, each one locked tight. It's a simple but efficient system for the apartment dwellers. I try the front door just in case but am not surprised to find it bolted tight. Next, I press the first few ringers, prepared to announce myself as delivery and see if I can get lucky, but no one answers.

Which leaves me with the direct approach. I hit 2B. After a moment, a male voice, younger, higher, answers. "Yeah?"

"I'm looking for Guerline Violette."

"She know you?"

"I'm here regarding Angelique."

Pause. Angelique has a younger brother, Emmanuel, also a teen.

I would guess this is him, particularly as his tone is already defensive with an edge of sullen. He sounds like someone whose been subjected to too many experts and well-wishers and been disappointed by all of them.

"You a reporter?" he demands now.

"No."

"Cop?"

"No."

"My aunt's busy."

"I'm here to help."

"We heard that before." I can practically feel the eye roll across the intercom. Definitely a teen.

"My time is free and I'm experienced."

"Whatdya mean?"

"If I can talk to Guerline, I'd be happy to explain in person."

Another pause. Then a female voice takes over the intercom.

"Who are you and why are you bothering us?" Guerline's voice ripples with hints of sea and sand. Her niece and nephew immigrated to Boston as young children a decade ago, along with tens of thousands of other Haitians after Port-au-Prince was nearly flattened by an earthquake. Emmanuel has grown up in Boston and sounds it. But his aunt has retained the music of her native island.

"My name is Frankie Elkin. I'm an expert in missing persons. I've been following your niece's disappearance and I believe I can help."

"You are a reporter, yes?"

"No, ma'am. I don't work for any news agencies or reporting outlets. My only interest is finding Angelique and bringing her home."

"Why?"

The question is not defensive, but quiet. It tears at me, the amount of weariness in that single word.

I wish I had an answer for her. Something simple like Because, or poignant, such as Every child deserves to be found, or defiant, like Why not? But the truth is, she's probably heard it all by now. A whole torrent of words and reasons. Instead of being given the one thing she wants most: answers.

The silence grows. I should attempt some line of argument, but nothing persuasive comes to mind. Then, a noise from inside the building. Stairs creaking as a light weight rapidly descends. Another occupant or . . .

The click of the bolt lock snapping back. The front door cracks open and I find myself face to face with a Haitian teenager. Tall, gangly, close-cropped dark hair and deep brown eyes a perfect match with his sister's. He takes a second to look me over through the slit of the open door, features as wary now as his voice had been earlier.

He turns, already dropping hold of the door. It's up to me to grab the edge, push through, and follow him up ancient wooden stairs to the second floor.

GUERLINE VIOLETTE STANDS in the middle of a cramped living room, her arms crossed over her formidable figure. I peg her age somewhere between forty and fifty, but her smooth, dark skin and classic features make it hard to determine. She's clad in purple scrubs seamed with orange trim and has bright green Crocs on her feet. She's a daunting woman, especially with her hair pulled into a thick bun on top of her head, calling attention to her high cheekbones and handsome brow. But upon closer inspection I spy the purple smudges of long nights and fearful days that bruise her eyes. She watches my approach with a mix of suspicion and dread. I can't say that I blame her.

Emmanuel closes the door behind me, then comes over to stand awkwardly by his aunt. At thirteen, he's already my height, with the slender build of a kid who's recently undergone a growth spurt. In contrast to his aunt's colorful ensemble, Emmanuel is wearing the official uniform of teen males everywhere—sneaks, jeans, and a worn T-shirt. He looks young, clean-cut, and determined. The man in the family, even if it scares him. These are the kind of cases that break my heart.

Belatedly I stick out my hand. Guerline clasps it briefly, more out of politeness than welcome. The one-bedroom apartment houses three people and looks it. Guerline gestures to the cramped family room that clearly serves as a common room, bedroom, and dining room all rolled into one. What the room lacks in space it makes up for in color. Yellow walls, an overstuffed red velvet chair, a sofa piled with bright-patterned sleeping quilts, all bleeding into turquoise kitchen cabinets to the right.

I go with the red chair, positioned in front of the window. On the wall beside me is a high wooden shelf bearing photos of gold-framed saints, some religious icons, and a single dangling rosary. Below it, running along first the tall bureau, then the long cabinet holding the TV, is a riot of green houseplants, adding to the room's ambience. Between a pocket of green leaves, I spy a discreet cluster of white candles, arranged in a semicircle with a bowl of water and fresh-cut flowers before them. Angelique's framed photo, the same shyly smiling picture used in the missing persons flyers, is positioned next to candles.

Guerline catches me eyeing the makeshift altar, and I quickly look away. According to what I've read, many Haitians practice a mix of Catholicism and voodoo, but it's not something I know much about.

I turn my attention to the other knickknacks littering the room. A clear baby food jar filled with sand—a touch of Guerline's island home? Then I spot the requisite school photo of Emmanuel, his teeth a flash of white. Next to it a smaller picture of an adult female, the colors faded, the background hard to make out. The woman's smile is familiar, however. If I had to guess—Emmanuel and Angelique's mother, who still lives in Haiti. Finally, I spot a photo of a graying couple, framed by palm trees. Guerline and her sister's parents, maybe taken outside their home before the earthquake destroyed it.

"You say you can help, yes?" Guerline states, moving to the sofa, her hand resting on the pile of quilts. Emmanuel follows closely behind. He is obviously protective of his aunt. I wonder if he was protective of his older sister, too, or if it was her disappearance that made him realize the need to guard his loved ones.

"My name is Frankie Elkin," I repeat for both of them. "I travel all around the country, handling cases just like your niece's."

Guerline frowns, trying to absorb what I said.

"You are a private investigator?" she asks at last in her French-lilted English.

"I am not a licensed PI. I'm a volunteer." I'm never sure how to explain this part. "There are actually quite a few people like me, laypersons who are dedicated to assisting in missing persons investigations. From search dog handlers to pilots to boots on the ground. There are organizations, missing persons boards where we follow cases like your niece's."

Guerline is frowning. "My Angelique . . . She is on some message board?"

"On the internet, *matant*," Emmanuel murmurs at her shoulder. "She's talking about reading details on the internet."

I nod. "According to reports, Angelique left school Friday, November fifth. At three fifteen P.M. No one has seen her since."

"The police looked and looked," Guerline assures me, her fingers twisting absently. "Ricardo, our community officer. He promised me they would bring my Angel home. But now, it has been many months since there has been any news."

"They found her backpack."

"Yes. Under a bush on school grounds."

"The backpack contained her cell phone, her school books, and the outfit she'd worn to school that day?"

Guerline nods. I glance at Emmanuel, wondering if he knew his sister had packed a change of clothes, that she must have been planning something that Friday afternoon. But his face remains perfectly expressionless.

"No sign of violence?" I prod, because not all details are made public.

Guerline shakes her head. "Nothing . . . They found nothing. Even on her phone . . . Ricardo tells me they can read the texts, see the phone calls. But there is nothing saying where she was going, what she might be doing. Her friends, they swear they don't know anything. LiLi went to school. Then she was to come home, start dinner. Except . . ."

Guerline looks as lost now as she must have felt eleven months ago. Her hands tremble. She clasps them tight, a model of grace, even in her grief.

"Did Angelique have close friends?" I push.

"Kyra and Marjolie. Good girls, too." But I catch an edge of hesitancy in the last statement, which intrigues me.

"Boyfriends?"

"LiLi keeps to herself. No boys, parties, those sorts of worries. She is a very good girl. A caring sister, a loving niece."

"I'm sorry, Mrs. Violette. Had she been having issues with anyone lately? Another classmate, teacher, coach?"

Guerline shakes her head. Emmanuel fixes his gaze on the floor with studied avoidance.

More questions for me to ask later.

"Girl drama?" I try one last time. "You know how it can be with teenagers. Bestie today, archenemy tomorrow."

"Not my Angelique. She has a good head on her shoulders, that one. She wants college. A future. You understand."

Guerline gazes at me directly and I get it. Angelique didn't want to return to Haiti. She wanted to get into college and hopefully be granted a student visa so she could remain in this country with all its opportunities.

"I am a CNA," Guerline tells me softly. "Nursing is a good job. But Angel, one day she will be a doctor. Maybe a surgeon. She is that smart. This is why my sister sent her children to me, though it hurts her heart for her babies to grow up so far away. They must have hope. Our beautiful Haiti . . . The earthquake took away too much, and rebuilding is slow."

Emmanuel clasps his aunt's shoulder.

"Do the police have any leads, maybe a person of interest?" I press.

Guerline shakes her head.

"Theories? Angelique left willing, unwilling?"

"She would never go willingly," Guerline informs me flatly. She crosses her arms over her broad purple-clad chest and takes on the slightly defiant look I already recognize from her nephew.

I don't push it. There's no point in arguing with a family's beliefs or perspectives. They have to get through each day, which makes truth a fickle companion.

"How can you help?" Emmanuel speaks up abruptly. His chin's up, also challenging me. "What can you do that the police didn't?"

"I'm sure the police did a fine job," I supply soothingly, though I'm not sure about that at all. "Bear in mind, however, that even the best detectives have dozens of cases that demand their attention.

Especially now, after so much time has passed. Whereas for someone like me, your sister is my sole focus. I'm here to find her, and I
won't leave until I do."

"You're living here, in this neighborhood?"

"I took a room above Stoney's."

The boy can't hide the look of surprise across his face, followed
almost immediately by a scowl. "You're crazy."

Guerline gives her nephew's shoulder a light smack. "Don't insult our guest."

"Come on. Look at her, *matant*. She's not police, she's not local,
she's not . . ."

One of us, I mentally fill in for him.

"No one is going to talk to her," Emmanuel continues relentlessly. "She will piss people off. How does that bring my sister
back?"

His voice raises stridently at the end, his anger a testimony to his
grief. I can tell his aunt understands, just as she can tell I understand. Briefly, we are bonded. Two older, wiser women sorry for the
pain the world is causing our children.

"I'm happy you say you're satisfied with the police efforts," I
offer. "The truth remains, it's been nearly a year. The police have
no new leads or you would've heard about them. So even if you
don't like me or don't understand me . . . What do you have to
lose?" I stare Emmanuel in the eye, as he seems the most hostile.
"You want your sister back. I want to help. Why not use me?"

Emmanuel doesn't have an answer for this; judging from his
expression, however, he still isn't convinced. His aunt, though, is
slowly nodding. I wouldn't say she believes in me either, but she's
clearly a practical woman. Forged by a childhood of deprivation
and an adulthood of uncertainty, she appears moved by my logic.

Deep sorrow brackets her eyes. Eleven months later, she's getting

desperate. She doesn't share it with Emmanuel; they are both staying strong for each other. Now I'm here, upsetting their fragile eco-
system by offering hope. Emmanuel isn't ready, but Aunt Guerline
knows better than to let it go.

Securing permission is not always this easy. I've been thrown out
of homes. Had beer bottles tossed at my head, vicious threats
spewed in my face. For some, rage is easier to handle. And many
families do have secrets to hide.

I don't think Guerline is one of those people. Emmanuel . . . He
knows more than he's saying, I'd bet. But I'd also bet he thinks he's
protecting his sister with his silence, meaning my real job will be
convincing him otherwise.

I rise. I don't want to overwhelm Guerline or alienate Emmanuel. Not when I can tell both truly want answers.

I focus on Guerline. "Ricardo, the community officer. Can you
give me his information and let him know I'll be in touch? Or I can
give you mine to pass along to him if you prefer?"

Guerline nods, and I scribble down the number to my Tracfone.

"If you could call Angelique's school, give permission for the
principal or a school counselor to speak with me?"

Another faint nod.

"I'm living above Stoney's," I repeat now, seeing the exhaustion
starting to take over. "I also work there several nights a week. If you
need to reach me in person, please feel free to find me there. I am
not just here for Angelique but also for you."

Emmanuel mutters something sardonic under his breath. But
Guerline grasps my hand firmly this time. I am unexpected and
unfamiliar to her, but she is a woman with nothing to lose.

This is how most cases start. With a bubble of desperate hope
and tentative trust. Where things go from here, how Guerline and
Emmanuel might view me months from now . . .

Emmanuel walks me back downstairs. He doesn't speak a word, relying on the rigid set of his shoulders to radiate disapproval.

"You love Angelique," I state softly when we reach the lobby. "She's a good older sister. She looks out for you."

He glares at me, but I see a bright sheen in his eyes. The pain he's trying hard not to show.

"You really done this before?" he asks roughly.

"Many times."

"How many people have you actually found?"

"Fourteen."

He purses his lips, clearly taken aback by that number.

"Good night, Emmanuel. And if you think of anything I should know." I stick out my hand. This time he takes it.

Then I exit the triple, out into the crisp fall night, where the sun has set. Bright lights wink in the distance. But on this block no streetlights are working. Not the best idea for a lone woman to be walking around after dark, but I hardly have a choice.

I square my shoulders and head briskly back toward Stoney's, grateful it hadn't occurred to Emmanuel to ask the next logical question:

Not just how many people I'd found but how many people I'd brought home alive.

None.

At least, not yet.

CHAPTER 4

LEAVING GUERLINE'S APARTMENT, I CAN just make out shadowy clusters of people on front stoops as I pass. I walk with my hands tucked in the front pockets of my olive-green jacket. It would be warmer if I buttoned it up, but I don't want to risk any restrictions to my movements. Especially as the first shape peels off from a front porch, exits the chain-link fence, and falls in step behind me.

I don't pause or turn around. I head straight to the end of the block, where the red crossing light forces me to draw up short. Footsteps behind me. Closer, closer.

I move to the side, clearing an opening beside me. The second person stops in the empty space. Black male. Anywhere between eighteen and twenty-five. Tall, broad-shouldered with an oversized Patriots hoodie that makes him appear even taller and broader.

He glances at me. I keep my gaze straight ahead.

The crossing light turns green. He steps off the curb, one of his strides easily twice the length of my own.

I'm just starting to relax, walking now in his wake, when I

realize I can still hear footsteps behind me. A second set, which I'm immediately paranoid has been there all along. I make it across the intersection only to realize the next block of triple-deckers is as dimly lit and ominous as the last.

Turn around and confront the person? Pick a door and pretend it's my final destination?

Options. I should pick one, exercise some kind of caution as the footsteps quickly close the gap.

I whirl at the last second, preparing to meet the possible threat head-on.

The Black girl behind me draws up short. She's wearing skinny jeans, a tight-fitting ribbed cotton shirt, and huge silver hoops, along with a black leather jacket and matching stiletto-heeled boots.

She lifts a finely etched eyebrow. "You nuts, lady? This is *not* a place to be walking alone after dark. Yo, Jazz, hold up."

Then she scoots around me, catching up with the broad-shouldered kid and looping her arm through his. They saunter down the block.

I tell myself I'm okay.

Mostly, I bolt quickly down the maze of streets to Stoney's bar.

I'M A RECOVERING addict. It's taken me a couple of tries, but I've now been sober for nine years, seven months, and eighteen days. And yet I still love walking through the doors and inhaling the scent of a tried-and-true local pub. It feels like coming home.

Many of my fellow AAs manage their recovery by avoiding booze and any situation involving alcohol. In the beginning I did, too. Well, kind of. I spent hours circling the outside of my local watering hole, wanting desperately to go in, willing myself to stay outside. That's how I met Paul. He recognized me, what I was going through. And for a while, he believed in me, when I wasn't ready yet to believe in myself.

I did the ninety-in-ninety drill. Got a sponsor. Got a new sponsor. Decided the program wasn't for me. Worried sobriety wasn't for me. Mostly, quietly, desperately understood that being me wasn't for me. I didn't know how to do it. I never had.

After more than a dozen years of AA and two reboots, I know firsthand there's more than one path to sobriety. AA's simple truth, however—admitting helplessness over alcohol and finding strength through a higher power—remains the best starting point that I've experienced. I attend my meetings. I read from the Big Book. I find comfort in the company of people living honest, messy, difficult lives without taking a drink and yet being okay. Even finding joy.

I had to go back to working in bars. Serving is one of the easiest and comparatively well-paying jobs, given my transient lifestyle. Besides, being around booze isn't one of my triggers. Nights like this one, when I'm feeling overwhelmed and lost and a little bit sad, are the challenge for me.

Stoney glances up when I walk through the front doors. So do a few others. The late hour has brought out dozens of customers. Most of the tables and barstools are now filled. Loners, couples, groups of friends. Those who are having fun, those who are drinking hard.

I don't mingle and I don't judge. There but separate. That part has always come easily to me. Like a lot of drunks, I've spent most of my life feeling alone in a crowded room. Drinking was one way of making it easier to take.

I head to the kitchen to take Stoney up on his offer of food. I haven't eaten since breakfast and now that the drama of the day has passed, I'm starving. I discover a short plump Black woman wearing a white apron and working the grill with a metal scraper in one hand and a wooden spoon the other.

She glances up when I walk in. "You the new girl?"

"I start tomorrow."

"Lord, you're a skinny thing. Hungry?"

"Always. But I can help myself. Looks like you're busy."

"No worries, hun. Burger or chicken? Long as I'm making four, five won't matter."

"My name is Frankie. And if you don't mind, I'll take a burger."

"Viv. Met your roommate yet?"

"Briefly. She stared at me like I was the devil. Or maybe that was the way I stared at her."

Viv lets out a low chuckle that shakes her entire five-foot-nothing body. "She likes me."

"Seriously?"

"Chopped chicken livers. Works every time." Viv flips four burgers and throws on a fifth frozen patty in the blink of an eye. I respect any person who can cook that fast.

"You a lifer?" I ask, meaning a lifetime of working in a kitchen.

"Yes, ma'am."

"Me, too. Behind the bar."

"Stoney says you don't drink."

"Twelve-stepper."

"Mmm-hmm. My husband does the same dance. Need a list of local meetings?"

"That'd be great." I'd printed out some info before my arrival, but in this matter, at least, I've learned to accept help. "What do you put on the burgers?" I push myself away from the doorjamb.

Viv nods toward the stainless-steel prep island, where I see a block of sliced cheese, a jar of pickles, and a bag of buns. Thin white melamine plates are stacked at the end, near canisters of silverware. It's a small kitchen, but efficiently set up. Viv moves straight from the grill to the fryolator and drops in a basket of fries.

I wash my hands, then plate the buns, dish out sliced pickles, unpeel slices of cheese. I add a fifth plate for me. Tucked in the kitchen with the smell of seared hamburgers and crisping fries, I'm famished.

"Lettuce and tomatoes in the fridge," Viv informs me in a stage whisper. "And my special sauce. Keep a batch just for Stoney. And friends of Stoney's."

"I like you already."

Happy hum. Viv tosses the four finished burgers onto the plates, flips the fifth, and grabs the fries. She is damn good.

I deliver the four plates to Stoney while Viv finishes up mine. Stoney doesn't bat an eye to find me standing at the end of his bar with food delivery. The three of us could've been working together for years. I both love the feeling and fear it. There's a reason I'm always the outsider. Many AAs talk about needing to replace one addiction with another as a form of coping. I gave up drinking and took up always being on the move instead.

A rolling stone gathers no moss. Paul used to tell me that all the time. Later, he'd accuse me of not listening. But I heard it all. I always heard it all.

Viv has moved on to deep-frying frozen chicken wings. She hums as she works, a sheen of sweat glistening across her brow. Her movements are unhurried, smooth. Stoney appears with two tickets in his hand. He glances at my burger, still midpreparation, then hands me the tickets and disappears.

I read off the orders for Viv, then smash the top on my burger and dig in.

"Stool in the corner," Viv sings out.

Sure enough, there's an old wooden stool tucked in the shadow of the fridge. I pull it up to the prep counter and take a seat. Since Viv has already proved she has no problems talking while she works:

"I heard there's a girl gone missing," I cue up.

"Angelique Badeau," Viv confirms. The sizzle of meat as she tosses two more ground beef patties on the grill.

"What happened?"

A wave of the metal scraper in the air. "Girl walked out of high school one day and bam, no one's seen or heard from her since."

"Drugs, gangs?" I ask.

Viv turns long enough to give me a look. "Cuz she's Black?"

"White kids have gangs, too," I assure her. "For that matter, so do most groups, including all the middle-class, middle-aged white guys suddenly becoming biker dudes. You could argue gangs are one of our common denominators."

"What are you, some sociologist lady? Or worse." Viv sniffs at me suspiciously. "Some white do-gooder here to save us from ourselves?"

"I would never presume that a woman who wields a wooden spoon with your degree of proficiency needs saving."

Viv gives a small nod, flipping two burgers, then raising the chicken fryer basket.

"Police still looking? For the girl?" I shovel in another bite.

"They say so. Hasn't been any news in months."

"What's the local take?"

Shrug. "Sounds like the girl was a good student, smart, not the kind for *gangs*. Then again, tough times to be an immigrant, especially one of the ten-year Haitians."

"Ten-year Haitians?"

"The ones that came after that earthquake. This area has always had a large community. So after the earthquake struck, people fled here, where they had family to help them out. Got in on some special visa for natural disaster survivors. But the visa was only good for ten years, and guess what, time's up. By now, lots of 'em, especially the kids, have lives here. Jobs, friends, community. 'Course they don't want to go back. But you've seen the news. These are tricky times to be an immigrant. Mass deportation would gut local healthcare, but that doesn't mean it won't happen. Some lawyers are now suing on the immigrants' behalf, so there's an extension while the courts sort it out. But after that . . ." Viv shrugs. "Plenty of local families don't know what the future holds anymore. And limbo ain't fun for anyone."

"So this fifteen-year-old girl ran off to avoid deportation?"

"She changed her clothes." Viv's voice had dropped lower. "Least that's what I heard. And left her phone behind. That sounds like a girl with a plan. God knows I'd never get a cell phone out of my grandbabies' hands."

I nod, chew my burger. Those details bother me, too. It did sound premeditated. The question remained, was it willing? As in, did Angelique place her backpack under that bush, or did someone rip it off her back and kick it there to avoid detection? If the police had any video of the event, they weren't saying. But I was willing to bet they didn't know that answer themselves. If there'd been solid evidence of abduction, the case would've rocketed immediately to an Amber Alert scenario. The fact that it took days for the police to fully engage told me there'd been doubt in the beginning. Maybe Angelique had a history of disappearing. Not something I'd wanted to ask the family during our first meeting. Our second meeting, on the other hand . . .

"So, the locals think Angelique skipped out to avoid possible deportation?"

"Girl's spent most of her life here. You think she wants to go back?"

"Her mother still lives there," I say, then add hastily, "At least that's what I read."

Viv rolls her eyes at me, pointing the metal flipper at the stack of white plates. Belatedly, I put down my half-eaten dinner, quickly wash my hands, and get back to plating. Viv bangs out the fries.

"The missing girl has a brother and aunt here. If she wanted to stay in the U.S., why leave them?" I ask, splitting buns onto the plates. "Now she's all alone." Viv tosses on the patties, I quickly add toppings. No custom orders, I'd already realized. Stoney ran a tight ship.

Viv gestures for two more plates. She splits the fry basket of chicken wings between the two, then adds more fries to all. From next to the silverware, she grabs a plastic squeeze bottle and squirts a deep red sauce into tiny bowls for dipping. The sauce smells slightly of barbecue, but is thinner, spicier.

"Your secret sauce?" I question.

"Stoney handles the wing sauce. Mine's for sandwiches."

"Do I get to invent one?"

"Gotta earn your stripes. 'Sides, what does a skinny girl like you know of cooking?"

"Not much." Especially given that I hadn't owned pots and pans, let alone a house, in nearly a decade.

I splay out three plates along one arm, grab the fourth in my right hand, and whirl out the door for delivery. Stoney nods his acknowledgment as he pours a beer at the tap, then jerks his chin toward a new ticket. I grab the order for more wings, then return to the kitchen, where Viv is already back to grilling.

"Pretty girl like that," Viv says, returning to the subject of

Angelique. "I'm guessing a boy. She falls in love. Doesn't want to leave him. So off they go."

"Wouldn't there be two missing kids, then?"

"Assuming he's a kid. Again, pretty girl like that."

Viv raises a good point. The family insisted Angelique didn't have a boyfriend, but as I'd already learned many times, the family is often the last to know. Better source of info on a teenage girl? Her friends.

I'm sure the police questioned them, too, but here's one area where I have the advantage: Plenty of people don't feel comfortable talking to cops. Whereas I'm just some random lady asking questions. Odd, but not threatening. Tracking down Angelique's best buds will be one of my first projects tomorrow. After getting some sleep.

Now, I gulp down the rest of my dinner, then tend to my plate. The kitchen is too small for a commercial dishwasher, but the powerful spray nozzle over the deep stainless-steel basin is blistering enough to sanitize just about anything.

"Need any more help?" I ask Viv, drying my hands.

"Tomorrow will be soon enough."

"I'll see you then." I hesitate. Time to head upstairs, my first night in my new room, with my new roommate. "Chicken livers?" I question.

Viv cackles. "No worries. Your roomie is out for the night."

"She has a social life?"

"She has a job. Rodent control. Why do you think Stoney keeps her around?"

"I was hoping he had a soft spot for strays."

"Hah. He's not called Stoney for nothin'."

I linger a moment longer. I like the kitchen, Viv's companionship. It's warm and cozy. Easy.

Then again, easy has never suited me.

A parting smile for Viv, then I determinedly head up the stairs. Home sweet home. I feel the booze beast stirring restlessly in my belly, triggered by my anxiety. Not tonight, I tell it. Tonight I'm strong enough. Tomorrow I will find a meeting.

I unlock the door to my new room, close and latch it behind me. Quick check under the bed. No sign of the cat. I take a moment to unpack my few belongings, set up my toothbrush, toothpaste. A ritual performed so many times, it leaves me both comforted and exhausted.

New town, new job, new case.

"Why are you doing this?" Paul demanded. "Why can't I be enough for you?"

Me, standing there, unable to answer.

"You're an addict." He answered his own question bitterly. "That's why. There will always be something you need more, some high you have to chase. Jesus, Frankie. I love you."

Me, still standing there, unable to answer.

Paul turning away. Paul walking away.

Me, not following.

Now, I change into the boxer shorts and worn T-shirt I wear for bed. I snap off the lights, then crawl beneath the sheets, which feel scratchy and unfamiliar against my skin.

The beast stirring again.

"Shhh," I whisper. To my racing mind, to my dangerous thirst. "Shhh . . ."

Then I close my eyes and will myself to sleep.

Later, I wake up with tears on my cheeks.

Later still, I rise to consciousness enough to register a rumbling weight on my chest and glowing green eyes staring down at me. "Shhh," I mumble again, then tumble back into the tumult of my dreams.

CHAPTER 5

WHEN I WAKE UP THE next morning there's no sign of Piper anywhere on the bed. I yawn, stretch, note the time. Nine A.M. Late by some standards, but not for someone who often works till three in the morning. I crawl across my mattress far enough to part the heavy black curtains and peer out the window. The crack of light is so bright I nearly recoil. Clearly a beautiful fall day. It should cheer me up. Instead, I feel slightly hungover, the aftereffects of lousy sleep and bad dreams. Not the first time, won't be the last.

I step off the bed. A white-tipped paw lashes out from beneath the mattress and rakes open claws across the heel of my bare foot. I howl, hop, bang into the edge of the kitchen counter, swear a blue streak. At least I now know where my roommate is.

I move to the end of the bed, where I gingerly lift up the edge of the blankets and peer beneath. Green eyes regard me balefully. Piper sits just under the mattress, in the perfect position to strike.

"Really?" I ask her.

She yawns, flashing sharp white teeth. Then she innocently sets about grooming herself.

"So that's how it's gonna be." Yesterday I hadn't been able to make out her coloring. Now I can tell she is mostly gray, with mottled splashes of orange, and a white chest and paws. She's not huge, but clearly dangerous enough. Time to start sleeping in socks, I decide, then hobble to the kitchen sink, where I bang out water, dampen a paper towel, and blot at my bleeding heel. The scratches aren't deep. More of a shot across the bow.

"You're not scaring me off that easily," I inform the shape under the bed.

I head to the ancient shower. Ten minutes later, shivering slightly from a spray that was more lukewarm than hot, I scrape my long hair back into a ponytail, fasten my fancy multi-tool clips to each side, then dab on facial moisturizer. The face looking back at me from the mirror isn't young or fresh or pretty. I have lean features, plain brown eyes, a dusting of freckles across my nose. Twenty years ago, my complexion may have glowed, but too many years of boozing have taken their toll. Even with moisturizer I have fine lines creasing my eyes, my brow, the corners of my mouth.

I look tired, I think, that kind of weariness where no amount of rest will ever make a difference. I finger my chin, feeling the prickle of random hairs that hadn't been there ten years ago, the soft pouch of skin sagging beneath my jawline. I'm not sure what I'm looking for. Some sign of the girl I used to be, or some proof of the woman I am now?

I wish sometimes I could see myself the way Paul did, all those years ago.

By the end, he wished the same.

I pull away from the mirror, exit the curtained-off bathroom.

After all this time on the road, I've developed a uniform. Two pairs of worn jeans, one pair of cargo pants, and one pair of black yoga pants. I have three short-sleeved tops and three long-sleeved, all interchangeable. My olive-green canvas jacket is medium weight—it lacks the lining needed for winter wear but should get me through the next month. It's easy enough to add a scarf or gloves if I need them. For shoes, I have one pair of sneakers and one pair of sturdy brown boots. Seven pairs of underwear, definitely on the dingy side. Seven pairs of socks, each a bit more worn than the last. I should stay here long enough to build the cash reserve necessary to refresh my wardrobe. But most of that depends on Angelique Badeau.

So far, I'm understanding why the media reports on her disappearance were thin and vague. There's no narrative. Angelique was a good girl. She might have run away. She might have had her backpack stolen. She might have abandoned it herself after changing into fresh clothes.

Who was this girl? What happened to her in the middle of one of the most densely populated neighborhoods in Boston?

And nearly a year later, how can she remain vanished without a trace?

I finish lacing my tennis shoes, then fill a bowl with water and place it on the floor. Stoney had said the cat needed nothing, but that feels weird to me.

I grab my key, slide my Tracfone as well as my photo ID and a modest amount of cash into my coat's inner pockets. Then I head out in search of breakfast.

I LOCATE THE nearest coffee shop, which turns out to be a vivid pink-and-orange Dunkin' Donuts. I haven't been to one in forever, but I remember the coffee as being excellent, the donuts okay. One large-coffee-loaded-with-cream-and-sugar later, I take a seat next to the window overlooking Morton Avenue and start planning out my day.

While I'd asked Guerline Violette to pass along my contact info to her friendly neighborhood cop, Ricardo, I don't feel like waiting for the phone to ring. Instead I call the B-3 Boston PD field office and request to speak with Officer Ricardo, community liaison. There's a pause.

"You mean Officer O'Shaughnessy?"

"Ricardo O'Shaughnessy?" Now I'm confused.

The phone attendant chuckles. "Yeah," he says. "Haitian liaison officer? We have a number of designated community contacts. Puerto Rican, LGBTQ, El Salvadoran?"

For a moment, I'm genuinely flummoxed. Most of the backwoods towns I've visited have been doing good to employ one or two officers to handle everything, let alone specialists for each community group. It's a whole new world out here, I guess.

I confirm Officer Ricardo O'Shaughnessy, then provide my name and number. As for my message, I hesitate, then state: "I'm calling with the permission of Guerline Violette to follow up on Angelique's disappearance."

I say it just like that. As if I know exactly what I'm talking about, maybe I'm even an old friend of the family.

The operator doesn't comment, just jots it all down. I leave my phone sitting out on the sticky tabletop while I nurse my large coffee and jot a list of initial questions I want answered. I've just underlined *cell phone* three times—I noticed two cellular provider stores last night, and what kind of teenager abandons her old phone without at least attempting to pick up another?—when my Tracfone rings.

I answer it quickly, discovering Officer Ricardo O'Shaughnessy on the other end, not sounding happy.

"Who are you?"

"My name is Frankie Elkin—"

"What's your angle? You looking for money? Cuz you're barking up the wrong tree."

"If we could meet in person—"

"This is horseshit. The family has been through enough."

"I'm here to help."

Snort. "Listen—"

"Meet me." My turn to interject. "Just five minutes. Jot down my driver's license number, general description, anything you need to check me out. But I'm sure when Guerline called you this morning, she said I had her permission to talk to you. For her sake, grant me at least a quick introduction. Then allow me one question. That's all. One question, then I'll leave you alone."

Another dubious snort, followed by silence. If Officer O'Shaughnessy truly cares about the family or the investigation, he'll feel compelled to interrogate me. His suspicion, my entry point.

Another moment, then a heavy sigh. "You know Le Foyer?"

"Sure." I have no idea.

"Meet me there in an hour."

"Absolutely."

He hangs up, which gives me a moment to chug my coffee, grab my notes, then approach the six employees clustered behind the serving counter, eyeing the white chick with open curiosity.

"Le Foyer?" I ask hopefully.

Four out of the six raise their hands. I offer up my map. The manager, an imposing-looking woman whose name tag identifies her as Charadee, takes my map, jots down some notes, then hands it over. And just like that, I'm off and running again.

I'M LEARNING QUICKLY that Boston isn't a town of neat and orderly streets. Instead, the lines on my map have me taking a diagonal here to a diagonal there. I stop and consult my directions often.

Walking down the sidewalks during daylight is a very different experience from last night. For one thing, I hardly see any other souls. For another, several of the winding streets offer rows of well-maintained freestanding homes, most looking straight out of the '50s and many with cars that I only wish I could afford parked on the driveway. I pass a blue-painted house whose white trim is decorated with cutout hearts, then a front porch with intricate red-and-gold woodwork carved into the shape of flowers. There is also more green space than I expected, from tended yards to community gardens to grassy parks.

I don't feel nervous at all walking down these streets. In fact, I'm beginning to think this quaint neighborhood might be one of the best-kept secrets in Boston. Maybe there's a whole other reason the locals want to scare outsiders away. This kind of charming, affordable housing I'd certainly want to keep to myself.

I'm just coming to the major intersection with Blue Hill Avenue when I pass a tall chain-link fence to my left. I'm thinking automotive repair shop, when I catch the first whiff. My feet stop on their own. I inhale a second time. Pastry dough, sugar, spice. My stomach is already grumbling as I realize the setback brick building is my target. Le Foyer Bakery. If it tastes half as good as it smells, I'm in.

I don't know what Officer O'Shaughnessy looks like. I'm guessing I'll recognize him by his uniform. As for me, I'm the only white person I've seen this morning, so I'm guessing I'm easy to spot as well.

I head into the bakery, where the intoxicating smell is even stronger. I note several display cases crammed full of huge, cracker-like rectangles that seem to be dusted in sugar. Then there are trays heavy with homemade peanut brittle, as well as cashew brittle. I don't see any labels, prices, or menus. Apparently, I'm supposed to know what I'm looking at and what I want.

The two people ahead of me are placing brisk orders in what I'm guessing is French or Haitian Kreyòl. A third is talking on his phone, also in Kreyòl.

The door opens behind me. A uniformed officer appears, midthirties, solidly built. Officer O'Shaughnessy, I would presume. He nods at me once, then breaks into a broad smile I realize belatedly is for the pretty young thing standing at the counter behind me. She grins back happily.

I have a feeling I know why we're meeting at this bakery.

"Frankie Elkin?" Officer O'Shaughnessy approaches, extends a hand. He nods at the two customers finishing up their orders, whether because he knows them or is being polite is harder to tell.

"It smells amazing in here," I say, shaking his hand.

"You ever eaten Haitian meat patties?"

I shake my head.

"Then you're in for a treat. Beef, chicken, or herring?"

"Um, chicken."

O'Shaughnessy approaches the counter, works his magic on his female friend. They both chatter away in French or a dialect I don't know, while she takes out a brown paper bag and starts doling out golden puff pastry squares from the warmer on the countertop.

The girl rings up the order. O'Shaughnessy takes the bag, which is already starting to darken with splotches of grease. A final dazzling grin for the pretty girl. Her blushing smile back. Then he returns to me, hefting up his bag of treasures. I don't see any place to sit inside so I follow the officer outside, where he takes up position on the concrete steps. He holds out the bag, I tentatively reach in and draw out one of the pastry squares. It smells wonderful.

He eyes me wordlessly while I take a first bite, followed quickly by another.

"Best damn food in the city," he informs me.

I nod enthusiastically. The pastry is light and flaky, the chicken filling both sweet and savory. I may have to eat several more just to place all the flavors. It's not a hardship.

O'Shaughnessy settles in more comfortably. He's purchased four of the meat patties. Now he dives in himself. "On the weekends, people drive in from all over to load up on Le Foyer's patties. Buy 'em by the dozen. Me, I stop in three or four times a week. Don't tell my mom, though. I'm required by filial law to swear hers are the best."

I nod again, his secret safe with me, as we sit in silence, chewing happily.

Officer Ricardo O'Shaughnessy looks much as his name suggests: a bit of this, a bit of that. His skin is lighter than Guerline's, his brown hair wavy, his features complicated. He's definitely a good-looking kid. The girl inside the bakery must be thrilled.

"Ricardo O'Shaughnessy?" I ask finally.

"Haitian mom, Irish father. Welcome to Boston."

"Father a cop?"

"Yep, and mother a nurse. Just to shake things up, though, I got one sister who's joined the force, and one brother in nursing school."

I nod in appreciation. "You're the Haitian liaison?"

"Grew up in this neighborhood. Known it all my life. Lotta my mother's family is still around, too. Point is, I have a relationship with this community. And plenty of the West Indies population in

Mattapan, from the old-timers to the newbies, feel more comfortable reaching out to a familiar face."

"Do you speak French?"

"Kreyòl. I can also do an impressive jig," he deadpans. He finishes up his second treat, goes to work wiping the grease off his fingertips.

I judge him to be a solid enough cop but still young. More attitude than experience. I want to pat his hand, tell him that no matter what I discover next with the Angelique case, it's not his fault.

"Photo ID?" he requests sharply, apparently ready to get down to business.

I dig out my driver's license from my front pocket with my left hand and slide it over to him. He checks it out. "California? You're a long way from home."

I shrug, finish one of the best breakfasts of my life, and reach for a napkin.

He places my ID on the step between us, snaps a photo of it with his cell phone. His fingers fly at the base of the screen. I'm guessing he delivered the photo to a buddy for basic background. I would if I were him. He tucks his phone in his jacket pocket, hands me back my license.

"Why you here?" he asks.

"A job. Cheap rent. A, um, cat." I sigh heavily. There's no good way to have this conversation. I'm a civilian, he's a cop. And most police will tell you no civilian has any business doing a cop's job.

I give it my best shot: "Look, you're going to get back a report on me telling you nothing of interest. I pay my taxes. I own only what fits into a travel bag. And I haven't bothered with a house, car, or credit card in nearly a decade. I am who I am. I do what I do. For the next few months, that will involve bartending several nights a week, while living above Stoney's and searching for Angelique Badeau."

"You know her?"

"Never met her. Just as I never met Lani Whitehorse, a hard-working mom from the Navajo Nation, or Gwynne Margaret Andal, proud Filipina and oldest of three children, or Peggy Struzeski Griffith, a slightly crazy, book-loving blonde. But I found them, too. Run the names. You'll see what I mean."

Ricardo frowns at me. "I'll run the names," he warns.

I spread my hands to indicate I have nothing to hide. Then I lean back against the metal railing, so I can see his face better, and he can see mine. "You and your officers won't like me," I state. "I understand. But I have the right to ask questions, just like anyone else. What I do learn, of course I'll share with the proper authorities. I don't have any jurisdiction here. It's not like I can search homes, or interrogate unwilling parties, or make an arrest. I simply want to learn the truth and gain closure for the family. I'll cooperate with the police every step of the way."

"You know how many murders we have around here?" Ricardo asks me.

"A lot. As well as a shocking number of nonfatal stabbings."

"You know why?"

"This area is a hotbed of gang activity."

He nods. "They're organized block by block. D Block. H Block. This street, that street. We're talking Black gangs, Haitian gangs, Puerto Rican—hell, we even have one corner held by the Chinese. You know what they all have in common?"

"They don't like cops?" I guess.

"They don't like outsiders." He rakes me up and down. "You, Frankie Elkin, are an outsider."

"My safety is my responsibility."

"Till you get yourself in trouble and good officers have to wade into a dangerous situation to save your ass."

"They took an oath. I don't believe it was to serve and protect only people who make intelligent life choices."

"Leave the family alone. They've been through enough."

"Isn't that for them to decide?"

"Drop the act. You're here purely to help? For how long? Till you get wind of some lead or witness who will reveal Angel's exact location, if only the family can raise the five hundred, one thousand, ten thousand dollars needed to seal the deal?"

"Run the background. I'm clean." I notice he uses the nickname Angel. As in he knows the family that well. And cares that much.

"Just because you haven't gotten caught, doesn't mean you're innocent."

"And just because *you're* suspicious, doesn't mean I'm guilty." I lean forward. "You think I'm here to make you look stupid, or even worse, exploit the family. There's nothing I can say that's going to change any community officers' or lead detectives' minds. So for now, let's agree to disagree. You do your thing. I'll do my mine. What I learn, I'll share. And maybe, just for the sake of argument, an outsider like me can shake loose a piece of information that will move the case forward. Win-win for all, but especially the family."

"Stay away from Guerline and Emmanuel," Ricardo informs me. He stuffs our grease-stained napkins inside the sack, rising to stand.

"Wait. What about my turn? Our deal was, you got to lecture me in return for answering a single question."

"The reward for any information leading to the discovery of Angelique Badeau?" he asks dryly.

I struggle not to lose patience, though given how many times I've had this same conversation in my life . . .

"Angelique went missing Friday afternoon after school," I state now. "But the police investigation didn't ramp up till Monday morning. Why that delay? What did you guys find, or not find, on Friday afternoon that kept you from immediately issuing an Amber Alert?"

Officer O'Shaughnessy regards me for a full minute. Then, "Dan Lotham."

"Who is Dan Lotham?"

"The lead detective on the case. He's who you need to ask."

"Don't suppose you feel like calling him on my behalf? Or I guess . . ." Meaningful pause. "I could always ask Guerline?"

The look Ricardo gives me would send a lesser person running. But I keep my face passive, my stare level. Nice doesn't always get the job done. And if this convinces Officer O'Shaughnessy once and for all that I'm a manipulative bitch, well, he won't be the first. Or the last.

Families always think they want the truth. But I've worked enough of these cases to know that sometimes cold hard facts slice deeper than expected. My contract is not with the cops. Not with the family. Not with the community.

My contract is with Angelique.

"Be careful what you wish for," O'Shaughnessy mutters now, as if reading my mind. "I'll give Detective Lotham your information. But between you and me, I wouldn't hold your breath."

The story of my life, I think.

O'Shaughnessy descends the steps and heads for his patrol car. I watch him drive away.

CHAPTER 6

THE BOSTON PUBLIC SCHOOL SYSTEM is a mystery to me. I grew up in a small community. One elementary school, one middle school, one regional high school. You stood at a corner, the bus came and took you where you needed to go with the rest of the neighborhood kids. Boston, on the other hand . . .

Public schools, charter schools, international schools. Forget local geography, such as Mattapan. From what I read, a high schooler could attend any public school in the city of Boston, using some crazy application process that probably made engaged parents want to shoot themselves and disengaged parents . . . well, that much more disengaged.

Given such madness, high schoolers didn't rely on the traditional yellow school bus. Instead, they had student passes for the city's mass transit system—the T. Reading about it gave me a headache. That headache returns now as I contemplate the map of Boston's MBTA system.

The articles on Angelique's disappearance listed her high school

as Boston Academy, a program that prided itself on helping minority students prepare for futures in healthcare, medicine, et cetera. If Angelique wanted to be a doctor, her school choice made
perfect sense. From what I can tell, Boston Academy is a mere
twenty minutes—and many confusing rail-bus-subway stops—
away. Just to make it more interesting, I've managed to catch Boston
in the middle of a massive update to the MBTA, guaranteed to cause
delays, shutdowns, and random moments of sheer chaos.

I follow one of my printed-out maps to a local station, where I
dutifully sit next to the tracks, watching garbage blow this way and
that. I make out some graffiti farther down the way, not to mention
random stickers adhered to benches and signs, now faded with age.
A tattered poster is fastened near the T sign. *MISSING,* it reads in
large print. Below, barely visible after eleven months of weather:
Angelique's official headshot. I feel a moment of fresh sadness. Not
just because this girl is missing, but because from here on out, she
will be defined by this one image. Was she happy the day this photo
was snapped? Thinking about school, dreaming about boys, or
plotting her next adventure with her friends?

Or, if her disappearance really was a planned event of her own
making, was she already working at the details even as this photo
was taken? Hoping no one would look too close? Fearing someone
might notice?

I try to study the smudged photo for answers, but of course it
offers none.

A rumble along the tracks, then my train arrives. Except it
doesn't look like a train to me. More like a vintage trolley. Orange,
single car, cute. I'm supposed to take the trolley a couple of stops,
then transfer to a bus. I once worked a case in a state park where
the entire search area was accessible only via horseback; how hard
could this be?

I screw up getting off at my first stop—ironically enough, because I'm studying the stupid map. I get off at the next and double back on foot, feeling frazzled and rushed as I don't have much time if I want to catch Angelique's school friends during their lunch break. My other option is to wait for them after school, but I have to be back at work then. I don't think Stoney will tolerate an employee showing up late for her very first day, even if she did survive her feline roommate the night before.

I make my second attempt to locate the right bus, only to find myself now headed in the wrong direction. Third stop, when I'm definitely starting to freak out and trying hard not to show it, an older African American woman with carefully coiffed gray curls and perfect red lipstick reaches up from her seat and gently tugs at the hem of my jacket.

"Would you like some help, dear?"

"Yes, please!"

I plop down in the seat beside her, handing over my now wrinkled printout. She eyes it carefully, then hands it back.

"I've never been any good with maps." She taps her temple with a manicured nail. "But I have it all right here. Tell me where you're going, child, and I'll get you there."

Her name is Leena. She's a retired receptionist, off to visit her sister for the day. She reminds me of a grande dame. Not just impeccably groomed, but with the kind of self-possession that comes from hard-fought battles and harder-won forgiveness. We speak for three minutes, long enough for me to decide I want to be her when I grow up.

Armed with her directions, I set off again. It takes me only a moment to realize Leena's right. If I hold in my head where I want to go, my feet take me in the right direction. One glance at the map, however, and all bets are off. Maybe because the transit map bears no resemblance to surface streets. It offers an oversimplified series of blue, green, red, and yellow spines that are far too neat for the reality of an overgrown historic city bristling with random byways.

I still make two wrong turns, but at last I find myself standing in front of Boston Academy in South Dorchester. The school sits atop a grassy knoll, one of the few touches of green I can see. If Mattapan is densely populated, high on crime, and low on the socioeconomic totem pole, South Dorchester appears to be its kissing cousin.

The academy boasts an imposing three-story façade with broad windows and huge glass doors that lead straight to twin metal detectors. Behind the carved granite entrance, the body of the building unfolds in a series of tall brick wings. Each exterior window is the same size, and they are equally spaced, row after row after row.

The grounds provide a perimeter of patchy green grass interspersed with clumps of woody shrubs. Some rhododendrons, hydrangea, and what looks to be forsythia. None of it is terribly well tended, but still a nice respite from brick and concrete. I hear a bell tone from deep inside the belly of the school, signaling something. Students don't come pouring out, so I continue my inspection.

I'm curious about a number of things. First, it looked to me like Angelique's daily school commute brought her within two blocks of the academy. From there, it's a fairly straight walk from her bus stop to the institute's front doors—which I'm certain, given the presence of the metal detectors, all students are required to use. One egress in and out. All schools, but particularly inner-city schools, are big on control.

I follow what I hope were her footsteps, passing a corner grocer, a liquor store, a nail salon, and a barbershop. I also note a sign for a chiropractor and a chain pharmacy at the opposite corner, doing bustling business.

Angelique had to cross the street to reach the front steps of her school. If she did that at the corner intersection, then her final stretch would be a hundred feet of grassy school grounds, tucked behind a low wrought-iron fence. Plenty of small bushes line the perimeter, but being right next to the street they are littered with disposable coffee cups, plastic water bottles, even nips of booze. I spot Fireball whiskey, three kinds of vodka, then Jim Beam, an oldie but a goodie. From the students or the neighbors? I'm not sure I want to know the answer to that.

Guerline had said Angelique's backpack was recovered from underneath a bush near school grounds. Meaning, if I were a student and wanted to hide something . . .

I look across the street at the row of businesses facing the school. An entire block of them. Meaning dozens of watching eyes, potential witnesses, and security cameras. Whatever happened that Friday eleven months ago, it definitely didn't happen here. This whole stretch is far too visible.

I continue around the block, down the side of the brick building. I have out my small spiral-bound notebook, jotting down a quick note of this, that. Mostly I'm counting security cameras, marking egresses, and mapping the bushes that fall in between. From time to time I stray onto school grounds, stepping over the low wrought-iron border to check out groupings of low shrubs. No trees, I notice. Nothing to interfere with the line of sight. Smart.

"Frankie Elkin?"

I glance up to find a big guy in a charcoal-gray suit staring at me from the sidewalk. He's tall, probably six two, broad shouldered, and with the build of a midforties male who was once super fit and is still fit enough. His erect bearing and buzzed black hair marks him as former military, while his complexion . . . maybe African American or Latin or some blend in between? I can't tell. Good-looking guy. Or would be if he weren't regarding me with exasperation. Now, he casually smooths back his jacket to expose the gold shield clipped to his waist.

"Detective Dan Lotham." I want to prove I can make educated guesses as well.

"Do you have permission to be on school grounds?"

"Um . . . My dog ate my homework?"

He gives me another look. I obediently exit the grounds onto the sidewalk. I already feel like a kid who got caught breaking curfew.

I don't expect Detective Lotham to like me. A civilian inserting herself into an official police investigation? I'm lucky if he doesn't start with handcuffs and proceed to criminal trespassing charges from there.

It surprises me then, how much I find myself studying his face. There's something about his eyes, the way he regards me, so coolly and patiently. He reminds me of last stands and a bastion against the storm.

I halt four feet back. For a moment, I'm tempted to close the gap. The instinct catches me off guard and I flush a little. It's my own fault. It's been a long time now since I've allowed myself human contact. And just because I choose to be alone doesn't mean I never feel lonely.

"Her backpack was here." My statement comes out tentative. I swallow, continue in a more assertive tone. "Fourth bush in. You can still see a slight hollow worn into the ground, plus some of the lower branches of the azalea are broken."

Clearly, my comment surprises him. The exact location of Angelique's recovered pack wasn't in the papers, proving I'm capable of learning some things all by myself. I continue quickly, without giving him a chance to demand I walk away, or lecture me on letting the professionals do their jobs:

"The front of the school is covered by at least six cameras between the academy's security system and businesses across the street. The other sides are slightly less monitored, but traffic cams still capture each corner, plus again, more establishments across the way. As perimeters go, the academy is well supervised.

"Until we get to here." I gesture to the area where we are standing. "No businesses across the street. No traffic cams midblock, no school surveillance."

He doesn't interrupt, just narrows his eyes at me. Meaning I probably do have it right, further pissing him off.

"There's a side door halfway down this stretch of the school, an emergency egress, which I'm guessing is locked externally as a matter of protocol. It forces the students to enter through the front doors, where they're subject to metal detectors and spot searches. Meaning there's either not a single weapon or ounce of drugs in this one high school, or . . ." I shrug.

Detective Lotham rolls his eyes. There's no institution in the world that's contraband free and we both know it. Administrations implement controls and almost nearly as fast, the inmates figure out how to circumvent the system.

I warm to my subject: "Looks to me like the students stash their guns, knives, narcotics under the bushes here, probably first thing in the morning, then wait for a break between classes. Then it's easy enough to prop open the side egress, scurry out, and recover the illicit goods with none the wiser. Meaning plenty of students know about this spot. Including Angelique."

"There's a second bolt-hole twenty yards down," Detective Lotham drawls, probably just to prove I don't know it all.

I shrug. Here, twenty yards from here—it doesn't matter. Angelique's backpack was left in a strategic location known by the students, not the administration. Meaning someone knew what they were doing. Meaning that someone might very well have been Angelique, stashing her personal belongings where she figured they'd be safe. Before she . . . ?

That's the part I don't know yet. The part nobody knows yet.

I ignore Detective Lotham and his relentless glower, turning in a small circle to sort out the rest in my mind. "Angelique had changed her clothes," I murmur. "The clothes she wore to school were in her pack, along with her cell phone. Meaning once she'd exited the front doors of the school, she came around the side of the building here to stash her school bag. Except, she had to change clothes somewhere in between . . ."

I look across the street, then up ahead to the corner, where there's a larger concentration of small businesses. I'm still trying to picture it in my head. "If Angelique had entered a store to change, she would've been caught on camera, and that would've been her last known location. Instead, the school is ground zero. So she must've walked around the block, school clothes on, backpack in hand, and then . . ."

My voice trails off. I glance at the detective. I think I know what happened. He doesn't confirm it in so many words, but his gaze flickers to the side door.

"She went back inside the school," I fill in. "Someone had propped open that egress. She rounded the building, ducked in this side entrance, changed, then exited back out. How long was she back in the school?"

Detective Lotham doesn't answer, then I realize he can't. This is the blind spot, of course. No way to see, to know exactly what had happened here.

But I'm starting to connect some dots. Not just what Angelique probably did, but what a cop might think of it.

Fifteen-year-old girl fails to return home. Several hours later, aunt reaches out to the community liaison officer. He comes over, asks a few questions. A teenager late for dinner . . . difficult to sound the alarm.

But protocol would've dictated a call to the local field office, reporting the situation. At which point a detective would've been called out. Maybe even Detective Lotham. He would've taken a statement from Guerline and Emmanuel. Maybe Guerline had already activated her niece's Find My Phone app, maybe the police pinged it. But that would bring the cops here, to a last known location with no sign of violence but plenty of evidence of local usage. A well-known student bolt-hole.

Brief canvass of businesses, maybe even an initial review of available security footage, enough to show that Angelique had exited the front door of the school, then walked in the opposite direction of her bus stop on her own volition. With no sign of violence but plenty of evidence of planning, which was bound to skew police perspective of her disappearance.

And on a Friday night to boot. Not just a night notorious for parties and teen mischief, but the end of a detective's normally scheduled workweek. A situation where a teen has only been missing for a matter of hours and probably of her own will would hardly win OT approval.

So the detective went home, leaving a few uniforms to continue canvassing neighbors, review security videos. Saturday. Sunday. Till Monday morning, when the detective returned to his job to learn the teenage girl remained missing and the trail was now forty-eight hours cold.

Then it became serious. Pity for the BPD. Pity for Angelique and her family.

"You're going to tell me to leave," I say shortly. "To mind my own business."

"Yep."

"It won't work."

"So I've heard."

"I have permission from the family. I also have the right to ask questions."

"Sounds like you have this all planned out."

"Not my first outing."

"So I've also heard."

"Did you call the names I gave Officer O'Shaughnessy?"

"I decided to check you out for myself. Then hear what others had to say."

"Good attitude for a detective."

"Not my first outing either."

"So?"

Detective Lotham shrugs his massive shoulders. "Sounds to me like you're about five minutes from cracking this case and finding a teenage girl the rest of us have clearly been too stupid to locate. Please continue."

I smile faintly. "Your original working theory was that Angelique had gone off on her own volition Friday night, to somewhere unknown by her aunt." I pause. "And most likely her brother. Because while Emmanuel clearly knows something, he also loves his sister and would've told you by now if he knew where she'd gone on Friday."

"And you got all this from meeting the family for what . . . five minutes?"

"More like twenty."

Detective Lotham regards me for a moment, his flat expression unchanged. "Go home."

"This *is* my home. I rented a room above Stoney's."

"It's wrong to give the family false hope."

"How do you know it's false?"

"Because you're out of your league. Because you *only* thought to check security feeds, when this area is surveilled by way more than cameras. This isn't the-middle-of-nowhere USA. It's fucking Boston, and we know what we're doing."

"So where's Angelique?"

"Go home," he repeats.

"Do you have LPR data?" A fresh thought occurs to me as I consider his surveillance comment. LPR is a license-plate reading system. Usually installed on police cruisers, parking enforcement vehicles, maybe even city buses. The technology continuously captures license plates as the vehicles drive around, creating snapshots of every single car parked at a given time in a given place. More surveillance data, as the detective said. I've heard of such things but never worked in an area sizable enough or sophisticated enough to have one.

"I'm not at liberty to discuss an active investigation," Detective Lotham informs me stiffly.

Meaning yes, Boston uses an LPR system. Which would've given investigators every car, van, truck, taxi, Uber driver, and city vehicle that had been in the area. Enabling detectives to identify the owners, run background, and tag criminal histories in the days and weeks following Angelique's disappearance. So much data. Way more than the-middle-of-nowhere USA, as the detective put it. And yet, eleven months later, not enough to help. I rock back on my heels, contemplating.

"All the cameras, surveillance," I consider out loud. "You should've been able to retrace Angelique's exact steps by now. Even if she exited the school in this blind spot, the minute she walked right or left, she would've appeared on camera. Whether she was on foot, in the passenger side of a car, tucked in the back of an Uber—*something.*"

Detective Lotham says nothing.

"She could've caught a bus or walked to the T stop," I continue musing out loud. "But you would've tracked that, too. Her path to the station, then standing around, backpack free, wearing her new clothes. Of course once she boarded and swiped her student pass, that would create yet another trail of breadcrumbs to follow."

"Assuming she swiped her card." Lotham appears bored with the conversation. "It's possible she used cash for a single-use ticket. Then again, we got cameras on buses, subways, and trains as well. And a whole MBTA police force well versed in studying such visuals. Boston is clever that way."

He's being sarcastic, but I take the assessment seriously. "In other words, Angelique didn't take mass transit because you would've spotted her. Likewise, she couldn't have walked away and she couldn't have driven away. Which leaves . . ."

I frown. Consider. Frown again.

"The sidewalk didn't just swallow her up," I say at last, frustrated.

"At this time, we've ruled out the sidewalk as a suspect," Detective Lotham intones. Wise-ass.

"Then you missed something." I announce firmly, never one to avoid a fight. "Technology is great, but it's not foolproof. Maybe fucking Boston, the world's cleverest city, has grown too dependent on its toys. I don't know. But a fifteen-year-old girl didn't just disappear off the face of the earth. There's an answer to this puzzle. There always is." I pause, then nod vigorously. "I'm glad I came. Whether you know it or not, you need me."

"Excuse me—"

"According to you, you have plenty of resources and experience, not to mention a shitload of technology at your disposal."

He glowers at me again.

"And eleven months later, how has that worked for you?"

"Listen—"

"I don't understand half the crap you do as a big-city cop; I've only ever read about LPR, let alone the other bells and whistles the BPD brings to the party. But it doesn't matter. Your best practices have failed you."

"Who the fuck do you think you are?"

"An outsider. But that's what it takes to find most of our missing children in the end."

"Stay away from my investigation," Detective Lotham warns.

"No."

"Screw with the family, mess up our case—"

"What case?"

"Fuck you!" He closes the gap between us, his arms out, posture aggressive whether he means it or not. He's bigger than me. Stronger, angrier. But it doesn't scare me. As a matter of fact, I like that about him. He *should* be pissed off. He *should* be protective of the family. It proves he cares. Though it worries me, too. Because police incompetence would've been an easy answer to this puzzle. And so far, Detective Lotham doesn't strike me as either burned out or lazy.

So what happened to a smart, shy teenager? She'd once stood right about where I am standing now. And then?

"I'll be in touch," I inform Detective Lotham.

His dark eyes nearly bulge out of his head with outrage. I smile. I'll be the first to admit that these kind of high-conflict moments aren't always fun for other people. And yet, they've always been fun for me.

"You don't have to talk to me," I say now, stepping back. "But you also can't stop me. So the real question is, do you want me running around on my own, or do you want to assert some control by offering a level of cooperation? That choice is yours. Either way, I'm gonna do what I'm gonna do. And that's find Angelique Badeau."

"You're nuts."

"A little bit of crazy never hurt."

"Asking the wrong questions can."

He has a point there. Another bell, ringing from inside the technical institute. This one is followed by more noise. The stir of hundreds of kids, squeaking back chairs, popping open doors, stomping down halls. Lunch break. Which brings me back to my original task, and yet another reason to ditch official police presence.

I signal my departure with a wave, then head back toward the street corner. Detective Lotham stays where he is, watching me go.

I disappear into the student traffic as it expels from the academy's front doors and pours down the steps. I count to five. When I look back, the detective is no longer in sight. Just as I'd hoped.

I allow myself a single smile. Then I go back to work.

CHAPTER 7

TEENAGERS ARE LOUD. IT FEELS to me like there are hundreds of them, swarming across the street, forming smaller pools on the sidewalk, then flooding into the corner grocer. No school uniforms. The kids wear ripped jeans or spandex tights, paired with sports tops, flannel shirts, or long fall sweaters. All in all, I'm not dressed that differently. Which, given the age gap, is probably not a good thing.

I try to focus on the girls, parsing out individual faces. Guerline listed Angelique's BFFs as Kyra and Marjolie. Unfortunately, I have no idea what they look like. Detective Lotham and his cohorts have most likely vacuumed Angelique's social media accounts for every crumb of information by now. They should know her life inside and out, from her family and friends to her favorite foods, zodiac sign, and nervous habits. I have none of that. At least not yet.

I consider myself old-school. I talk to people, versus reading tweets. I ask questions, versus consulting forensic reports. Obviously, it's harder for me to get that kind of access. On the other hand, by the time I arrive on scene—months, maybe years later—none of those leads has made a difference. So I stick to my Tracfone and my gumshoe spirit.

I pick a place near the epicenter of teenville and resume my recon. The student population is the most diverse I've seen in a bit. Dozens of African Americans interspersed with pockets of Indian, Latin, and Asian kids. I think most are speaking English, but given that I can't follow any of the conversations, it appears to be some dialect known only by teens. I notice that other pedestrians are now crossing the street to avoid the mass of high schoolers. I don't blame them.

Angelique was fifteen at the time of her disappearance. It follows that her friends would've been fifteen then as well, making them sixteen now. So two sixteen-year-old girls. Except most of the females in this crowd look to be anywhere from eighteen to twenty-one. Did I ever look that fresh and pretty?

In high school, I'd never been one to hang with groups or join teams. My father told me I was a free spirit, but really I was awkward and self-conscious. Until I had a couple of beers. Then the world was my oyster. I fucked the quarterback, blew off classes, and danced with abandon.

I remember feeling like my hometown was too small and my skin too tight and I wanted to simultaneously burst upon the world and lock myself inside my room. I loved my drunken, irresponsible father. I hated my demanding, critical mother. I wished for bigger boobs and a smaller waist and that girl's hair and this girl's gorgeous skin. Whatever I had wasn't what I wanted. But what did I want? I had no idea.

These poor kids, I think now. Like this whole age isn't confusing enough without adding in a missing classmate.

Yellow ribbons. It takes me a minute to spot the pattern. Not just a random accessory pinned to one girl's top or stuck on one guy's shoulder, but half a dozen of them attached to various students.

In honor of Angelique, has to be. Last winter, most of the student body probably had worn them. But now, one month into the start of a new school year without any fresh developments . . .

Her friends would still be making the effort.

I spy two ribbon-wearing girls standing side by side in animated conversation with a third teen. One of the girls has beautiful Black skin, high cheekbones, and thickly lashed eyes. She is clutching the blue straps of her backpack on her shoulders, her gaze constantly working the street even as she chatters away with her classmates.

Hypervigilant. I know how that feels.

I work my way through the cluster of kids. A few nod. Most cast suspicious glances. I'm definitely persona non grata. I close in on the trio of girls. The restless one notes my approach first. Her dark eyes narrow. She stops talking, then whacks the girl closest to shut up.

Bit by bit, the kids nearest to us fall into wary silence. I feel like a gazelle, walking through a pack of lions. Same rules of survival apply. Make no sudden moves. Show no fear.

I come to a halt in front of the strap-clutching girl. She stares straight at me, expression already set.

"Marjolie? Kyra?" I ask.

"Who wants to know?"

"I'm Frankie Elkin. I'm here to find Angelique."

The girl laughs. It's a harsh sound. "Lady, if you're looking for the suburbs, you already made, like, four wrong turns."

"Kyra?" I guess.

The shorter girl next to her startles. My target rolls her eyes. "Marjolie. But nice try."

She's lying. I know that instantly. Both by her tone and by the response of the kids around us. Some are surprised, but most are smirking. A challenge for the crazy lady, who's clearly dumb as shit to think she can barge into their world demanding answers for things she can't possibly know anything about.

I know how to take a hit. Now is not the time for fighting back.

"Angelique's aunt Guerline suggested I speak with both of you. If I could have a moment . . ."

The third girl backs up and away, but Kyra and Marjolie remain planted.

"Gotta get back to school," the tall girl states. Her dark hair is fixed into a complicated mix of braids, pulled back from her face and fashioned into a wrapped crown, which further emphasizes her stunning cheekbones. The girl is drop-dead gorgeous. Never an easy trait in a best friend.

"Ten minutes." I gesture to the ribbon she has pinned to her deep purple top. "Or is that just for show?"

"Fuck you."

The shorter girl stirs. She's pretty but not stunning. No doubt she and Angelique formed the background for their flashier friend. But that also meant of the three, she and Angelique shared the tighter bond.

"Please," I say quietly. I spread my hands in a show of submission. "Just a couple of questions." I direct my gaze at the tall stunner. "Kyra." I address her directly just so she knows that I know that she's already lied to me.

The shorter girl, Marjolie, gazes up at her friend. Her glossy black hair is a riot of unbelievably tiny ringlets. It's a nice fit with her round face, clear brown eyes. I want to lean in and tell her that she's beautiful, too, but I already know that's not how the world feels to her. Her friend is gorgeous. She's cute. Kyra leads, Marjolie follows. She must miss Angelique terribly.

"Fine," Kyra exclaims suddenly. "But you're wasting your time."

"Because Angelique doesn't want to be found?"

"Because we don't need some skinny-ass white lady trying to save her soul by slumming it in the ghetto. Come on, have you looked in a mirror? This ain't your neighborhood." She delivers this with the kind of disdain only a teenager can muster.

I take the second hit, surrendering the battle but focusing on the war as I lead Kyra and Marjolie away from the pack. Their classmates have already grown bored with the show. My initial appearance had been interesting, but Angelique's case is old news. Nothing of interest here.

"How long have you known Angelique?" I ask casually.

"Six years." Marjolie speaks first, her voice soft, her gaze cast down. "I live near her in Mattapan. My family is Haitian, too."

Kyra shrugs. "Two years, when we both started at Boston Academy. I used to steal Angel's notes. Eventually she began giving them to me. Told me she never minded helping a friend. So then, you know, we became friends. Angel's like's that. She has this way . . ." Kyra shrugs again. "She's way too good to be, like, missing, you know? But she's got hidden reserves. She's gonna come home, just you wait and see." Kyra's nostrils flare. I get the impression this has been a lot of words for her, and she meant every one of them. Beside her, Marjolie is nodding.

"I've worked fourteen missing persons cases," I volunteer. "All around the country. Missing kids, missing adults. You know the one thing they all had in common?"

The girls wait. I have their attention now.

"The victims' own families, even the ones they loved and who loved them, still didn't *know* them. Not all the pieces, the jagged edges, the still-forming dreams. I think in the end, no parent or sibling truly can. That's where friends come in. Angelique's aunt, her brother, they see what they've always seen, combined with what they want to see. But you two . . . You *knew* Angelique. You are the family she chose for herself."

Marjolie looks like she's going to cry. Even Kyra has lost her edge. She appears younger. Less certain. She glances at Marjolie, who now appears scared. Why scared?

A bell rings, shrill and insistent. Behind us, the kids begin gathering up their belongings.

I make it quick. "Did Angelique have enemies at school? Kids who threatened her? Kids she threatened?"

"We stuck together," Kyra says. "Watched each other's backs. And don't you go talking smack about my girl—Angel never threatened no one in her life."

"What about gangs?"

"No way. Academy's neutral ground. Principal Bastion says first time she catches wind of a gang sign or threat, that's it, we'll be wearing school uniforms."

I translate that to mean the uniforms are the threat, and Kyra and her peers are taking it seriously.

Marjolie adds, "Angel wasn't the kind to call attention to herself. She's woke, you know. Sensitive to others, but unlike some *others* who always gotta be making a fuss." She and Kyra exchange knowing glances. Marjolie continues. "Most of the kids in our school, they didn't even know Angel's name till the police showed up asking questions."

I understand about half of what Marjolie said, but with the sea of kids preparing to exit, now is not the time. "Boyfriend?" I prod.

The girls exchange a glance. Marjolie is uncomfortable. Kyra sets her jaw.

"Yes, Angel had a boyfriend," I fill in.

"No," Kyra corrects. "At least . . ."

"We don't know," Marjolie clarifies quickly. "Angel came back to school last year . . . different. We teased her—"

"Had to be a boy," Kyra interjects flatly.

"She said no—"

"Lost the big V. Still think so." Kyra glances haughtily at her friend. "Not gonna convince me otherwise. Good for her."

"She would've told us," Marjolie insists. "Why keep it a secret?"

"Maybe he's batshit ugly."

Marjolie huffs out a breath, turns to me. "Kyra just likes to pretend she knows Angel the best. Summer before last year, *I* was the one who spent two months with Angel at the rec center; there were no boys. I mean, no one special."

"Did Angelique have a job?"

"Babysitting. But she also helped out with her brother, so it's not like she had tons of time."

"But you're saying she returned to school in the fall different? How so?"

More exchanged glances.

"I think Stella found her groove," Kyra drawled.

Marjolie shook her head. "She was just—"

"Distracted. Big-time." Kyra again. "She started giving me class notes with only half the material. And when I asked, it was like she didn't even know. She'd, like, space out or something. From Mrs. Brain Trust to Mrs. Wish You Were Here."

"Did she seem *scared* distracted? Or *dreamy* distracted?"

"Distant," Marjolie murmured. "She seemed distant, but also like . . . more solidly herself. Like she was alone, even when she was with us, but to her, maybe that wasn't such a bad thing."

I think I understand. Together but separate. I know that feeling well.

Across the street, the bell tones at a more insistent volume. The girls edge toward the street. Their classmates are already departing, exhorting fierce gravitational pull. I speak faster.

"She changed her clothes that Friday after school. Do you know why?"

Both girls shake their heads, take a couple more steps. I quickly follow.

"Did you see her after she changed? Maybe she'd put on a dress, date clothes?"

More negative head shakes. More shifting sideways.

"Okay, okay, one last question, side door of the school. The one you guys use for smuggling in contraband, how do you prop it open? Is there a rock, stick, pencil for jamming the lock?"

Both girls startle, stare at me.

"You need to go, I need answers. Quick."

My insistent tone, combined with the demanding bell, does the trick.

"Can't prop it open," Marjolie murmurs rapidly, voice low. "The janitor checks. Kids bring a friend or two. Couple of kids do the spotting, while the third runs out and grabs . . . whatever."

"So when Angelique went back into the school Friday afternoon, which of you held the door?"

Kyra and Marjolie draw up short, faces paling.

"What?" Marjolie asks first.

"The police know she reentered the school using the side door in order to change her clothes. Then she hid her backpack. The police already know that. You're not ratting her out. Please. Eleven months is long enough. It's time to put it all on the line."

"The police never mentioned—" Kyra, already sounding angry.

"The police don't disclose information. But I can. Help me, and

I'll keep you informed." I'm begging, pleading. One last shrill alarm from inside the school, followed by cars honking on the street, where we're now holding up traffic.

I want to grab Marjolie's arm but will myself not to. They know something. Not about the side door, which has appeared to catch them completely off guard. But about the new Angelique who returned from summer vacay. I need to know that something. Detective Lotham has his surveillance videos. I have this.

"It wasn't us," Marjolie says suddenly. "We didn't do it. We didn't even know she went back inside. When the police said they found her backpack on the school grounds, we wondered." She flickers a glance a Kyra. "But we honestly had no idea."

"We're her friends," Kyra mutters stiffly. "Her *best* friends."

"Then I have to ask again—who are her enemies?" More honking, while the last of the bell fades away.

"The police are wrong," Kyra declares flatly. "Angel wasn't like that. She wouldn't keep secrets, she wouldn't backstab her friends, and she sure as hell—" Whatever the girl is about to say, she bites it off. One last glare at me, then she grabs Marjolie's hand and they both bolt for the academy steps.

I'm alone in the middle of the street with plenty of cars willing to tell me about it. I take the first step back toward the sidewalk, still thinking.

They're lying. Angel's friends, her brother—they all know more than they're saying. And yet they also seem genuinely concerned and want her back. Meaning?

I make a quick stop in the corner market to grab water and dash a bunch of notes in my spiral notebook. Then I realize I need to do some hustling of my own in order to get to work on time.

I exit the grocer and round the corner to what I hope is the correct bus stop, casting a glance over my shoulder out of sheer habit.

Which is when I see him. A tall, skinny Black male standing across the way, staring straight at me. At least six foot four. Anywhere from late twenties to late thirties. Wearing a blue nylon tracksuit, with a thick gold chain around his neck, like he last got dressed in the early 2000s.

Cars zoom between us. When they've passed, he's gone. But the shiver of unease follows me back to the bar.

CHAPTER 8

Returning to Stoney's dim interior feels like a balm after spending half the day out in the big city. I draw in a lungful of grease, salt, and hops, as I tie a white apron around my waist and prepare for battle. I know this bar's fragrance as well as I know the feel of the beer taps and a sound of a bell: *Order up!* I like Stoney's. Not just because it's a no-frills joint where you get what you get but because it's the local watering hole.

I've worked in dozens of bars across dozens of cities. I could make much more in some upmarket, aspirational place. But I remain partial to the kind of pub that feels like home.

When I check in, I find Stoney tucked inside a tiny office next to the kitchen. He looks me up and down, maybe checking for Piper damage. "Got three menu items," he says, ticking off on his fingers: "Cheeseburger and fries ten dollars, chicken wings and fries ten dollars. Only fries, five dollars."

He turns back to his archaic desktop. At least that explains the lack of menu.

I linger for a second, in case he wants to walk me through setup, maybe review some custom drinks. Nope, nothing. Apparently three minutes of instruction is all it takes to run this joint. Fair enough.

I unstack the chairs from the tables. Wipe every available surface. Napkin holders, check. Salt and pepper shakers. Cheap promotional coasters.

Then it's time to check keg lines and clear the soda gun. Followed by drying and stacking glasses, filling bowls of spicy peanuts, slicing up lemons and limes.

I like the work. Quick and mindless. It allows my attention to wander.

Emmanuel Badeau and his look of suspicion. Detective Lotham and his look of hostility. Angelique's friend Marjolie and her look of fear.

I don't know my own expression at this stage of my investigation. Confusion? Intrigue?

Most of my work has been in remote areas where there's been a lack of resources or small-minded police departments stocked with good old boys who don't want to waste their time. Or, say, tribal police who really believe outsiders need not apply. As a city, Boston is definitely not that, and yet some of the same defensiveness applies.

Did I once feel the sting of barbed comments? Or fear being shut out, told I was wrong or stupid? Did I feel guilty for ruffling so many feathers? If I did, it was a long time ago.

Before I was stopped on an open road in the middle of the desert, the blacktop wavy with heat, as a county sheriff and his three deputies climbed out of their cruisers, smacking their batons in cadence with their approach.

Before the crack of a rifle shattered the rear window of my rental car and I skidded sideways into a bank of heavy trees, more windows imploding, airbag deploying, my nose breaking.

Before a screaming uncle pulled me from his sister's front porch, punching me and crying that it was all my fault, then falling to his knees and simply crying because his six-year-old niece was never coming home and maybe he shouldn't have drunk himself into oblivion the night he was babysitting.

Memories sear. I have so many of them now. They're not precious moments, but burning-hot coals I keep picking up and turning over in my mind. They hurt. I study them harder. They burn deeper. I come back for more.

Paul accused me of remaining an addict even after I stopped drinking. I don't think he understood that's exactly how it works. I am my demons, and my demons are me. Some days I do all the talking and some days my monster does all the drinking, but every day it's all me.

Viv arrives with a hum and a wave, as the first few customers walk in. I receive wary glances from most of my customers. I am, for the moment at least, the only white person in the room. But I keep the alcohol coming and as hour speeds into busier hour, with me smoothly drawing down draft beers, pouring out shots, tossing in limes, everyone settles. I deliver food slips to Viv, pick up waiting plates for tables. Stoney and I fall into an easy shorthand of numbered fingers as he splits his time between back kitchen and front counter.

We pass quickly from an easy happy hour to a hopping dinner rush to the late-hour locals who have nowhere else to be at ten o'clock on a work night. I zip back a tray of dirty glasses, placing them in the bottom of the vast stainless-steel sink and topping them with steaming-hot water.

Then I'm back to the bar, looking for the next drink order.

Detective Lotham takes a seat in front of me. No gray suit, but jeans and a navy blue sweater that stretches across his broad chest. Off duty, then.

He regards me. Friend or foe? He's still debating the matter. Which means time for more fun.

"What can I get ya? Wait, let me guess: bourbon, neat."

His brow furrows. "Good God, no."

"Corona?" Though he didn't seem the type.

"RumChata."

"Seriously?"

"Around here, real men drink rum."

I shake my head, reach up for the simple white bottle. I'd never even heard of the liqueur till this evening. Now, I'd received multiple orders for it. It reminds me of a Caribbean version of Baileys except it's lighter in color and smells like rice pudding topped with cinnamon. I'd asked Viv about it during one of my kitchen excursions. She'd muttered darkly about Crémas, Christmastime, and I'd better demand a raise by then.

Now I get out a half glass, scoop in ice, douse it in white boozy sweetness, then push it toward the detective.

"One girly drink for the big guy. I'll be back." I head to the other end of the bar, topping off water for one customer, pouring fresh beers for three more. I keep my movements easy, my face bright, and pretend I don't feel Detective Lotham's stare burning a hole in my back.

A wave from the corner booth. I walk around to take an order for three burgers from a trio of elderly gentlemen who seem to be having a very good time. The one closest to me gestures me closer. "You the new girl Viv was talking about?" He has gray whiskers, sparkling brown eyes, and a mischievous smile. I'm willing to bet he was hell on wheels back in the day. And that day might've been yesterday.

"I'm the new girl," I confirm.

"Mmm-hmm. I tell you what, girlie. That Viv give you any trouble, you come find me. I'll set her straight."

"Viv? You're offering to protect me from Viv?"

"That's right. She can be uppity. Bossy, too. And I should know; I'm her big brother."

"That so?"

"Albert."

"Nice to meet ya, Albert. But I'm afraid I'm gonna have to be blunt: We both know that you're no match for Viv. Thanks for the offer, though."

The man's friends chortle across the table. My customer's grin broadens. Whatever the test, apparently I passed it. A parting wink, then I deliver the order slip to Viv, informing her that she has a table of admirers, including older brother Al. She merely rolls her eyes and drops down another bucket of fries. I escape before the greasy steam coats my skin.

Back at the bar, I notice Lotham's drink has been barely touched. Apparently, he's planning on staying for a while. With the bar pared down to the night owls, there's nothing that demands my immediate attention. I plop my elbows on the counter across from the Boston cop.

"So . . . of all the gin joints in all the towns in all the world?"

He smiles briefly. "I had some time on my hands, wanted a drink."

"Really? Because I think you're still rankled that the new girl is sniffing around your turf."

"You didn't leave the school after our conversation."

"Never said I was gonna."

"You talked to students. Kyra and Marjolie."

"I liked their yellow ribbons."

Detective Lotham takes a sip of his RumChata. When he sets it down and exhales, his breath smells like cinnamon.

He has dark eyes, thick eyebrows, and battered features. His nose has definitely been broken, probably a couple of times, and he's missing a piece of his ear, as if someone took a bite out of it. There's a story there, no doubt. I like that about his face. That it's a road map of been there, done that. It's interesting.

In my drinking days, I devoted my share of nights to drunken hookups. Even back then, it wasn't about the sex for me, which was generally a clumsy and forgettable affair. I liked the quiet right after. When neither of us were speaking. Just the sound of chests heaving, heartbeats slowing. That short, fleeting moment that occurs right before regret. When you can smell the sweat on your body, now mixing with someone else's, and wonder again how you can remain so disconnected. Like it wasn't your arms, wasn't your legs, was never your body to begin with.

I wouldn't invite a man like Detective Lotham up to my room for sex. But even now, I wouldn't mind tracing the line of his chewed-up ear, his weathered jawline.

I stand, putting distance between us, then pour myself a glass of water and down it.

"I called the names you gave O'Shaughnessy," Lotham offers up casually.

"And?"

"Wouldn't say they sang your praises, but it does sound like you're legit. I mean, as legit as an inexperienced, untrained civilian can be."

"I'll take that as a compliment."

"No seeking of financial reward, or attention from the press."

I shudder automatically. "I don't care for the press."

Lotham nods before he can stop himself, then scowls, as if I tricked him in to having something in common with me.

"Are you a good detective?" I ask Lotham.

He doesn't take the bait.

"I think you are. You and the BPD have all the bells and whistles you could ask for. Not to mention access to way more information than I can get. For example, I had to interview Marjolie and Kyra to learn if Angelique had a boyfriend. While you probably know every detail from dumping Angelique's phone, searching her laptop, surfing her social media. And yet you still stopped by tonight to learn what her two friends told me. Interesting."

I push away. Drift down the bar to take a new drink order, settle a bill.

When I return, Detective Lotham has sipped infinitesimally more of his drink. This time, he doesn't bother with pretenses.

"What did Marjolie and Kyra have to say?"

"I'll show you mine, you show me yours?"

One arched bushy brow.

"Let's both pretend that means yes." I plant my elbows on the countertop. "Something changed in Angelique's life the summer before she disappeared. She returned to school more . . . self-possessed, distant, distracted. Kyra thinks a boy, and serious enough to be sexual. Marjolie disagrees, but mostly because it hurts her feelings to think her bestie kept such a secret."

"How long did you talk to them?"

"Five, eight minutes before lunch break was over."

"And they told you about their friend's sex life?"

"Think of it as girl talk. See, a civilian investigator isn't so bad."

Lotham takes a pointed slurp of his drink.

My turn: "I'm sure you have copies of Angelique's text messages, but what about Snapchat? That's what most teens use for communicating away from prying parental eyes. I imagine they think it's covert, disappearing messages and all that. But is it? Can you recover a message that vanishes the moment it's read?"

"The police can get Snapchat info."

"How?"

"The messages pass through the closest server, the server captures the data."

"But how do you know which servers to access when people use their phones walking all over the place?"

"It's never a bad idea to start with the areas closest to home, school, and work. Won't get everything, but will get enough."

"What about messages sent in an app? You know, utilizing Instagram or some of the specialized messaging apps?"

"That's what search warrants are for."

I nod. Makes sense. For every new medium of communication comes a new way to capture that form of communication. "All right. Let's say it's been, I don't know, eleven months since an investigation first started. By now you have your search warrant results, server data, cell phone dump."

"Unless it involves something being unlocked by Apple. In which case we're still in court."

I smile. "Man, you're a pain in the ass. Tell me, did all this new information scored by the search warrants and recovered from miscellaneous servers confirm your initial theory of the case, or alter it completely?" I look him in the eye. "Do you still think Angelique was changing clothes Friday night to meet a mystery lover?"

Lotham's turn to smile. He sips his drink.

He's not going to answer that question and we both know it. It's okay. Whether he intended or not, he's done me a favor, as just knowing what information is out there is half the battle. Some of the reports received by the police I can request copies of through the Freedom of Information Act, things like that. In this case, that probably won't work. But I can also ask Angelique's aunt Guerline if she'd be willing to ask for copies. Most families have no idea what the police have been doing behind the scenes and are frustrated about being left in the dark. Meaning my suggestion that they ask for a specific document almost always leads to instant results, and yet more cops who hate me.

"You're thinking boyfriend," I say now. "I can tell by the look on your face that what Kyra and Marjolie told me wasn't news. You probably already read the messages, buzzed through the photos. Good lord, the hour after hour of teen drama you must've had to wade through. Kids keep everything on their phone."

I pause for dramatic effect. "Except not Angelique. That phone in her bag wasn't her *real* cell. She's got a backup, probably a cheap burner. Where her real life happens, which is why she was comfortable leaving her parentally approved model behind."

In front of me, Lotham thins his lips, flares his nostrils. I've been working on the thought all afternoon. Judging by Lotham's expression, I'm right. But where does that leave us?

I have a second thought. Sadder, more sobering. Why Detective Lotham is really here. Because he gets it, too, that nearly a year later he's no closer to the truth. And he's troubled by that—both by what he's seen and by what he can't see. He doesn't want me getting involved, no detective wants that. But at the same time . . . What if my blundering jars something loose?

Detective Lotham doesn't approve of me. But he's also desperate. And like any good detective, he knows he doesn't have to like me to use me as a resource.

I push away from the bar again, nodding at the customer trying to get my attention. While I'm up and at it, I deliver Viv's burgers to the flirty trio, noticing all three burgers are topped with her special sauce—family connections paying off. I wipe down two recently vacated tables. Scrubbing the surface with my fraying dishtowel gives me more time to think.

It's after eleven now. Only half a dozen customers and forty-five minutes left till closing. I return to the bar and my position across from Lotham.

"Officer O'Shaughnessy was warning me about the gang activity in this area, dozens of them willing to kill over a single block of real estate. I did some reading of my own, you know, before I waded inexperienced and untrained into the lions' den. There was a local case a few years back. A gang needed to lure out a rival in order to kill him. But their faces, their girlfriends, were too well known. So they recruited a new girl with no history of gang activity—had one of the females befriend her. Couple of months later, at her new friend's request, that girl invites the rival to meet her at the park for a date. He shows up . . . Further statistics ensue."

I tilt my head at Lotham. "Angelique would be a good target for that kind of scheme. Shy, quiet girl, also innocent and pretty. Maybe she was befriended, maybe threatened, but for whatever reason, she ended up in a situation beyond her control."

"I remember that case." Lotham nods. "There was a retaliatory shooting shortly thereafter. Killed three more."

"But if that's what it was," I contemplate, once again leaning in close, "why didn't she come home when it was over? Unless something worse happened? A shooting followed by a retaliatory shooting, like you mentioned? But in that case, you'd have a bunch of cops deployed to those scenes, and one of them should've seen or heard about Angelique."

"True. Plus, there's another problem with that scenario."

"Do tell."

"Gangbangers don't fly."

It takes me a second, then I get it. If Angelique were meeting up with new friends, and/or gangsters, there should still be some image caught on video. Maybe cameras missed the blip of a moment when Angelique appeared here, or crossed there. But for her to head deeper into the hood, traversing neighborhoods and parks, whether by foot, subway, or car . . . No way some camera somewhere didn't capture her image. By now, I wouldn't be surprised if Detective Lotham hadn't personally viewed all possible video feeds dozens of times. I've done it myself, poring over maps again and again.

It's how I found Lani Whitehorse, because in the end the lake was the only place she could've gone, regardless of the tribal police saying there were no tire marks in the mud, or flattened bushes along the shore to indicate an accident and justify the cost of a water search. I don't know why that was, or how an ancient Chevy went from a hairpin turn to thirty yards out into a lake without leaving any trace behind. Maybe not all things are meant to be understood.

Of course, in Angelique's case there remains one other terrible, awful scenario.

"Sex trafficking," I murmur now. "Innocent girls are often lured into the life. Angelique fits the description as that kind of target as well. Meaning maybe she thought she was going on a date with the new man in her life, except . . ." I shrug. "She never got to come home."

Lotham doesn't answer right away. He spins his drink, watching the white liqueur coat the chips of ice. "Boston has a human trafficking unit. They can reach out to CIs, run facial rec against all the local sex services sites, partner with the National Center for Missing and Exploited Children. Prostitution is no longer a street game. It's gone digital just like everything else. Customers log in, peruse the 'menu,' place the order. Sick to be sure, but it does allow us to cover a lot more ground using cyber tech. Let's just say the human trafficking unit has nothing new to report."

Stoney appears at the end of the bar, clad in his usual worn jeans and blue chambray shirt. He looks at his watch. Two minutes to midnight by my count, but apparently close enough for him, as he raps the bar three times hard with his fist.

Last call. Customers toss back drinks, rise to standing, cash out accounts. One by one. Till only Detective Lotham remains. Stoney gives him a look, seems to decide he's nothing to fear, then retreats to the kitchen.

I yawn. "Gonna help me clean?" I ask, starting to stack up dirty glasses.

"I'm trying to figure you out."

"If only someone could."

"You really don't work for money."

"And give up this kind of reckless abandon?"

"You literally go from place to place, case to case, no time off, no life, no loved ones in between? Like what, some kind of modern-day gunslinger?"

"Yes, there are that many open missing persons cases out there. I could travel from town to town, investigation to investigation for the rest of my life, and still not make a dent in the number."

"Why?" Lotham downs the last of his drink. He stands up from the stool, then makes his way around the bar till he's standing right in front of me. His eyes aren't so flat now. They're dark and deep and endless. He really does want to know. If only I had the answer.

"I think Kyra and Marjolie were right," I murmur. "If Angelique had met a boy, she would've told them. Maybe not her aunt and her brother, but her two best friends? They would've known. But most likely, she had met someone. And what kind of someone would a teenage girl hesitate to introduce immediately to her inner circle?"

"An older man?"

"Or a new female friend. Someone who might be good for Angelique but threatening to her posse. Teenage girls don't always take that kind of change well."

Lotham's studying me intently, still trying to turn me inside out so he can understand all the gearings. See exactly what makes me tick.

I wish it were really that simple. But he remains frustrated and I remain my same old self, thoughts whirling, skin humming, anxiety flying.

He steps back. Away. Heads for the door.

I follow him, preparing to lock up behind. Beyond the bar, the street is cast in pools of light and shadow. The air is colder, the pedestrian traffic scant with roamers keeping their heads down and feet fast.

"I'm gonna focus on potential new friends in Angelique's world, as well as her missing burner phone," I tell Lotham as he steps into the night.

"Can't buy a prepaid cell in Mass under the age of eighteen."

"Never stopped a teenager before."

He shakes his head, clearly annoyed by my persistence, but not surprised. "Be careful out there. Bad things can happen, even in daylight."

"It's cute you think I'm waiting for daylight."

I shut the door, firing the bolt home while Lotham is still whipping around in shock. A final wave, then I head back to the bar to finish cleaning up, before starting my next adventure.

CHAPTER 9

THE WORLD WOULD BE A better place if more people spent time drinking cheap coffee in church basements. So many think we must share the same beliefs to get along. In my experience, sharing the same fear is a far more effective strategy.

By the time I find my way down the stairs of the congregational church, I'm slightly out of breath. I claim a folding metal chair toward the back where I can get the lay of the land. The room, like so many I've sat in before it, has commercial-grade carpet, a drop ceiling, and walls covered in a combination of children's art and framed Bible passages. It smells like coffee and mildew.

Once more, I'm the only white person in the room. Here, however, I can shed the label of outsider. In this room, race, gender, age, ethnicity, income level—these things don't matter. Interestingly enough, neither does religion. While AA was founded on the principle of God, over the years its lingo has evolved to recognize a more general higher power. Call it what you want; even atheists have some kind of spirituality. The point is we're all here because we recognize we have a problem with alcohol. We desire sobriety, and understand that, in this matter, we need help to get the job done.

Already, other AAs are turning to offer a nod of greeting, a hand in welcome. From a grizzled old war vet in an army jacket to a young Black kid in a T-shirt to a woman still folding up her cook's apron. We introduce ourselves, even before the meeting has started. I have a hard time catching all the names or understanding all the accents, but I smile and mean it. Another basic tenet: All are welcome and we welcome all. We are comrades-in-arms, waging a mutual fight with the enemy. And we've come together tonight to share the horrors of war, while shoring one another up for another day of battle.

There's power in humility. It's one of the toughest lessons I've had to learn. Like the other souls in this room, I live on unsteady ground. Each moment is a choice and for all my good choices, I'm a single mistake away from having to start my journey all over again. As someone who's relapsed twice, I know better than anyone I can't afford to be cocky or negligent. No matter where I go, these meetings, this group, these strangers-who-aren't-really-strangers, are my key to survival.

Meetings have different focuses. This meeting was listed in the pamphlet as Big Book, meaning we'll take turns reading out loud, followed by discussion. I've lost count of how many times I've gone through the giant tome at this point, but this format is still one of my favorites. There's something soothing in revisiting words written eighty years ago that still resonate today. I can already feel my shoulders coming down, the pressure in my chest easing. I'm finally with my own people, all dozen of us young-old-Black-white-rich-poor-devout-atheist drunks.

An older gentleman sits at the head table. He has the look of a long-timer. He starts us off with the Serenity Prayer, which sounds even more beautiful in French-accented English, then we shift into meeting mode. I take my turn reading out loud, though my voice is slightly shaky. We are at the beginning of the Big Book, the chapter introducing the true nature of the disease and the terrible treachery that lies in the alcoholic mind.

I agree wholeheartedly. My mind is a traitorous beast I must monitor at all times. All those thinking games I used to play: I need a drink, I deserve a drink, I swear I'll stop at just one.

Mad, sad, or glad, as the saying goes. We drink because we're lonely, we drink because we fell in love. We drink to help ourselves go to sleep, we drink to wake ourselves up.

I drank because it made me feel alive. Then I drank because I didn't want to live anymore.

Now, I sit here. One day at a time.

It feels to me that meeting-goers fall into two camps—those who find comfort in sharing their stories, and those who find comfort in listening to others share stories that could be their own. I'm in the second camp. I rarely talk during the discussion time or volunteer my journey. I genuinely appreciate hearing about others, though. The ways we are all different and yet alike.

Tonight, talking about the nature of the disease, allergy, whatever you want to call it, I recognize the classic story elements from my own life. A family legacy of alcoholism. A parent who was a chronic drunk, another parent who was a chronic enabler. Hitting that awkward, anxious phase of high school, not knowing who I was or where I belonged—and consequently tossing back a beer at that party, or stealing a shot of my parents' liquor before boarding the school bus. That magical melting feeling that immediately followed. That sense of almost primal recognition. I like this. I want this. I *need* this.

Even now, I remember those first few drinks with longing. Those blissful early days of love, before I realized just how toxic and abusive the relationship was about to become.

The army guy shares his story of bottoming out. His wife kicking him to the curb, his kids refusing his calls. Spending months sleeping on the streets till another vet found him and dragged him to the hospital to begin detox. More nods around the room.

I didn't bottom out, as much as I crashed in a series of waves—low, lower, lowest. By my twenties, my entire lifestyle revolved around booze. I existed to drink and drank to exist. Mostly I have dark, spiraling memories of neon lights and a strange, hideous laughter ringing in my ears. When I sobered up, it was only to realize that laughter was my own, so of course I drank again.

Then there was Paul. Holding out his hand. Offering to save me.

In the beginning it was enough.

Later came the hard knowledge that no one can save you from yourself.

The meeting reaches the hour mark. We each produce a dollar, toss it in the basket, then rise to standing. I'm curious if this is a Lord's Prayer group or not. The traditional meetings end with it, but more and more groups have drifted away. This is a traditional group. I take the hand of an older Black woman to my right, and a cabdriver with an accent I still don't recognize on my left. We recite the words together and I use the moment to focus on the feel of a neighbor's hand gripping mine, to remind myself that this hour counts, that my sobriety is worth it. That we are all worth it.

The meeting breaks up. We help pile up books, pick up coffee cups. The army vet had coffee-prep duty. I move to his side to rinse out the coffeepot while he puts away creamer and sugar. His name is Charlie. I introduce myself again while we clean up together, explaining I've just moved into the area.

The meeting leader comes over. He has two pamphlets in his hand plus a torn piece of notebook paper.

"A list of daily meetings," he informs me, handing over the

green pamphlet. "More information on upcoming AA events." The blue pamphlet.

I wipe my hands with a paper towel and peruse both brochures. The nice thing about major cities—they have robust AA populations. I didn't have nearly this many choices at my former location. Especially these middle-of-the-night meetings, targeting those of us in the restaurant industry who get off after midnight and need support before heading home.

"Arnold," the man says, sticking out his hand again. Copious introductions is an AA way of life. We all know what it's like to feel lost in a crowd.

"Frankie. And thank you also for the phone list." I hold up the notebook sheet.

"Top one's mine. Third is Charlie's." The vet nods at me. "Second here, that's Ariel." He points to the woman who'd been wearing a chef's apron. She crosses over to shake my hand.

"You need anything . . ." Arnold gestures to the phone list, indicating I should feel free to use it.

"Thank you," I say, and I mean it. Ten days, ten months, ten years, you never know when the next craving is going to hit, and in those moments, a single connection can make all the difference.

Even after our relationship ended, I'd often call Paul. One A.M., two A.M., three A.M. It hardly mattered.

I'd dial his number. Hold the phone next to my ear. Listen to the sound of ringing, followed by the click of someone picking up on the other end.

He didn't speak. He didn't have to. He knew it was me just as I knew it was him.

We'd lie in silence together. I'd focus on the sound of his breathing, feel it like his heartbeat against the palm of my hand back in the days when we were still together, and I pressed myself against him in the middle of the night to keep my body, my thoughts, my very sanity from spinning apart.

Minute into minute. Until it was enough.

Then I'd hang up the phone and be separate once more.

Two weeks ago, after Lani Whitehorse's funeral, when the work was done and my goal accomplished and I lay in bed in my cheap motel room, feeling all the emptiness and sadness crash down upon me, I called his number again.

Except this time there wasn't silence on the other end.

This time, a woman picked up. She said, "You need to stop this." Then, not unkindly, "You need help."

I hung up the phone, my heart racing wildly in my chest. Then I curled up in the fetal position and burst into tears.

The truth can be like that.

"Hey," I say now, addressing the three people before me. "I need to buy a new phone. Something simple and cheap, like a burner. Do you know where I can go?"

"There's a T-Mobile around the corner," Ariel mentions. She's buttoning up a light jacket.

"Sounds expensive."

Arnold doesn't say anything, but Charlie the vet nods. I figured it would be him. Funny, how any addict can spot a dealer. We are crazy-good judges of character. Just don't ask us about ourselves.

I hang back with Charlie, as Arnold and Ariel hit the stairs.

"How cheap you looking?" Charlie asks, moving over to the light switch.

"Very. I'm just now back to work, so extremely low on funds."

"I do some volunteering at the rec center," Charlie says, flipping out the lights and herding me toward the stairs. "I've heard the kids talk about after-hours phones."

"After-hours?"

"After closing hours. You'll find a guy or two lurking outside the mobile carriers. They have old phones with new SIM cards. Now, I mean *old* phones. Flip phones, that kind of thing."

I nod.

"Lotta kids pick those up. Can use them for a month or two, at ten, twenty bucks a pop."

I'm thinking if I'm a teenage girl embarking on a secret life with limited funds, that's an excellent price point.

I drop my voice in a pseudo whisper. "Do I ask for Marco or just look for the guy in the trench coat?"

Charlie grins at me. I like his beard. It fits nicely with his broad face, hulking build. He would make an excellent teddy bear.

"Little thing like you needs to be careful asking around. Some of these kids are in the life for sure."

I'm assuming he means gangbangers. Which makes sense. Additional funding for illegal activities.

"I'm not threatening," I assure him. "Any kid looking to build his rep is hardly going to bother with a scrawny middle-aged white woman. Frankly, it'd be too embarrassing."

Charlie grins again. "Not so wrong, little lady. Not so wrong."

"You work at the rec center?" I ask as we exit the church. He locks up behind us.

"Volunteer three afternoons a week. Try to do my part to set these boys straight. I've lived here most of my life. Seen the good, the bad, the ugly. I know what they're going through."

"Ever meet Angelique Badeau?"

"The missing girl?" Charlie stops, looks at me. "Why are you asking about her?"

"I heard about the case. It's made me curious."

"I saw her around the center," Charlie says slowly. "But can't say that I know more than that."

"Could I stop by, look around?"

"Don't see why not. Best time is after school hours or on the weekend. If you're looking to see the kids."

Charlie studies me. Maybe he hopes I'm looking to mentor girls or volunteer my time or talk responsible drinking with teens. He's not sure about my questions, however, some internal radar clearly pinging to life. Liars are very good at spotting other liars. He doesn't push it, though. Maybe the next time we meet.

We're outside the church now, standing on a broad avenue. I have eight blocks between here and Stoney's to cover. The first of those streets is bathed in streetlights but quickly fades into a tunnel of black. I stick my hands in my jacket pockets, square my shoulders. Now or never.

"I can walk with you," Charlie offers.

I shake my head. "I'm good. I don't have far to go, and I have a few tricks up my sleeve."

Charlie is clearly torn on the subject. But we've just met and part of being an addict is learning the importance of boundaries. His job is to take care of him, just like my job is to take care of me. We will both be the better for it.

He finally shrugs, heading in the opposite direction. I let him go first, watching his bulk shuffle into the dark. Then I set off at a much more rapid pace.

The first block is empty of pedestrians. Just cars passing by, some slowing down, some speeding up, all of which I pointedly ignore. Off the lighted boulevard now, onto a smaller, darker residential street. No shadows peel off from the dark. No footsteps echo around me.

I keep hustling, block by block. Two streets from my destination I spot four figures ahead. They are clumped near a tree at the corner of an overgrown lot. Definitely men, but other than that it's too dark to tell. Their attention is on one another, not seeming to notice me as I cross to the other side to put more distance between us.

There is something so furtive about the group that the hairs rise instinctively on the back of my neck. One of them has his pants down around his knees. I don't want to see more, yet I can't look away.

Then I spy it, faintly illuminated by a distant porchlight. A needle jammed into the inside of the man's thigh. Followed by an ecstatic look on the man's face. His companions shift closer, one already reaching for the needle, anticipating his turn.

I pass on by. They never notice. Just five addicts sharing a brief moment that four of them will never remember.

I make it to my apartment. Close the door behind me. And remembering to leave my socks on, finally crash exhausted into bed.

THE LOW RUMBLE of an engine. I hear it, followed by a weight, solid and warm on top of my chest.

"Good night, Piper," I murmur.

More rumbling.

Then we both fall asleep again.

CHAPTER 10

I N THE MORNING, PIPER HAS once again vanished off the bed. Not wanting to repeat yesterday's mistake, I climb off the end of the mattress, taking as big a step as possible onto the floor. No claws lash out. I move gingerly around the bed to the kitchen area, and notice two things at once: The water bowl needs to be refilled, and there are two disemboweled mice in the middle of the ancient hardwoods. Viv hadn't been kidding; Piper earns her keep.

"Am I supposed to be impressed?" I call out to my roommate. "And what do I do now? Throw away the corpses? Fashion the ears into a necklace?"

I find a plastic grocery bag in one of the kitchen drawers and reluctantly use it to pick up the remains. That still leaves me with a brownish red smear. Definitely gross. I jump quickly into the shower before my feline roommate can make any more statements.

Ten A.M. I have five hours before I need to report to work, and many investigative paths to pursue. I want to follow up on after-hours cell phones, though it sounds like that might have to wait for a free evening. I also have more questions for the family, now that I'm getting the lay of the land. I wonder if Guerline would let me go through Angelique's room, till I remember Angelique doesn't really have a room. But she must still have stuff in the living room, that sort of thing.

Most people don't realize what a financial luxury privacy is. An individual bedroom, time alone, designated workspace—these things cost money. Angelique got to sleep in a shared family room, while probably doing homework on the kitchen table on a refurbished laptop after her brother had his turn.

Meaning that if she wanted to keep secrets, a diary might not be out of the question. The police had to have gone through her things; her aunt and brother, too. But this is where a fresh pair of eyes doesn't hurt.

Maybe I could get Guerline to meet me at the apartment on her lunch break? Which would make this morning a good time for the rec center. Even if there aren't kids around, it would be helpful to meet the staff who work there, some of whom may remember Angelique from the summer before she went missing.

It's worth a shot.

I lace up my tennis shoes, throw on my olive-colored jacket, and head down the stairs and out the side door.

Where I receive my next surprise of the morning.

Emmanuel Badeau, who's clearly skipped school, is waiting impatiently for me.

"I have something to show you," he says without preamble, pushing away from the side of the building. "But you can't tell my aunt."

I don't have time to say yes or no, before he unzips his backpack and removes a battered laptop.

I turn back around, unlock the door, and lead him into Stoney's bar.

"You do not know my sister," he starts. "People think because she's a teenager she must be silly or stupid or impulsive. She's none of these things."

"Water?" I ask.

"Coffee," he orders.

"What are you, thirteen?"

Emmanuel looks up at me blankly. Apparently drinking coffee at thirteen is not shocking in his world. I head to the kitchen to brew up a pot, because I certainly need a cup, giving him time to boot up the laptop. By the time I return, he's seated at the booth farthest from the front door, frowning over the screen on his laptop. The machine is making a funny whirring noise that doesn't sound particularly healthy to me. Idly, he lifts up the slender instrument and bangs it down on the table. The grinding noise stops. The battered case, I notice, is covered in stickers. Everything from favorite coffee shops to the Haitian flag to the Red Sox. You can learn a lot about a person from their stickers. So far, I've deduced that Emmanuel has the same interests as an average teenager.

"Cream, sugar?" I ask.

The answer turns out to be all of the above. Emmanuel pours enough extras into his mug to turn it into a coffee-flavored milkshake. I take my first sip of shuddering-hot brew, and remind myself it would not taste better with a shot of Baileys. Or Kahlua. Or maybe even that RumChata stuff.

Emmanuel turns the laptop till I can see the screen from my side of the table. It takes me a moment to understand what I'm seeing.

It's like a virtual bulletin board, filled with photos of his sister, and plastered with what appear to be scanned copies of newspaper articles. There are bubble comments here and there and fierce words scrawled across certain sections in bold.

Big Sister. Caring Daughter. Star Student.

It's a digital collage. Without asking for permission, I take the laptop and pull it over to me. I study each image, each pull-out quote.

A faded photo of a baby with her face covered in smeared bananas. A photo of a little girl sitting on an old couch next to an infant, patting his head like one would pet a dog. Next photo, Angelique and her toddler brother are holding hands, beaming in front of a homemade swing.

Then the most recent photos. Angelique sitting at the table in the apartment, head over her schoolwork. Angelique on the sofa, holding up an exasperated hand, as if to ward off the photographer. Angelique curled up asleep on the sofa, colorful quilt pulled up to her neck, an anatomy book splayed beneath her chin, where it must've fallen when she dozed off.

Angelique smiling that same shy smile from her missing poster. But also Angelique laughing, Angelique working. Fifteen-year-old Angelique, growing up in front of my eyes.

Then, I start scanning the words, and I understand everything.

"It was you," I murmur, looking up at Emmanuel. "You're the one who keeps posting online, visiting the message boards. You—your posts—you're the one who brought me here."

"I didn't mean you." He scowls darkly.

"Tell me about this." I push the laptop back to him. "How did you do this? Why?"

He takes a moment, clearly gathering his thoughts. "That Friday, when my sister didn't come home, when my *mamant* called Officer O'Shaughnessy . . . I could see they didn't take the situation seriously. She will come home, they said. Maybe she had to run an errand or made plans with friends. Don't worry, don't worry, don't worry. These things happen with teenagers. But these things don't happen with my sister. Not with LiLi."

His personal nickname for his big sister, from when he was little and couldn't pronounce Angelique. I had read about it online. A detail provided by Emmanuel, I realize now, in order to humanize his sister. Make her real not just for sympathizers, but to any predator who might be holding her.

"Officer O'Shaughnessy promised he would ask around. He even called a detective, to make my aunt happy, and more officers arrived to question our neighbors. But I could *tell* they didn't believe anything was wrong. That they thought at any moment, the door would open and my sister appear."

"They interviewed your neighbors?"

"Up and down the block. The ones who would answer the door."

"Knock-and-talks," I murmur, the beginning of any search.

"I conducted my own knock-and-talks." Emmanuel feels out the sound of the official words. "Except I reached out to LiLi's friends. When they said they didn't know where she could be, I knew she was in trouble. And I knew the police would not be able to help us. But I can't knock on every door. I can't make adults talk to me or force the police to listen. So I made this. To keep my sister alive. To let the world know who she is, so that maybe if someone sees her, they will call us. Or"—his shoulders square—"if someone has her, they will see she is a daughter, sister, niece. She is kind and smart. And that person will let her come home again."

"What about Officer O'Shaughnessy? I thought your aunt liked him."

"She likes that he speaks Kreyòl. That he drinks soursop and brings over his mother's homemade meat patties. He's familiar, but he's not the same. He's an American whose family came from Haiti.

My aunt, my sister, myself, we are Haitians who now live in America. He has never felt the ground shake beneath his feet. He doesn't understand that it can happen again."

The way Emmanuel says this, I realize he's not talking strictly about the earthquake that flattened Port-au-Prince ten years earlier. He's speaking of their life even now, filled with an uncertain future.

"Are you happy here?" I ask. "Do you—did Angelique—want to stay?"

"We want to be Americans. Very much. LiLi talks of nothing else."

"I've heard of the complications of your visa status. That it's already run out once, and may still be revoked. Was Angelique scared that she would have to return to Haiti? Does she even remember your home island?"

"You do not understand my sister," Emmanuel repeats.

"I would like to," I tell him honestly. "I would like to, very much."

Emmanuel sighs. He leans forward, gets that look on his face people reserve for speaking to idiots. "I do not remember Haiti. I was three when we left. Even my own mother, I know her face from photos, her voice from the phone. The rest, it's been too long now."

I nod.

"What I do remember is the dark. Waking up to a noise that scared me. I didn't know what, I was only a little boy. But I woke up and I knew, without seeing, that something very bad was happening. Then I heard my mother, crying, pleading. 'No,' she was saying over and over again. Then I heard a terrible sound again. Smacking. Like flesh hitting flesh."

I'm not sure what to say.

"I couldn't get up. I peed the bed in terror. Then, LiLi took my hand in the dark. She told me it was just the TV, even though we both knew it wasn't. She sang me a song, one of our favorites, and after a while I sang with her."

"She would've been what, six at the time?"

Emmanuel nods. His gaze is far away, his young face grim. "Later, the earth started to shake and pictures fell off the wall and my sister was there again, grabbing my hand, pulling me outside into the open yard. 'Stay,' she ordered me. Then she disappeared into the house. I wanted to follow. I was so scared. People were screaming. I thought I would die. I thought we would all die, and there was nothing I could do."

"You were three," I remind him gently.

"When I saw my sister again, she was holding my mother's hand. I don't think my mother found my sister. I think LiLi went back for her. I think LiLi brought *her* out of our home, right before it collapsed."

Six-year-old Angelique. It's possible, I suppose, but I also wonder how much of this memory is clouded by a baby brother who idolizes his big sister.

"We had a father," Emmanuel tells me. "I've never seen pictures of him. LiLi, my aunt, my mother, they never speak of him. I remember his voice. I remember his fists. And I remember LiLi did *not* lead him out of our house."

This catches me off guard. I sit back, trying to understand what Emmanuel clearly believes. That six-year-old Angelique not only saved him and their mother during the earthquake, but she— deliberately?—left their abusive father behind.

"People say LiLi is shy. She's not shy," Emmanuel tells me fiercely. "She's focused. She has her friends, but they're foolish girls with foolish dreams. LiLi has a mission. Not just to save herself, but to save both of us."

"She had a plan to protect you two against deportation?"

"She started taking classes online." Emmanuel gestured to the laptop. "Two extra courses a semester. She said she could not count on her visa lasting three more years till graduation. But she could work harder to graduate earlier, so she could get into the college and have a student visa. Then she would be safe."

"What about you and your aunt?"

"My aunt has a green card. She's been here a long time. But she said if LiLi and I go, then she will return to Haiti as well. We have been together too long for her to want to be apart. We are hers, the children of her sister's body and her heart."

I imagine that sounds even more beautiful in Kreyòl. "So if Angelique had a student visa . . ."

"Then she and my aunt would be safe. Maybe then, they could petition for just me, or buy some time. LiLi told me not to worry. She always told me not to worry."

"You don't think she simply took off to avoid deportation?"

"Never."

I point my chin at the laptop. "Did you and she share that?"

"Yes."

"The police must've examined it."

"They took it, kept it for months till Officer O'Shaughnessy asked for it back. He knew I needed it for my schoolwork."

"They find anything?"

"No. But I knew they wouldn't."

I regard Emmanuel seriously. "Because you had the laptop for at least a full weekend before the police became serious about their efforts, and in that time . . . ?"

"I didn't remove anything. There was nothing to remove." Emmanuel touches the keyboard lightly. "My sister loves math and science. She would read codebreaking books and do endless number puzzles to wind down. She will become a doctor. None of us doubt her. But this is my superpower." His fingers dance across the keyboard. "By midnight Friday, when LiLi still hadn't come home, this is where I first started looking. I tore apart every gigabyte of data on the hard drive. Nothing. By the time the police requested it on Monday, what did I care? As usual, they were too late."

"But your sister is very smart. And aren't there a ton of apps designed solely to help teenagers avoid their parents' spying eyes?"

Emmanuel merely shrugs. "LiLi might keep secrets from our aunt, but she wouldn't keep secrets from me."

"What about her phone?"

"We don't have it. It was in her backpack, or I would've checked it, too."

"You ever see a different cell phone around the house? Maybe something old-school, like a beat-up flip phone . . ." I let my voice drift off.

"An after-hours phone. Many kids have them."

"Then you all know about them, including Angelique?"

"Yes." Emmanuel hesitated. "Once, I noticed what I thought might be a phone, tucked underneath Angel's school papers. But then it was gone, and I never saw it again."

"When was this?"

"Over a year ago. September maybe, last year."

"Two months before Angelique went missing?"

He nods.

"What about the rec center?"

"What about it?"

"I understand Angelique spent the summer before school started there."

"They have a day program for teens." Emmanuel nods. "We both attended."

"With your friends from school?"

"Our friends from the neighborhood. Most of our classmates live too far away."

"So, lots of new kids?"

"Yes."

"Did you make new friends?"

"Yes."

"And Angelique?"

A shrug. "No one she mentioned. She had Marjolie, of course. They walked over together each day."

"What about a young man?"

Emmanuel flops back in the booth. "Now you sound like the stupid police."

"Sorry."

"My sister did not meet some boy. She would not leave me or my aunt or her dreams of medicine for some *boy*."

There is so much disdain in his voice, I wonder if Emmanuel is protesting too much. But what he says next catches me off guard.

"'I think that God's got a sick sense of humor and when I die, I expect to find him laughing,'" he suddenly quotes.

It takes me a moment. "Wait, isn't that Depeche Mode? But what do my high school memories have to do with anything?"

"Eighties music is very popular," Emmanuel states seriously.

"I still don't get it."

Emmanuel looks around, as if expecting the sudden appearance of eavesdroppers, then whispers quietly, "LiLi doesn't believe in love. She doesn't believe in God either. 'No one will save us, *ti fre*.' She told me that all the time. When I woke up with nightmares, when I first cried with homesickness: 'No one will save us, *ti fre*, but it is okay, for we will save ourselves.' That's what my sister believes in. Her strength, her determination, her plan. She was not waiting for our aunt to magically secure our visas, or for some lawyers to sue on our behalf. LiLi believes in LiLi. We will be okay, because *she* will work hard enough to make it so." A pause. "You cannot tell my aunt this. It would break her heart."

I nod slowly, leaning back in silence. The sister he describes, a girl who at the tender age of six supposedly had the fortitude to save her own mother and brother, who was still actively in pursuit of a better future for them all . . .

I think I would've liked that girl very much. And I don't want to believe she could've been derailed by something as fickle as male attention. Then again, fifteen is that age. And maybe the girl who didn't get to act like a normal six-year-old wanted for one moment to be foolish and giddy. I couldn't blame her for that.

"Are you continuing to update this site?" I ask Emmanuel.

"Yes. The police . . . They were too slow to start. And now, all this time without any progress . . . We do not see or hear from them so much anymore. Even at school . . . It's a new year. The other kids, teachers, they move on. It's not their home that is empty."

"You're hoping this might gather national interest. Maybe get your sister's case on a major news program, re-ignite the investigation."

"I send letters and e-mails every week. They don't answer. But my sister . . ." His voice breaks slightly. "She's worth it. The whole world should know her. The whole world should be looking. Why . . . Why aren't they looking?"

Then he can't talk. Emmanuel looks down at the table, blinking rapidly. I reach across, lightly fold my fingers over his hand. He doesn't pull away, but we both know it's not my comfort he wants.

"I'm not *GMA*," I say. "Or *48 Hours* or any of those national shows."

"No," he states bitterly. Nothing like a teen to give it to you straight.

"But I can promise you," I continue, "that I do care, and I am looking, and I won't leave till your sister comes home."

"She's not your family."

"I choose her anyway. According to you, she's worth it. That's good enough for me."

He glances up, his eyes damp with tears. "She did *not* run away."

"I believe you."

"She did not leave us for some boy."

"Okay."

"But something has changed."

"Clearly."

"No, I mean recently. The past few weeks. Before, when she first disappeared, I monitored the internet for signs of activity all the time. But . . . It's been a while."

I nod.

"I'd stopped paying attention. But then you came, and you asked questions and last night . . ."

"What happened last night, Emmanuel?"

"I logged into one of her classes," Emmanuel murmurs. "I just wanted to picture her leaning over the computer, tapping away. I wanted to feel close to her again. But I couldn't."

"You couldn't log in, or you couldn't . . . feel any hint of your sister?"

"The course was closed."

"Like you said, it's been eleven months."

"No, not suspended or canceled. *Closed.* As in the work completed, so the class is no more. Sometime in the past month, my sister logged in. She submitted the homework. She passed the test."

Emmanuel stares at me. "Last week, my missing sister . . . I don't understand . . . I can't explain . . . but of all things, LiLi completed her online class. She's out there, somewhere, still doing her school-work. But not coming home to us. Why? Of all things . . . Why?"

CHAPTER 11

DETECTIVE LOTHAM IS NOT HAPPY to hear from me. The news that I'm with Emmanuel and the teen has something to share doesn't improve his mood.

"What, you talked to him for four minutes this morning and now he's bared his soul?"

"Actually, he came to me. First thing. No four minutes required."

The detective growled. I have that kind of effect on law enforcement.

"Why?"

I treat the question as rhetorical. The answer, that Emmanuel brought his discovery to me because I'm *not* a cop, is hardly going to improve Lotham's mood.

"Stay," the detective orders. "I'll call up the crime scene techs and be right there."

"You don't need crime scene techs."

"You said he found something on the computer—"

"The internet. His computer is just the access point. And if you seize—for the second time—the laptop he needs for his schoolwork, then he's definitely not sharing anything with either of us ever again. Bring yourself, Detective. That'll be enough."

More grumbling, but surprisingly enough, twenty minutes later Detective Lotham knocks on the front door all by his lonesome. I've taken the time to brew another pot of coffee and make two giant plates of French fries. I haven't had breakfast yet, and you can never go wrong with fries. Given how quickly Emmanuel inhales the first batch, he agrees.

"This is cozy," Lotham mutters to me as he stalks in, inhaling the scent of coffee and grease.

"Which would you like first: caffeine or sarcasm?"

"Caffeine."

"At least you have some common sense." I leave the wide-eyed detective to sort himself out while I pour a third mug. Emmanuel is already regarding Lotham warily. If I didn't know any better, I would say the teen looks hurt.

Had he been grateful when the detective finally arrived at his apartment? The presence of so many officers, forensic experts? A kid who'd grown up watching American crime shows, he must've assumed the next scene would include his sister's tearful return.

Except eleven months later, Detective Lotham hadn't brought home his sister.

I don't expect this conversation to be fun for anyone. I eye the wall of booze with longing. Feel your feels, as the saying goes. Except so many feelings are hard to take.

While waiting for Detective Lotham, I'd convinced Emmanuel to call his aunt. She couldn't answer her phone at work, he told me, so he left a message explaining where he was and what he was doing. Odds are she'd listen to the recording during her lunch break.

Which gave us maybe an hour before she came barreling through the door as well. Stoney's bar is one happening place.

"French fries?" I ask the detective, pushing the second plate in his direction as he slides into the booth across from Emmanuel. This morning he's wearing a dark blue blazer over a light blue shirt and a patterned indigo tie. Sharp dresser, I think, but I still prefer his broken nose and tattered ear. If clothes are camouflage, then scars are exclamation points of honesty.

Lotham lifts his coffee mug, gives me a look, then picks up a fry.

I offer ketchup. Emmanuel and Lotham reach for it at the same time. And we're off and running.

"Start at the beginning," I tell Emmanuel. So he does. Lotham, to his credit, doesn't interrupt or make any more scowly faces. He drinks his coffee, scarfs more fries, and listens, face intent.

When Emmanuel's done, Lotham produces a little spiral notebook and his cell phone. With his phone, he takes a photo of the laptop screen, with the web address of Angelique's school site clearly visible. Then he pushes his notebook across the table and has Emmanuel jot down Angelique's username and password.

"So Angelique registered at this GED Now site to take online courses?"

Emmanuel nods.

"In order to graduate high school early?"

A fresh nod.

"And this U.S. history class was what she'd started before she disappeared?"

"She'd been taking it over the summer."

"Who knew this?"

Emmanuel shrugs. "My aunt and me, of course. I don't know how much she talked schoolwork with her friends."

Lotham is staring at the computer screen. "I don't remember this from our original conversations or having seen anything in the reports on the forensic exam of the computer."

"You wouldn't. An online class is an online class. The computer doesn't matter, the codes to access the class do."

Lotham picks up his notebook. Angelique's username is a basic Gmail account, which makes sense. Her password, however, looks like a string of random numbers followed by an exclamation mark. Lotham shares it with me. I glance up at Emmanuel.

"You can remember this?" I ask him.

"It's a code," he murmurs. "The numbers stand for letters, from a cypher LiLi made up when we were younger. It reads *Doc2Be!*"

"As in doctor-to-be?"

"Exactly."

Lotham makes another note. "This her primary password? The one she uses most of the time?"

"I don't know. I understand her cipher. We'd send each other coded notes using it. But we share this laptop, and I've watched her log in enough times. She knew I knew. What did it matter?"

"Can you see when she logged into the class?" Lotham asks. "Or how many times?"

Emmanuel takes the computer back. "Normally you would check browser history, but given she didn't log in from this computer to complete the coursework . . ." He chews his lower lip, dark eyes narrowed in thought. "Ah. Here. When I first logged on last night, it told me the last time I'd accessed the course." Emmanuel taps the screen, showing a record of date and time.

Lotham makes more notes while I peer closer. "Two weeks ago," I say. "Three-oh-three P.M." I glance at Emmanuel. "Does that mean anything to you? The date significant? The time of day? You said your sister likes codes."

Emmanuel's fingers fly over the keyboard, but then he shakes his head. "I don't think so."

"Walk me through how this works," Lotham requests, attention back on us. "Angelique logs in to get assignments off the site, then what—completes them in some virtual classrooms, or uploads them from her own computer for her teacher to review?"

"Written essays she completes on her own, then uploads, yes. Tests are more complicated, with additional codes that must be entered by an adult, like my aunt, as protection against cheating."

"So for this class to be completed, the final must've been some kind of written work?"

"Yes."

"Which she had to upload from a computer," Lotham muses, "which would give us an IP address. Now that's something."

He has his phone to his ear in the next instant, talking to someone about the website, user codes, and issuing a subpoena for additional records. Emmanuel nods along with the conversation, so apparently the technical mumble-jumble makes sense to him.

I have a different question. "When Angelique disappeared, did you or your aunt contact this site, tell her teachers she had vanished?"

"My aunt gets e-mails from the site, keeping her notified of Angel's progress. The courses cost money, so the school wants guardians to be informed. When assignments stopped being turned in, she would've been notified. But of all the things for my aunt to answer, worry about . . ."

"What did Angelique post?" Lotham is off the phone, looking at us again. "Can you pull up the essay?"

Emmanuel shakes his head. "The class is closed out. I can't enter the course to look at past work."

"Could you contact the course instructor?" I ask. "I mean, you have your sister's e-mail and password. Can't you just . . . be her and fire off an e-mail asking for a copy of the final assignment back? Your computer crashed right after sending, a virus ate your hard drive, something?"

Both Emmanuel and Lotham appear impressed, so apparently my basic internet skills have some merit.

Emmanuel works the keyboard again. "I can Instachat," he declares after a moment. "The class professor is listed as being available. Hang on."

I sip my coffee. It's almost noon now. I wonder when Stoney is going to arrive and realize I've turned his bar into some kind of investigative headquarters. And what he might do or say about that. This may be the shortest job I've ever had.

Well, there was that place I was employed at for all of twenty minutes. Probably the fact I'd showed up totally loaded and crying hysterically hadn't helped. Then that restaurant where I'd caught my hair on fire during the first shift . . .

Emmanuel frowns at the screen. "The teacher is Dr. Cappa. She says she thought she might hear from me."

Lotham and I exchange glances.

"While the essay doesn't reflect the quality of my previous work," Emmanuel reads out loud, "there's no need for a redo given my passing grade."

"Get the damn assignment," Lotham growls.

Emmanuel types more furiously. I have no idea what he's saying to the teacher, if he's still pretending to be Angelique or now explaining the situation, but minute rolls into minute, Lotham shifting restlessly beside me. Then:

"She sent it. I had to open the messenger system. Okay, here we go. The file was uploaded when Angelique last accessed the site.

From . . . from an internet café." Emmanuel pushes the laptop across the table to Lotham, who snaps a photo of the file's information, and once again starts working his phone.

"You can tell all that from the upload?" I ask Emmanuel.

"Cybercafés have certain string codes," he murmurs, already back to work. "Hang on. Here it is. The essay. Except it's not a .doc file. It's a PDF—a scanned image."

The laptop screen fills with an image. It takes me a few moments to digest.

It appears to be a copy of torn pieces of yellow legal pad paper. It was scanned in color, revealing fold marks and smudges in the background. *Western Expansion* is written across the top in a small, neat script, followed by the body of the essay.

"Is that her?" I ask.

"It's LiLi's penmanship," Emmanuel confirms, still scanning the screen. "But she would not handwrite school work."

We all resume studying. I can't tell what Detective Lotham thinks, but I'm confused. Everyone has described Angelique as a gifted student. This essay, on the other hand, not only looks clunky and awkward as it unspools down two sheets of paper, but reads that way as well.

Never has a moment been as important in American history as the westward movement.

Going forward was the only option for settlers in search of land and a new government that needed

To expand resources. President Andrew Jackson refused to

Give up plans to eject Indians from lands west of the Mississippi even when

You would've thought otherwise . . .

I don't understand. Eleven months after disappearing, this is what Angelique cares about? Finding a way to crudely complete and post an essay for high school credit? Which assumed she had at least some access to the outside world. Yet hadn't returned home?

I've encountered some strange behavior in my line of work, but this has me stumped.

"Did she sign up for additional courses?" I start to ask, just as Emmanuel bolts upright and slaps the table.

"It's code! I knew it. She sent a code! My sister sent us a message!"

"What code?" Lotham is already pulling the laptop closer, trying to decipher the riddle.

"The capitalized words at the beginning of each line on the page. Look at them." Emmanuel starts circling words on the screen with his finger. I follow along, reading out loud.

"Never. Going. To. Give. You." I stop. Glance at Lotham. "Isn't that a song—"

"'Never Gonna Give You Up' by Rick Astley, 1987, yes, yes," Emmanuel says quickly. He's grabbed the detective's spiral notebook without asking and is already jotting down the first word of each line on the page. Lotham doesn't stop him.

"Rickrolling," Emmanuel informs us in answer to our unasked question, still writing furiously. "It was an internet meme prank years ago. People would embed the link to the music video in various websites or news clips. It was really funny." He waves his hand. "I told you the eighties are big."

Lotham looks at me. I shrug, confirming we are both that old.

"LiLi didn't care about the memes. She got excited about the paper."

"The paper?" Lotham takes the bait.

"A quantum physics essay written by a student. It perfectly incorporated the lyrics from the entire song. LiLi loved it—the idea of a brilliantly written paper also being a joke. How clever, you know?

And she liked the song, used to sing it while getting ready in the morning."

Emmanuel's writing suddenly falters. He glances up, his expression stark.

"These capitalized words are from the song, right?" He shows us the list of lyrics he's scrawled down. "If you were to pay attention, knew what to look for, the message is funny. Some stupid things kids do."

He said it, not us.

"But two words don't belong. They're capitalized, but they're much further down in the essay, and they're not part of the lyrics. She tucked them in. Hoped whoever was watching wouldn't notice." Emmanuel's voice drops to a whisper as his gaze rises to meet ours. "*Help Us*. My sister wrote *Help Us*. That's the message. Except who is *us*?"

CHAPTER 12

LOTHAM IS BACK TO HIS phone, a major detective working a major case. He paces the entire length of the tavern as he rips off strings of commands. I don't have minions to order about or experts to call in, so I remain with Emmanuel. His face has shuttered. He stares at his laptop as if trying to see through it. Maybe he's wishing he'd logged on sooner to find the note. Maybe he's sorry he found it now.

I give him thirty seconds, then start stacking our used coffee mugs on the empty plates. "Come with me."

"What?"

"Time to clean up."

Emmanuel's eyes widen. What kind of crazy person worries about dishes at a time like this? But I don't make it a request, and he's too well trained to defy direct orders. He follows me into the kitchen. I set him to work with the high-power spray and industrial-grade dishwashing detergent.

While he tends to the dishes, I go to work on the coffeepot, then clean up around the fryolator.

"Your sister sent that note for you," I say.

Emmanuel pauses momentarily, then picks up the next coffee mug.

"She sent that note to you," I continue. "She posted it, knowing you would see it. Who else would be logging into some virtual high school? Who else would think to look there, other than the younger brother who knew her that well?"

"I don't understand. Where she went. What happened. Who she is with now. I don't understand."

"None of us do. But this is good, Emmanuel. It's contact. If she did it once, maybe she'll have a chance to do it again."

"My sister has been kidnapped." He says the words as if testing them out. "She made it to the internet café, but she must still be fearful if she couldn't just ask for help. Why wouldn't she be able to ask for help? Who is *us*?"

"This is good," I repeat. "She's alive."

"LiLi's not safe," he says. "Help us, help us, help us." His shock is wearing off. I know what comes next.

I move to the sink. I shut off the spray, taking the mug from his now shaking hand and setting it down.

"We don't know what we don't know," I tell him, my fingers holding his, as his breath starts to hitch and his shoulders tremble. "She's thinking, Emmanuel. As you said, your sister doesn't dream, she makes plans. Disguising a plea for help as a history essay, then waiting for the right moment to upload it to the internet for her brother to discover—that's brilliant. Your sister found a way to reach out to you. And you were there, Emmanuel. Whatever happens next, you got the message. You were there for her."

His eyes well. He wants to cry. He doesn't want to appear weak. He's nearly broken with fear. He's desperate to remain strong.

Then, noises from the dining room behind us. Guerline appears in the kitchen doorway, coat still on, bearing still imposing. She doesn't so much as glance at me but sweeps through the tight space and enfolds her nephew into her arms.

Emmanuel's shoulders shake harder, though no sound comes out. His aunt strokes his hair and murmurs soft words. A family unit of two that used to be three.

I leave them to their shared grief as I go to find Detective Lotham and figure out what I should do next.

AN HOUR LATER, Guerline and Emmanuel are ensconced in the booth, heads bowed together, while Detective Lotham stands in the opposite corner in deep conversation with Officer O'Shaughnessy. They keep their voices low, but the intensity of the discussion has me and Angelique's family straining our ears.

Finally both cops pause, mutter something I can't quite catch, then break from their police huddle and make their way over to them. I'm behind the bar, pretending to stack glasses and clean already scoured surfaces simply to give myself something to do. The French fries have settled queasily in my stomach, or maybe it's the growing implications of what Angelique's hidden *help* message must mean.

"Does the name Tamara Levesque mean anything to you?" Detective Lotham asks Aunt Guerline and Emmanuel.

Both shake their heads as Officer O'Shaughnessy slides into the booth opposite them. He clasps the aunt's hand, and she lets him.

"All right, this is what we know." Lotham doesn't take a seat but remains standing. I've already noticed that about him. He's one of those people who do their best thinking while moving. He's restless and, especially under stress, radiates a certain raw presence.

"Two weeks ago, a Black female entered an internet café in Roxbury. She produced this driver's license." Lotham reveals a black-and-white photocopy of the license. From this distance, I can just make out the name as Tamara Levesque. The picture is too small for me to see how much it resembles Angelique, but judging from everyone's expression, it must be damn close.

"According to the attendant, he'd just logged her in and copied her license when her phone rang. She talked for a second, then abruptly handed over a note to the attendant along with twenty bucks. She said she had to go right now, but her class assignment had to be posted or she'd fail the course. Could he follow the instructions and do it for her? Please. Thank you. Then she was gone before he even had time to answer. Annoyed him, but twenty bucks for two minutes' work? He went ahead and did it. Never saw the girl again."

"My Angelique," Guerline says.

Lotham squats down to match her seated height. "He couldn't identify the girl as Angelique. She was wearing a red baseball cap, pulled low, and he wasn't paying that much attention. But if you look at the photo on the fake ID . . ."

"My Angelique," Guerline states again. She sighs, and there is a wealth of sorrow in that single exhale.

"Was she alone?" Emmanuel asks. Smart kid.

"The attendant doesn't remember seeing anyone else. We're grabbing video from inside the store, as well as the general area." Lotham rises once more to standing, knees popping in the silence. He rubs one absently.

"So . . . She was walking around the street alone. She entered the store alone. She had a phone alone . . ." Emmanuel looks at the detective, his pain and confusion clearly evident.

"We are taking this very seriously." O'Shaughnessy speaks up from the table. "We're going to find her."

"Emmanuel," Detective Lotham says more quietly, "even if your sister was alone, it doesn't mean she wasn't under duress. If she's feeling threatened enough to write a coded message, it may mean she knows eyes are on her at all times. It may mean she feels like she must do whatever it is she's doing in order to keep others safe."

"Help us?" Emmanuel asks. He looks too young for this conversation. I truly wish he were too young for this conversation.

"My niece has been kidnapped?" Guerline speaks up. "Somebody . . . took her? After school? And others? But her friends . . . We have seen her friends."

"What's important is that Angelique's alive and has some level of autonomy," Lotham states. He doesn't address the issue of Angelique's friends being accounted for, because sadly, there are too many other terrible possibilities. Human trafficking. Angelique being abducted with other pretty young girls. Or swept up in something beyond her control. Maybe she had met the wrong boy. Or made the wrong new friend. The *help us* message is an important break in the case. But it's also an ominous development. That we are dealing with a situation far graver than a lone teenager having disappeared or run away.

"Have either of you seen this fake ID?" Lotham asks Emmanuel and Guerline. His gaze lingers on Emmanuel. But both shake their heads.

I bring over four glasses of water to the booth, passing them out in a show of hospitality that also allows me a closer look at the black-and-white photocopy of the fake ID.

At a glance, I can tell this ID is an old-fashioned Massachusetts license, versus the newer Real IDs that are required for airport security. The photocopy is of the front of the ID only and not a good-quality reproduction. Clearly, the attendant at the cybercafé had been purely going through the motions.

"Ahem," Lotham says. I glance up to find him staring at me, my water delivery not having fooled him for a second.

"Does that cybercafé still have the original ID?" I ask. As long as I'm busted, I might as well go all in.

"No."

"What about the essay, login instructions, other notes she handed over?"

"Attendant threw them away. They were scanned and uploaded. No reason to hang on to the hard copies."

"Why Roxbury? Has she used that internet café before?"

Lotham doesn't object to this question. Instead, both he and O'Shaughnessy glance at the family. Once again, Emmanuel does the answering.

"She never mentioned it to me. It's not close to our apartment, or on the way home from school. Or"—he is a thoughtful young man—"near her friends."

"What about her new friend?" Again, as long as I've joined the party. "The one she met at the rec center that summer?"

"I do not know that friend," Emmanuel says.

Guerline speaks up. "What new friend?"

That I stay out of. Though it's difficult given the glare I receive from Lotham. The police like to withhold as much information as possible, even from the families. I understand; nine times out of ten, the family is part of the problem, not the solution. But I've also worked cases where such communication gaps led to stalls in the investigation. If someone had just mentioned discovery A to family member B, then investigator C would've learned immediately about the impossibility of that claim.

Being an untrained, inexperienced civilian, as Detective Lotham likes to put it, I'm not bound by department policy. Instead, I get to follow my gut. Given the genuine shock, grief, and fear I see on Guerline's and Emmanuel's faces, I think they have no idea what happened to Angelique. Whatever mess she'd made or stumbled into or gotten tangled up in, they would like to know as much as anyone.

I also like to think: They would love her anyway. But maybe that has more to do with my needs than theirs.

"Angelique's friends claim she was different the fall she disappeared," Lotham provides at last. "Distracted. Maybe by someone she'd met during the summer program at the rec center. Did you notice anything?"

Guerline doesn't answer right away. On the table, O'Shaughnessy is still clasping her hand in his. Now, he gives her fingers a reassuring squeeze.

"My Angel, she was . . . quieter," Guerline concedes at last. "On her computer more. I assumed it was school. Her classes are very demanding, yes, and she insists on taking even more, over the internet. She wants to get ahead. This is a good thing. I did not worry. I did not think to worry."

Emmanuel leans his head against her shoulder.

"Did Angelique have her own money?" I ask now.

Guerline glances at me. "She babysat, had small jobs. Not a lot of money. But for her own spending."

"Did you find that money after she left? In a handbag, stashed in a lockbox?"

"Angelique carried a small zippered wallet. It went missing with her. But . . ." Guerline is frowning.

So is Detective Lotham. "When we searched the apartment," he provides, "we didn't find any cash. Nor was the wallet in her backpack. Most likely, she had it on her when she disappeared."

"How much in savings, Guerline? Hundreds? Thousands? I mean, if Angelique had been babysitting for a bit, and wasn't one to spend money on frivolous things . . ."

But Guerline shakes her head. "Angelique spent her money on her extra classes. I did not like that. I would have liked to pay for them, let her keep her money for fun. But . . ." Guerline shrugs. "It is only me to buy our food, pay our rent, plus send money back home."

I nod. So does O'Shaughnessy.

"Would a couple hundred dollars be out of the question?" I push now.

Guerline still seems uncertain, but Emmanuel nods. I turn my attention to Lotham.

"That's a lotta cash for a person to be carrying around these streets," I murmur. "For her to have all of that in her wallet the day she went missing . . ."

Lotham clearly doesn't like this thought any more than I do. A girl as smart as Angelique definitely wouldn't be roaming around with hundreds of dollars in cash as a matter of habit. And yet, if all the money was gone . . . She must've taken it out of its hiding spot for that Friday and brought it with her to school. For the something special she was planning to do afterward.

"I don't understand—" Emmanuel begins.

"Could I come over to your apartment?" I ask Guerline. "Not today, I know you're exhausted. But maybe tomorrow? Just . . . to glance around. Get a feel for Angelique. A fresh pair of eyes never hurts."

"Wait a sec." Lotham, using his unhappy voice.

"You and my Emmanuel, you find this note?" Guerline speaks over the detective. "This message for help from our Angel?"

Emmanuel did the heavy lifting, but I don't hesitate to share the credit.

"Then you should come. Today. Now, please. This message was sent weeks ago. That is too long. My Angelique needs to come home now."

The starkness behind her words nearly breaks my heart. I don't know how I can blow off my second day of work already, but I also can't deny her. Even the cops, twin faces of disapproval, don't say a word.

I hear a distant rattle from the back. A second later, Stoney walks in from the side entrance, both hands on his light jacket. He stops when he sees the strange little grouping sitting in his closed tavern. His gaze goes from the police to the family to me.

I open my mouth, searching desperately for some kind of explanation. No words come out.

He waits.

"Your cat killed two," I state finally.

He nods, as if this makes perfect sense.

"Then Emmanuel Badeau—do you know Emmanuel? One of your neighbors? He made a discovery on the laptop he shares with his sister, Angelique, the missing girl? So he came over, and I called Detective Lotham and then his aunt came, and Officer O'Shaughnessy, and, and . . ." I run out of steam.

Stoney nods again. He turns and heads toward his office.

"Do I still have a job?" I call after him. "Cuz if so, I'm gonna need a couple of hours off . . ."

No answer.

"It'll be fine," I tell Guerline and Emmanuel. "It'll be fine," I repeat to Detective Lotham.

Then I stop talking because no one believes me and we all have bigger problems anyway.

CHAPTER 13

I FINISH SETTING UP THE BAR, just in case that saves my job and maintains my lodging. Stoney, being Stoney, is hard to read. I tell him I should be back before things get too busy. He nods. I tell him no later than five. He nods again. I tell him I'm so sorry, but I have to do this.

He gives me a long look.

I decide that's enough conversation for now and head out the door. I'm not surprised to find Detective Lotham waiting for me.

"Aren't you supposed to be watching videos from outside Angelique's cybercafé?" I ask him.

"Real police work takes longer than . . ." He waves his hand in my general direction.

I smile. "I'm growing on you, I can tell."

He rolls his eyes.

We've arrived at his standard-issue detective's vehicle, an unmarked Chevy. I shake my head. "What is it about police cars that even the unmarked ones can be made a mile away?"

"At least it's not the ice cream truck."

"The ice cream truck?"

"Department bought it a few years back. For Operation Hood-sie Cup."

I can't decide if he's pulling my leg or not. "To break up some evil frozen custard cabal before they took over the world?"

"More like for cruising around Roxbury handing out free ice cream to kids. We can't be arrogant, incompetent authority figures all the time."

"I didn't say you were incompetent. Now arrogant, on the other hand . . ."

He sighs, pops open the passenger-side door for me, but I shake my head.

"Beautiful day like this, I think I'll walk."

"Now you're just being difficult."

"So I've heard. Still, a pretty afternoon and given the rest of my evening will be spent in a dank bar . . ."

He concedes the point, leaving his vehicle to fall in step beside me. "We went through that entire apartment with a fine-toothed comb," he warns me.

"I know."

"Even brought in search dogs." He emphasizes the word enough for me to understand he means drug-sniffing canines. Yet another detail he most likely never told the family. I think Angelique Badeau's case still keeps him up at night, and this afternoon's revelation didn't help.

"What do you think of Angelique's message?" I ask him. "*Help us.* Clearly, it implies there's more than just her safety at stake. But as Angelique's family pointed out, all of her friends are accounted for. So who is the *us*?"

Lotham doesn't speak right away. His expression is troubled. "For the record, Angelique Badeau is our only active missing persons case at this time. So even looking beyond one teenage girl's social circle . . ." He shrugs.

In other words, there's not an immediate or obvious connection between Angelique and other possible victims. Interesting.

"Could be she's being abducted and held with a group of runaways," I brainstorm out loud. "Or, given the prevalence of human trafficking, other girls, immigrants who were smuggled into the country to be put to work. That's an entire victim group that would never even cross investigative radar screens until it's too late. Though how Angelique became part of such an operation, what exactly she stumbled into . . ." My voice trails off. This is all purely speculation. At the end of the day, Angelique's ominous message changes everything—and nothing.

The investigation remains as it's always been—stuck. Lacking a cohesive theory. A fifteen-year-old girl disappeared after school. How, why, where? The possibilities are endless. Mostly, we now have proof that Angelique is alive. Though if she was driven to risk delivering a coded message at this stage of the game, her fate— and those of the mysterious *us*—could very well be hanging by a thread.

"I don't know what I'll find when I search the apartment," I say at last. "Mostly, I'm just hoping I find *something*."

Lotham nods as if this makes perfect sense. We lapse into silence, easily covering block after block.

I like walking beside him. The comfort of his larger bulk, the ease of his stride. People move over slightly on the sidewalk, though that might be in deference to him being a cop as much as anything else. He is very present, and several brightly dressed women watch him out of the corner of their eyes as he passes.

"Football or baseball?" I ask him now, because I can't decide.

"Neither."

I chew my lower lip, then realize I've been stupid. The broken nose, battered features. "Boxing," I state.

"I've been known to spend some time in the ring."

"Is that when someone went Mike Tyson on your ear?"

"That's from my older brother when we were kids. We fought a lot. Just, you know, to have something to do."

"How many brothers?"

"Three."

"Good God, your poor mom."

"Exactly."

"Where did you grow up?"

"Foxborough."

"Is that around here?"

"South of the city. My parents were teachers. My mom taught English, my father was the classic gym instructor by day, school coach by night. He was at a middle school, so he coached across the board, football in the fall, basketball in the winter, baseball in the spring. But his first love was boxing; he took my brothers and me to the gym on the weekends. Your turn."

"Grew up West Coast. Mom worked hard, Dad drank hard. Both are now dead."

He stares at me hard enough as we pause at a crosswalk that I finally add: "Car accident. The other vehicle was at fault, which was a total shocker given my father's drinking and my mother's rage. The driver drifted over the center line, hit them head on. They died instantly. It's funny, my parents had a terrible marriage. I don't remember either of them ever being happy. And yet the fact they died together brings me comfort."

He nods in understanding.

"Military," I deduce next, inspecting his haircut. "Possibly army, but I'm thinking with those looks, former Marine."

"No such thing as a former Marine," he says, answering my question. "Post high school?" he quizzes me.

"Excelled at partying. I spend a lot of time in church basements now."

"But you work in a bar."

"Being around booze isn't such a big deal for me. And bartending is my only life skill."

"You don't have a home. Or a husband, or kids. You just travel all around doing . . . this."

"Inserting myself into other people's problems?"

"Exactly."

"Definitely growing on you. And your deal? Wife, kid, white picket fence?"

"My job is a demanding enough spouse, and my nieces and nephews keep me busy."

"You're the favorite uncle, aren't you? Swoop in, hop them up on video games, sugar them up with soda, then ride off into the sunset."

"Guilty as charged." He arches a brow. My turn. Everyone has someone, don't they?

"Ghosts of Christmas past," I tell him lightly, all I'm going to say on the subject. "Okay, bonus round: In this day and age of racial tension, gender fluidity, and political polarization, how do you most define yourself?"

This earns me serious contemplation. After a moment: "Black male. Not African American because, according to my mother, there's more in the mix, including Portuguese, though I don't know any more about that culture than Africa. Definitely, I'm a Boston cop. Not southern, not West Coast, purely New England. After that . . . good son, amazing uncle. And you? White, female, heterosexual . . . ?"

"Fishing, are you?" My turn to tease, then become serious. "Demographically speaking, I am white, female, heterosexual, agnostic, progressive, Californian. But first and foremost, I'm an addict. Which has taught me enough of my own weaknesses to be more understanding of others."

"And this is why strangers magically talk to you?"

"Maybe I'm just that good a listener."

We've arrived at the Badeaus' apartment. Lotham pauses before climbing up the front steps. He has a piece of white lint on his indigo tie. I have to repress the urge to reach out and flick it off. He defines himself as a Black male Boston cop, but to me he is a port in the storm, whether he wants to be or not.

I would like to step into the silence that surrounds him. Lay my head against his shoulder. Discover if his stillness could seep into my own wild, restless being.

I find myself leaning closer.

"Why do you do this?" he asks me softly, dark gaze pinning my own.

"I have no idea."

"What is it you're looking for?"

"The truth."

"Even if it's ugly?"

"It's always ugly."

"Try not to hurt the family too much," he murmurs.

And I have to smile, because I understand completely. Missing persons cases . . .

I turn and climb the front steps. After another moment, he follows.

GUERLINE IS AT the stove when Emmanuel escorts us in, throwing a flour-dusted drumstick into the pan of sizzling oil. The spattering drumstick is quickly followed by four more.

The moment we appear, however, she pulls herself away from the stove and produces a pot of coffee. She doesn't ask, but pours out two mugs, handing one to each of us. Having just consumed my body weight in caffeine, I'm tempted to wave off, but the look on her face stops me.

Stoic but welcoming. She is going through her steps, just as earlier today, I did mine.

As if reading my mind, Lotham murmurs beside me: "Take it. It's a Haitian thing. Drink up."

I take the mug, thanking her profusely. Given she hadn't offered me coffee the first time I appeared, I appreciate that I've now risen in her esteem, while already wondering how long that will last.

The living area is too small for four, especially when one of them is supersized. Lotham takes the hint. He downs his mug, then disappears back to the second-floor landing, where I can soon hear him yapping away on the phone.

Emmanuel remains with me, his hands fidgeting in front of him.

"What would you like to see?" he asks at last.

Guerline moves away from me in the tiny space to throw more chicken into the skillet. More hissing and crackling.

"Walk me through the living arrangements."

Emmanuel shows me the doorway leading to the single bedroom, which belongs to his aunt. Across from it is a cramped bathroom with a single vanity, toilet, and tub-shower combo. There is a mirrored medicine cabinet above the sink, a cheap shelving unit over the toilet. Shared space is cluttered space, which leaves me with much to sort out.

For now, I follow Emmanuel back to the family room. He gestures to the couch. "For LiLi," he explains. Then to the floor. "For me." A nightstand next to the sofa. "For my sister." Followed by a dresser wedged next to the TV stand, then the lowest shelf of the entertainment unit, which is lined with books. "Also for my sister."

That leaves two pieces of furniture, which must be Emmanuel's.

It's not a large search area. But it's a lot to process, given the riot of personal possessions, family photos, and miscellaneous knick-knacks. It's like peering into a dense forest, then slowly trying to pick out a single leaf.

I take a seat on the sofa, then stand up again. "Where did your sister sit?" I ask Emmanuel. "Everyone has their spot."

He gestures to the end, closest to the wall, where an oversized ceramic lamp tops the nightstand, excellent lighting for a serious reader.

"How did she sit?" I ask Emmanuel next. "Straight up, sideways, curled up? Can you show me?"

Emmanuel moves to the couch. He appears to consider the matter, then settles himself into the cushions, striking a pose. Sideways, curled up. Again, closer to the lighting.

Emmanuel bounces up. I nod in his direction as I take over Angelique's position on the sofa. Then, for a long while, I don't do anything at all. I just sit there and try to see what Angelique would see. Not rows of clutter, but pieces of memory. A fifteen-year-old girl, her family split between this country and the island she used to call home.

Emmanuel drifts into the kitchen, taking a seat at the kitchen table, where his heavily stickered laptop is up and running. Doing homework or updating his sister's digital memorial or monitoring her virtual high school? I wonder what his friends think. If he has anyone he can talk to.

I refocus my eyes on the wall ahead of me. Eventually I get up. I open each dresser drawer and work my way through. It feels intrusive, pawing through someone's piles of clothes. Having the family in the same room doesn't help. I keep my movements brisk and my attention focused. It's hard enough to do this once; I don't want to have to repeat.

I don't stumble upon any hidden notes, photos, diaries. I feel out each drawer for false bottoms, then peek behind the dresser itself. There are routine places, contraband 101. Items tucked under floorboards, taped beneath shelves. Under this object, behind this piece of furniture.

I take down the framed photo of Angelique's mom and, with my back to the kitchen, delicately dismantle it. My efforts are rewarded by the discovery of a scrap of thick white paper. It's covered by a child's crayon drawing of a heart and flowers. Written across the top in large, looping script are the words *Mwen renmen ou.*

I don't have to know Kreyòl to guess it reads *I love you.*

I return the note to its place behind the photo, feeling even more intrusive. I wander the bookshelves, the makeshift altar, the riot of green houseplants. I worked a missing persons case once where a thumb drive of illicit photos was slipped inside the pot of a fake ficus tree. These plants involve moist loamy soil, however. And none appear recently disturbed.

I move to the bathroom, where I check the medicine cabinet and beauty products littering the shelves above the toilet. I shake aerosol cans for fake bottoms. Open up makeup containers just in case. There is nothing in the handle of the hairbrush, taped inside the toilet tank, or bolted to the underside of the sink.

I account for the wooden baseboards, then check the doorframe, before emptying out the contents beneath the sink. Lot of cleaners, toilet paper, and feminine hygiene products. Given that a classic travel hack is to hide cash inside sanitary pads or tampon wrappers, I pull out every item in the boxes. When I look up, Detective Lotham has returned and is shaking his head at me. I shrug, get back to it.

Other classic hiding spots. Inside the freezer. Inside the door of the freezer. Tucked between wall cabinets, or behind crown molding. I once found a stash of dope inside a vacuum cleaner. Turned out to belong to the mother's boyfriend and had nothing to do with her son's disappearance, but he was pissed at me for months. And yes, my relationship with the entire family went downhill from there.

I eventually discovered the body of the nine-year-old locked in the trunk of an abandoned car on his grandfather's property. The murder trial is due to start sometime next year.

I return to the living area, confront the couch. I take it apart cushion by cushion. Fortunately, it doesn't include a sofa bed, so I don't have to rearrange the entire room.

Then I return to my perch at the end of the sofa, and resume thinking like a fifteen-year-old girl. This is where I watch TV, surf my phone, hang with my family. This is where I stay up late, tuck into bed, confront each morning. In this entire apartment, this corner of the couch, this nightstand, that bureau, are mine alone. Slivers of privacy in an arrangement where my younger brother is also living, sleeping, waking right beside me.

And maybe I don't mind. I protected my baby brother from our father. I led him from our collapsing house. Even now, I have promised us both a better future.

But maybe I met someone? Or someone found me?

Maybe, for a moment, I wanted my own dream, my own secret,

my own life. But how? In a place this small, in an apartment this crowded, where even my computer is shared . . .

I leave the photos and inspect the row of books. I take down each one, reading the title, fluffing the pages. A few are in French, but most are English. None of them are books that I understand. Apparently Angelique liked to read everything from bios on Madame Curie to Elizabeth Blackwell. I flip through an anatomy book where I discover inserted sheets from Angelique's sketch pad, incredibly realistic renderings of skeletal systems and muscle groups. She was clearly a gifted artist, at least to my untrained eye.

I give up on that mission and return to the couch. It's already been more than an hour. The chicken is done and currently warming in the oven. If I wasn't intruding before, I am now. Guerline has joined her nephew at the table, both of them clearly anxious. I should leave them so they can finally collapse in peace.

One last try. I'm fifteen. I've met a female friend . . . boyfriend . . . exciting stranger . . . I am . . .

I don't know what Angelique was into, that's the whole problem. But I know one thing she had—a second phone. Which she would've had to hide from her aunt and brother. But would want to check frequently . . .

I twist around. There's nothing tucked in the sofa cushions. Nor taped beneath the coffee table, nor under the sofa.

I lean closer to the nightstand, snapping on the brightly colored lamp, and then—just like that—I know. Her spot on the sofa. The way she sat, not leaning forward or slouching down, but angling toward the wall.

Better light to read by, I'd thought. But maybe, it was just plain better light.

Now I reach up and snap off the bulb. Then I pick up the entire lamp, with its large ceramic base covered in checks of red, purples, and turquoise. When I shake it, there's no rattling sound or sense of movement. But the weight of it, so solid, so heavy. I feel beneath it until my fingers close around the large bolt that holds the whole thing together. I don't need a tool. The bolt is already loose, waiting.

I twist the nut. I slowly pull off the base. And just like that, banded rolls of bills go thumping out on to the floor. One two three four five six. Not hundreds of dollars, but thousands in tightly bundled cash.

A screech at the kitchen table as Emmanuel shoves back his chair. A terrible gasp from Guerline, hand flying to her mouth.

Detective Lotham appears in the doorway.

I shake out three more rolls. We all watch them roll across the rug. Thousands and thousands of dollars in cold, hard cash. Way more money than any teenager could have accrued by legal means.

Guerline places her head in her hands and starts to cry.

CHAPTER 14

THE HAPPY HOUR CROWD IS firmly entrenched by the time I return to Stoney's pub. I grab an apron, wash my hands, and get straight to work banging out beer and running plates of food.

My mind keeps returning to the rolls of cash hidden in Angelique's lamp. When I left, Detective Lotham was bagging the evidence. The fact that Guerline and Emmanuel weren't protesting his removal of large sums of money from their humble apartment confirmed that the money wasn't theirs and the implications troubling.

Not being an official investigator type, I can only guess what kind of forensic tests will be conducted on the cash. Fingerprinting, for sure. My understanding is that new bills can often yield useful prints. Anything in circulation too long, however, has been touched by too many greasy hands, leaving behind a mess of smudged partials.

They'd test each bill for chemical residue. Traces of drugs. Maybe some cool random mold that could only be found in one basement in all of Boston. Or not.

I'd read about a case where the serial numbers on the bills were traced to a particular ATM, which allowed the police to pull video and identify the person who withdrew the funds. That would be great. Given how tightly bound the money was, however, I don't have an impression of crispness, consecutive serial numbers, or, really, any useful information.

It looked like rolls of hundreds, maybe thousands of dollars per bundle. Making the total stash worth tens of thousands. What in the world could a teenage girl be doing to earn that kind of money?

Prostitution is the first thought that comes to mind. And would fit with an overall story line of human trafficking. But I certainly hadn't seen any sign of sexy clothes or paraphernalia. Let alone, when? Angelique shared her sleeping quarters with her brother. If she was sneaking out, surely he'd be sharing those details by now. Not to mention tens of thousands is a lot of money for that scenario. No pimp wants the hired help to achieve financial independence.

"Umm, lady, you gonna keep pouring that beer?"

A voice jolts me from my reverie. Sure enough, I've topped off the glass and am now gushing foam down the sides. I flush, knock off the tap, deliver the beverage.

When I return, Stoney looks like he's wondering if no help might be better than mine. Fair enough.

"Illegal income," I tell him. "What are the local options?"

He appears to take my inquiry seriously as he stacks dirty glasses on a tray for delivery to the kitchen. "Drugs."

"No sign of product, plus narc dogs would've sniffed out the cash if it had been in contact with meth, dope, whatever." I line up four half glasses, toss in ice, start doling out rum.

Stoney doesn't question this statement. "Sex."

"Possible but not probable."

"Stolen goods."

Hadn't thought of that. I top the rum with Coke, then swing back around the bar to deliver the drinks to the waiting table. When I return, Stoney has finished with the dirty glasses and is now ringing up an order for a waiting patron.

"What kind of stolen goods?" I ask him.

"Electronics. Cell phones. Guns."

"Not sure our girl has that skill set or resources. She's the studious type. Wants to be a doctor when she grows up." Viv appears from the kitchen, one of her rare appearances, and hands me three plates. I shoot them to the end of the bar, picking up an order for a pitcher of beer on my way back.

"Sell off a kidney?" Stoney asks next.

"Think the family would've noticed." I go to work filling the pitcher. I could ask about any recent surgeries. Maybe Angelique had suffered appendicitis that wasn't really appendicitis? Or had tonsils that weren't really her tonsils removed? Seems far-fetched, however, that she could pull off such a ruse in such tight quarters.

"Credit card fraud," Stoney supplies next. "Or identity theft."

Worthy of consideration. We know Angelique had a fake ID, why not a credit card in someone else's name? She could charge items online, have them delivered to her home, then return them to local stores for cash or credit. Seems like the kind of activity, however, that would've drawn attention and been shared with the cops by now. Unless she used someone else's house for delivery? A co-conspirator? The other half of *us*? Interesting.

Of all the options, white-collar crime sounds like the best fit with the picture of the Angelique I'm building in my mind. Then again, my image is based on information from her family and friends. And clearly, they don't know everything about her.

Angelique went to high school by day, and took online courses by night. A lot of school, actual and virtual, for a teenager. Could that be a hint? Illegal activity disguised as schoolwork? Maybe she sold exam answers and/or term papers? But tens of thousands of dollars' worth? Are there even enough kids in high school or at GEDNow.com to supply that kind of income?

I keep turning it over in my mind but still can't come up with a venture, illegal or otherwise, that can account for Angelique's level of cash.

What if she found the money? Or stole it? Maybe she wasn't a dope dealer, but say she babysat for a drug kingpin, discovered a stash of cash, and thought she could get away with helping herself. Until the dealer found out and . . .

Now I have too many possibilities to consider, though most of them result in Angelique being shot as a message to others, versus being kidnapped for eleven months. Drug dealers are not the subtle sort.

I dole out shots, top off drinks. I operate on muscle memory, a woman who's spent the majority of her adult life in bars, while my mind whirrs and chugs and ponders.

None of it brings me peace.

Help us, Angelique had encoded into her school essay. A girl clearly in trouble and desperate enough to take a shot at reaching out. I agreed with what Detective Lotham had said—just because someone hadn't walked into the cybercafé with a gun pointed at Angelique's head didn't mean she wasn't under duress.

Then another possibility came to me, scarier and sadder than all the others. She could've been kidnapped to serve as recruitment bait. A quiet, pretty immigrant teen. Held against her will, then sent out to bus stops and train stations to meet other unsuspecting teens and lure them over to meet her "friends": sex traffickers, pimps, dope dealers. How much would that erode a natural caretaker such as Angelique, a girl who'd rescued her own mother and brother?

If the threat against her family either here or in Haiti was significant enough, she wouldn't have a choice but to obey.

This scenario wouldn't account for why Angelique had rolls of bills stashed in a lamp, but it would explain her disappearance, as well as her sudden reappearance seeking help.

As for how she might have gotten involved in sex trafficking, all I can think of is the rec center. According to her friends, she'd become distant after attending the summer program there. Because she'd met someone? Seen something? I have no idea, but it seems as good a starting place as any. First thing tomorrow, I'll find my new friend Charlie and head on over. Like Angelique, I do best with a plan.

Which makes me wonder where Angelique is right now. Terrified or determined? Longing for her brother, or resigned to her fate?

And the mysterious *us*? Another girl? Several girls? Dozens of girls? All waiting for someone to rescue them from the dark?

The implications of that, the responsibility for all those lives, when I've never even rescued one living soul . . .

I can't think about it.

Angelique. Others. Out there alone.

Please, please, please, for their sakes, let me get this right.

BY THE TIME the night owls have been shown to the door, my mood is subdued. I scrub and polish, stack and sweep in silence. Viv is in the kitchen, scouring down, while Stoney closes out the register.

It's been a long day. I should head to a meeting, then get some sleep. Or maybe I could go for a run. It's late and dark and dangerous, but that's never stopped me before. Sometimes my blood flows too close to my skin. I can feel my own nerve endings spark and snap, the pressure building in my chest.

Once upon a time, I would head to a bar, slamming back shots of tequila and dancing with abandon. Dance drink dance. Or maybe it had been drink dance drink. Oblivion. That's what I sought, what I still seek.

One precious moment when I'm no longer trapped inside my own head. Knowing things I don't want to know. Remembering things I don't want to remember. Worrying about things I can't change.

As I do too often, I think of Paul. The feel of his lips whispering down my neck. The tickle of his hair, the strength of his hands. The beginning, when he made me feel safe. The end, when I broke his heart and shattered the last of my self-respect.

I don't want to go to a meeting. I don't want to run. I want to grab a bottle of Hornitos, crawl upstairs, and dial his phone number. The pain will be swift and brutal. Like a razor to the soul. Then I can lie there and feel myself bleed, while guzzling tequila. Drink and wallow. Maybe Piper the homicidal cat likes pity parties, too. You never know.

Viv comes charging out, already thrusting her arms into her coat. Her husband is waiting just outside the door to walk her home. It's sweet and charming and salt on my gaping wound. Addicts are particularly good at this game. Everyone else's life is easier, better, happier. If we could be those people, then we wouldn't need to drink again.

It's everyone else's fault. The universe's. Never our own.

Go to a meeting. Just walk out the front door and go. I eye the rows of bottles that line the back wall. I feel the beast stir to life in my belly, opening its eyes, stretching out its claws.

It's been a hard day. And I'm tired and alone. And *white*. Dear God, when did I become this impossibly glow-in-the-dark neon white, so that everyone stares at me and no one knows me? My skin color has made me the enemy, a walking advertisement for entitlement and privilege except I don't feel like any of those things. I feel like I've always felt. Broken. As if the whole rest of the world knows something I don't. Feels things I can't. Connects in ways I've never learned how.

Of course, I've spent enough time by now in marginalized communities to understand there's more to that story. That for all my internal angst, the truth is I grew up with limited fears and unlimited dreams. I had implicit faith in authority and never thought to question the system. I had an innate understanding of the world and my place in it. Let alone a roof over my head, food in the fridge, and a safe neighborhood to grow up in.

Which is a privilege indeed.

I should go to a meeting. Just walk out the front door, find my people, and set down my burden. Breathe.

The restless dragon, fully awake now, uncoils. It whispers memories of my very first drink, a sip of my father's Jack and Coke fetched by my eight-year-old self for my already slurring parent. The feel of caffeine and bourbon sliding down my throat, both hot and cold, melting and jolting. The slow-spreading euphoria that brought a flush to my impossibly young face.

Not a bottle. Just a shot. Or two or three. Then I'll sleep. Sleep is good. I'll feel better after a good night's rest.

"Sit." Stoney stands in front of me. He grips the chair I just stacked on the table, flips it back down, points at the hard wooden seat. "Sit."

I do.

A second chair, slapped down next to the first. Then a pause, as he disappears and I close my eyes, count to a hundred by fives, then when that doesn't work, by sevens. I'd just hit eighty-four when Stoney reappears with two mugs of coffee.

"Decaf." He keeps one, hands over the other. He takes up position across from me. We both sip our coffee in silence.

"You married?" I ask him at last. The pressure is easing in my chest, but I grip my coffee mug hard, like an anchor. Another trick. Rattle off five things you can see right now in as much visual detail as possible. "I spy with my little eye" as a grounding exercise. If that doesn't work, then five things for five senses. The smell of freshly brewed coffee. The sound of the buzzing overhead lights. The feel of the warm mug. The look on Stoney's impassive face. The taste of regret.

Stoney takes his time answering. "Was. She died. Ovarian cancer."

"I'm sorry."

"Had thirty amazing years. Appreciated every minute. Makes me luckier than most."

"Kids?"

"Three. Two girls and a boy. One of my girls lives in Florida now. Keeps asking me to join her and her family. But this is my home."

"You grow up here?"

"New Jersey. But moved here when I was in my teens. Close enough."

"This neighborhood, this bar, these are your memories."

"I see my Camille everywhere," Stoney affirms. "And I'm not complaining."

"Grandkids?"

"Four. Ages three to eight. Two in Florida, two in New York."

"All three of your kids are married?"

"My two girls. Jerome, my son, died at sixteen. Not easy to be a young Black man. Harder still, when you're sixteen, stupid, and susceptible to your peers."

As usual with Stoney, it's what he doesn't say that matters most. "Gangs or drugs?" I ask at last.

"Drugs. Broke his mother's heart." His father's, too, but that went without saying.

"Gonna die in this bar?" I ask him.

"That's the plan."

"What's it like?" I whisper. "To know exactly what you want? To know this is your home? To feel like you belong?"

Stoney doesn't answer, but then, I don't expect him to.

"You know the family?" His turn to question. "The missing girl, Badeau?"

"No. This is what I do. I look up cold cases involving missing persons. Then I find them."

"How many?"

"Fourteen."

"How long?"

"Nine years. More or less."

"How'd you get started?"

"Fluke thing. I had just joined AA. One of the women was struggling with the disappearance of her daughter. The police thought she'd run away. Margaret didn't believe, but couldn't argue. I asked a few questions, which led to a few more, then a few more. Addicts are prone to obsession. I ended up tracking the daughter to a flophouse where she was holed up with her abusive boyfriend. The girl was underage, so I called the cops. They closed in for the arrest, but not before the boyfriend shot her, then himself. Classic murder-suicide."

"Not a happy story."

"No, but maybe that's why I keep coming back for more. I don't trust happy. These cases, these situations, I understand."

Stoney nods, sips more coffee.

"Thank you," I say at last.

No comment.

"You know your cat is crazy, right? And/or a serial killer?"

No comment.

"But she does have a nice purr," I allow.

Stoney smiles. We both drain our mugs. Then, together, we restack the chairs, wash out our cups, rinse the coffeepot.

Stoney goes home. And, no bottle in hand, I head upstairs.

IN MY DREAMS, Angelique appears. She is running down a long, dark alley that gets longer and darker with every step. She is a blur of frantically pounding limbs, dark hair bouncing beneath a bright red ball cap.

"Help me," she screams, disappearing around a corner. Except when I get there, she's already flying around the next sharp turn. So I run left, then right, zigging and zagging, zagging and zigging but never gaining any ground. I can just hear the echo of her footsteps, the sound of her breathing as she races ahead.

"Help me help me help me."

Abruptly, the dark alley is gone and I'm standing at the grassy edge of a road, peering at the crumpled remains of my parents' car, their bloody faces slammed wide-eyed into the crackled windshield.

No, I'm underwater, fighting to get away from Lani White-horse's skeletal grasp, as she pulls me down, down, down.

I try to pinch my skin. I try to scream at myself to wake up, but it doesn't work. I remain trapped in a nightmarish slideshow, where the scenes go from bad to awful to terrifying to . . .

Paul. His head on my lap, his body bathed in blood.

"What did you do, Frankie?" he screams at me, his fingers reaching out like talons. "Dear God, what did you do?"

Shh, I want to tell him. Save your strength.

But it's too late. A kid is screaming, a gun is booming. No place to go, nothing we can do. I reach for his hand.

"What did you do?" he asks me one last time as the life drains out of him. So much blood. Too much. And yet still he grips my hand. Still he looks to me.

"I loved you."

Then I close my eyes, as light explodes around us, brilliant, excruciating, searing. I scream. In my dream. In my sleep.

I pray the pain will be quick.

Now, as then, it isn't.

CHAPTER 15

ORNING DISORIENTS ME. I WAKE up with a feeling of dread and a pit in my stomach. For a moment, I lie still. I drank. That must be it. I caved, I gave in to the beast, and now I have to start my sobriety all over again.

Tears are already leaking out of the corners of my eyes before my mental fog lifts and I remember I didn't break. Stoney pulling down the chair. Stoney talking to me. And then I do cry, from sheer relief, because my sobriety is my one and only accomplishment in my whole fucking miserable life and to lose that . . .

I will go to a meeting today. Before work, I promise myself. There must be a noontime gathering somewhere. There always is.

I sit up and swing my legs over the bed. Then I realize what's different. No claws slash my bare skin. No rodent carcasses decorate the floor. For that matter, I have no memory of a comforting rumble easing my chronic nightmares.

I peer beneath the mattress. No glowing green eyes. I check the water bowl. It appears untouched.

Apparently, my roommate never returned home last night. Given we've only been together a matter of days, that shouldn't bother me, but it does. I brush my teeth, shower, pick out the day's wardrobe, all with half an ear listening for sounds from the cat door. By the time I'm ready to go, there's still no sign of Piper. I feel like I should leave some food out for her, but I haven't gone grocery shopping and there's not a scrap of sustenance in my kitchen.

I head down to the kitchen, where I rummage till I find the brick of cheese. I peel off a slice. I don't think Stoney or Viv will mind. I shred the cheese into smaller bits, then return to my apartment, where I place the cat snack next to her water bowl.

I'm not sure what else I can do, so even though I still feel unsettled, I get on with the day's business.

I don't know much about the rec center. It's on my printed map, a large structure to the north in a sea of green. Once again, the presence of such a large park in the middle of inner-city urban density surprises me. But yeah, if I were a bored teen, I'd probably go there.

It's a far walk, which means I should take a bus. Which means I have to once again figure out Boston's mass transit system. I feel overwhelmed already. What elderly lady is going to save me today?

I head for Dunkin' Donuts first. I need the coffee as well as the advice.

Given the late-morning hour, I'm the only customer, the shocking white woman passing through the glass doors. I recognize the crew of older Black women behind the counter from before, including the manager who'd helped me with directions to Le Foyer. Most of them appear to remember me, too. It makes it easy to order a large coffee, then plunk down my map and request assistance.

This time they all gather round, and I get bus routes and pickup times.

"Where you living now, girl?" the manager, Charadee, asks me. She is tall and round and somehow impressive despite the brown-and-fuchsia uniform.

"I'm working at Stoney's, live above the bar."

"You a bartender?" Arched brow. A silver star winks at the end. Stud or sticker, I can't decide.

"I make an excellent mojito," I inform her. "You should come by some time. I owe you for the help with directions."

Charadee nods at me. The other women appear pleased.

"Why the rec center, hun? You got kids?"

"No, but I've heard good things and want to learn more. I'm an alcoholic," I volunteer, having learned that in many situations it helps break the ice. "I was wondering if there was something I could do to help. You know, having been there, done that, myself."

Nodding heads. Charadee flips over my map and jots down some notes. She has a large looping script that is much prettier than mine.

She murmurs some questions in what I assume is French to her companions. Various French replies produce more scrawled notes. In the end, Charadee divides my paper into three sections. The first contains numbers, the second contains names, and below the mid-way line dividing the page are a whole mess of names and numbers.

She walks me through it: the bus schedule, which I'd recognized; the names of her "boys" at the center, who can help me out; and a list of the best restaurants.

"Skinny girl like you needs to eat," Charadee provides as explanation. In a culture that prides itself on curves, I must look particularly pathetic. Honestly, I've been begging God for breasts since the day I turned thirteen. Any time now.

I thank her sincerely. High fives to all.

There's a chime as a car pulls up to the drive-thru. They return to their stations and I head once more for the door, armed with coffee and my new and improved local guide.

I GET ON and off the right bus. It makes me smile so brightly even the bus driver, a stoic Black man who appears to be somewhere between old and ancient, grins back. I smile larger and he shakes his head. "You take care of yourself, you hear," he says, and the fact I got him to speak feels like my second triumph of the day.

Forget Detective Lotham. Maybe I'm growing on the entire population of Mattapan.

My heady sense of success lasts until I make it to the front of the vast rec center complex. Again, much larger than I expected, and given the surrounding park, tennis courts, and running paths, nothing like I imagined. Sure, the rec center looks slightly tired and stooped, a giant metal hangar that had probably been very impressive in its heyday, and appears in need of a good power-washing and paint job. But the size, the access to the outdoors—I've visited plenty of neighborhoods with less.

Of course, I can't figure out how to get in. If what my new AA bud Charlie said was true, the center's hours would be mostly after school, evenings, and weekends. Which probably explains the locked front doors. However, a taped sign advises deliveries around back.

I'm a delivery. Of sorts.

I wander around the massive building. This close, I can see the pitting in the metal side panels, more signs of age. I'd guess the faded blue structure was built in the seventies or eighties. Maybe some government initiative to provide more opportunities for inner-city youths. I wouldn't mind having these paths to run on. Or basketball courts or soccer fields. They are all empty now, but I'd guess around three in the afternoon, this place really comes alive.

I discover a side door, give it a tug. No luck. Keep on walking, all the way behind the building now. A second set of double doors, twin to the first. This time when I pull, the tinted glass door gives way. I step inside the cool, shadowed depths, seeking signs of human life.

There's a check-in counter directly across from me. When I get closer, I see bins with various kinds of sporting equipment stacked behind it, locked behind metal grates. So this is where the kids check out the goods before heading out into the vast green park.

I follow the shadowed corridor deeper into the building. Given the lack of overhead lights and the deep hush broken only by the sound of my tennis shoes on concrete, the whole place is slightly ominous. Outside was filled with promise, but as for the inside . . . I spent a few days in county lockup once, and this makes me think of that. I wonder if the kids feel the same.

I walk past double doors leading to an indoor gym, but both are locked. Next up, I spy what appears to be a weight room, followed by some kind of kitchen area. Again, all shuttered tight. With the exception of the open back door, they appear to take security seriously around here. Belatedly, I realize I should've looked for cameras, outside as well as in. I wonder if I'm being recorded as I continue my path down the central corridor, still searching for signs of life.

Next up, a smaller gym with mats on the floor and a boxing ring in the middle. It makes me think of Detective Lotham, and I wonder if he ever came here to help out. Certainly, Officer O'Shaughnessy must know this place well, being the community liaison.

Voices. Finally. I follow the sounds to the end of the corridor, where light floods out from two separate offices.

I poke my head into the doorway on the right first, encountering two African American men, one short, one tall.

"Hi," I say.

They stare at me.

"Are you in charge here?"

They stare at me.

I consult my notes from my new Dunkin' Donuts friends. "Is one of you Dutch? Or maybe Antoine?"

"Dutch," the shorter one concedes. He wears a whistle around his neck. I didn't know that kind of thing was done anymore.

"Excellent. Charadee recommended that I talk to you about the rec center programs. I just moved into the area and would like to learn more."

I deliver my best I'm-completely-harmless smile, then I stick out my hand. They take turns shaking it, which seems to break the ice.

"I understand you run an after-school program for local youths?"

"Yes, ma'am." The shorter man, Dutch, confirms. His accent sounds pure Boston, no trace of immigrant anything.

"Please, call me Frankie. And you are?" I turn to the taller man, who appears roughly forty years old and has the erect bearing of a natural leader.

"Frédéric Lagudu," the man says, with a trill of sand and sea. I gravitate toward him immediately.

"I'm a friend of the Badeau family. I understand from Ms. Violette that her niece and nephew came here often."

"You are here about Angelique Badeau?" Frédéric asks, dark eyes narrowing.

"Yes."

"She did not go missing here. She was back in school. That is what they say."

"They say?"

He flushes. "What I know to be true."

"That's what I've heard, too," I assure him. "I'm curious about the summer before school started. When Angelique and her brother, Emmanuel, were both here."

The two men exchange glances again. I understand their natural distrust. I'm not the police, which makes me an unknown variable.

"Ms. Violette put me in touch with Officer O'Shaughnessy," I volunteer now. "He recommended I talk with you."

A stretch, but effective. Both men relax. O'Shaughnessy probably did help out around here, as I'd suspected. And while it might be a white lie, even if the men called O'Shaughnessy directly to check me out, I doubt he'd throw me under the bus. I've stirred up more activity in Angelique's case in the past two days than the BPD did in the past two months.

"I know Angelique and her brother," Frédéric confirms now. "Please. Come to my office. We can talk there."

I think that's a marvelous offer. I follow him across the hall, to a small, straightforward setup. Desk, ancient computer, coat rack, half-dead office plant. Frédéric has a brightly framed poster of a coat of arms on the wall. A palm tree upright in the middle of two golden cannons and what appear to be bayonets, cannonballs, anchors, bugles, all in patriotic colors of green, blue, and red. Below it reads *L'Union Fait la Force*.

"Our national emblem," Frédéric tells me, following my gaze. "From Haiti, the country of my heart."

"When did you immigrate?"

"Twenty years ago."

Meaning he wasn't caught up in the current visa turmoil of the earthquake survivors. "Do you still have family back on the island?"

"One brother, two sisters."

"They don't want to come here?"

"Maybe their children. For school. It's better here than there."

"I understand Angelique and her brother are good students. And Angelique is looking forward to studying medicine at a U.S. college."

Frédéric shrugs. "I'm the executive director. We serve over five hundred families through our various programs. I know all a little, but none very well."

"How does summer camp work? Do the kids sign up for specialized activities, something?"

Frédéric lays it out for me. Youths register for specific programs based on age and interest. After consulting his computer, he can tell me Angelique signed up for fashion camp while Emmanuel pursued basketball. I'm not sure why future doctor Angelique would choose fashion till Frédéric produces the program description. Apparently, fashion camp involves lots of sketching and art. Remembering the highly detailed medical drawings I'd found in in the teen's collection, that makes sense. The activity director is a woman named Lillian, who is an art teacher from a local middle school and works for the rec center during the summer. Frédéric doesn't want to give me her contact information but promises he'll pass along my phone number to her.

He pulls up the program registration, showing eighteen kids: sixteen girls, two boys. Sure enough, Marjolie's name is right after Angelique's. Most likely they signed up together, the way friends do.

"Do you remember Angelique hanging out with anyone in particular?" I ask now, not giving away Marjolie's name.

Frédéric pauses, leaning back his long frame and steepling elegant fingers together as he considers the matter. "There was one girl. They sat together. Also Haitian. Shorter, pretty. They seemed to know each other well. But this other girl didn't care about fashion class so much. She spent more of her time in the gym."

"Like playing basketball or something?"

"Like watching the boys playing basketball." He arches a suggestive brow.

"Boyfriend, or boy crazy?"

"One boy in particular. I once had to interrupt a . . . social situation that had gone too far."

I take that to mean Marjolie had been making out with said love interest in some random corner. Frankly, if I'd been at summer camp in this vast building at that age . . . Had to be secluded spots everywhere and I bet the kids knew every single one.

"What about Angelique? Ever interrupt one of her . . . social situations?"

Frédéric shakes his head.

"Did she have a tendency to drift out of her program to, say, watch basketball, boxing, baseball, whatever?" I'm pursuing the theory that Angelique had a secret romance. Especially with her best friend distracted by some basketball player, maybe Angelique had felt compelled to do likewise.

"She would go on occasion to watch her brother," Frédéric supplies. "During breaks, though. She never missed class. At least not that I ever heard, and it is my job to hear such things."

His picture of Angelique is consistent with everything else I've been told about the teen. For now, I table the boyfriend idea and return to my own thought from the night before: "What about another girl? A new friend Angelique bonded with while Marjolie was off drooling in the gym?"

Frédéric frowns, hesitates. "This was two summers ago . . ."

"And yet Angelique went missing shortly thereafter. Don't tell me you haven't thought about it."

He winces. I can't even imagine how hard his job must be, trying to both corral and inspire hundreds of at-risk teens. Wanting to make a difference, knowing there are limits. And then when one of the kids who by all accounts should make it simply vanishes one fall afternoon . . . I have a feeling Frédéric has done nothing but replay the memories he has of Angelique over and over again.

"I wish I had noticed more," he concedes now. "Paid more attention, made more effort. But Angelique, she was a good kid. She came on time. She stayed with her program. She produced many beautiful drawings. Lillian posted several around the halls. I remember congratulating Angelique on her work. She seemed shy, but again, not one to get into trouble. My time, my job, is spent more with those teens." He shrugs. "It is regretful, but it is what it is."

"You have problems with gang activity here?" I change gears.

"We are zero tolerance. Any gang signs, colors, activity leads to immediate expulsion. The kids know. Off the grounds, yes, there are problems. But when they enter this property . . . If they want to shoot hoops, they play nice. It works more effectively than you think."

"Are there times all the kids intermix? I mean, regardless of fashion camp versus boxing camp or whatnot?"

"Lunch is within each group. It makes it easier for us to monitor. But there are breaks during the day. Kids wander. Some might go watch a part of a soccer game or gather to enjoy the sun outside. They are teens, and we want the programs to be fun, not just . . ." He struggles for the word.

"Glorified lockup?" I volunteer.

He sighs but doesn't disagree.

"Can I get a copy of this list?" I point to the registration list for fashion camp.

"The police have it."

"I don't want to bother them. I'm trying to find new leads to move us forward, not make them go backward."

He hesitates again, but my argument is a decent one. He prints me out a fresh list.

"One last thing. If you don't mind. A simple memory exercise. You know Angelique's face?"

He nods.

"Now picture her, here, the last time you saw her. Where is she?"

It takes him a moment, but he complies, even going so far as to close his eyes. "Angelique is sitting outside on a yellow bench. She has her sketch pad on her lap, her head bent over as she draws. As I walk by, making my rounds, she doesn't look up but continues to sketch, very fast, very focused. I can hear the scratch of charcoal against the page. I remember thinking she looked like a true artist, with a vision in her head she must capture immediately, before it disappeared forever. I was impressed."

"Could you see the drawing?"

"No, but she was wearing her hair down. She had thick ringlets that hung in front of her like a curtain."

"Were there other kids around her?"

Silence as he digs deeper into his recollection. "I see three boys. They have a hacky sack and are kicking it around. Two more girls, sitting on another bench. One is giggling. There are other kids lounging in the grass. The weather is very beautiful."

"Who is closest to Angelique? A boy? A girl?"

"I see only the three boys and they are busy with their game."

"Anyone else? Someone near Angelique, or maybe—like you— noticing Angelique even if she doesn't notice them?"

Slowly, he says: "There's another girl. Seated on the ground further down, her back against the building. She is also drawing, but she is in the shade, not the sun. She is looking in Angelique's direction. She is watching Angelique draw. When I walk by, however, the girl ducks her head quickly. Too quickly, I think. I'm about to stop, push a little, then I hear yelling in the soccer field. I turn and head there."

"What does this other girl look like?"

"Another teen. I remember seeing her in the fashion camp as well." Frédéric opens his eyes, shakes his head. "But I don't remember her face. I'm not even sure I ever saw it fully. I could always find her in a crowd, however, by looking for her hat. Every day, regardless of weather or conditions, she wore the same red ball cap. And yes, now that you mention it, she was often staring at Angelique."

CHAPTER 16

I'VE BARELY LEFT THE REC center property, heading back down the main boulevard with a vague notion of finding my bus stop, when a white car goes roaring past me in the opposite lane. It slams on its brakes, performs a hard U-turn, and zips up beside me.

"Get in," Detective Lotham orders.

I stare at him for a moment, not trying to be belligerent, but definitely disoriented.

"I know you like to walk," he growls.

"Actually, I was headed for the bus."

"Stop being so damn contrarian and get the hell in."

The moment he calls me contrarian I naturally want to protest. But the urgency in his voice, underlaid with anger, and maybe even a hint of fear, catches my attention. I get in. I've no sooner shut the door than he floors the gas. The sudden acceleration slams me back against my seat and I scramble for a seat belt.

"What do you know about counterfeiting?" he asks me, both

hands on the wheel, eyes fixed forward. He's leaning forward, as if throwing his whole body into his aggressive driving.

"As in money?"

"U.S. currency to be exact."

"I thought that was very hard to do."

"Exactly. Meaning it's not a small-time DIY enterprise. The good fakes generally come from overseas. Europe, Russia. You need the right equipment and a master tradesperson to pull it off. Computers have simplified the process some—the good forgers scan hundreds of images of, say, a Ben Franklin, then create a 3D master plate based off the composite image. Provides the bills with the same printing imperfections the U.S. Treasury installed on purpose. Still, there are watermarks and special paper and reflective dyes. Not something for the average criminal to execute."

I nod, then start to connect the dots, why Detective Lotham is suddenly an expert on forgery. "The bills from Angelique's lamp," I murmur out loud. Of all the findings from the hidden cash, this is not one I'd expected.

"A tenth of them are counterfeit. Almost exactly. Which, according to the Secret Service agent who showed up in my office this morning, is how it's usually done."

"They mix in fake money with real money so it's less noticeable?"

We've come to a red light. Lotham hits a switch on his dash, issuing a shrill *whoop*, *whoop*, and we scream on through. I grab hold of the oh-shit handle, still not knowing where we are going with such urgency.

"Angelique's stash isn't as large as it appears. We're talking rolls of twenties, wrapped in hundreds."

"Okay."

"It's a popular trick among the streetwise to appear richer than they are."

"Give me a total."

"Stashed in that lamp was about twelve thousand dollars."

"Still an impressive haul."

"Yep. But the outer layer, the Ben Franklins—"

"Those were counterfeit?"

"Exactly. To make matters more interesting, these particular counterfeits have been in circulation for years, apparently. They're called the Russian notes, because the U.S. Secret Service believes they were first printed there. Using an offset printer, probably in a giant warehouse with specialized dyes, acids. Again, not a local job."

I nod, though more to register I've heard the words than I understand them. We hit another intersection, and with a fresh *whoop*, *whoop*, we slice through two lanes of traffic before instigating a hard left across oncoming traffic. My stomach tightens. A fresh boost of speed, then we clear imminent death and sail down a narrow side street.

"Are the counterfeiters actually chasing us?" I ask Detective Lotham. "Or is this your competitive streak now that a federal agency is involved?"

"Forget Secret Service. They already have the bills and—based on the serial numbers—they already know the source. For them, this is mop-up from a decades-old operation. Some Russian syndicate executed tens of millions of near-perfect fakes. They sold them for ten cents on the dollar to a distributor who sold them for twenty-five cents on the dollar to various middlemen in various countries who finished the food chain by selling them locally for sixty cents on the dollar. According to Agent Ford, they'll be recovering the fake Benjamins for the rest of his life and from all over the world."

"So how did Angelique end up with them?"

"That remains our problem. How, who, why? According to Agent Ford, any one of us might be carrying a counterfeit without knowing it. But a dozen of them? Each wrapped around a bundle of real twenty-dollar bills? That's not random. We certainly have Russian gangs in Boston, which might explain how we ended up with these fakes in this area. But not too many Russian crime bosses are hanging out with Mattapan gangbangers. Criminal enterprises are notoriously snobbish, and our local gangs aren't sophisticated enough for Russian interest."

I have no idea what to say to this. It's okay. In the way Boston works, a random street has appeared ahead, forking a right diagonal, not to be confused with the three other diagonals flaring out around it. Lotham hits that turn as hard as he hit the others. Apparently, he's in a temper this morning.

"Did you sleep last night?" I ask him.

"Does at a desk count? Minute I logged those bills into evidence, my phone started ringing off the hook. And *then* my sergeant called me into his office . . ."

"So it's your sergeant we're running away from?"

"Don't be a wise-ass."

"I'm more worried about becoming a soon-to-be-dead dumbass. Why the bells and whistles?"

"We have a sighting."

"What?"

"A teen matching Angelique's description just tried to purchase a fresh burner phone using a fake ID. The ID bears the same name, Tamara Levesque, as the one given to the cybercafé clerk two weeks ago. Officer O'Shaughnessy is already there, fanning out with a few other units, hoping to get lucky."

"We're joining the hunt?" I don't know which surprises me more: that there's an active search after all these months, or that I've been invited to participate.

"*We* are not doing anything. *I'm* interviewing the sales specialists. You." Lotham blew out a hard breath. "Heaven help me," he muttered.

"I'm there for moral support?"

"No. You're there because one of the witnesses, some guy named Charlie, asked for you."

BY THE TIME we come to a screeching halt, the scene in front of the wireless company is a pile of blue uniformed officers, a crowd of gawkers, and, if I'm not mistaken, a number of corner dealers back-pedaling furiously down the street.

Detective Lotham spares the retreating youths a look but doesn't acknowledge or pursue. Today is their lucky day: The police have bigger fish to fry.

I spot Charlie almost immediately. He stands outside the storefront, his large size and authentic army jacket making a statement. Next to him stands a female beat cop, clearly waiting.

Detective Lotham ushers me through the crowd. Once on the other side of the madness, he pauses long enough to state, "When you're done talking to your friend, remember who drove you here." Then he disappears into the store, leaving me to cross the remaining space to Charlie.

I feel suddenly awkward, unsure of what to say. We've met only once, at an AA meeting. In the midst of this hoopla, why ask for me?

Charlie doesn't speak right away, but nods his greeting.

Then he stares at the female officer. She gives me a look as if to say he's all my problem now. She drifts off five feet. Still monitoring, but allowing some privacy.

"Detective Lotham said you asked for me."

Charlie stares at me. He has his hands in his coat pockets. It makes him look bigger, broader. I don't think he's trying to appear intimidating as much as he simply can't help it. But I still don't find him threatening. The man joined the service because he has an instinct to protect. And some things, no matter the trauma, can't be shaken.

"You asked about cheap cells," Charlie says now. "You asked about the missing girl, Angelique Badeau. Just last night, you asked these questions."

I nod.

"I stopped by the store today, to take care of some business. But as long as I was here, I started thinking, I started wondering. About you and your questions. Then I look up and I swear to God, there she is."

"Angelique Badeau."

"And she's trying to buy a phone. I couldn't help myself. I stared straight at her. Next thing I know, she's snatching back her ID, tossing the new phone on the counter, and booking it out the door. Then the damn salesman starts yelling for security and the idiot runs right into me. By the time I get out onto the street, I can't see her anymore. But she was in there. I swear it. Trying to buy a phone." His eyes narrow. "How? You tell me. How did you know that?"

"I didn't," I tell him honestly. "Not that she'd buy a new phone. But I'd read in the paper that the police had recovered her original mobile eleven months ago. Figuring no teenager can be without a cell, stood to reason she'd bought a replacement along the way.

That's why I was asking about cheap burners. If I were a teenager with secrets, at least that's what I'd buy."

"You're no teenager," Charlie tells me.

I smile wanly. "But I do have secrets."

"Who are you?"

"I am Frankie Elkin. I'm an alcoholic. I work as a bartender at Stoney's, having just moved into the area. But I also have another passion—I work missing persons cases. Particularly cold cases. And yes, I came to Mattapan because of Angelique Badeau. I would like to find her."

Charlie doesn't speak right away. Neither does the female officer, who's been shamelessly eavesdropping.

"Did you really spot Angelique Badeau?" I ask now.

"I've been looking at her photo for eleven months. Hell yes, I saw the girl."

"Was there anyone else with her or did she appear to be alone?"

"Alone."

"And when she exited? Anyone waiting outside?"

"Didn't get that far. Had to drag some fat-ass mall cop off my foot before I could follow."

Now our cop chaperone smirks.

"Did she walk away or get into a car?"

"Don't know that either. But—" Charlie points up, to below the store awning where I can see two different cameras. "Cops should be able to answer that question soon enough."

"What was her mood?" I ask, still trying to understand.

"Didn't notice right away. But once I started staring, she got fidgety. Then she bolted and ran."

"You ever meet her before, Charlie?"

"Not so much for a hot minute. This city ain't that small, and our paths don't exactly cross."

"Charlie, I went to the rec center today. Talked to the director, Frédéric. You said your and Angelique's paths didn't cross, but she attended the summer program there, and you volunteer there."

"I help out after school, mentoring young Black males, teach 'em skills like cooking, so they can get a job and stay out of the life. Maybe that girl was also in the center, but I never saw her. Not like she'd be in one of my groups. She in trouble?"

"I think so."

"So why run? She's out buying a phone on her own. Why not ask for help?"

"I don't know."

"But she's clearly alive and still hasn't returned home. Meaning maybe she doesn't want to. Maybe she has a good reason to stay away."

I understand his point. Two public sightings of Angelique in two weeks. Both times she's bearing fake ID and appears to be acting independently. And yet, it still doesn't make any sense to me. The Angelique her family knew would never willingly disappear. Let alone her coded message: *Help us.* I simply don't believe she's a runaway. But as to what is going on . . . ?

"How did she look?" I ask at last. "Tired? Rested? Well fed? Starving?"

Charlie has to think about it. He shrugs at last. "Looked like a teenage girl. Blue jeans, light gray sweatshirt. Had an emblem on the front, but I couldn't make it out from my angle."

"And her face?"

"Couldn't see it. She was wearing a hat."

"A red hat?"

"How did you know that?" His tone is suspicious again.

"I'm sorry, I can't honestly say, Charlie. The police have their reasons for making only some details public."

He scowls at me but doesn't press. "I woulda helped her," he says abruptly. "All she had to do was ask. I woulda helped her."

"Maybe she couldn't ask. Sometimes, in these situations, the bad guys threaten a person's loved ones."

"Or get the girls hooked, so they don't wanna wander."

I can't deny it. "Did she look like an addict?"

"Nah. Moved too quick. Darted right out the door. Addicts don't have that kind of control."

I nod. "I think she got tangled up in something. But I don't know what, and I really don't even have proof of that. If you see her again, though, I do think she needs help, Charlie. One last thing: Could you make out an emblem or logo on the hat?"

"Not that I saw. But I didn't get a good look head on. Dark red cap, don't see so many of those around here."

"Why do you say that?"

"Kids generally wear hats from their favorite teams. Patriots, Red Sox, Bruins. Those hats are navy blue or black. Just look around. You'll see 'em everywhere."

Now that he's mentioned it, I have been seeing dark blue ball caps everywhere. Belatedly, I remember my slip of paper from the rec center. I pull it out of my back pocket, unfold it, and hold it out.

"Do you recognize any of these names, Charlie? From the rec center, around town, anything?"

Charlie studies the list of fashion camp kids for a while. He grunts twice, then points at the two teenage boys. "Seen them around. One is the younger brother of one of my kids. Good boys. Trying hard to stay out of trouble, as much as they can. Wait a minute. This name here." He points to one of the females on the list. "Livia Samdi. I've heard this name. Recently." He scratches his beard, appears thoughtful.

He drops his voice abruptly as the connection hits him. "At a meeting. Months ago. Pretty sure now. Her mom was there, had recently relapsed after nearly a year sober. Going through a tough time, she said. Lost her job, had her son arrested, then on top of all that, her daughter ran away."

"Her daughter ran away? As in Livia Samdi went missing?"

"That's what the mom thought. And not for the first time either. Apparently, Livia's one of those kids—wherever she went, trouble soon followed. But no doubt about it. She's definitely gone. The mom said so herself."

CHAPTER 17

I REMAIN ON THE SIDEWALK with Charlie and our police chaperone till Detective Lotham reappears from the wireless store. Whatever he's learned inside, it hasn't improved his mood.

He spots me, then Officer O'Shaughnessy, who is deep in conversation with two other uniforms. I watch the debate play out over Lotham's face. He abruptly turns and strides toward me.

"So," he states. He looks from me to Charlie back to me.

"This is Charlie," I say by way of introduction. I don't know Charlie's last name so I don't offer it. The lapse creates an awkward moment, then Detective Lotham extends his arm, shakes Charlie's hand.

"Army?" Lotham asks, gesturing to Charlie's coat. Then, when Charlie nods: "Marine, Force Recon. Thank you for your service."

"Thank you, sir."

"You saw Angelique Badeau?"

"Yes, sir."

"And you're sure it was her?"

"Yes, sir."

"And you know Ms. Elkin how?"

Charlie doesn't immediately respond to this sudden change in questioning but looks to me.

"Are you doubting I have friends?" I ask the detective, doing my best to sound indignant.

"You arrived in the area three days ago."

"All the more reason to reach out. Just ask Charadee at Dunkin' Donuts or Viv at Stoney's or Frédéric at the rec center." I search frantically for more names. "And my roommate, Piper. Though she didn't come home last night and I'm worried about her."

Detective Lotham looks like he has a headache. Whether it's the case or just me is open to interpretation.

"Charlie has other news," I add quickly now. "Earlier I was at the rec center—"

"With your friend Frédéric."

"There you go. He gave me a list of all the kids who were at fashion camp with Angelique during the summer program."

"I've seen the list. Even interviewed the teens."

"Including Livia Samdi."

"Probably. We're talking eleven months ago."

"So she hadn't gone missing yet. Interesting."

"What? Hang on." Detective Lotham pinches the bridge of his nose. I swear he's both taking a deep breath and muttering shit, shit, shit, but I can't be sure.

"Charlie heard a rumor at least." I glance at Charlie for confirmation. "Livia Samdi's mom said she ran away. And um, just to make things interesting, according to Frédéric from the rec center, Livia is known for wearing a red baseball hat."

Detective Lotham turns his gaze to Charlie, who immediately nods. "Livia ran away," Charlie supplies.

"Where did you hear this rumor?"

"Doesn't matter," I interject quickly. "What about Officer O'Shaughnessy? As the community liaison, maybe he knows more. We should ask him."

"You know what I learned inside?" Detective Lotham speaks up abruptly.

"What?"

"Nothing. No, not entirely true. I learned some kid named Warren couldn't describe his own mother if his life depended on it, and oh yeah, the security cameras haven't worked properly for months though they've been meaning to do something about that. You, on the other hand, standing out on the sidewalk . . ."

"It's a gift," I assure him. Then, noticing that Officer O'Shaughnessy is now looking in our direction, quickly wave him over before Lotham spontaneously combusts.

Detective Lotham steps back, takes a moment to consult with O'Shaughnessy. Now Charlie, the female cop, and I all eavesdrop shamelessly. This is what we hear: The uniforms had spread out and canvassed the neighborhood. According to witnesses, a girl in a red baseball cap had booked it out of the store and headed north. One officer had discovered her fake ID where it had dropped on the sidewalk two blocks from here. But no sign of Angelique herself.

Lotham brings O'Shaughnessy over. Charlie repeats his news. O'Shaughnessy frowns thoughtfully.

"I know the Samdi family, but not well. Dad's MIA. Mom's a drunk."

Lotham glances from me to Charlie, seems to connect the dots. I shrug as if to say, finally. He sighs again.

"Hadn't heard about Livia, though," O'Shaughnessy continued. "Her oldest brother recently got pinched for dealing. Small time, and not exactly news, but hardly a surprise either. The family . . .

Let's just say they're not the type to get the police involved in their business."

Lotham nods. "We're going to need to talk to them. Learn everything about Livia, including last time she was seen, relationship with Angelique Badeau, et cetera, et cetera."

"*Us,*" I murmur. "Or maybe the beginning of *us.*"

O'Shaughnessy gives me a funny look. "Angel's family has never mentioned Livia's name. So I'm not sure what 'us' you're talking about."

"I don't think they knew. I don't think anyone knew."

"Knew what?"

"About their friendship. Or whatever it was." I turn over the pieces in my mind. "They met at the rec center. Angelique had signed up for the summer program with her bestie Marjolie, but it turns out Marjolie was more interested in a certain basketball player than fashion camp. So Angelique ended up on her own. Until she made a new friend, Livia Samdi, who, for whatever reason, Angelique felt compelled to keep secret. Maybe because Livia had a history of getting into trouble? Or the nature of their relationship? I don't know all the details yet. But Livia was definitely aware of Angelique. The executive director, Frédéric, reported that he caught her watching Angelique on several occasions. You should talk to him."

"I *have* talked to Frédéric," Lotham practically growls.

"Then you should've asked him more questions relevant to teenage girls," I retort, starting to feel hostile myself. It's not my fault he didn't pick up on the details. Maybe he should've invested more time in a misspent youth. Certainly, I make most of my discoveries by asking what would my former, reprobate self do, and voilà, I get answers.

"Have you eaten?" Lotham asks me abruptly.

"No . . ."

"Great. Follow me."

He doesn't wait, just turns and heads up the street. I glance at O'Shaughnessy and Charlie. Both appear as confused as I feel. Charlie finally gives me a little nod. I take that as a hint and scamper after Lotham. He doesn't slow down or turn around, as he cuts his way through the slowly dispersing crowd of gawkers.

I realize several things at once. It's already after one in the afternoon and I'm starving. Also, I'm two hours from reporting to a job I can't afford to miss for the second day in a row. And yet, to pull away from the case now . . .

Lotham crosses the street. I follow, barely on his heels. Up ahead, a giant battered sign appears. It looks like an enormous ice cream cone perched on top of a roof. I can just make out the word *Simco* running down the peeling white cone. The words across the ice cream top are harder to make out; maybe *hot dog*? Though why a giant ice cream cone to advertise hot dogs?

Lotham has picked up his pace. I hustle to catch up.

Simco's World's Largest Hot Dog does appear to be our destination. It's a long, stand-alone building with a row of windows for ordering takeout. Half the windows are covered in photos of food. In addition to hot dogs, there's everything from a fried whiting dinner to Caribbean flavors to frappés, fried dough, and raspberry-lime rickeys. I'm so mesmerized by the options, I barely notice that Lotham has stopped in front of one of the open windows, where a middle-aged Black woman waits impatiently for our order.

"What do you want?" he asks me.

"Everything! I've never had a lime rickey. Sounds amazing."

"We'll take two dogs, one rickey, and a chocolate frappé," Lotham orders.

"Perfect. What are you going to have?"

He rolls his eyes, clearly onto my witty repartee by now.

There are toppings to be sorted out. I have no idea so I let the local have at it. Soon enough we have a greasy bag of food and two freezing-cold drinks. I'm excited.

"If I'm a good girl and eat all my food, can I have fried dough afterwards? Or maybe the banana boat. Dear God, this is better than the county fair."

"County fair?"

"Trust me."

We stand on the sidewalk to eat. Cars roar past, some beaters, some so custom you have to wonder about the driver's profession. Lotham seems immune. He keeps chewing and swallowing, his eyes half-mast with happiness. The hot dogs are super long, the fries salty, and the raspberry-lime rickey a refreshing hit of icy tartness.

"Number six," I inform Lotham as I munch away. I'm never going to finish the world's largest hot dog, but it'll be fun to try.

"Number six what?"

"Best meal I ever had."

"You rate them?"

"It's good to note key moments. And food is often a source of happiness."

"You're saying eating a hot dog standing roadside is your sixth all-time favorite meal?"

"Precisely."

"I don't understand you at all, Elkin."

"Because I'm simple when you want me to be complicated. And I'm complicated when you want me to be simple." I shrug. I've lived with myself for a long time now. And part of maintaining my sobriety is being honest even when it hurts.

Lotham has already finished his dog. He goes to work on his fries with mechanical precision.

"You piss me off," he states.

"I got that memo."

"We asked questions. I personally visited that fucking rec center. For that matter, I was there when we searched the apartment, interviewed family and friends. And yet you . . ." He seems at a loss for words. "Three days into it, and you've turned this whole damn thing on its head."

"Would you rather have no leads at all?"

"No, dammit!"

"Then you'd rather all discoveries be the product of your greatness?"

"I'm not that petty!"

"Then what the hell is it you want? I'm here. I'm sharing. Frankly, you're the one being an asshole."

Lotham scowls, eats more fries. "I'm trying to figure out your secret. Or what to do with you. Or what to make of you. Maybe all three."

"Hah. Good luck with that."

"Why are you here? Why this case? Why this girl? What exactly it is you're looking for?"

He's ruining my mood and my appetite. I shutter the clamshell container of hot dog and fries, take a sip of my lime rickey instead. It's melting fast now. Probably doesn't like angry conversations any more than I do.

"You want to know who I am."

"Precisely."

"Maybe it's more important to know who I'm not."

"I have such a headache right now, and this . . . is not helping."

But he started it, and now I won't be put off. "You want to know me, Mr. Big-Shot Detective, Mr. Fucking BPD and Expert on All Things Local? You ran my background. You already know what you need to know. I'm a woman who can't stay in one place for very long. I don't have close, lasting relationships. I have no sense of material possessions or financial stability. And I fight every fucking day not to take a drink. You know what I can do? This. Locate missing persons. Work cold cases. I don't know why. But this is what I've got, pretty much the only thing I've got, so I'm sticking with it."

"Some modern-day Sherlock Holmes."

"Sherlock sees the answers. I just have a gift for asking the right questions." I take the bag from him, jam my container of food back in. "I don't know where Angelique is. I don't know why she has a hidden stash of counterfeit money or what's her relationship with Livia Samdi or why she's running around the city with a fake ID leaving coded messages. But I'm also okay not seeing that far ahead. As long as I have the next question . . . I'll get there."

Lotham has finished his lunch. He takes the bag back, adds his own trash. His eyes are dark and intense. He stands much closer to me than necessary. I can feel the heat from him. Roiling waves of rage and frustration.

"You want answers," I say quietly.

"Of course!"

"You're all about the finish line."

"Bringing home a missing teenage girl, hell yes."

"I'm about the process. Once we cross the finish line . . . that's where I get lost. That's when I stop understanding things so well."

He frowns, appearing genuinely puzzled. "You're really never going to settle down? You're really just gonna do this—drift from city to town to city?"

"Will you miss me?" I smile. It's a bit sad, though. I would honestly like the good detective to kiss me. No, I'd like him to drag me around the back of the building and fuck me senseless, because that's the kind of intensity I crave. But he's all solid and stable and Marine Force Recon. The calm in the storm. While I'm the hurricane that destroys everything in its path.

Lotham must read some of it on my face, because he suddenly grabs my chin. His hand is warm, his fingertips calloused. I part my lips. His thumb brushes over the lower one and I clamp down on his finger gently, touching the pad of his thumb with the tip of my tongue.

His eyes darken. Here's something else I know: Good guys like him have a weakness for train wrecks like me.

Just ask Paul.

"Do you want to take me home?" I ask him softly, releasing his thumb. "I'll go. We can fuck on your sofa, your kitchen table, maybe even your bed if we get that far. You can work out all that turmoil. Maybe you'll even feel in control. Like you got a handle on me, at last. Got me right where you want me."

He doesn't speak, but takes a step closer.

"I love sex. The harder the better. A moment where I don't have to think, where I can escape my own mind? Afterwards, I might even get a good night's sleep. But the minute it's over, you're gonna want what you're gonna want, and I'm still gonna be me. And that will piss you off all over again."

"Maybe you don't know me as well as you think."

I smile. And I can see Paul so clearly, it's like a hole being ripped in my chest all over again.

What did you do, Frankie? Dear God, what did you do?

I loved you.

"I have to go to work now," I tell the detective honestly. "I get off at midnight. If you want to find me. We can talk about the case. Or not. I'll be there."

I step back. Then, because one step doesn't quite do the trick, two, three, four, more. He watches me retreat, staying rooted in place with the remnants of our shared lunch. When I'm sure he's truly going to stay, I turn.

I walk rapidly back to Stoney's. I tell myself I am okay. I tell myself I'm not rattled. I tell myself I can handle it.

Because no one can be honest all of the time. Not even me.

CHAPTER 18

POP UPSTAIRS TO MY apartment to clean up before work. And possibly, though I don't want to get carried away, because I'm worried about Piper. But given that I'm greeted with a giant ball of vomit in the middle of the floor, I can see my concerns are misplaced. I check under the bed, and sure enough, glowing green eyes stare back at me.

"We need to discuss your communication style," I inform her.

She blinks slowly.

"I find the gutted mice and pile of ick to be passive aggressive. If you need a bit of personal space, just say so."

She yawns, flashing canines. Maybe her communication style is direct, and I just don't like the message.

I get out the paper towels and mop up the mess.

Tomorrow, I'll hit the grocery store, I promise myself. After I survive my work shift, attend an AA meeting, and . . . well, whatever comes next with the good detective.

I really wouldn't mind a night of mad, passionate sex.

Then again, I'm not convinced Lotham is the type who can handle the morning after.

I sigh heavily. Scrub my hands and face, rake a comb through my hair, then report downstairs for work.

Stoney is his usual silent self. I appreciate that today. My mind is racing. For all my big words to Lotham, I hate having this many questions. Livia and Angelique. Angelique and Livia. Am I being too naïve? Maybe instead of secret besties, they were lovers and Angelique wasn't ready to disclose her sexuality to the world?

In my experience, teenagers today are pretty open-minded about these things. Certainly compared to my generation. Though maybe sexual orientation isn't as accepted in Haitian culture? Or in Angelique's family? How do I ask that question?

It matters, though. What is the relationship between Angelique and Livia, and what drove both of them to disappear within months of each other?

Us. Help us.

And again, just how many people is *us*? Is a presumed runaway girl the end of that question, or just the beginning?

The knowledge of a second missing teen does help with some answers. For example, Angelique's obvious autonomy to move around the city, but her continued need for secrecy and refusal to come home. Human trafficking 101 is to play the girls off one another. You can have freedom for the night. But one false move, and your friend will pay the price. Given Angelique's reputation for caretaking, she would be particularly vulnerable to such control tactics. Especially if Livia was a new friend, more-than-friend, whom she wouldn't want to betray.

Meaning that eleven months later, Angelique had acquired some level of trust and independence from her kidnappers—while remaining terrified for her safety, and the safety of at least one other girl.

Angelique didn't believe in dreams, Emmanuel had said. She believed in making plans. Like sending a coded message. Like appearing at a major wireless store where maybe she hoped she'd be captured on security cameras. Two sightings in two weeks.

Whatever her plan was, it involved a definite sense of urgency. Meaning what had changed? What was about to happen if we didn't pick up on her trail of breadcrumbs and fast?

I unstack chairs, wipe tabletops, slice up lemons and limes, and still come no closer to any answers. Clearly Angelique is trying to communicate. Unfortunately, I still didn't get the message.

Viv appears through the front door. She stops when she sees me.

"I hear you're looking for that poor missing girl."

"Yes, ma'am."

"You some kind of private eye?"

"I'm gonna go with *some kind.*"

She hums her approval in her Viv-like way. "Honey, no child should be missing from her family. Any way I can help, you let me know."

"Do you know the Samdi family? Their daughter is Livia."

"Doesn't ring a bell, but I can ask around. Mattapan ain't that big, but it's crowded enough. Was a time when I felt like I knew my neighbors, but not anymore."

Viv disappears into the kitchen, hollering out a greeting to Stoney, who grunts in reply. I just finish setting up the bar in time for the first few customers to arrive. I already recognize a few of the regulars, and no longer earn so many dark scowls. I take that as progress as I start banging out drinks and delivering plates of hot food.

I keep myself busy. I tell myself I'm not glancing at the door every time it opens. I promise myself I'm not some giddy schoolgirl anxiously waiting for her crush to appear.

It doesn't really work, but thankfully the combination of cheap beer and low-priced food has the tables filled and the orders coming. I'm a good bartender. I like the steady rhythm, the adrenaline rush of juggling dozens of customers, followed by the quieter times where I restock, clean up, and prepare for the madness to return.

The hard-core drinkers aren't ones to talk, but I like that, too. More of them make eye contact with me tonight. Another few days, and I'll be worthy of them learning my name. Then my list of growing social contacts will really piss the detective off.

Nine P.M. Dinner crowd done, tables thinning, demand easing. No detective.

Ten P.M. Down to a few tables of rowdies, enjoying a big night out. No detective.

Eleven P.M. Tables are pretty much cleared. The bar is left with the hard-core stragglers, who will stay to closing.

I scared him off. Not everyone appreciates bluntness, and not every man can deal with the hot mess that is me.

Or he's exhausted, having spent most of last night working. Or he's still on the job, as today's revelations have led to even more breaks in the case.

I want to hear about new breaks in the case. I want . . .

The door opens.

Lotham appears.

And despite all my bold declarations, my stomach flip-flops and my hands tremble, and I do feel like a stupid schoolgirl, even though I, of all people, know better.

The detective has showered and changed. Dark jeans, paired with a rich turquoise button-down shirt stretched across his broad chest. He radiates cop and authority figure and military man all rolled into one. As he approaches the bar, several of the hard-core drinkers beat a retreat. I don't blame them.

"Girly drink?" I ask as he takes a seat.

He gives me a look. "I'll take a glass of water."

The order unsettles me. Because he's still working and needs a clear head? Or because he wants complete focus for our future interlude?

I dump ice in a glass, add water. Stoney wanders over, greets the detective with a nod. This time of night, never bad to have a cop nearby. Then Viv bustles out, takes in my impressive new customer, eyes him, eyes me, then delivers a not-so-subtle "You go girl."

I turn red, which frazzles me more. I never did the giddy school-girl thing. Frankly, I was much too hammered most of the time to care. Manic, yes. Destructive, certainly. Giddy, never.

I place the water in front of Lotham. He takes a sip. At the end of the bar, one of the regulars flags me down to settle up his bill. I'm grateful for the distraction.

More beer here. A final round of rum punch there. Clearing plates. Cleaning tables. Moving, moving, moving.

I really would like a drink right now—and that, as much as anything, pisses me off. Time to get over my own fucking self.

By the time I return to the bar, my nerves have settled and Lotham has finished half his water.

"Food?" I ask him.

"Honestly, I've had nothing but grease for days. What I could use is a salad, but that's not exactly on the menu."

"Viv has been known to do special orders. For her favorites."

"Viv, from the kitchen?"

"That's her. And judging by the way she was looking at you, you're already one of her favorites."

That earns me a grin. Briefly, the detective appears ten years younger. His job is a burden he never sets down. It is both extremely attractive and kind of sad. Trying to save the world can be as much a compulsion as drinking, except Lotham doesn't have a twelve-step program to save him from himself. I wonder if he will burn out, become embittered with the job, the life he never took the time to build. Maybe one day he will envy me, but I doubt it.

I pop into the kitchen. Ask Viv if she wouldn't mind making a garden salad for a friend. That earns me so many cackles and knowing winks I have to leave before I start blushing again.

But the salad comes and the detective turns his attention to his food. The bar empties out and soon enough, Stoney is there, ready to lock the front door. He eyes the detective questioningly.

"He's going to stay for a bit."

Stoney nods, locks up, then pockets the key before making a point of disappearing to his office. I don't know how to close out the register, so eventually he'll have to take care of that, but for now I start stacking chairs.

Without a word, Lotham slips off the table and carries his plate to the kitchen.

"Hello, handsome!" Forget about me, he's officially made Viv's night.

"Thank you, ma'am. That was exactly what I needed."

"You come again, let me know and I'll make you a steak. Then you'll know exactly what you've needed."

From the back room, I hear Stoney make a strangling sound. Then Lotham reappears, looking slightly wide-eyed and red-faced. At least it's not just me. I hand him a broom. As long as he's here, he might as well be useful.

He starts from the back, working his way to the front while I wipe down the last of the tables and finish with the chairs.

"Did you learn more about Livia Samdi?" I ask him finally.

"She's definitely missing, and the family definitely doesn't care for police involvement."

"Wait, is that your way of saying there might be value to my particular approach?"

"A good cop would never encourage civilian involvement in a case."

Which is not the same thing as no.

"When did Livia run away?" I continue.

"January. Nearly three months after Angelique."

"And the circumstances?"

"Went to school and never came home again."

"That sounds suspiciously familiar. And they never contacted police?"

"According to the mom, Roseline, it wasn't the first time Livia had disappeared. Sometimes the girl wouldn't come home on Friday but would show up to school on Monday like nothing happened. Lost weekends. Even a week here and there. Let's just say, given the . . . nature . . . of the household, I'm surprised they noticed that much."

"What did Livia take with her?"

"That's the thing. According to the mom, Livia's clothes, personal possessions are mostly accounted for. She didn't own a computer, just a cell phone, which disappeared with her. We tried pinging it with no luck. But we're now pulling a record of calls and texts from the provider. Will be interesting to see if the phone is genuinely no longer in use, or just activated in short intervals."

"Had they heard of Angelique Badeau?"

"The mom recognized the name from the news, that's it."

"So they didn't know she and Livia were friends?"

"To be honest, I'm not sure the mom knew any of Livia's friends. Or hobbies, or favorite color. Not that kind of family."

"In other words, the complete opposite of Angelique's family." I pause, my hands still on a back of a chair. "I wonder what brought the girls together? Opposites attract? Angelique the caretaker think-ing she could help out with Livia's sad life?"

Lotham shrugs.

"Livia have a history of drinking and drugs?"

"Given the family, I would say yes to both. But they aren't talking about it."

"Maybe a school guidance counselor can tell you more."

"Which is where I'll be first thing in the morning."

"So much for sticking around for a late breakfast," I grumble.

That earns me the detective's full attention. His eyes darken. He stands ten feet away, still holding the broom, but there's suddenly not enough air in the room.

"This is what we do know," he says softly. "Angelique is alive, and she needs help."

I nod.

"She is somehow connected to Livia Samdi, another missing girl. And we are absolutely, positively, not mentioning anything about red hats to the press."

"Your hold-back detail."

"Not to mention, we don't need dozens of sightings of people in red ball caps tying up resources."

"What about Angelique's appearance today? Will you ramp back up the investigation?"

"We are taking the sighting very seriously. But as far as the pub-lic knows, we have no confirmation that was Angelique in the store today. Which works well with the clerk's *maybe, kind of, not really sure* statement."

"You don't want to involve the public?" I ask in surprise. "Reis-sue the Amber Alert?"

Lotham leans against the broom. "Angelique clearly has some freedom of movement but doesn't feel like she can come home—"

"She needs help! *Help us*. She said it herself."

"Exactly. She feels threatened and in danger. Until we understand more about that threat, who and what it involves, the safest approach is to follow her lead and keep things quiet. We're adding more officers to the case, don't worry. But our official position, which I need to know you will support, is that there's nothing new to see here."

"Don't insult me," I tell him harshly. I return to stacking chairs. I honestly can't decide what I think of this.

"You're going to inform Angelique's family of the new sighting," I say after another moment.

"The fewer people who know, the better."

"Are you kidding me?" Now he does have my attention. "You have a significant lead and you're *not* going to notify Guerline and Emmanuel?"

"When we know more, have something specific to share—"

"Oh, come on. You wouldn't even have these latest discoveries without Emmanuel. The family trusts you, they came to you—"

"Actually, Emmanuel came to *you*—"

"And you wonder why? They knew then that you were holding back, and it did nothing but fuel further mistrust."

Lotham remains calm and controlled: "Look me in the eye and tell me you've never lied to a family. Never omitted a detail, buried a lead. You do this work, you know how it is."

I scowl. But I can't look him in the eye and we both know it. I've made this judgment call before myself. I just don't agree it's the right approach with Angelique's aunt and brother.

I stack more chairs. Lotham returns to sweeping. Stoney appears and tends to the register.

Viv finishes first. Her husband no sooner appears on the other side of the smoked-glass doors than Viv comes bustling out, putting on her jacket. Telepathy after so many years of marriage? Or does he text her upon arrival? I don't know why I prefer the more romantic option.

Stoney takes off next. One last glance between Lotham and me. Then with some sort of mental shrug, he disappears out the side door. Lotham puts away the broom. I finish up cleaning the bar area.

Then that's it. Work is done. The customers and other employees gone. There's just this man and me, and a homicidal cat upstairs.

Lotham walks toward me. He's light on his feet. A boxer. In hindsight, I should've known instantly.

He stops right in front of me, and I can't help myself. I raise my hands. I dance my fingertips across his face, feeling out the line of his jaw, the soft, ragged edge of his mangled ear, then find another scar, just over his left eye. He has ridiculously long, thick eyelashes. Why do men always have the best eyelashes?

His buzzed hair scrapes against my palm. Closer in texture to his end-of-day stubble and nothing at all like his silky eyebrows. He has furrowed lines in his forehead. I trace each one. Another sign of his stressful job? I like the mystery of those lines. What they communicate but cannot say.

My hands fall to his shoulders. Heavily muscled, rigid to the touch. Same with his arms. A boxer who still spends plenty of time in the ring. Up this close, I can see the pulse pounding at the base of his throat, hear his ragged breath.

I whisper my lips across the hollow of his throat. He smells of sandalwood, tastes like salt. The cleaned-up version of the man, but I would find him compelling either way.

"Good night, Frankie," he says.

"Good night, Detective." Then I raise my lips and kiss him properly.

For a moment, he unleashes. A storm of wild attraction and raw power as he crushes me against him. His mouth devours. His tongue ravages and I respond eagerly. This is not drunken fumbling or mindless fucking. This is feeling your feels.

I don't protest when he pulls away, releases my arms, and steps back.

"Good night, Frankie," he says again.

"Good night, Detective."

Then I let him out the front door, and watch him walk away.

CHAPTER 19

IT IS A BRIGHT, SUNNY morning as I head down the final few blocks to the Samdis' apartment. Even with daylight on my side, I find myself hunching my shoulders and gazing around nervously. If Mattapan is a mix of good and bad neighborhoods, this isn't one of the good ones.

Rusted chain-link fences buckle and gape, revealing modest yards long on neglect—abandoned piles of battered kids' toys, drifts of dead shrubs, borders of shattered beer bottles and used condoms. Each triple-decker seems determined to appear even more broken down than its neighbor. I honestly can't tell who's winning.

This isn't the place to be after dark. I'm not even sure it's somewhere I should be now, as I feel eyes starting to fall upon me, and more and more human-sized silhouettes appear at the windows to monitor my progress. I am definitely an outsider here.

Deep breath. In through my mouth. Exhaling through my nose. Not the first time I've been through this. Stay calm, relaxed, focus.

I'm not a threat. I have no issues. Just a couple of questions for the family.

On my right, the front door opens and three African American males come strolling out, crossing their arms over their muscled chests and pinning me with their best thousand-yard stare. Followed by similar movement from the house across the street. Then up ahead to the right. Then left.

Am I *this* unwanted here?

I arrive at the Samdis' building, which is neither the best nor worst on the block. The narrow triple-decker has shed huge flakes of dark green paint, while the stacked front deck sags dangerously forward. A giant piece of plywood patches a hole along the right side. Two more are nailed on the roof.

I don't have to open the front gate. It's already collapsed, the front corner gouged deep into the earth. I shimmy around it, kicking a deflated soccer ball that plows into a pile of empty booze bottles. I startle from the noise, snag my jacket on the rusty chain link, and tear a hole.

"Shit!" I curse, then belatedly catch myself. Relaxed and focused. The family I need to speak with are looking for reasons not to like me, excuses not to help. My job is not to give them one.

I pick my way up the front steps. One of the boards is so rotted, I skip over it completely, landing harder than I would like on the one above. I feel it shake upon impact, and clamber up the remaining stairs in a burst of adrenaline.

The second I hit the landing, the front door opens. A young Black male stands before me in a white tank top, and sagging dark jeans. He wears his hair in a million braids, curving back from his face before falling like a curtain to his shoulders. He has a giant diamond stud in one ear, and enough ink sleeving his forearms and twining around his neck to serve as a second shirt. Even looking straight at him, it's impossible to see behind the confusion of tattoos, jewelry, and hair extensions. Urban camouflage.

"We don't want you here," he states. His eyes are dark and flat.

"I'm looking for Mrs. Samdi," I say.

"We don't want you here."

"It's regarding her daughter, Livia."

"Get the fuck off my property."

"Do you own the whole house?" I ask him curiously. "What a great accomplishment. And at such a young age, too."

A single slow blink. "No white bitches wanted here."

"Okay, but I'm a cheap white bitch. Surely that counts for something? My specialty is locating missing persons, free of charge. I'm already in the area looking for Angelique Badeau. Maybe you know her?"

"Fuck off."

"Are you Livia's brother? Uncle? Random acquaintance? I understand from the police the family believes Livia ran away. I respectfully disagree. I think her vanishing act has something to do with Angelique's disappearance and I'd like to help both of them."

"You hard of hearing, lady? Go. The fuck. Away." Two steps forward now. His tough words aren't getting the job done, so he's throwing his body behind them. He's five ten and a solid one eighty of sculpted muscle. I have exactly . . . nothing . . . on him.

"I'm here for Mrs. Samdi," I repeat, more quickly now. "If she wants me to go, I'll go. But not before I see her. Look, I'm not here to jam you up or judge your family. I don't work for the police, the press, anyone. I'm here solely for the missing and I need just a few minutes of your mother's time. Five. Five minutes. Who knows, by the end, maybe both she and I can do some good."

The boy—who has to be Livia's older brother—opens his mouth again. His hands are fisted, his throat corded. I'm already leaning back, wishing I'd left about two seconds earlier, when a tired, ragged voice comes from inside the house.

"Let her in, Johnson."

My greeter scowls, loosens his fists.

"Johnson?" I mouth at him, one brow arched.

"J.J.," he snaps back.

J.J. lets me pass by, nodding across the street at the many loitering, heavily muscled youths still keeping watch. His friends? His gang? It doesn't really matter. O'Shaughnessy had pegged Livia's brother as a drug dealer. Which makes it in my own best interest to keep my head down and eyes on the floor as he leads me down the hall to the rear of the building.

We emerge into an open area, hazy with cigarette smoke. To my right is a kitchen, with almost every available surface covered with discarded food containers and supersized bottles of booze. Something big, brown, and shiny skitters across the floor. Then two more somethings.

I swallow slowly. Going from Guerline's bright-colored, homey apartment to this makes it hard to believe Livia and Angelique had much in common. And yet . . .

I turn my attention to the card table positioned against the wall on the left. A gaunt African American woman sits there, her face wreathed in smoke from her burning cigarette. She wears a faded blue floral housedress and the heavily aged features of a lifetime drinker.

I pull out the folding chair across from her, and have a seat. "Roseline Samdi?"

The woman takes a long drag, then taps the ash off the end of her cigarette in the remnants of a beer can. "You're the woman? The one looking for Badeau?"

Roseline's first few words sound typically Boston. But when she delivers *Badeau*, her island heritage gives her away. The name comes out both hard and soft, an echo of palm trees and drifting clouds.

"Did you immigrate as a child, or more recently?" I ask. I'm trying hard not to wrinkle my nose against the stench of spoiled food, unwashed clothes, and human sweat. If I lived here, I'd smoke all day, too, just to cover the smell.

"When I was little. I came with my *mamè*, thirty years ago."

It takes me a moment to figure out that Roseline isn't that much older than me. But to look at her . . .

On impulse, I reach over and clasp her hand. She's too startled to pull away.

"Nine years sober. Nine years, seven months. I still miss it all the time. It sucks, doesn't it? To want something so badly, when you know you shouldn't."

She doesn't speak right away. Her skin is jaundiced. Her expression bleak. But in her eyes, I think I see a flash of gratitude.

"I made it a whole year once. Can't say it was my best year, spending every damn day hurtin' and wantin'. But afterwards." She takes another drag of her cigarette, nods slowly. "Afterwards, I was sorry I let it go."

"We've all been there."

"So that's it, then? You're an addict, I'm an addict. I might as well tell you *everything*?"

The bitterness in her words is sharp enough for me to release her hand and sit back. This isn't going to be an easy conversation or a friendly one. Might as well get it done.

"Did Livia know Angelique Badeau?"

"No." It's a hard sound. Like she's exhaling very quickly, getting the word as far away from her as possible.

"Did Livia ever mention Angelique from the summer camp at the rec center?"

"No."

"Why fashion camp?"

Roseline pauses, blinks. Her cigarette is almost burned down. She bangs out a fresh one from the pack beside her, using the old to light the new, without even the slightest pause in between.

"Why not?" she asks at last.

"She didn't talk to you about it? Say how much she wanted to go, loved going, was so happy she went? I mean, you paid for it, right? Surely you wanted a reason."

Roseline pauses. Inhale. Exhale. Tap. She didn't pay for it. I can see that from her expression. Livia must've qualified through some program for low-income families. Meaning her mother never thought to ask a question about her enrollment?

In the end, Roseline offers a single, fatalistic shrug. In other words, Livia did go to fashion camp, and her own mother never bothered to find out why. I notice Roseline's cigarette is now shaking slightly in her hand. She's not as impervious as she wants to appear.

"Did Livia have a friend who was taking it?" I press. "Or maybe an obsession with *Project Runway*? Aspirations to design for a living?"

Inhale, exhale, tap. Finally. "Livia liked to make things."

"Make things . . . So fashion camp was the closest she could come to . . . making something?" Which is interesting, because I'd already assumed Angelique hadn't been into fashion either. For her, it appeared to be about the opportunity to do art. Maybe for Livia, it had been design?

"Who are Livia's closest friends?" I ask.

"She doesn't have none." But the assertion is halfhearted. As in, her own mother once again doesn't know the answer.

I wait, in case she clarifies. In the silence, she takes a drag of her cigarette, so deep that for an instant her face appears skeletal. "We're not the friendly type," she says at last, exhaling slowly.

"Did Livia like school?"

"She went."

"What was her favorite subject?"

"I dunno." Inhale, exhale, tap. "She'd bring home these little projects she'd made. Like this fake pumpkin. Tiny, carved from orange plastic. Even the eyes were cut out. It was cute enough. Worthless, though. What the hell am I supposed to do with such a thing?"

I have no idea what kind of class at school leads to minuscule plastic jack-o'-lanterns. "Do you still have it?"

Roseline glances at the floor. There is more movement beneath the expansive layer of trash. I can't look anymore.

"Maybe you could show me on Livia's computer? It must have a record of her schoolwork."

Roseline bangs her cigarette against the remnants of the beer can, shakes her head. "You see a computer? Girl had to use whatever they had at school."

"So she liked school? Her other classmates—"

"She went. Every morning. Got up, got out. That's all I care."

But I can hear it in Roseline's voice. That's not all she cared. That's not all she was worrying about.

"Sounds lonely," I prod now. "Going to school each day without any friends."

"The girl stayed out of trouble."

"She's shy?"

"She's clever. Always where you don't expect her. Seeing things she shouldn't see. Hearing stuff she shouldn't hear. Even when she was young. But then, you'd turn around, and she'd be gone again. Learned from her brother not to be in one place too long. Gonna be sneaky?" Roseline stares at me. "Better also be fast. Livia had skills."

Meaning Angelique's new acquaintance from fashion camp was habitually subversive? Or maybe, by virtue of snooping where she wasn't wanted, in some kind of serious trouble?

"In the weeks leading up to Livia's disappearance, did anything seem different?"

"Was what it was."

The answer I expected. "Your son, Johnson? Is he more or less interested in his sister?"

"Johnson wouldn't hurt his sister!" The answer is reflexive, and not entirely devoid of dread.

"Why not?"

"Family's family. 'Sides." Roseline's first moment of levity. "Drama's not good for business."

I get her point. Except according to O'Shaughnessy, Johnson is pretty low level. Meaning he probably reports to higher-level gangsters who probably report to highest-level drug lords. Would they consider a fifteen-year-old girl off limits? Especially one who had a tendency to be where she shouldn't?

"Where did Livia go to school?"

Roseline rattles off a name that is definitely not Angelique's school. "Is that . . . ?"

"A trade school. Nothing wrong with that. Kids need a life skill. Or . . ."

They'd fall back on the family business of dope dealing.

"Did she have a favorite teacher?"

Inhale, exhale, tap. Shrug.

"Favorite subject?"

"She liked making the pumpkin."

A commotion now. Noise from the front of the house. Roseline sits up suddenly, stubs out her cigarette. The first time she's stopped smoking since I entered the room.

"Time's up."

"Wait—"

"You gotta go. Door's behind you. You know the saying, don't let it hit you on the ass on your way out."

Apparently, I'm not allowed out the way I came in but must flee through the rear door. I want to argue, but suddenly Roseline is standing, her nicotine-stained fingertip an angry punctuation as she jabs it toward me.

"Out!" Her tone is suddenly commanding.

I hesitate. "Come with me. I'll take you to a meeting. We'll go together. I'll hold your hand, you hold mine."

"Go!"

"One step. Remember that year? Even now you miss it. Come with me. I'll help you."

"*Now.*"

"Mrs. Samdi—"

Her left hand snakes out, grabs my shoulder, and clenches it with a strength that is surprising. "You're not safe."

I don't have words. The spit dries up in my mouth, while her clawlike fingers skewer me in place.

"Livia was not safe."

"Mrs. Samdi, are you saying you're grateful she's gone? Is that why you never reported her having gone missing to the police? You hope she has run away. You think she's safer that way?"

"This is no place for girls."

"I can handle Johnson—"

"It's not my son you should fear."

The noise turns into a riot of pounding feet and streaming ex-pletives. Heading straight at us.

I want to ask more questions. I want to understand. But Roseline is already shoving me toward the back door.

"If you find my Livia," Mrs. Samdi hisses, wrenching open the door.

"Wait—"

"Do not bring her home to this."

Then Roseline Samdi shoves me straight out. I stagger down the steps, arms pinwheeling for balance. I've just come to a stop, when I hear male voices, shouting behind me.

"Mom!"

"Stop her!"

"What the fuck, J.J.!"

I don't spare a moment to look back. I bolt away from the house. I run fast, then faster, not even glancing behind me when I hear the rat-a-tat of footsteps chasing me. Though just for a second, out of the corner of my eye, I spot a shockingly tall, skinny Black man wearing a red tracksuit and loads of gold chains. Retro man, I recognize. The guy from Angelique's school who's dressed like a time capsule from 2002.

There's a look on his face. A warning.

I add a fresh burst of speed just as a gunshot splits the air. Followed by another.

I dodge left, hunching my shoulders to make myself as small a target as possible as I pound down the sidewalk, gasping through my tears. Another left, another right. Keep on trucking. Don't look back. Don't ever look back.

Paul, I think wildly. Then the giant hole in my chest gapes open, and I run through that, too. Faster, faster, faster.

Don't look back don't look back don't look back.

I run so fast my tears dry before they can stain my cheeks. I race so hard I'm not even in this city, but somewhere far away where the trees are sinister shadows and the moon is snatching at my hair and I have to squeeze my eyes shut against the sheer terror.

Don't look back don't look back don't look back.

Next thing I know, I'm plowing into the Dunkin' Donuts, where my new friends are staring at me.

"Call the police, call the police, call the police!" I scream at Charadee.

Which she does, except I don't remember the rest; I'm crying too hard, my mind a wreck of then and now, what was and what is. What will never be again.

Eventually Lotham bursts through the door. He takes one look at my devastated face and pulls me into his arms.

"Paul," I sob hysterically against his chest.

He lets me collapse against him, and holds me as I weep.

CHAPTER 20

I SIT IN A BOOTH at Stoney's. On the table in front of me: a mug of coffee, a glass of water, and a giant box of Munchkins that Charadee shoved into my hands as I was leaving. The box is open. I've managed to eat two, which explains the powdered sugar on my fingers, lips, and cheek. Lotham disappeared long enough to retrieve a damp washcloth. Now, he uses it to wipe gingerly at my snot- and tear-stained face. I don't make a move to stop him or assist.

My brain has short-circuited. My heart has exploded in my chest. That nothing actually happened to me is the least of my worries.

"Coffee," Lotham orders.

I lift the mug, take a sip.

"Sugar."

He provides a chocolate Munchkin. I chew obediently.

"Water."

I move on to the glass.

"Repeat."

So, I do. Two, three, four more times. Till my coffee mug is dry and the water gone and a suspicious number of donuts missing as well. Judging by the smear of red jam at the corner of Lotham's mouth, I'm not the only one using pastries to self-medicate.

"Start at the beginning."

I try. I'm not really sure what there is to say. I met with Mrs. Samdi. I asked her a variety of questions about her daughter, Livia, most of which she couldn't answer. Meaning I basically learned what Detective Lotham had surmised the day before—Livia's family wasn't exactly the loving sort.

"She ordered you to leave," he repeats now.

"Someone arrived. At the front. I could hear a commotion. I never saw who, but Mrs. Samdi's demeanor changed. She shoved me out the back. She said . . ." I draw a shaky breath. "She said the house wasn't safe for girls. She told me if I found her daughter, *not* to bring her home."

"Why isn't their house safe for girls?"

"I don't know."

"The son, J.J.—"

"Johnson."

Lotham arches a brow.

"You should call him that," I insist. "Really pisses him off. Apparently, you can't score any street cred as a Johnson."

"Definitely not."

"But she also implied he wouldn't hurt his sister. Family doesn't go after family. Someone else, I'm guessing one of Johnson's acquaintances, bosses, I don't know. Higher on the criminal food chain."

"Okay. So Mrs. Samdi shoves you out the rear door. You take off and they—"

"I didn't see."

"—give chase. And fire a gun?"

"I heard gunshots. But I didn't stop to look. Firing at me, firing at someone else, someone else firing at them firing at me. Your guess is as good as mine."

"And guess is as good as we got," Lotham grumbles. "Uniforms already canvassed the area. As the saying goes, nobody saw nothin'. On that block, that's how it goes. Crime techs recovered a fresh slug from the side of a porch probably two feet from where you passed. Trajectory indicates it didn't come from behind you, however, but from across the street."

"Oh goody. So it was one of the neighbors who wanted me dead."

"First time being shot at, Frankie?"

"No."

"Want to talk about it?"

"No."

"Want a drink?"

"Is it a day ending in *Y*? Hell yes."

"Then talking is what you get to do instead."

I have to smile. Man is smart, his manipulation well played. But I'm not going to talk to him about my meltdown, or PTSD or whatever you want to call it. It's too personal. And maybe, all these years later, still too intimate. It belongs to Paul and me. To talk about it with anyone else . . .

I will call his number. Listen to it ring. The click of him picking up. The reassuring sound of his breathing, syncing with my own. My heartbeat. His heartbeat. Intertwined.

Then a woman's voice: "You need to stop this. You need help."

Don't we all?

I get up from the booth, head to the kitchen for more coffee. I'm already so caffeinated I teeter on the edge of nausea. Ironically, this is not when I'm most at risk for falling off the wagon. I'm too exhausted to self-destruct. If I finally pour that drink I've been craving for nine fucking years . . . Trust me, I plan on remembering it.

When I turn around, Lotham is standing behind me in the kitchen. He takes the mug from my violently trembling hand, and leads me back to the booth.

"Talk to me," he says.

"I don't think Livia and Angelique meant to be friends."

"Okay."

"I think something else brought them together. Neither one of them enrolled in fashion camp because they were that into fashion. Angelique's a future doctor who likes to sketch. Livia, apparently, is a sneaky survivor with a penchant for making things. But then Angelique's bestie bailed on her for a basketball player, and Livia never had a friend to start with. So you have two lone girls, both quiet but smart. Maybe they simply sat side by side for a bit . . . I don't know. I think they became friends in spite of themselves."

"Yet never mentioned each other's names to their families?"

"Livia doesn't have that kind of family. As for Angelique . . ." I hesitate, glance at the detective. "In the beginning, I thought Angelique kept Livia to herself so as to not alienate her other friends. But given how connected Angelique and Livia must have become, for both of them to have now gone missing . . . What if we were right in the beginning? Angelique did fall in love. It just wasn't with a boy."

"You think she and Livia were dating?"

"It would explain the secrecy. At fifteen, trying to figure out who they are, how they identify. Livia with her fucked-up family. Angelique with her much more traditional one." I shrug. "None of this stuff is easy. But clearly there's a connection between the two girls. And yet, as you say, Angelique never mentioned Livia's name to anyone. In her world, that's a pretty big omission."

"Unless Livia got her involved in something criminal."

"You really think Angelique wouldn't talk to Marjolie and Kyra about illegal activities? Please. Best buds are by definition co-conspirators. No, this level of secrecy smacks of something more personal."

Lotham nods slowly. "All right. But even if we assume Angelique and Livia's relationship was intimate, it still doesn't explain how both wound up missing, three months apart. Let alone why Angelique had thousands of dollars, including counterfeit hundreds, stashed in a ceramic lamp."

"Details, details," I mutter. But the detective does have a point. "Let's back up for a moment. What do we know about each girl? They both live in Mattapan, but they didn't attend the same high school, meaning they probably met for the first time at fashion camp. Angelique was there due to her interest in art while Livia liked to make things. Both come from very different family backgrounds. Both, apparently, are good at keeping secrets."

Lotham nods. His hand remains next to mine on the table. Now, he idly rubs my thumb. I'm not sure he knows he's doing it. But I don't move and he doesn't stop.

"What kinds of things did Livia make?" he asks.

"Her mom talked about a plastic jack-o'-lantern that Livia brought home from school. Eyes cut out, whole nine yards. Though I have no idea what kind of class teaches plastic pumpkins."

"Livia attended a trade school. I was talking to her guidance counselor when I got the report of shots fired. Livia had courses in basic construction, metalwork, and some computer design class. I don't remember anything involving plastic. Wait." Lotham pulls his hand away, snaps his fingers. "Her computer design course. They have a 3D printer. That would do it. Maybe for Halloween. Design and print your own jack-o'-lantern."

"Counterfeit money," I murmur. "Any way you can get from design and print pumpkins to design and print U.S. currency?"

"Absolutely not. Remember that whole spiel on counterfeiting being a very sophisticated operation, involving printing presses, master tradespeople, and extremely rare and specialized inks—"

"Yeah, it's coming back to me now. But still . . ."

"We have two missing girls with at least a personal connection, not to mention complementary skill sets in art and design." Lotham shakes his head. "Honest to God, the more I learn in this case the less anything makes sense. But having said that, I think we should return to Livia's school. Determine exactly what kind of mad skills she had, not to mention if she ever had Angelique with her in the classroom after hours. The fake bills have to mean something, though I'll be damned if I know what."

"We are going to visit Livia's school?"

"In the interest of public safety, I think I should keep you close. Can't have too many shootings in one day."

He says the words lightly, but he's tossing me a bone and we both know it. I'd like to say it's all due to the power of my charm, but more likely it's pity. Beggars can't be choosers, so I don't argue.

I push slowly out the booth. A final chug of coffee. A last cinnamon sugar Munchkin. My hands are still shaking from the morning's misadventure. My stomach has a hollow, sick feel. But my job is my job. And given all the past mistakes I can't change, thank God I still have this.

I rise to standing.

Lotham slings on his blue sports coat and leads me out the door.

CHAPTER 21

M R. RIDDENSCAIL IS LIVIA'S AUTOCAD teacher at Boston Poly-
tech. A tall white guy, he has a lanky build and an absent-
minded expression. He's dressed casually in worn jeans, a thin
T-shirt topped by work flannel, and battered boots. A spoon and a
fork protrude from the top of his right boot, but he doesn't appear
to notice. He moves across the room, dodging workstations with
quick efficiency born of practice, as he leads us to the front. He
doesn't seem all that concerned to have a police detective and associate appear in his classroom during lunch hour. A very been-there-
done-that sort of dude.

"Yes, I know Livia Samdi." He nods as he reaches his desk, pulls
open a drawer, and takes out a metal lunchbox that looks straight
out of the 1950s.

"Did she make a plastic pumpkin in the course of your class?"
Lotham asks him, his gold badge clearly on display.

"Sure. That's a traditional fall assignment."

"How would you describe her?"

"Good student. Solid. But I have a feeling that's not why you are asking these questions."

"When did you last see her?"

"January. I reported her absence to the administration, if that's what you're asking."

"No judgment here," Lotham says, which is great because I'm full of judgment. How did you not worry about her? How did you not reach out in any way possible to this teenager who clearly needed you? Having seen firsthand the conditions of Livia's house, the dealings of her family . . .

"Describe her as a student." Lotham again.

Riddenscail pauses in the act of unwrapping his sandwich, obediently considering the matter. "Umm, she had natural aptitude for picturing things in an X-Y-Z plane. Can't say the same for too many of my kids."

"But was she a good student?"

"Excellent. But also quiet. She wasn't one to speak up, or help out her fellow classmates. I'd describe her as a sleeper student."

I raise my hand, unable to help myself: classroom, conditioned response. "What does that mean?"

Mr. Riddenscail turns toward me. "She had a natural aptitude but she existed in her own self-contained bubble. She knew what she knew, did what she did, then moved on."

Detective Lotham: "How adept was she?"

"Oh, I would describe her as one of my best students." Mr. Riddenscail hesitates. "Look, I work with a lot of at-risk kids. For many of them, discovering the right trade represents their ticket out. Meaning once they find the right fit, they go all in. Bond with me, work with their classmates, log extra hours. These kids . . . You wouldn't believe the talent. Give them the opportunity and man oh man! Livia Samdi, on the other hand . . . I tried to engage her on multiple occasions, give her special assignments to build her confidence. But in the end, she wasn't taking the bait. And yeah, I was concerned by that."

Detective Lotham: "She ever talk about her family?"

Mr. Riddenscail shakes his head.

Me: "What about friends?"

"Couldn't give you a single name. She was a loner. At least in my class."

"Did she stay after school?" Lotham again. "Spend extra time in your class?"

"I'd pushed her to enter a SkillsUSA technical drafting competition in the spring, which required preparation. So yes, she often logged time here after school. I'd say several days a week. At least, you know, till she went missing."

My turn: "Did you ever see anyone waiting for her? Or maybe she brought a friend with her to your classroom while she worked?"

Mr. Riddenscail gives us both a look. "Never."

"Tell us about this competition," Lotham orders.

"Livia's specialty was designing plastic molds for the manufacturing of thermoplastic materials. Basically, using 3D printing to help create replacement parts. Think of it this way. In various manufacturing processes, say your average laptop computer, dozens of the component parts are plastic. The ability to design the right part, or create a mold for the ongoing manufacturing of such parts, is highly valuable. Livia had a mind for such things. She could naturally picture what made something work. Better yet, she could see how each piece worked within the whole. From there, it was easy enough for her to design the necessary part, or on a great day, design a whole new setup that dramatically improved the operational whole. Like I said. She's crazy talented."

"Can you show us an example of her projects?" Lotham asks.

I nod vigorously, because so far, I can't picture any of this. Then again, science was never my strong suit.

"Didn't she use one of your computers?" I add.

"Sure, but you're talking last year. I don't have her work saved on the computers anymore. Then again"—Mr. Riddenscail taps his nose thoughtfully—"I didn't clean out her drawer. That should still have some of her drawings, not to mention smaller samples of her work."

Lunch forgotten, he leads the way over to a huge metal cabinet. The doors open to reveal a series of shallow drawers. Bending all the way down, Riddenscail pulls out several large sheets of design paper, followed by what appear to be several plastic thingamajigs.

Lotham takes the drawings. I explore the thingamajigs. A cube that has movable sides, a series of spirals that spin here, spin there. The items are fashioned from plain white plastic and rough to the touch, clearly prototypes of something. But the fact that I can work the cube and play with the spirals is fascinating to me.

"She was fifteen?" I ask incredulously, because this is way beyond me as a functional adult, let alone the drunk teen I used to be.

"Ah yes, Livia's specially designed fidget gadgets. The pumpkin assignment for her was fun, but hardly a challenge. Most kids spent a week on it, whereas Livia designed her jack-o'-lantern in a single day, then designed two of those with the time left over. Several of her fellow students expressed interest, but like I said, she wasn't one to share."

Because I just can't help myself, I raise my hand again. Clearly Livia had mad skills. Which meant she also had a way out of her impoverished, drug-dealing, crime-ridden family life. Her education combined with her natural ability—the sky should've been the limit.

So what went wrong? Why wasn't she still at school, perfecting more pumpkins and fidget doohickeys and manufacturing molds while preparing to launch the next great exciting chapter of her life?

And how did it involve Angelique?

"This was easy for her?" I ask, holding up the fidget gadgets. "As in, totally natural?"

"Absolutely."

"And she could make plastic molds? For manufacturing, something like that?"

"Sure. Rudimentary ones, but she was only going to get better. Especially given her gift for total system overview—how one part related to the next. That kind of process perspective I can't teach; you get it or you don't."

Beside me, Lotham nods. "She ever play around with, I don't know . . . plastic stamps of images, flowers, U.S. Treasury symbols, whatever."

Mr. Riddenscail taps his nose again. "Umm, no."

"But she had the ability. Could've even been working on some side projects at home?"

"Ability, yes. Side projects, no. Whatever work Livia did was performed here. The design software is licensed; the kids can't access it on their own computers. Let alone, for any of these products"—he nods toward the plastic chunks in my hand—"you need a 3D printer. Again, not the kind of thing Livia would have at home."

"And you knew every project your kids worked on?" Lotham presses, while I stare at the spirals in my hand and digest this latest statement.

"3D printing isn't cheap. Of course I monitor it. Have you seen our school budget? Plus, my job is to review my students' drawings over and over again. You only want to print when you're absolutely ready. Otherwise it wastes time and materials. Have you seen a 3D printer, Detective?"

Lotham shakes his head. Without another word, Mr. Ridden-scail turns and leads us to a side door in the classroom, which opens to a smaller room dominated by a large, fully enclosed glass box with all sorts of mechanical parts in the middle. It looks to weigh a ton and cost a fortune, which I guess goes to Mr. Riddenscail's point that it's not the sort of thing any teenager is going to have at home.

"This is the uPrint," he says.

"Can't you print a plastic gun?" I ask, because thinking of Livia's family and my own recent encounter with them, this strikes me as a highly valued commodity.

"Can you fashion a plastic gun? Yes. Do we do that here? No." Mr. Riddenscail sounds firm on the subject.

"But it would be highly valuable," I press. "Particularly in this neighborhood."

"No."

Lotham raises a brow at the reply, causing Mr. Riddenscail to elaborate: "Most plastic guns are good for a single shot. And given the lack of rifling on the barrel, it has to be up close and personal. Now, if you needed to sneak a gun through security—either at an airport, courthouse, for a Jason Bourne kind of deal, okay. But I know my kids' lives, and no gangbanger wants a small, single-shot pistol. They want firepower. The bigger, the better. Nothing made here is going to be impressive enough for their needs. Plus most of the drug dealers out there, just because they can pull the trigger, doesn't mean they can aim. Hence their love of automatic rifles. Plastic guns are a finesse tool. Around here"—Mr. Riddenscail shrugs—"that's not what's needed."

Lotham nods shortly. It does make a crazy kind of sense but also leads us back to where we started. Livia had a talent, involving complex design and this enormous 3D printer. Which translates to what?

Plastic molds to assist in counterfeiting money? Except that's only a tiny step of a highly involved and elaborate process. Let alone what kind of European counterfeiting ring is going to recruit a fifteen-year-old girl from inner-city Boston?

And yet, Angelique had counterfeit hundreds while also having a relationship—intimate or otherwise—with Livia. Angelique disappeared, and three months later Livia went missing. The girls were connected. The money was connected, which made it stand to reason that all of this—Livia's skills, Angelique's ambitions—also had to be connected.

Except how?

"Are there other teachers or classes Livia mentioned?" Lotham asks now.

A shrug. "You can check with Mrs. Jones, the school guidance counselor. She might know more."

Lotham nods. He'd mentioned talking to a school counselor earlier this morning, so I'm guessing he's already covered those bases.

"Anyone seem rattled or particularly bothered when Livia stopped coming to school?" I speak up.

Mr. Riddenscail shakes his head. "Which is a shame. She was a good kid. I'm sorry I can't be of more help."

There doesn't seem to be much more to say or do. Lotham shakes the teacher's hand. I follow suit. Then we're once more in the hallway.

"Where does this leave us?" I grumble out loud.

Lotham frowns, purses his lips. "I don't know," he says at last.

"Livia's and Angelique's disappearances have to be related."

"I don't believe in that big a coincidence," Lotham agrees.

"The cash in Angelique's lamp, the burner phones. The girls were up to something that put them in contact with fake currency while helping them earn real dough. Something that clearly got them in trouble. Leading to Angelique's disappearance, then Livia's. Except why the vanishing act three months apart? *Help us*, Angelique's note said. Meaning they're together now? And in even more danger eleven months later? Held against their will? By whom? How . . ."

Suddenly, I stop walking. I grab Lotham's hand. "The footage. Angelique's last day of school. All the cameras that *don't* show Angelique exiting the school or walking down the street."

Lotham regards me quizzically.

"You didn't know about Livia then. You watched all those video frames looking for Angelique. This whole case, back then, was about *one* missing girl. *One* disappearance. But knowing what we know now . . ."

Lotham comes to a dead halt as well. "We gotta watch those tapes again."

I smile. "We should absolutely do that," I say, with just the barest emphasis on *we*.

He doesn't deny me. Together, we rush out the door.

CHAPTER 22

Lotham is the dedicated, workaholic detective I suspected him to be. He doesn't take me to some evidence lab or special countersurveillance expert. He drives us to the BPD field office in Mattapan. *District B-3*, the blue sign reads, perched outside a fairly new-looking brick structure. It has a towering front façade that reminds me of Angelique's high school. Apparently New England architecture is all about first appearances.

Inside the station, things are a bit more "TV cop show." The drop ceiling, cheap flooring, security desk. Lotham waves at the front desk sergeant, having me sign in, while not offering an explanation. The female officer—older, with a hawkish face—looks bored. But I'm wide-eyed. My last few investigative gigs have involved places where the local police outpost was barely more than a double-wide. In comparison, this is swanky. Boston fucking PD for sure.

Lotham weaves his way down the hall, up the stairs. Once more, my job is to scamper behind him. I catch a glimpse of walls covered with Most Wanted photos juxtaposed with tributes to officers fallen in the line of duty. I don't get to study any of it, as I quicken my pace to keep up with a boxer on a mission.

When we finally arrive at Lotham's workspace, it turns out to be a desk in an open bullpen. The low walls of the cubicle bear everything from a few tucked-away photos of beaming schoolkids—his nieces and nephews, I would guess—to various police agency patches to several framed Muhammad Ali quotes. Angelique's missing poster is pinned up in one corner, right where he'd see it every time he sat down in front of his computer. He doesn't comment, and neither do I.

But I have a curious flushed sensation. I was right. He is who I thought he would be. Which is much more than I can say for most people.

Lotham fires his desktop to life. He disappears briefly, returns with two plastic cups of water. Then he snags a desk chair from the unoccupied cubicle behind him and drags it over. He doesn't speak, just gestures. I take a seat. Pick up my water. Watch his fingertips fly across his keyboard.

I have only limited technical skills. But befitting a big-city detective, Lotham appears just as at home in front of a computer as he does out on the streets.

Next thing I know, he's shoving back his chair, while gesturing me closer. "First—and best—camera angle," he states. "Taken from the corner grocer across the street. You'll see all the kids exit at end of day, Friday, November 5. Day of Angelique's disappearance."

I nod and focus on the screen as he hits play. I don't get to hear the school bell, as the video offers images only. But I can pretty much fill in the audio, as on the screen bodies start pouring out the doors and down the steps.

It's a fluid mass of teenage humanity. Almost all of it African

American and clad in the same uniform of jeans, hoodies, flannel shirts. In the end, it's not Angelique I spy first, but her curvy friend, Marjolie. Which leads to Kyra, and then, following shortly behind her, Angelique. The girl is wearing denim leggings with an oversized sweater in deep red. She has a bright-colored knit scarf wrapped tight around her neck, thin black gloves on her hands, and untied duck boots on her feet. Her navy blue backpack is slung over one shoulder. The weather is sunny but clearly cold.

Lotham taps the screen, in case I missed our target. I nod to let him know I see her. As we watch, she and her besties grow slightly larger, walking across the street toward the corner grocer. Then they disappear from view.

"After-school snack," I mutter. Or drink, as it might have been in my case.

Lotham hits arrows. The video fast-forwards. Now we see all three girls reappear. There appears to be laughing, hugging. One dark head peels away. Taller, so I'm guessing Kyra. That leaves Marjolie and Angelique. Marjolie must return inside the store, as she simply disappears from the frame. But Angelique appears more fully, crossing the street toward her school. She doesn't head for the front steps, however, but disappears, backpack slung over her shoulder as she strides down the long right side of the brick building, toward the infamous bolt-hole and side door, where she vanishes completely.

It's a disconcerting feeling. A girl. There—with her friends and favorite scarf and school bag—then gone. Until she reappears at a cybercafé eleven months later.

I want to reach out and touch her image on the screen. I wonder if her family still does the same. Strokes the framed photo of her smiling cheek before heading to bed each night. Places two fingers against her matte lips upon waking again each morning. How can a person go from being so present, so *alive*, to vanished without a trace?

I focus my attention back on the screen. I try to think past the image, to the Angelique I now know. A smart, serious student. A caretaker for her brother, her aunt, and her mom back home. In her brother's words, not a dreamer but a planner.

What I notice now is how she walks. Straight, direct, not a trace of uncertainty. Angelique didn't wander down the side of the building to whatever would happen next. She strode purposefully forward. A girl on a mission.

"What the hell are you doing, Angelique?" I mutter.

Lotham nods slightly. He's asked the same question a million times.

He hits stop. "I can already tell you how this video ends: without any more sign of Angelique. Which brings us to half a dozen more cameras, including traffic cams at each major intersection, none of which show her either."

"From what I can tell, neither of Angelique's friends reentered the school after her. It appears that Kyra heads off to the left, while Marjolie spends more time in the little grocer."

"Actually, in a matter of minutes, Marjolie heads down the block in the opposite direction of the school, to the bus stop Angelique normally uses. I traced her route back home utilizing various video feeds. Kyra, as well. Both go from here to various buses to their individual residences."

I nod, impressed. That must've taken no shortage of time to sort out, given all the cameras involved. But it's also good info to have. Whatever happened next *didn't* involve Angelique's best friends.

Which leaves us with? "All right. So we know where Angelique goes—down the side of the school. We know where Kyra and Marjolie head—home. Which brings us to new friend . . . associate . . . *something*, Livia Samdi. What about her?"

Lotham obediently rewinds the deli-mart footage. Once again students pour down the front steps into the broad city street. This time, I keep my eyes out for a red hat. I don't know Livia's features much more than that.

Lotham rewinds six more times. We devise a system. I stare at the upper left quadrant while he does lower right. We work our way toward each other. The end result: No red baseball cap. No Livia Samdi.

I sip more water, rub my eyes. Lotham closes out that video, loads up the next.

"This is from the traffic cam on the intersection to the west of the school."

I nod, grateful I don't have work tonight, as apparently, there's enough footage here to last at least a week.

"How did you go through this the first time?" I mutter.

"Painfully. Our video tech also ran facial recognition software against it, though given the number of kids and how few gaze directly at the camera, that was a low-probability play."

"Leave no stone unturned," I murmur.

He agrees.

The traffic surveillance starts a minute before the end-of-day exodus. I watch a couple of cars pass through the intersection. Then there's a sense of movement at the edge of the camera: the students, descending. Then, individual shapes become clear as dozens of students trudge toward the intersection, headed for bus stops, whatever. None are Angelique or her friends, which makes sense as we already know they're at the grocery across the street.

I study the faces anyway, looking not just for Livia Samdi but anyone who might suddenly strike a spark of inspiration or magically answer our millions of questions. Nothing.

We watch this video for a solid fifteen minutes. Until the last of the kids have disappeared and only cars zoom into the camera's field of view.

I yawn, cracking my jaw, as if that will get my eyes to focus again. Honestly, this is tedious work.

"Next camera?" Lotham asks.

"Next camera."

Repeat and repeat. I earn new respect for Boston detectives. This is draining work and I still can't be sure I'm not missing something. With so much to see on a busy city street, it's hard to know where to look, let alone to sustain focus.

Lotham switches up videos; he must've downloaded all these feeds to his computer months ago. Where he could watch them again and again, deep into the night, searching, searching, searching.

We break the screen into quadrants again, as that seems the most scientific approach. We study, stare, grunt, groan. No luck.

An hour later, we both shove back our chairs and rub our eyes.

"This is pissing me off," I say.

"Welcome to my world."

"I was so sure Livia was the missing link. Knowing about her involvement now, you'd load up these videos, we'd spy her hat, her face, something and *kapow!* All the pieces of the puzzle would fall into place."

"Kapow?"

"I like a little drama in my narrative." I rub the bridge of my nose. My stomach growls. I'm starving. Lotham must be as well, but I can tell from his face he's not ready to take a break any more than I am. We want something to show for all this effort. It's human nature.

"Let's talk it through," he says. "What do we know from the footage?"

"Angelique definitely heads down the side of the school to the emergency exit and hidden bolt-hole. Marjolie and Kyra don't."

Lotham nods, laces his fingers behind his head, and stretches out his shoulders. "Our assumption has been that Angelique reenters the school via the side exit. So, if Marjolie and Kyra are headed home, as we know they did, who opens the door?"

I sigh heavily. "I asked about it being left propped open. Apparently, the school is wise to that trick and monitors the door. So the kids use an inside man. Only person I can think of is Livia Samdi. Angelique's brother goes to the middle school, right?"

"Yep."

"So it can't be him."

Lotham swivels his chair to face me. "Livia isn't a student. So how would she get into the school?"

"After hours," I begin.

"Can't. Front doors are locked and monitored. Students have to show their ID if they want to reenter. Welcome to today's school security."

I frown, chew on my bottom lip. "What about during school hours?" It hits me, what I'd witnessed myself without really noticing. "After lunch." I speak up excitedly. "The mass exodus from the deli-mart back into the school. With all the kids headed inside at once, and rushing to make it before the final bell . . . Even the best security guards are probably looking more at backpacks and security screening than at individual faces. And Livia is a high schooler. It would be easy for her to blend in."

Lotham lowers his arms, pulls his chair back up to the driver's position in front of his monitor.

"I have twenty-four hours of surveillance on this tape. Let's check it out."

It takes a bit to find lunchtime, where again, the exodus of kids from school to sidewalk to across the street is eerily familiar. Thirty minutes pass. Then, just like that, kids appear again, clogging the street as they trudge back to school. I keep my eye out for Angelique and her friends. Sure enough. "There."

Lotham nods, having spotted her. Being only a few hours earlier in the day, she's wearing the same sweater and scarf, walking between Marjolie and Kyra. They all appear to be chattering away, paying no particular attention to anything.

But then, just as they hit the sidewalk in front of the school . . . Angelique pauses. Angelique looks back.

And there, on the lower edge of the video. A red hat comes into view.

We watch in total silence as Livia Samdi crosses the street, clad in ripped jeans and a gray hoodie. Angelique and her friends are already climbing up the stairs to the front door. Angelique doesn't glance behind again, but I know she knows Livia is there. It's in the rigid line of her posture. The way she keeps commanding her friends' attention, keeping them focused ahead as well.

Angelique, Kyra, and Marjolie disappear inside the glass school doors. Then a few minutes later, Livia follows behind them, a blue pack slung over her shoulder that looks suspiciously close to Angelique's.

Lotham rocks back in his chair. "I'll be damned."

"I think I know what happened," I whisper.

"No shit, Sherlock."

Without another word, Lotham loads a fresh video, the traffic cam from the closest intersection. He finds the end-of-school-day flood. Then advances five, ten, fifteen minutes. Pauses. Glances at me. Hits play.

It takes several more minutes. Then amid the now random pedestrian traffic, a new form appears from the side of the school. Walking straight toward the intersection, head down, red cap plainly visible. Ripped jeans. Gray hoodie. Blue backpack.

But looking closer, I can see the hat now sits awkwardly. Because the mass of hair underneath is considerably bigger. Angelique's curls, stuffed beneath the brim. Not to mention the distinct gait. Direct, purposeful, determined. Angelique's.

"Angelique changed clothes with Livia Samdi," Lotham murmurs. His fingers dance across the keyboard. Other videos appear, disappear, but none improve our view.

"That would explain why Angelique wasn't missing any clothes. She put on Livia's clothes. But why?"

Lotham doesn't answer. Instead, he returns to the corner grocer camera, except now twenty minutes after the end of the school day. Five minutes after Angelique—dressed as Livia—appears and disappears from the frame, a new female emerges from the side of the school. She moves totally differently than Angelique. Hesitant, self-conscious, almost skulking as she hugs the inside edge of the sidewalk.

Livia Samdi, now dressed in black stretch pants and a navy flannel shirt. Her shorter hair is held back with clips and for the first time I can see her face. She appears younger than her fifteen years.

A pause at the intersection, waiting for her turn to cross. She glances up. A single heartbeat, where she stares directly at the video camera.

She looks terrified.

———

THEN SHE CROSSES the street and disappears from view.

Lotham hits stop. He once again pushes back his chair. "Fuck me," he states.

For a change, I don't go with the obvious retort. "Angelique took Livia's place. The clothes, the hat. She's not trying to hide herself. She's trying to *appear* as Livia Samdi."

Lotham sighs, scrubs his face with his hand. "I've been working the wrong damn missing persons case."

I get it then, the full implication of Angelique's deception, her and Livia's plan. Serious, hardworking, caretaker Angelique. She didn't engage in high-risk behavior or lifestyle choices, which had made her disappearance such a puzzle.

Because she hadn't been the one in danger.

She hadn't been the target.

Livia Samdi had been.

And now, she was gone, too. The girl with a gift for visualizing X-Y-Z planes. The girl who lived with a known drug dealer. The girl who clearly feared for her life.

"What the hell were they up to?" I ask quietly.

But neither one of us has the answer.

CHAPTER 23

'M AT MY BEST WHEN I'm busy. After leaving Detective Lotham, I head back to Stoney's. The pub is up and running with the regulars. Tables half full. Noise half volume. It's only been a matter of days, but it still feels strange not to take up position behind the bar. I drift up to my studio apartment, where I discover that Piper has abandoned me for the night. Given it's my night off, I could catch up on sleep or finally tend to household tasks such as laundry and grocery shopping.

Instead, I do the sensible thing: I attend a meeting. Given the earlier hour, I'm surprised, but not unhappy, to discover Charlie also there. I take the empty seat beside him, sipping on coffee as we run through introductions, then get down to business. This meeting is about the twelve steps, step nine in particular. Making amends. I've never gone through all twelve steps. It's not the apologizing for the wrongs I've done—I get that completely. It's cataloguing all my sins that has me hung up. For all my talk of honesty, there's only so much scrutiny I can handle. Though asking for forgiveness is also an issue. How do you apologize to the dead?

I get through the meeting, content to once again be in the company of like minds, even if the topic isn't my favorite.

I help Charlie clean up after the meeting, working in companionable silence. Then, almost in sync: "Would you like to grab a cup of coffee?"

AA-speak for would you like to talk?

We smile in unison. "Yes."

I follow him from the church basement into the fall-tinged night. He seems to know where he's going, so I don't worry about it as we weave from block to block. Finally, we arrive at a tiny little diner I never would've found on my own. When Charlie walks in, with his telltale bulk and army jacket, he's clearly recognized and greeted as a friend. I earn a glance or two from the staff, but his welcome expands to include me. I smile openly, happy for friendly faces after my morning adventures.

Charlie takes a seat near the back. He doesn't even have to ask before a mug of rich, dark coffee is set before him. I nod I'll take the same. I still haven't eaten, so I ask for a menu. Charlie says he's fine. After a brief contemplation, I go with the Greek salad, which makes me think of Lotham and other things I don't want to consider.

My salad arrives in a matter of minutes, given we're the only two customers around. I dig in, munching happily on romaine lettuce and kalamata olives, while Charlie sips his coffee.

"Thank you for yesterday," I say finally. Charlie's sighting of Angelique Badeau at the wireless store. His personal request for me at the scene. His tidbit on Livia Samdi also having disappeared.

"Any news?" he asks.

"Nothing tangible yet. I visited Mrs. Samdi this morning." I hesitate, not sure what to say.

"There by the grace of God go I," Charlie intones.

I nod vigorously and we lapse into a silence, weighted by the shared horror of that one single drink that can undo our hours, months, years of hard work. There's no judgment in AA; only mutual fear.

"I tried to get her to leave with me," I venture at last. "Join me in attending a meeting."

"Can't help someone who doesn't want to be helped."

I nod, chewing slowly. "Her house, her son . . . I don't know if I could do it in those conditions."

"For the longest time," Charlie says, "I figured I couldn't get clean, not living on the streets. But then, later . . . I wondered if homelessness wasn't easier. Took all the responsibility, the agitation of daily life away. Mad, sad, or glad . . . We don't need a reason to drink. It's just easier to blame it on something else."

I nod. He's right. Mrs. Samdi's living conditions are deplorable, but not impossible. AA teaches us that our worst enemy lives not outside the gates but inside our souls. We need no excuses to drink. As long as we have air in our lungs, it will always be a temptation.

And yet I'm sad for her in ways I can't fully explain. She's a prisoner of more than just her disease. Her family, poverty, lifestyle choices—the causes are endless.

"You seem to be . . ." I'm not sure exactly how to state this, ". . . in touch with street life around here."

Charlie grins, a flash of white against his heavyset face. "Yes, ma'am."

"Is there a gang, criminal organization around here sophisticated enough for counterfeit currency?"

This raises a brow. "U.S. dollars?"

"Hundred-dollar bills to be exact."

The brow rises higher. "That's some fine work. How high-quality are you talking?"

"Very high end. Extremely well done."

Charlie takes another sip of his decaf coffee, appears to seriously contemplate the matter. "Aren't you talking special paper, metallic threads, watermarks, all sorts of crazy stuff?"

"Exactly."

"Then no. We got our fair share of crime, and some of these boys . . . Don't let an appetite for violence fool you into thinking they aren't smart. But that kind of technical know-how, specialized equipment . . . Nah. Not in a million years."

I nod, share with him what I learned about counterfeiting operations from Lotham: bills printed in Europe, then sold to middlemen for pennies on the dollar, eventually sold to end users for sixty-five cents on the dollar.

"Thirty-five percent markup," Charlie deduces, nodding. "Makes sense. Person who spends the money should get the highest percentage as they bear the greatest risk." He sips more coffee. "End users . . . Now *that* I could see around here. Drugs and guns require cash. If some new player arrived and said I could sell you cheap money . . . Yeah, plenty of players would go for that." He pauses. "And plenty of other players would kill their sorry asses once they realized they got paid in fake bills. Risky proposition all the way round."

"But given the demand . . ."

"No pain, no gain, as the saying goes. I imagine at least a few would be willing to try it out."

I lean forward. "Any players in particular?"

Charlie has to think about it. "Can't say off the top of my head. But I can think of a few people to ask."

"If it doesn't jam you up."

"I don't mind. But I'd like to ask why."

Briefly, I explain to him the counterfeit money discovered in Angelique's lamp, not to mention her friendship with Livia Samdi and Livia's expertise with 3D printers, which may or may not have anything to do with anything. And that Angelique was dressed up as Livia when she disappeared.

"You're thinking Livia was the real target?"

"Maybe. Possibly. When I'm arrogant enough to know what to think."

"But then Livia still went missing. And Angelique's still alive."

"Yes."

"Hell, that doesn't make a damn lick of sense."

"Exactly."

Charlie drains his coffee mug, waves over the waitress for a refill.

"All right. So if Livia was the target, and the girls are still alive—"

"Angelique smuggled out a message. *Help us.*"

"Damn, that's scary. But . . ." Charlie considers the matter. "If the girls are still alive but can't come home, are like, held against their will?"

I nod.

"Then they must be worth something, right? Only reason to keep them alive, cuz the girls know something or are doing something their captors need."

I like the way he puts that. Simple, logical. The girls know something or are doing something. "Which brings us back to Livia's skills with AutoCAD and 3D printing. But that's still not enough for counterfeiting currency, and apparently plastic guns aren't nearly as valuable as we thought."

Charlie's turn to nod. "If counterfeiting currency is like advanced math or something, then what about other kinds of forgeries? Starting with fake Real IDs. Now that would be worth some serious dough."

"Explain."

"Back in my day, a fake driver's license was a simple matter of prying apart the lamination and inserting a new photo. More recently, I've heard some of the kids at the rec center talk about buying fakes online, especially foreign IDs. Say from Ireland, places like that. You wanna sneak into a bar, it gets the job done. But now, with states transitioning to Real ID . . ."

"Which is very sophisticated, right? Watermarks, hidden images, reflective ink. Isn't that why it's now the new standard for TSA?"

"Exactly. The old model of fake driver's licenses just doesn't cut it. World's getting serious, meaning everyone, including criminals, gotta get serious. I'm not saying faking a Real ID would be easy, but compared to forged bills, gotta be a step down." Charlie shrugs.

I think of Angelique, showing up at the cybercafé with a fake ID. Then trying to buy a cell phone from the wireless store with the same ID. Letting it fall to the ground in her escape.

I wonder suddenly if we hadn't missed the obvious. She hadn't been trying to leave us a coded message. The ID itself was the clue.

"I'll be damned," I mutter.

"Not as long as you keep from drinking."

"Charlie, are there any new players in town? I don't know. New gangs, or criminal enterprises? Even something that seems like a whisper of a ghost story. Keyser Soze, that sort of thing?"

Charlie arches a brow. "Street loves a good ghost story. But not that I've heard."

"What about a newer gang rising to sudden prominence? A power grab?"

This takes him longer to consider. "Maybe," he says at last. "For all the evils in Mattapan . . . Most of our gangs are small. Fractured. Got not just Blacks versus other Blacks, but El Salvadorans versus Asian versus Haitians. Can be a block-by-block sort of thing. Keeps the violence high as someone is always shooting someone, but also keeps the level of sophistication low. Nobody gets big enough or lasts long enough to do too much damage. What you're suggesting . . ."

"I don't know what I'm suggesting."

"Quality fake IDs, quality fake money, or at least access to quality counterfeits . . ."

I wait.

"Off the top of my head, I'd say it doesn't have to be a new gang," he says slowly, "but maybe a traditional player with a new connection. I can do some digging."

"Don't put yourself at risk."

Charlie glances down at his imposing size. "I've been around a long time, little girl. Grew up in this town. Lived on these streets. Don't you worry about me."

"But I do."

"Aren't you sweet for a woman who doesn't stick around?"

"Doesn't mean I'm not sentimental."

"Think it means exactly that."

"No." I shake my head seriously. "I just know how to live with the pain."

He doesn't have an answer to that.

"You really think these girls, Angelique and Livia, are caught up in some sort of criminal enterprise?" he asks at last.

"I think . . . I think Livia was clearly terrified of something. You can see it on her face on the security camera. And the fact that Angelique left her school disguised as her friend . . . Angelique's been described as a nurturer. Let alone, she clearly had a close relationship with Livia. Maybe a *very* close relationship."

Charlie arches a brow, doesn't say anything.

"I can imagine Angelique trying to devise a plan to help her friend. Save Livia. Except." I sigh sadly. "They are just kids. And you know how it is with teens. They get in trouble first."

"Figure out the real danger later," Charlie finishes for me.

"Exactly. Whatever usefulness they've had for their captors, I'm wondering if it's nearing an end. Hence Angelique's desperate attempts at contact. Posting a coded message, appearing in the wireless shop. Something's changed, the clock ticking down in a genuinely terrible, dangerous way. Given the two have been missing this long, nothing to stop their captors from disappearing them completely."

"Damn," Charlie mutters. "I'll keep an ear out." Then, more softly, so only I can hear "But as long as we're talking danger, you should know I did learn a few things, but it wasn't about them."

It takes me second. "About me?"

"You're asking too many questions. Your visit today to the Samdi household got people riled up."

"Who? And is that why he shot at me?"

"You need to be more careful, my friend."

"Why? If Livia's brother is just some low-level dope dealer, who cares about my visit?"

"You can get killed for looking wrong around here. Don't trust you're as immune as you think."

I tilt up my chin in an impressive display of false bravado. "I'm here to find a missing girl. Or girls, as the case may be. I'm gonna keep going till that job is done. You can start your own rumor on the streets—they want the skinny white chick to go away, then produce Angelique and Livia. I'll be gone within a matter of hours. On my word."

"Doesn't work like that."

"Does for me."

Charlie smiles, but it's a briefer expression this time. He leans forward. "Watch your back, little lady."

"I've been in tough places before."

"Not like this."

"How do you know?"

"Because I've been to war, and it still wasn't as scary as living around here."

I don't have an answer to that. I finish my salad. Charlie finishes his coffee. I pay for both of us—then, despite my protests, Charlie walks me home.

Even then, I'm suddenly aware of all the dark shapes around us, noises from side streets, small gatherings in the dark. One kid with a gun. All it would take. Quick, dirty, effective. Charlie's not wrong about that.

At the side entrance to Stoney's, I kiss my newfound friend on the cheek in gratitude, then retreat upstairs and hole up in the solitude of my apartment.

I CALL LOTHAM. It's late, but it doesn't surprise me that he picks up immediately.

"You should pull the fake ID Angelique dropped yesterday. I have reason to believe the ID itself might be a clue."

A pause, the weight of many unasked questions, such as why

did I believe such a thing now and who might I have been speaking with. Then: "I'll retrieve it from evidence first thing in the morning."

"Thank you."

Then, we don't speak. I stay on my puny little flip phone. I listen to him breathe. And it's like knives flaying my skin. The sense of déjà vu. The harsh knowledge that this is the only way I know how to connect. All these years later, nothing has changed. I am me, and the rest of the world, the good guys like Paul, like Lotham . . .

"Good night," I say at last, my voice thick. I might be crying, but I don't want to be.

"Good night," he agrees.

He ends the call. I sit in my threadbare room, holding my phone against my chest and telling myself I have no reason to be sad when this is the life I've chosen for myself. Eventually, I change into my sleeping clothes, brush my teeth, and climb into bed. Lights out. One day done, another soon to begin.

But once again, my dreams haunt me.

Paul: "Are you going to tell me what's really going on?"

Me: "I just have work to do."

"Are you drinking again?"

"No! It has nothing to do with that."

"Then why all the secrecy, the disappearing act?"

"I told you, I'm looking into something, a friend's missing daughter . . ."

"What's it to you?"

Me, hostile: "What's it to you?"

"There you go again. I'm trying to ask a question, you make it a war."

"I'm not making it a war!"

"You keep secrets, Frankie. You enforce boundaries, erect walls.

Then turn around and try to pretend it doesn't matter. What's it going to take for you to be honest with me?"

"What's it going to take for you to trust me?"

"You're an addict. You really have to ask that?"

Me, staring at him, feeling my throat thicken and my chest compress. "It's not always about drinking!"

"Then what's it about?"

My mouth opens, but the words don't come out. I stare at his kind, earnest face. I gaze into the eyes of the man who loves me. And once again, I feel nothing but my own frantic heartbeat. I gotta go. I gotta get out. I can't handle this.

I found this man. I fell in love with his kindness, his patience. He saw me, all of me, and he didn't turn away. He let me in. He held back my hair while I puked my way through detox. He spoon-fed me broth while I slowly fought my way back to living. He crawled into bed beside me, all those horrific nights, when I shook uncontrollably and prayed for death but never actually let go because I didn't want to disappoint him.

He is my anchor. The best person I've ever met. If I think of life without him, I feel pain, way down deep in the place that alcohol once took away, and now I will always get to live with.

And yet, day after day after day. This life. This existence. I don't feel joy or contentment or everlasting peace.

I think, most of the time, don't look at me, don't look at me, don't look at me.

I think, all of the time. I wish I could disappear. Vanish without a trace. Never to be seen again.

My hand, on the doorknob, trembling slightly. "I'll be back later."

Paul, his handsome face now contorted. "Don't bother."

"Okay."

"*It's that easy for you? Just walk away, never look back? For God's sake, I love you, Frankie.*"

Me, twisting the doorknob. "*Okay.*"

"*Okay? That's all you have to say? Fucking okay? You break my heart.*"

"*I love you,*" *I whisper finally, though it's not enough. We both know it's not enough. I so wish I were on the other side of the door. I so wish . . .*

"*Get the fuck out, Frankie.*"

"*Okay.*"

"*It's not,*" *he says bitterly.* "*It never was.*"

And me, a stupid broken record. "*Okay.*"

I leave.

He lets me.

Okay. Okay. Okay.

And then, mere hours, days, an entire lifetime later:

"*What did you do, Frankie? Dear God, what did you do?*"

Now I'm the one crying. I'm the one cradling his head in my arms. The blood, the blood, the blood. Dear God, the blood.

"*I love you. I love you, I love you. I promise I loved you.*"

But there's just so much blood. As his eyes close, and his breath starts to rattle.

"*What did you do?*" *Paul asks me, one last time.*

"*I loved you . . .*"

I WAKE UP screaming. Or maybe I'm sobbing. It's hard to be sure which. Piper is curled up against my lower back. I focus on the sound of her rumbling purr as I stare into the dark, willing my breathing to ease, the horror to fade.

Paul is gone.

Two girls are missing.

And I am still me. Afraid of everything. Of anything.

I will find Angelique and Livia, I promise myself, hands fisting the sheets. I will bring them home. I swear it. Because I need this. *Need* it.

Which explains the phone call I get next.

CHAPTER 24

"THIS IS EMMANUEL," he says.

I'm groggy, still rousing from my troubled night. "Emmanuel?"

"I'm here with my aunt. We need to speak to you."

Talk. Now. The victim's family. "I can meet you at your apartment."

"We're outside, at the side entrance."

Of course they are. "Five minutes," I mutter, which is a total lie. I'm buried in bed, still wearing my nightshirt, breath foul, feral roommate long gone.

I hang up the phone and stagger my way to the shower. I subject myself to an ice-cold spray, then throw on jeans and a long-sleeved shirt and head downstairs before I think better of it. Angelique's family. They might have new information for me. Or new information to demand of me. Either way, their pain matters.

I crack open the side door of Stoney's establishment long enough to identify Emmanuel and his aunt. Guerline is wearing traditional turquoise hospital scrubs, but there's something about the expression on her face . . .

I blink against the harshness of daylight, glance at my watch. Ten A.M. Late by many standards. Way too early for the night shift crowd. I open the heavy metal door wider. "Are you hungry?" I ask.

"We've eaten," Guerline speaks up.

"Coffee?"

No one says no to coffee. Plus, Lotham had said it was an important part of Haitian hospitality, and I want to be as welcoming as possible. Guerline nods. I allow her and her nephew entrance. Emmanuel, a pro by now, leads the way to the exact same booth he occupied before, while I disappear long enough to activate machines that produce caffeine. My stomach is grumbling. I inspect Viv's fridge, hope she will forgive me as I select two eggs, fire up her griddle, and scramble away.

I return with the pot of coffee, pouring out three mugs with the deft practice of a lifelong waitress. Emmanuel goes to work with the cream and sugar. I return to the kitchen, where I wolf down the scrambled eggs to settle my stomach, then give myself a brief and silent pep talk. I head back to the dining room.

"The police," Guerline says at last, clutching her coffee mug. "They ask, but they do not tell. You must have word."

I understand. The families so often live in anguished limbo—not trusted, not informed, not represented in their own loved ones' missing persons investigations. I've worked plenty of cases where the suspicions regarding the family's involvement have been borne out, but my gut tells me Emmanuel and his aunt aren't part of that group.

Briefly, I tell them about the findings involving Angelique's recovered stash of money—that some of the bills appear to be high-quality counterfeits. Guerline's eyes widen in genuine shock, while Emmanuel pauses with his coffee mug in midair.

"Counterfeit?" he asks.

"Probably printed in Europe and imported."

"We don't have counterfeit money," Guerline says. "We don't have . . . money."

And yet, Angelique had.

"Did Angelique ever talk about her friend from the summer camp, Livia Samdi?"

Twin *no*s.

"Do you know Livia?"

More head shakes.

"Ever hear her name mentioned, maybe when Angelique was talking to another one of her friends, or maybe you came home early to find a new girl visiting your apartment?"

Guerline shakes her head, more emphatically this time.

Emmanuel hesitates. "One day, I overheard LiLi, on the phone. She was trying to calm someone down. 'I know, I know,' she kept repeating. Then, 'I'm working on it. Please trust me.'"

"And?" I prod.

"And then Angelique spotted me. She turned away, ended the call. It was only later that it occurred to me, the way she was holding the phone, it wasn't right."

"What do you mean?"

"Her iPhone is flat, like everyone else's. This phone, the way she had her hand wrapped around it . . . It had to be smaller, thicker. Like a flip phone."

"An after-hours phone," I fill in.

"What is an after-hours phone?" Guerline asks.

"Like a burner phone. We suspected Angelique had a second phone, hence she left her original phone in her backpack."

Completing her disguise as Livia, I think, while also eliminating the chance her personal cell would be discovered on her or used to trace her movements.

"Are you sure she wasn't speaking to one of her other friends, Marjolie or Kyra?" I say to Emmanuel.

"I don't think so. Her tone . . ." He shrugs. "When she saw me, she looked guilty. Why would she feel guilty about talking to her friends?"

Emmanuel is an astute young man. I'm willing to bet he's right, Angelique was speaking on a burner phone with Livia, and once again, I'm struck by her level of secrecy regarding that relationship . . . But I don't think now is the time to go into that level of detail with Angelique's family.

"I don't think Angelique was trying to run away or disappear," I say at last. "It sounds like she had befriended a girl, Livia, from the summer rec program. Livia's own background . . . Let's just say it appears she was in some kind of trouble and Angelique was trying to help her. So much so, Angelique was dressed as Livia that final afternoon in November. That's why the police originally couldn't find evidence of Angelique departing her school. She did it disguised as Livia Samdi."

Guerline's eyes widen. She clearly doesn't know what to say. Beside her, Emmanuel appears equally shocked.

"What does this Livia girl have to say for herself?" Guerline asks at last.

"She also went missing. A few months later. Except her family never reported it, which is why the police didn't make the connection. The family assumed the girl had run away."

"This girl is trouble?"

"I don't know. But her brother is a known drug dealer."

"My Angelique did not do drugs!"

I hold up a placating hand. "No one is saying she did. For that matter, there's no evidence Livia did drugs either. Like Angelique, Livia was a gifted student, except her talents were in computer design and 3D printing."

Guerline appears even more lost. Emmanuel recovers first.

"LiLi was smart. And she could draw, but like freehand. I never saw her do anything on a computer."

"This girl, with the drug family," says Guerline. "Could the fake money be hers? Because my Angelique . . . Children make mistakes, yes, but she is a good girl. That kind of money only comes from bad things. And LiLi is not that kind of bad."

Now it's my turn to feel stupid. When we'd found the money, we hadn't known about Livia yet. But in retrospect, it does seem more probable that the money came from Livia or her drug-dealing brother. Maybe Angelique was keeping it safe for her.

Or as a safety net? That kind of money, thousands of dollars, would definitely be something Johnson—fine, J.J.—would want back. But more to the point, the fake hundreds . . . Had Angelique and Livia realized they were counterfeit? Two intelligent girls, both known for their attention to detail?

Had Livia realized her brother had gotten himself into something much more dangerous than street-corner distribution? She could have stolen the money, asked her friend Angelique to hold it for her. Or . . .

My mind is starting to spin. I feel like I suddenly have too much information to work with—except again, how to make sense of it all?

I rest my elbows on the table, peering hard at Guerline and Emmanuel. "Anything else you might have heard or remember from the time leading up to Angelique's disappearance? The smallest little thing that maybe didn't seem like a big deal at the time, but now, looking back? Snippets of conversation, e-mail? Hurried exchanges? Odd behavior?"

"She was quiet," Emmanuel volunteers at last. "I found her one day curled up on the sofa. Just sitting . . . No TV, phone. When I asked, she said she was tired. Another afternoon . . ."

He hesitates, ducks his head.

"Speak," Guerline demands.

"She was holding the picture of our mom. She'd taken it down and was staring at it. She looked . . . sad. Very sad. When she saw me, she put it back. Clearly, she'd been crying. I assumed she was feeling homesick. Sometimes, I am homesick, too, and I don't even remember home anymore."

Aunt Guerline reaches over and takes her nephew's hand.

"When was this?" I ask.

"I don't know. We were back in school. Fall sometime."

I nod. I'd already inspected the framed photo during my first search of their apartment, seen the love letter tucked behind the faded picture. Neither child had seen their mother in nearly a decade, but clearly, they still yearned for her. Maybe enough that whatever was going on in Angelique's life, she didn't feel she could tell her aunt, so had sought comfort from her mother's photo instead.

I take a deep breath. "Two mornings ago, Angelique was spotted at a wireless store in Mattapan Square."

Guerline gasps, then appears outraged. Emmanuel as well. This little disclosure is going to get me into a truckload of trouble with Lotham, but I feel it's necessary. "As she was walking away, she dropped a fake ID. They're studying it now. I think you should look at it, too." I point my chin at Emmanuel. "In case she used some kind of code again. You know her best."

Emmanuel nods immediately. Despite his young age, he's serious, even solemn. In this moment, I see shades of the older sister he described to me. Problem solvers, doers. Life hasn't always been kind to them, but it's made them stronger, more determined. Opportunity isn't given, it must be made.

Which makes me wonder again what Angelique had been up to. Helping a friend made sense, and explained the stash of money as well as her deception, dressing up as Livia to head for some mysterious meeting that Friday. But what had happened next to keep Angelique away from home permanently, while still not being enough to save her friend, who'd disappeared three months later?

I think back to what Charlie had said. If they were being held against their will, but still alive, then they must have value. But what kind of value did two fifteen-year-old girls have? Beyond the obvious, of course, in the sex trade. I felt like it had to have something to do with the counterfeit money, which was our other outlier. Maybe their captors knew the girls had fake hundreds, wanted them to fetch more? Make more? Except that was a pretty tall order given it took highly skilled experts to pull off quality bills.

My mind spins through possibilities, but none of them make sense.

Livia is the key to understanding what happened in the past, I decide now. She's the missing girl no one even knew was missing, and yet was probably also the original target. Which leave us with Angelique, given her recent appearances, as the best hope for finding both girls in the future. Before time runs out.

With that in mind, I finally organize some semblance of next steps.

"I'm going to call Detective Lotham," I announce, rising from the booth. "Ask him to bring over Angelique's fake license. Emmanuel, you stay here to study it."

I hesitate, glance at Guerline.

"I must make some calls," she volunteers. "Return to work. I can come back . . ."

"It's not a problem. Emmanuel will contact you when we're done." I imagine she doesn't get many vacation days, and after the events of the past year, she probably can't afford to take any more.

Guerline climbs out of the booth and heads for the door.

I step away from the table to call Lotham. I update him on the morning's developments, then hold my phone far from my ear as the yelling begins.

CHAPTER 25

LOTHAM SEEMS OVER THE WORST of his tantrum by the time he arrives at Stoney's. He skewers me with a single glare when I let him in, then stalks over to the booth where Emmanuel remains seated.

I've made a second pot of coffee. Wordlessly, I pour out a mug for Lotham. I take a seat next to Emmanuel, while Lotham slides in across from us.

Lotham removes a clear plastic bag from the inside of his charcoal gray sports jacket. A thick stripe of red tape screams *EVIDENCE* across the top. Lotham doesn't open the bag, but sets it on the table.

I scan the bag's contents—a single Massachusetts driver's license. I remember Emmanuel and me studying the black-and-white photocopy of this same license, used by Angelique at the cybercafé, days ago. The real thing is much more distinct, and will hopefully provide better details.

"No opening the bag, no touching the license, no removing it from my sight," Lotham states. The rules of engagement, which are important for preserving the chain of custody.

Emmanuel nods. His young face is once again deadly serious as he picks up the bag, peers at the front of the ID, then flips it over to study the back.

The picture is of a young African American female, black hair scraped back from her face in a tight ponytail. Dark brows, dark eyes, full face, much more heavily made up than I would've imagined, while huge beaded earrings provide further distraction. Mostly, I notice her eyes. They don't gaze ahead with the deer-in-headlights stare of so many official IDs but seem to peer straight into the viewer. They radiate intelligence.

"This is my sister," Emmanuel confirms. "But . . . I've never seen her with this jewelry. And . . . LiLi hardly ever wore makeup. It's her, but different."

"We see that often in fakes," Lotham says. "Tricks for making the subject appear older, or to obscure her real features. On this license, Angelique is supposed to be Tamara Levesque, age twenty-one."

Emmanuel cocks his head to the side. "She used this license to post her class essay. But why Tamara Levesque? That name means nothing to me."

"Do you know how to check an ID to tell if it's fake?" Lotham asks him presently.

"No, sir."

"This is modeled after the current Massachusetts driver's license, which involves a fairly sophisticated design. Not as high-tech as the Real IDs now required for airport security, but still, no joke. So here's what to look for. First off, feel the weight of it. Genuine licenses are high quality, decent weight, nearly impossible to bend. Try it."

Emmanuel fingers the license through the plastic bag. Experimentally, he squeezes the ends together. Nothing.

"In other words," Lotham continues, "the initial structure is solid. That's some skill right there. Now run your finger along the printing. Should be slightly raised. It's a specialized laser technique."

Emmanuel frowns. "I can't feel it well enough through the bag."

"Then trust me to tell you, they got that right, too. Which brings us to the more difficult elements. You see the watermark of the golden dome from the State House? Then we get to the embedded image of the state bird and state flower."

Peering from across the table, I interject. "Wait, is that the brown blob in the middle? I thought that was a dragon."

"It's a chickadee."

"Huh."

Lotham gives me a look. "The hologram is off, not a true hologram if you hold it up to the light. Instead, they've created a visual illusion done with particularly bright inks. I've seen this approach before. Also, under blue light, several things should appear on a real license. But the producers substituted reflective dyes for the proper UV ink in this model. All in all, I'd consider this a drinking-class license, so to speak, not flying-class."

Emmanuel nods.

"Now this is the part that's interesting. Final significant feature, the bar code. Upon scanning, it should verify the info already shown on the licenses. Plenty of fakes show a bar code, but it's nothing but garbage. This bar code is genuine. Which is a decent accomplishment. Whoever made this put a lot of care and technology into it. A few more iterations, and maybe flying-class would be within reach."

Emmanuel nods. I'm desperate to get my hands on the piece, but Emmanuel's still clutching the ID in a way that speaks of more than an academic interest. This is the last thing his sister touched. One more tiny link to her. He's not going to set it down anytime soon.

"Which brings us to the information on the ID itself," Lotham states. "Name, address, date of birth. Best practice is to keep the user's day and month of birth, just change the year. That way, when a suspicious bouncer asks questions, the holder can rattle off the correct answer off the top of his or her head. Knowing your sister's info, I can already tell you that's not true. Look. Does the date of birth mean anything to you? Code? Another cry for help? Something."

Emmanuel's eyes widen. "That is our mother's birthday!" he blurts out. "But . . . why? As you say, just changing the year would be easier."

"I was hoping you could tell me."

But Emmanuel doesn't have an answer.

"Okay, next few lines. Height, weight, eye color. Anything jump out at you?"

"The address," Emmanuel speaks up shortly, his voice excited again. "P.O. Box eighteen-oh-four."

"That's too short to be a valid box number around here," Lotham provides.

"It is an important date for us in Haiti. The year of our independence."

I frown at the revelation. Another inside joke on Angelique's part? But to what end?

"There's a physical address as well," Lotham says. "Check it out."

Emmanuel studies the print. "I don't know this address."

"Because it's not valid. At a real DMV, the system wouldn't even accept it. That street doesn't exist in all of Boston, let alone Mattapan."

"I . . . Can I show my aunt?"

"For chain-of-custody purposes, this can't leave my sight. But you could write down the info. Now, I need you to study the license number itself. Normally, the string of numbers communicates information to law enforcement; yet another point of verification. Trust when I say, this license number is nothing but a string of gibberish. Which doesn't make sense. They get the bar code right, only to screw up the license number? Which makes me wonder . . . Could this be another code meant for you?"

Emmanuel scrunches up his face. His lips move as he reads off the numbers to himself, then repeats several times. Slowly, he shakes his head. "This is not obvious to me. But LiLi had several ciphers. If I could compare these numbers with her notes in her codebreaking book, I might be able to figure it out."

"Add it to your address notes." Lotham produces a scrap of paper, pushes it across the table.

Emmanuel gets to work.

"Emmanuel." I speak up. "Is there something from Haiti that might be relevant? A reference to a belief, religion, custom. I don't know. But the fact that Angelique chose your mother's date of birth, as well as a mailing address that marks your country's independence. Surely that's not accidental."

Emmanuel smiles slightly. "You mean like pointing at a rainbow brings bad luck or eating the top of a watermelon will cause your mother to die? There are many superstitions in our culture, most of which my sister and I have heard from our aunt. But for us . . . LiLi believed in science. And I've lived my life here, not there. These are stories to us, nothing more."

"It's not personal to Angelique," I fill in. "At least, not personal enough."

Emmanuel nods. He fingers the evidence bag, then sets it down.

"I can study the license number, the street address. For now, all I can say is that LiLi must be thinking of our mother."

Lotham exhales, tries not to look as frustrated as I'm sure he must feel. I turn to him.

"You're saying this is a decent-quality ID, possible to produce with a computer and printer, but requires some advanced skill. So how did Angelique get her hands on it?"

"Probably bought it on the streets. This area has some known providers. Wouldn't be too hard to ask around, make it happen."

"You think? Because this is a girl who takes extra high school courses in her free time. She's not exactly lurking on street corners."

Emmanuel suddenly flushes.

"Emmanuel?" Lotham's voice holds a low growl of warning.

"Other kids, in high school, the rec center, they speak of fake licenses."

"Purchased from the internet," I say. At least that's what I'd heard from Charlie.

"Maybe some. But . . ." That awkward teen pause again.

"Who, Emmanuel?" Lotham demands.

The kid relents with a sigh. "Marjolie. Angelique's best friend. She has a fake ID. I heard her talking about it one day with LiLi. She was bragging about getting into a club. When LiLi asked her how, Marjolie started giggling. I couldn't hear her answer. But Marjolie has a fake license, and she definitely could've gotten one for my sister. Once, I would've said my sister didn't have the money to waste on such things. But, after what you found in the lamp . . ."

Emmanuel looks at me. "I must accept I didn't know everything about my sister. I must wonder . . . Maybe I didn't know her at all."

"You did, Emmanuel. You know her and she's counting on that.

The coded school essay, the particulars of this license. Your sister is out there. And she's talking to you. She's counting on *you*."

But I can tell the kid doesn't believe. And after all the cases I've been through, I can't really argue.

I clear the coffee mugs and carry them to the kitchen. I already know where we're going next.

CHAPTER 26

THIRTY MINUTES LATER, I STAND across from Angelique's high school, waiting for the bell to ring. Having spent hours yesterday staring at the same view through the corner grocer's security camera, it feels like I've known this place forever instead of just a single afternoon.

Lotham had wanted to march into Boston Academy, gold shield flashing, and drag Marjolie straight down to the station for questioning. Fortunately, cooler heads had prevailed.

Now I have the honor of meeting up with Marjolie and coaxing her back to Lotham's vehicle, parked several blocks away, where we can all chat privately. I'm due for work sooner versus later, so I need this to go quick and easy. No pressure.

I hear the bell start its run. There's a roughly five-minute delay, then the front doors of the academy heave open and the first wave of students pour out, hefting their packs and bolting to freedom.

Couple of minutes later, Marjolie appears, head bent close to Kyra's as they descend the front steps deep in conversation. Once again I'm struck by the contrast between the two. Kyra, tall and stunning even from this distance. While Marjolie walks with her shoulders hunched self-consciously. Pretty to Kyra's drop-dead gorgeous. Softer to Kyra's hard-edged attitude. One leader. One follower.

I feel the first prickling of unease, just as Marjolie glances up and spots me. Across the street, rows of traffic and rivers of kids between us, she falters. So many expressions flicker across her face: shame, fear, regret. Guilt. A whole boatload of guilt.

She knows that I'm here for her. That finally, this is all about her, and that stupid summer program at the rec center, and all the secrets teenagers feel the need to keep.

She turns away from her friend, already debating her options. I lean forward, preparing to give chase.

Then Kyra spies me. She grabs her friend's arm, totally missing the nuances. She tugs Marjolie forward, and after a final tense moment, the shorter girl gives way. She lets Kyra guide her across the street to me.

This is it. Eleven months later, it's finally time for the truth.

"I HAVE SOME questions for Marjolie involving the summer program she attended with Angelique at the rec center." I keep my voice light, tone matter-of-fact as I rattle off the story Lotham and I had concocted to justify culling Marjolie from the herd.

"Okay." Marjolie stares down at her feet, her fists tightly clenched around the straps of her backpack.

"Whatdya want to know?" Kyra prods.

"I think it would be better if we spoke alone. Don't you agree, Marjolie?"

The shorter girl still won't look at me, while beside her, Kyra blinks in confusion.

"Why do you want to know about summer camp? Did you learn something more about Angel?" Kyra leans forward eagerly. "Tell us! We're her friends, we deserve answers."

I keep my gaze on Marjolie. "Fashion camp. You and Angelique signed up together?"

The girl nods.

"And there was this other girl, Livia Samdi, also in the class? Prone to wearing a red baseball cap?"

A look of pure misery sweeping across Marjolie's face. "Yes."

"Come with me," I say gently. "It won't take long. I just have a few questions. Nothing special." I glance at Kyra, while Marjolie nods.

"I'll um, I'll catch up with you later," she tells her friend.

Kyra isn't stupid. She looks from Marjolie to me to Marjolie.

"I'll go with you—"

"No!" Marjolie, tone sharp, eyes wild.

"Marjolie . . ." Kyra, her voice pleading. She's scared, I realize. But not about what she knows, but about what she's now realizing she doesn't know. And she's worried for her friend.

"I'm sorry," Marjolie whispers. But I can tell Kyra still doesn't know who or what her friend's apologizing for.

"She'll call you later," I intervene, then I place my hand on Marjolie's shoulder and guide her away, before Kyra can continue pressing the issue.

Kyra lets us go. I can feel Marjolie shaking beneath my touch as I lead her down the first block. Then the second. We walk in total silence, tension building.

Lotham has his tricks, I have my mine.

Around the corner, to the unmarked car. I pop open the back door, just as Marjolie's head snaps up.

"I didn't mean it!" she exclaims wildly. "I swear I didn't mean to hurt her! I had no idea!"

Then she bursts into tears.

"You're welcome," I tell Lotham, as Marjolie collapses in the back seat and the show officially begins.

IT COMES OUT in fits. Starting with a boy, because so many stories do. The basketball player. The one Marjolie followed to the rec center because she needed to protect her territory.

Lotham and I sit in the front seat of the car, Marjolie in the back. Forget driving to the station. Our target is already pouring out her sins. We don't have time for traffic.

Lotham has his phone on, discreetly recording away. He's looking at anything but the sobbing girl in his back seat, so I continue to do the honors:

"You convinced Angelique to sign up with you. Your wing man—or woman, in this case."

"She wanted to work, earn extra money babysitting. But I begged and pleaded. That was the thing with Angel. She'd do anything for her friends, and we'd been best friends since fifth grade."

"So you and her signed up for fashion camp. Except it was never about fashion camp."

"DommyJ." Marjolie sighs, sobs.

"Heartbreaker?" I ask.

"I thought he loved me. I thought . . . I should've known better." Poor girl, I don't think she could look any more miserable.

"How old's DommyJ?" I ask.

"Seventeen."

To Marjolie's then fifteen. "Hot?"

Lotham gives me a look, but I stand by my question.

"Totally. All the girls wanted him. But he chose me. He said he liked my smile."

I nod sympathetically. I already know where this story's going, and I feel terrible for Marjolie. For all the vulnerable, self-conscious girls out there who dared to believe the cool guy wanted them, when really . . .

"What happened, Marjolie? You met DommyJ, convinced Angelique to sign up for fashion camp, and then . . ."

"Angel didn't like him. She warned me. Worse"—Marjolie smiles bitterly—"she told me I could do better. But of course, who could do better than him? I didn't want to hear it, I didn't want to believe."

Marjolie presses her lips together. More tears slide down her cheek. I whack Lotham till he belatedly produces a travel pack of tissues.

"Dommy's older, you know. He's not the type to be sitting around at home at night, plus he has all these college friends. Hoops players who know the hot spots."

I nod.

"During the day, at camp, he was really sweet. He'd call me his girl, walk around with his arm around me. He made me feel special. I'm not gorgeous like Kyra, or smart like Angel. I'm just me." Marjolie shrugs. "Except when Dommy was around. Then, I was the girl other girls stared at. I was the one everyone else wanted to be. So when he said he wanted to go club hopping and I should go with him, of course I'm gonna go. Him, out on the town with his buddies, in places like that? No way he's going home alone."

"But you were only fifteen . . ." I prod gently.

Marjolie's chin comes up. "I can rock it. Little more makeup, right hair and clothes. I just need an ID to back it up. And that's okay, cuz DommyJ knows this guy. Fifty bucks for a fake. Nights out with my man, priceless." Her lips twist sardonically. She starts dabbing at her smeared mascara.

"I didn't tell Angel, not at first. I knew she wouldn't approve. And she was mad at me. I'd made her sign up for fashion camp and then DommyJ's breaks were different than ours, and I kept sneaking out to see him. She said I'd abandoned her. I didn't mean it that way. Just . . . I was the girl making out with the hot guy in the hallway, you know. I'd never been that girl before."

"How'd you get the fake ID, Marjolie?"

"Dommy got it. I gave him the money on Tuesday. He brought me the ID Thursday. That night we're at his favorite club, hitting the dance floor with all his friends. He's got moves. I got moves. He's buying me shots. Everyone's happy." She hesitates, voice dropping low. "I felt like I was flying. Like it was the best night of my life. Like it would never get better than this. Then, DommyJ took me out to his friend's car."

She pauses. Her expression goes flat.

"Did he rape you, Marjolie?" I ask the question. Lotham's jaw has set, his hands fisting.

"Nothing like that. I gave it up. I thought . . . I thought this is what I'd been waiting for. I thought this was the special fucking moment with that special fucking guy." She laughs now, but it's a harsh sound. "The next day, at the rec center, I tell Dommy I love him. I tell him, I can't wait to go out again. Have fake license, will travel, you know. Dommy says I should bring a friend. It's awkward, him with me, then all the guys. He says . . . He says maybe I could bring Kyra."

Marjolie's drop-dead-gorgeous friend. Of course. "Oh, honey. I'm so sorry."

Marjolie doesn't cry anymore. She is too gutted for tears. She's right, first love feels like flying higher than the sun. And inevitably leads to the mother of all crash landings.

"I asked Angel instead. I didn't want to believe . . ." Marjolie glances up at me. "I thought if I brought Angel, that would be good enough."

"You asked Angelique to come with you club hopping?" Lotham is startled enough to finally ask a question.

"I showed her the ID. What's the big deal? Even if she didn't love partying, this is the girl who never stops talking college. She could use her fake license to sneak onto campus, take classes, whatever. It'd be good. I begged her. But she was angry. So then I told her everything. What Dommy and me did, how much I loved him. How much I needed her to do this, because I couldn't bring Kyra. Obviously. And I couldn't . . . I didn't want it to end."

"What did Angelique say?" Lotham again.

"She didn't. She just grew quiet. Then she hugged me, like really tight. And I started to cry, because . . . I knew. I just didn't want to know."

Marjolie closes her eyes. Takes a big shuddery breath. "Turns out, DommyJ's a collector. V cards. Like, is even in a competition with his buddies over who has the most. And having gotten mine . . . He broke up with me two days later. Clubbing, dancing, true love. None of it meant a thing."

"Oh, honey . . ." I say again.

"That's when things got weird."

Lotham frowns, gives me a look as he twists back around in the driver's seat. "Weird how?"

"Next week, bright sunny day, everyone's sitting outside. Angel walks right up to DommyJ. At first, you can't really hear them. She's like whispering furiously, he's totally blowing her off. Even giving me dirty looks like this is all my fault. Then she suddenly raises her voice. She starts talking, in as loud a voice as possible, that he's a cheat. That the fake IDs he sells aren't even worth the plastic they're printed on."

She has our full attention now.

"I had showed her mine to convince her to buy her own. But now she's yelling that fifty bucks is a total rip-off. A mall cop could tell they were fake and DommyJ's gonna get all his friends arrested. Then, she says, super loud, he owes everyone a refund."

"A refund?" Lotham presses.

Marjolie nods solemnly. "DommyJ was *furious*. She doesn't know what she's talking about. Take her fucking mouth and get out of his fucking way. Which is when that other girl, Libby, Liv—"

"Livia Samdi."

"Yeah. Totally quiet, like never speaks at all. Everyone knows her older brother got kicked out of the program two years ago for drugs. J.J., something like that."

"Johnson."

"Seriously?"

"Mmm-hmm."

"She suddenly joins Angel, yelling at Dommy. Except she knows all this stuff. The fakes DommyJ is dealing don't have the right hologram, laser printing, I don't know. All sorts of shit. Basically, she's also insisting DommyJ has cheated all his friends.

"Now *everyone's* listening, and things are getting really intense. I mean, Dommy's got all his buds there. Who knows how many fakes he sold them."

"*Do* you know how many fake licenses he sold?" Lotham pushes.

Marjolie shakes her head.

"What about others being involved? Some of his friends also selling the IDs?"

"I just know Dommy. And he doesn't make them. At least, I

don't think he does. He said a friend did. But when we were at the nightclub, all his buddies were using them. It's not like they're twenty-one."

At fifty bucks a pop. Lotham and I exchange another glance. "Do you have your license on you?" I ask.

Marjolie hesitates, as if finally remembering she's talking to cops. Lotham arches a brow. She relents, digging into her pack until she finds her wallet, then produces the ID. She hands it to Lotham first, who tests the weight of it in his hands, then twists it around in the light. He doesn't say a word, just passes it to me.

Marjolie has been telling the truth. It's cheap work. Too thin, blurry photo, not even an attempt at the holograph. In comparison, the fake license Angelique dropped the other day is a masterpiece. Fifty bucks for this? I see Angelique's point.

"So Angelique and Livia accuse DommyJ of ripping off his friends," I prod. "In front of everyone."

"Angel's trying to get back at him for what he did to me. The other girl, Livia, I don't know what her deal is. But this stuff, Dommy J, the crowd he hangs with . . . It's no joke. Angelique shouldn't have been talking to him like that. Especially in front of others. Dommy gets real serious real fast. He shoves them back. Tells them to shut the fuck up or they'd be sorry."

"He threatens them?" Lotham, clarifying.

"I guess."

"And then?"

Marjolie shrugs. "The director guy came out. Mr. Lagudu. Break's over, everyone back inside. Angel was still shaking, really upset. I knew she'd done it only for me, but I told her to knock it off. She was going to get herself in trouble. And I . . . I was embarrassed. Maybe I hoped DommyJ might still change his mind, take me back. But after that little display . . ." Marjolie exhaled roughly. "Angel and me had some words. Big fight, really. Angel . . . She couldn't see it. Sometimes she was *too* smart, *too* capable. She didn't understand what it meant to be just a regular girl like me. She didn't understand that sometimes, her being her, just made me feel bad."

Marjolie swallows, falls silent. "Things weren't the same between us after that. She kept sitting with the Livia girl. Sometimes I swore they were whispering about me. I wanted to apologize, make things right. I hurt, too, you know. I'd loved this guy, then he'd gone and done . . . I don't know. Summer camp really sucked. When it ended and school started again, things settled. Livia was gone and it was the Angel, Kyra, and Marjolie show again. I figured more time would pass, we'd grow close again. Like we used to be. Except then one day, Angel was just gone. And we never got our second chance."

"Did you see her with Livia Samdi again? After the summer program?" I ask.

She shakes her head.

"What about DommyJ?" Lotham presses. "Any more altercations between those two?"

"Not between Angel and him."

"But between . . . ?"

Marjolie took a deep breath. "The last week of the summer program. I'm just leaving, when I see DommyJ at the street corner. So I slow down. Cuz . . . Cuz I'm stupid, that's why. Then I see Livia, in her red baseball cap. She's standing right in front of him, but she's not the one yelling this time. He's clearly pissed off, ranting away, and she's like cowering, trying to just weather the storm. Then he grabs her arm. I'm startled. I've never seen him get physical with a girl before.

"Suddenly, she gets this look. She plants her feet and stares right at him. She says loudly, 'You know who my brother is, don't you?'

"He says he's doesn't give a flying fuck about J.J. Which makes her shake her head. 'Not J.J.,' she says. 'My *other* brother.'"

"Her other brother?" Lotham asks sharply.

"Exactly. She glances across the street. That's when I see him. Some super-tall dude in a blue tracksuit and gold chains. He didn't look all that scary to me. But Dommy now, his reaction . . . DommyJ drops Livia's arm, and backpedals so fast I thought he was gonna trip over his own damn feet."

"He saw this guy across the street, and he ran away?" Me this time, because I'm suddenly remembering my first visit to the school, the guy I spotted watching me. And possibly spied standing outside the Samdi residence, before bullets started to fly.

"DommyJ looked like he was gonna shit his pants. I've never seen him look that scared."

Lotham stares at Marjolie. "What did Livia do?"

"That's the thing. Second Dom let her go, she scampered off. But not toward the dude. In the total opposite direction. I saw her face, right before she took off down the sidewalk. I swear, she looked just as scared as Dommy. I mean, if this guy is her brother, why is she so freakin' anxious to get away from him?"

CHAPTER 27

T HREE P.M., WE PULL AWAY from the curb and head once more into Mattapan. I'm going to be late for work, but with a little bit of traffic luck, hopefully not too late. I'm agitated. The thought of spending the next eight hours serving drinks and wiping down tables when I have so many questions regarding Angelique and Livia *right now*. When I feel we're so close to learning the truth *right now*.

Alcoholics are notoriously obsessive. Particularly involving something as stimulating as *right now*.

"What do you make of Marjolie's fake ID?" I ask Lotham, my fingertips thrumming restlessly on my knee.

"Definitely cheap. Surprised it got them into any kind of nightclub. Then again, some places, slip a little cash into the bouncer's hand, and the deal is done. They just want plausible deniability if things go sideways."

"Angelique's ID is definitely better quality than the one Marjolie had."

"Significant step up."

I purse my lips, angling myself in the passenger seat to better face him. "Isn't that kind of interesting? That she complains to this DommyJ about the quality of his work—"

"About the way he treated her friend."

"And a year later, Angelique herself is running around with a superior fake."

Lotham nods thoughtfully. We've come to a red light. He glances over at me, his face hard to read. "You think Angelique made that license? Or helped someone make it?"

"I think if Marjolie's story is true, Livia Samdi knows a lot about fake IDs, while also having the skills to do better. Fifty dollars a pop . . . I mean, if DommyJ can unload hundreds of dollars' worth of shitty IDs during a summer rec program, imagine how much Livia could make off quality merchandise?"

"Of all the counterfeiting we've discussed, a fake ID is the most feasible DIY project. With the right software, and a specialized printer, I could see two teenage girls pulling it off." Lotham frowns. "Unfortunately."

"Maybe the money in Angelique's lamp came from their own business enterprise? Livia probably enjoyed the design challenge, while Angelique had personal incentive to run DommyJ out of business."

"Why the counterfeit hundreds?" Lotham countered, making a hard right into a stalled stream of city traffic.

"Maybe someone paid them with fakes. Maybe they didn't know they even had counterfeit bills."

"So they're smart enough to see the flaws in fake IDs but not forged bills?"

He raises a valid point. But damned if I can figure out how we get from Russian-printed Ben Franklins to locally manufactured fake driver's licenses. I'm also curious that the executive director of the rec center, Frédéric Lagudu, never mentioned a huge confrontation between Angelique and Livia and this DommyJ. Unless he came upon it at the very end and had just enough time to break it up while writing it off as another day in paradise? Because surely once Angelique went missing, her screaming match with a wannabe hoodlum would be worth noting?

"Let's say Livia Samdi knows something about production, given her design talents," Lotham muses. "After the confrontation with DommyJ, she and her new bestie Angelique start scheming. They'll make their own fake IDs. Superior quality that will drive dumbass Dommy out of business, while earning them extra cash."

"Livia is manufacturing, Angelique marketing and sales."

Lotham nods. Cars are not moving. He gives it another ten seconds, then flashes his grille lights. The car in front of us does its best to squeeze over. Lotham threads through a narrow opening between the clogged lanes, gets to the first turnoff, and takes it. I have no idea where we are, but I like his style.

"Here's what I don't get," Lotham says. "Wouldn't Angelique's first customers be her own friends? Think of the DommyJ model. He probably signed up for the summer program just so he could sell to his fellow teens. Enter Angelique, who we're saying sold enough to have thousands in cash but never approached her own social circle? That seems odd."

I sit back grumpily. Then, remembering my conversation with Charlie: "Maybe she and Livia sold online. The international IDs are done that way. And these are two girls who've both been described as quiet. Internet sales would work, while further compartmentalizing this new criminal activity from their real, college-aspirational lives."

"Possible. But that introduces more infrastructure. How are

they getting paid? Money transfers? Bitcoin? They'd need to have bank accounts and they're both underage."

"Not according to Angelique's fake alter ego, Tamara Levesque."

Lotham eyes widened slightly. "Shit." He bangs the steering wheel with his hand. "Of course. We examined the Levesque ID for forensic clues, then overanalyzed it with the help of Angelique's brother for coded messages. Maybe, all along, the breadcrumb was the name itself, Tamara Levesque. A lead on Angelique's secret life, which has clearly gotten her and her friend in trouble."

"Oooh." I finally get it. "As in Angelique doesn't have bank accounts and Livia Samdi doesn't have financial records, but Tamara Levesque . . . Oh, oh, oh."

"Damn sleep deprivation," Lotham mutters. "I'll get on it, the second after I drop you off."

I sigh heavily. So much happening *right now*. On the cusp of so many answers *right now*.

"We still have a problem," Lotham says, finally able to pick up a little speed as he cuts through a maze of tiny side streets. "Assuming Livia and Angelique were doing this together . . . Why did Angelique go missing first?"

"She was posing as Livia. Trying to protect her from . . . someone."

"And it took that someone three months to realize he had the wrong girl? That's not a very bright someone. Besides, if you're a criminal who wants to move in on their new and improved fake ID business, wouldn't you just grab both of them?"

I have to think about it. "If Livia is the design genius behind their operation, then she'd be more valuable than Angelique. Maybe that's why she appeared so scared. Maybe Angelique volunteered to take the meeting in Livia's place. When the bad person discovered the subterfuge, they kept Angelique and used her as leverage to force Livia to work for them."

"Then why take Livia three months later?"

"Ummm . . . coercion only works so long? Or operations had grown so fast they needed Livia at their immediate disposal? Maybe they have Livia shut up somewhere, designing a million fake IDs a day, I don't know. And Livia's now the collateral being held against Angelique. Hence Angelique has resurfaced to perform other, smaller tasks, because as long as they have Livia, they know she'll return to them."

"There's a lot of assumptions in that theory," Lotham informs me. "On the other hand, playing the girls off each other is a tried-and-true strategy. Used by human traffickers everywhere. In fact, it's often easier to kidnap two people rather than just one, as it gives the kidnapper more leverage over both of them."

"Those poor girls," I murmur. "For Angelique this whole thing probably started as a way to strike back against the asshat that hurt her bestie. For Livia, maybe it was all about impressing her new friend, inserting herself deeper into Angelique's world. And for their troubles, the two of them have now been kidnapped, while most likely being forced to engage in some kind of criminal activity, license forgeries, something. I don't know if I could handle that kind of stress. Especially eleven months later."

Lotham nods, arrives at last by the side door of Stoney's. "So, to recap, we have the victims, Angelique Badeau and Livia Samdi. We have a possible criminal activity—fake IDs. Which still feels small potatoes to me. Thousands a month, versus the hundreds of thousands that can be netted through drugs. So who would be into something like that and have enough incentive to kidnap and hold two teenage girls for nearly a year?"

"What about this brother? Not Johnson. The other Samdi brother who appeared at the rec center?"

"The tall, sinister guy?" Lotham shrugs. "I'll do some asking around. Chances are the gang taskforce has a name."

"I saw him."

"You *saw* him?"

"The first time I visited Boston Academy. Skinny Black dude, with a fashion sense that's at least twenty years out of date. I'd just wrapped up talking to Kyra and Marjolie when I spotted him across the street. He was watching me."

Lotham turns in the driver's seat, his shoulders massive in the confined space. "And you were going to mention this when?"

"What was there to mention? I was at a public school in Roxbury and a Black guy stood across the street. Hello, there's a shocker. Frankly, he had more grounds to report the strange white woman accosting students in the corner deli. I didn't realize his presence had any kind of significance. Let alone that he might be Livia Samdi's long-lost brother. For that matter, I didn't know about Livia Samdi. But he definitely knew I was there." I hesitate. "I might have seen him a second time, as well."

"Where?"

"Outside the Samdi house, when I was being shot at."

"Are you fucking kidding me?"

"I wasn't exactly paying attention to the scenery. I was hightailing it down a sidewalk trying to save my sorry ass. But for a moment, out of the corner of my eye, I thought I saw him across the street."

"In other words, where the shot was fired from." Lotham sounds beyond pissed off. I'm not exactly sure why, given I was the one who'd been the target.

"It's possible," I allow.

"I'm gonna send techs back to the scene. Have uniforms perform a fresh canvass."

"Nobody's gonna say a thing. Especially if it's some mysterious scary older brother."

Lotham shakes his head. His mouth is set in a grim line. "You're here tonight?" He gestures to Stoney's.

"Till midnight."

"I don't want you out by yourself. You need to attend a meeting, call me. If I can't come, I'll send a patrol car."

"To drive me to AA? Wow, talk about making a statement."

"Frankie . . ."

But I've had enough. There's only so much of this kind of male fretting I can take. I have been on my own for a long time. And I'm not an idiot.

"I'm gonna go to work," I inform him. "Then, given the day, I'll probably retreat upstairs to my studio apartment and incredibly hostile roommate. Forget a guard dog. I dare any evildoer to take on Piper. That cat bites first, asks questions later."

"Call me when you're done with work," Lotham orders.

"You call *me*." Now I *am* being a bitch, but I don't care.

"If that's what you prefer."

"And what will you be doing this evening?"

"Running down financial accounts for Tamara Levesque and a family tree for Livia Samdi."

"Do you think you might need an attack cat?"

"I'm a police detective, for the love of God—"

"And I'm a woman who's lived in more scary neighborhoods than you'll ever get to visit. We both have our skills."

"Frankie—"

"Lotham."

"I wish I understood you."

"Detectives like puzzles. Which means the moment you figure me out . . ."

"I'm not as shallow as you seem to think."

"And I'm not so complicated. I'm here to find a missing teen, which is now two missing teens. This is what I do. I am experienced, and I have handled situations like this before. These kinds of cases . . ." I shrug. "They always involve secrets and there's generally at least one person willing to kill to keep those secrets safe."

"Do you carry a gun?"

"I have a whistle. A very loud whistle. Though if it helps, Stoney has a baseball bat behind the bar."

"Take it upstairs with you tonight."

"Fine." I glance at my watch. Three thirty. "I gotta go." I pop open the door, climb out onto the sidewalk.

"Frankie," Lotham calls from the driver's seat. "Be careful, okay? Just, be careful."

"Back at you."

I shut the car door and head to work.

CHAPTER 28

STONEY IS NOT HAPPY WITH my late arrival.

"Sorry, sorry, sorry," I say.

He gives me a look. The look. No one likes that look.

I don't provide an explanation or an excuse. I already know it doesn't matter. Instead, I do the best damage control I can: I get to work, and I work fast. Thirty minutes later, when the front doors open and the first wave of locals arrive, I'm already pouring spicy cocktail peanuts and pulling beers. Today, I get a few nods in recognition. Not words yet, but physical acknowledgment that I'm still here. I'll take it.

The night busies up. Which is all well and good in my world. I don't want or need the constant buzz of too many thoughts in my head.

Nine P.M., the first break arrives. I head back to the kitchen long enough to request a garden salad from Viv. She looks me up and down.

"You're not getting laid."

"Sorry."

"Whatdya waiting for? No man's gonna be better looking."

"Don't tell your husband that."

A snicker. "Enjoy your salad. But live a little, too. Life's too damn short, or haven't you heard?"

More food deliveries to various tables, more pitchers of rum punch. Then I get fifteen minutes to inhale salad. "Love it," I inform Viv. "Thank you very much. Have I mentioned that I stole your eggs and fries?"

"Not my eggs and fries."

"I stole Stoney's eggs and fries."

"Better work hard, then. He's fussy like that."

I take that to heart, turning into a whirling dervish of hospitality. Tables served, drinks delivered, smiles extended. I'm like the Wonder Woman of food and beverage. By eleven, when things have settled and we're down to the die-hards, Stoney says:

"Easy now. You're starting to freak me out."

"I really am sorry."

"You are a piss-poor employee."

"Good news, though. I'm not so bad on the missing persons front."

"Angelique Badeau is coming home?"

"Hard-ass. Maybe tomorrow."

He gives me a look.

"Maybe," I insist. Then, more thoughtfully, "Stoney, you must've seen a bunch of fake IDs in your time."

"It comes up."

"What'd you think?"

"About what?"

"The market, quality, et cetera."

He shrugs, gathers up dirty glasses. "Don't have an opinion. Ones I saw, I seized, per the law. Plus, I don't have any interest in serving kids. Then again, you've seen our crowd; not exactly the college type. I don't get the big deal myself. If you can die for your country at eighteen, why not have a beer?"

"Victimless crime?"

He shrugs. "Plenty of bigger things to worry about."

"What if it's not all about drinking? I mean, an ID can get you access to all sorts of things."

"Like what?"

"Well, if you're under eighteen, your own cell phone."

"After-hours phone," he states, no prompting required.

"You know about those?"

"Everyone knows about those."

I scowl. "Then it gets you . . ." I honestly falter. Being eighteen or twenty-one, depending on your preference, is worth the right to vote, the honor of joining the military, and . . . well, access to Boston's night life.

"How many kids you think want a fake ID?" I ask him, changing gears.

"Plenty. Boston's a college town. Most of the freshmen want to drink or party. And owners like me take carding seriously or risk losing our licenses. You know what it costs to get a liquor license?"

"A small fortune?"

"A large fortune. Enough most establishments aren't playing it fast or loose anytime soon."

"So there's a decent enough demand for fake IDs. A person could make some cash."

Another Stoney shrug. "If you're into counterfeiting, why not just print money?"

"Turns out that's really hard."

"No shit. Well, what about stocks or bonds or bank notes on one particular ancient neighborhood bar?"

I hear what he says. "Might be possible. I don't know."

"Green card." A voice speaks up from the end of the bar. One of the regulars. Michael Duarde. I've served him several nights, but this is our first conversation. His accent is definitely not from here, though I'm hard-pressed to pick a country. The fact that he's slightly slurring his words doesn't help. "Gonna fake something, fake a fucking green card. Or work visa. That's what everyone wants."

Michael raises his beer and takes a long pull. Both Stoney and I watch him.

"You have TPS status?" I ask him. As in Temporary Protected Status, which is what most of the Haitian immigrants, such as Angelique and her brother, were granted post-earthquake.

"Not me. Plenty of others."

"Can you fake a visa?" I ask Stoney, genuinely curious. Because the drunk guy raises a good point.

"Can you fake a passport?" he asks me.

"Not without a lot of expertise."

"There you go."

"Harder than a hundred-dollar bill?" I ask him.

"Beyond my pay grade."

He's right, but he's got me thinking about Lotham's point from the car ride home. Even if Angelique and Livia were making thousands a month dealing fake IDs, that's small potatoes compared to illegal drug revenue . . . Why kidnap two girls over small potatoes?

Counterfeiting green cards or work visas would be big leagues. Crazy amounts of money. Except if you can't nail a hologram on a Massachusetts driver's license, how the hell are you going to fake a document on par with a U.S. passport? Forging a visa is terrorist-cell kind of crazy. Or Russian-printed-bills kind of savvy.

It feels to me it all boils down to one key question—Angelique and Livia were clearly involved with something illegal, but *how* illegal? What kind of crime would incentivize kidnapping and holding two teenagers for nearly a year?

I mull the possibilities as I wrap up for the night. Closing out tabs, carrying the last of the dirty dishes to Viv, cleaning.

"Where's your handsome hunk?" she asks me as she finally bustles out, pulling on her coat.

My phone hasn't rung. I refuse to admit how many times I've checked it. "Working."

"Mmm-hmm."

"Been a long day."

"Mmm-hmm."

"Oh look, there's your husband waiting for you."

"Mmm-hmm."

"Stop that!"

Finally a smile. "Girl, you gotta get your priorities straight. None of us have forever. You know what I'm talking about?"

"My eggs have petrified in my ovaries?"

"Forget that, honey. I'm talking fun. You hear me?"

She's not wrong. But it doesn't help my cause as I let her out the front door, then lock up behind. I watch as her husband takes her arm. They look adorable. Two peas in a pod. Viv shoots me a final cheery wave. I do my best not to vomit in her general direction.

Stoney closes out the register, brings me my tips. I wave him off. "I keep eating out of the kitchen. My bad."

"You're both eating my food and showing up late?"

"What I lack in discipline I make up for in personality."

He gives me a look.

"Hey, I'm confessing my sins up front. Offering you money back. As employees go, that's not too shabby."

He seems to accept this.

"I even clean up after your homicidal cat."

"Piper's a good worker. Complains less than you do."

"I haven't bitten off anyone's toe lately."

He shrugs. Apparently that's not as impressive a feat as I'd hoped. "You gonna bring that little girl home?" he asks me.

I'm feeling reckless. "Hell, I'm gonna bring two little girls home: Angelique Badeau and Livia Samdi."

He hands over the fifty bucks in tip money, cash I sorely need. "You do that, and we're even."

"You love this community, don't you?"

"It's my home."

"I don't have a home, but I still know what you mean."

We both finish up our work in silence. Then Stoney exits stage left and I climb up the stairs to my apartment. I meant what I said to Lotham; today had been a long day. Best to retire early.

Yet I still check my phone. No calls, no messages. I feel restless, thrumming with the edge of unfinished business. What has Lotham learned about Livia Samdi's other brother? Or what about possible bank accounts for Angelique's alter ego, Tamara Levesque? I hate being in the dark.

Pacing my tiny apartment back and forth, back and forth. Feeling my restlessness grow, my skin start to tingle, my scalp pull tight. Maybe I should head to a meeting. Nights like this are exactly when I need a meeting.

No need for a fucking police escort. I've lived tougher, seen neighborhoods more dangerous. I wasn't lying to Lotham when I said as much earlier. I can do this.

I pull back my curtain. I stare at the street outside.

That's when I see him.

Standing there, directly in a wash of light where I'm certain to spot him. Very tall, lanky build, red sweatsuit, multiple gold chains. His hair is pulled back from his face in an intricate pattern, revealing a face that is lean, callous. Cruel.

He stares right at me. I see him. He sees me.

I let the curtain drop. I tumble back onto my bed.

I think wildly, I need Piper. Where's my attack cat?

But when I check under the bed, Piper's gone.

I order myself not to panic. I tell myself I'm strong and capable and I've been in deep shit before. Then I nervously work the lock of my door, easing it open long enough for me to creep downstairs and grab Stoney's bat. As long as I'm there, I check the front door—still secured. Then the side door—also bolted. The side door is unmarked and solid metal. No one is getting through that. The bar's front door, however . . . Smoked glass. It can be shattered. Would probably set off an alarm, but maybe noise doesn't matter. A determined predator on the hunt. In, out, done.

I recheck the locks, then head upstairs, holding the bat stiffly before me.

Once in my apartment, I hit the bolt lock. I gingerly move the curtain back. I see retro dude still standing on the sidewalk, staring up at me.

I should call Lotham. And say what? Livia's evil older brother is watching me? And why haven't I heard from Lotham anyway? Surely Boston's finest has learned something by now. So why the radio silence?

One A.M. Two A.M. I sit on the bed facing the door, bat across my knees, phone within easy reach.

I doze off. Dreams of blood and Paul and screams so primal they shiver up my spine. I'm chasing Angelique Badeau down a long corridor, never able to catch up. Except then I turn a corner and the tracksuit man is there pointing a gun.

"Couldn't leave it alone," he says.

He pulls the trigger. Angelique screams and falls to the ground, a bloody hole in her gut. He pulls the trigger again and now I'm falling to the ground, a bloody hole in my gut. A third booming shot. Paul screams the loudest, blood everywhere, as he collapses beside us.

"I'm sorry," I gasp.

"But you killed us." Now they're both angry and it's all my fault and so many things I should've done differently, should've done better. I'm falling down down down. Into an abyss of tortured souls and clasping hands and guilty consciences, mostly my own.

A cat appears, growling low. She leaps into the fray, slashing out with her claws. I feel pain, startlingly harsh, refreshingly clear, just as I bolt upright, clutching my arm against my chest. My phone is ringing.

I spy Piper, now on my bed, twitching her tail crankily as she grooms her right front paw. I glance down at my forearms to discover fresh scratches.

I don't have time to consider the matter. Three A.M. My phone still chiming. I answer it.

At long last, I hear Lotham's voice.

He says, "We have a body."

And just like that, I've failed again.

CHAPTER 29

LOTHAM SITS IN THE REAR booth. He's wearing yesterday's snazzy ensemble with his tie loosened and dress shirt wrinkled. He looks gutted.

I pour him a cup of hot coffee. When he stares at it blankly, I head to the bar, grab a bottle of rum, and add a shot. Just because I'm an alcoholic doesn't mean other people can't drink.

I return the rum, take a seat across from him. I'm still wearing my oversized T-shirt with a pair of men's boxers. They were Paul's, once, but we're not here to discuss that.

"Speak," I order.

"What happened to your arm?"

I look down at the blood-crusted gashes. "Piper."

"Did you try to spoon with her or something?"

"Or something. Speak."

Lotham takes a fortifying gulp of rum-laced coffee. His hand is shaking. I'm not sure he notices till he tries to set the mug down and sloshes coffee over the edge. "Sorry."

I wait.

"I didn't even know she was missing," he mutters at last. "Fifteen-year-old girl, and we didn't even know she was lost till a couple of days ago."

Which is how I learn we're talking about Livia Samdi, not Angelique Badeau.

"Where did you find the body?"

"Franklin Park. Dumped behind a tree."

I wince. "Harsh."

"She was fully clothed," he says.

I get it. There are other options. "Cause of death?"

"Bruises around the neck. Petechial hemorrhages in the eyes."

"Strangulation."

"Park was the dump site. Forensic gurus will have to perform some magic to see if we can narrow in on place of death. Homeless guy flagged down a patrol car. Poor man was just looking for a place to crash for the night, when he found a body instead."

I nod. Lotham keeps talking.

"Initial analysis, wherever Livia had been staying, it wasn't on the streets. She was too clean for that. She was dressed simply— jeans, a Patriots T-shirt, sneakers. None of the items were brand-new, but none appeared that old either. She was noticeably thin, her fingernails chewed down to the nubs, her back molars worn from repeated grinding. Definite signs of chronic stress, according to the ME, though not necessarily physical abuse. No bruises, fresh lacer-ations, healing fractures, that sort of thing. She looked pretty good, all things considered. You know, other than her neck." Lotham exhaled heavily, chugged more coffee.

"Angelique?"

"Homeless man didn't see anyone in the area. We're still reviewing video footage now. But that section of the park is off the beaten path. I'd say whoever dumped her knew what he was doing."

It's such a sad term. Dumping. Like trash or unwanted goods, instead of a teenage girl.

"Livia's family?" I ask.

"I did the notification myself. Her mother didn't appear surprised at all. Just flat—that parent who's always feared the worst and now doesn't have to be afraid anymore."

"I know how it is."

"J.J. was there."

"Johnson," I say. I don't know why. Just to get in one last dig.

"Of the two, he was the more emotional. Initial response, stricken, followed by pissed off, followed by driving his fist into the wall."

This gives me pause. "He didn't suspect his sister was dead?"

"No. More to the point, he was enraged. Whatever's going on with that family, I would bet my shield Johnson didn't want his sister harmed. If he even knows what happened to her."

"You ask about an older brother?"

"I know my job," Lotham speaks up sharply.

He's had a rough night, so I let it slide. He takes another gulp of spiked coffee. "Fuck," he says at last.

I can't disagree with that, so I say nothing at all.

"J.J. had already taken off by the time I broached the subject of an older Samdi sibling; I thought being alone would make it easier to talk with Roseline, but she shut down. If she hadn't kept sucking the life out of each cigarette, I'm not sure I would've believed she was even there. I'll take another run at her later, but given her love of the police . . ."

Lotham isn't asking for me to get involved. As a detective he would never ask for a civilian to insert herself in an investigation, let alone visit a residence where she's already been shot at. And yet, that's my mental takeaway. Mrs. Samdi doesn't talk to cops. Meaning if we want to learn about Livia's mysterious other brother . . .

"Red baseball cap?" I ask.

"Not with the body."

In other words, Angelique is still wearing it. "Something's changed," I murmur.

"No shit."

"Seriously. Angelique disappeared eleven months ago. Livia a couple of months after that. But it's only been in the past few weeks that Angelique's resurfaced. Sending a coded message for her brother. Dropping a fake ID. The girls were clearly being kept alive for some purpose. Producing semi-decent fake licenses, I don't know." Though even as I say the words out loud, that sounds like a dubious master plan. What kind of criminal enterprise kidnaps two girls and holds them against their will to manufacture less-than-brilliant forgeries? I don't get it.

For now, I press on. "Clearly things are going downhill. The signs of Livia's acute physical stress, Angelique's frantic overtures. Now . . . Livia's murder. I think whatever purpose the girls had been serving . . . time's up. And they both knew it. Know it." My own voice ends shakily. Is Angelique even still alive? Or is it just a matter of time before we find her body? And if she is still breathing, dear God, what must she be going through? After everything she did to try to help her friend.

Where have these girls been hidden? What the hell has been happening to them for the past year?

And why the fuck couldn't we have found Livia in time?

Lotham downs half a mug of rum-laced coffee, his grim expression a mirror for my own dark thoughts.

"Were you able to trace Angelique's alias, Tamara Levesque?" I ask at last, trying to marshal some semblance of professionalism. "Did it lead to a bank account?"

"Yes, I was able to trace it. No, it didn't lead to a bank account stuffed with ill-gotten gains. What I did discover: Tamara Levesque is a college student. Enrolled in Gleeson College, to be exact."

"Seriously?"

"Do I look like a guy with a sense of humor?"

I'm this close to fetching more rum, this time for both of us. Instead, I rub my temples furiously. "So Tamara Levesque is Angelique's alter ego. And Angelique used the fake identity to go to college? When will the case make any damn sense?" I mutter to no one in particular. "Is it a medical school?"

"Nope. Some small liberal arts college in Western Mass. It'll take some digging to learn more. You know how many colleges exist in Mass?"

"A lot?"

"Hundreds."

I nod, as if any of this makes sense. "I asked Stoney about fake IDs tonight. He assures me there's a market. But he's not convinced it's on financial par with say, drug dealing."

"He's probably right about that."

"And yet, we now have evidence of two girls who may have been involved in producing fakes, and at least one was murdered for it. What would make such forgeries worth killing over? Especially considering they weren't even top-quality knock-offs."

"I have no idea."

"You know what would be priceless and worth killing over? Green cards. Or work visas. A guy at the end of the bar suggested it. You have thousands of immigrants whose temporary status is about to expire, all of them have local roots, and none of them want to go home. Making a forged visa worth a small fortune."

Lotham, however, is already shaking his head. "Can't be done. Certainly not by two teenagers. Hell, we might as well go back to counterfeiting currency. It'd be about as easy."

"Is there something in between? More valuable than a fake license? Not as complicated as a visa?"

"Off the top of my head . . ." He pauses, closes his eyes in thought, exhaustion, something. Opens them again. "Fake credit cards, I suppose. But that's getting into identity theft, which is a whole different ball of wax. And I don't know why anyone would need to kidnap two girls for that. There are several Russian gangs in Boston who are known for it. They already have recruits roaming the streets, internet cafés with data miners to record financial data straight out of someone's wallet. Later, the data is transferred to a cloned card. For those operations, kidnapping would cause more trouble than it's worth."

I get what he's saying. Unfortunately, it only adds to our confusion. I take it from the top.

"Angelique and Livia were abducted for a reason. First Angelique, who was most likely held hostage to force their original target, Livia, to do whatever it was they wanted Livia to do. Most likely this something involves computer design, 3D printing, parts manufacturing, whatever. But eventually, Livia disappeared, too. For the sake of argument, let's assume it was because operations reached a point where they needed her on site, or desired more control. So now both girls are under wraps, but alive, fed, clothed, housed. Angelique doesn't dare make a break for it or contact her family over fears they'll hurt Livia, and vice versa.

"And the girls are working. Doing something important because otherwise why be kept alive at all? Maybe it started with the forged licenses, which showed off Livia's skills. But it must've migrated to something with higher revenue potential to justify holding two kidnapped girls for nearly a year. Not to mention they'd need a space to keep the girls, plus have at least a couple of guys serving as guards, while overseeing operations . . . They wouldn't necessarily require an entire warehouse for computer-generated forgeries, but space is still space."

Lotham nods.

"For eleven months, the girls have been working on this . . . something. It's gotten so intense and stressful. Livia's breaking down, while Angelique's terrified enough to risk making contact and dropping breadcrumbs. Except it's still not enough. Angelique's worst fears come true. Livia is killed . . ."

My voice trails off. "Meaning, whatever the project is, it's nearing completion. They don't need Livia anymore. Or Angelique."

Lotham doesn't disagree. "Except these are still questions, not answers. Nearly a year later, we're no closer to the who, what, or where. Best lead we got is some mythical older brother of Livia's who inspires fear."

"I saw him again tonight."

"Who?"

"Our mystery man. He was standing across the street from my apartment. When I pulled back the curtain of my apartment, he stared straight up at me."

"Goddammit!" Lotham slams down his coffee mug. "You didn't call me?"

I merely shrug. "And say what, he was just standing there. Except . . . If he was outside my apartment, then he couldn't have been the one killing Livia. Could he?"

"I wouldn't jump to that conclusion. We don't have time of death. Meaning he could've very well killed Livia, then come to monitor your actions. Dammit. Everything about this case. Dammit, dammit, dammit!"

"You need some sleep. We both need some sleep."

"Because it'll look better in the morning? It *is* fucking morning and a girl is dead!"

I don't say anything, just take his hand. I feel his rage, his frustration. I've been there myself. Fourteen times. And it doesn't get any easier to take.

"Angelique is still alive," I tell him.

"Maybe."

"She needs us. Whatever's happening . . . it's all going down fast. We have to figure this out. We *will* figure this out. But not like this. When's the last time you even closed your eyes?"

He doesn't answer. By my calculations, it's probably been days. And exhaustion is clearly taking its toll.

"Come on. I'm taking you upstairs. Grab an hour or two of rest. Then we can review this again. When we're both a little less insane."

Lotham glowers, but doesn't resist as I take his hand, lead him upstairs. My own thoughts are churning. A mix of crushing sorrow for a girl I never met and didn't save. A deepening despair over too many questions and not enough answers. A growing dread that the clock is ticking, mercilessly now, and if we don't figure this out . . .

Help us, Angelique had written.

Except we didn't.

I make Lotham sit on the edge of the mattress. He removes his sidearm and gold shield, placing them neatly on the bedside table. He moves on autopilot, his eyelids already lowering, his body collapsing as I divest him of everything but his T-shirt and boxers. His chest is broad, and heavily muscled. I do not trace his collarbone with my fingertips. I do not trail my lips along the hollow of his throat.

Instead, I lift his legs and tuck him into bed.

"Good night, Detective."

"Who's Paul?"

"I didn't say Paul."

"Yes, you did."

"Good night, Detective."

I put him to bed. Then I take up watch in front of the window, pulling back the curtain just enough to peer out. But no gold-chained gangster is staring up at me.

"I'm going to learn your secrets," my guest says sleepily.

"Shhh . . ."

I let the detective sleep. Then I rest my forehead against the cool glass of my window, and think of Livia Samdi, and Angelique Badeau, and what it means to be a teenage girl. The mistakes we all make. The moments we'll never get back again.

Then, I do say his name. "Paul."

And I smell blood and I feel pain and I let it wash over me, the price of my sins.

"I'm sorry," I whisper. But I'm not talking to Paul anymore. I'm talking to Livia Samdi, and all the girls like her.

Then I pray, as hard as I've ever prayed, for Angelique Badeau. For us to find her in time. For her to be out there, still alive, still okay.

For her to please, please, please, come home again.

CHAPTER 30

I DON'T SLEEP. MY THOUGHTS are spinning too swiftly. Five A.M., Lotham tossing restlessly, I give up and tiptoe out of my room. Stoney has an ancient desktop in his office. I fire it to life, hoping it might provide some insights.

I brew a fresh pot of coffee as I wait for it to boot up. Then I take a seat and have at it.

First, I Google the name Tamara Levesque. It has to mean something, I think. Though, why a college student in Western Mass? But Emmanuel said his sister didn't dream, she made plans. So what was Angelique trying to tell us? What did we need to know?

I get four hits. Three of them are Tamara Levesques who live in other states. The fourth is a mention on an Instagram page.

I have plenty of experience with social media; in this day and age, it's impossible to search for missing persons without following their digital footprints. Now, I log in and look up Tamara Levesque.

Immediately, a page for Gleeson College loads up. I discover dozens of photos of a college campus surrounded by rolling green hills and old brick buildings. There are pictures of laughing kids sitting outside, more smiling students inside classrooms. It takes me a bit to pick out Tamara. She's pictured in a lab, her face partially obscured by goggles as she handles a flask over a Bunsen burner. Her black hair is pulled back tight—Tamara's image on the license, versus Angelique's heavy ringlets from her missing poster. But it's the same girl.

Which leaves me even more confused. Angelique is using her fake ID to enroll in college? That makes no sense at all. So what did Angelique need me to see here? What's she trying to tell us?

Gleeson College is listed as a small liberal arts college. It appears to rest at the foothills of the Berkshires, with the address given as some town I've never heard of. It offers online classes as well as a traditional classroom education. I peruse photo after photo of beaming college students, then read a note from the president—a stern-looking white dude in thick black glasses and gray three-piece suit. I didn't know people still wore three-piece suits.

I review each photo in detail, then return to the collection as a whole. All in all, Gleeson College looks just like any other New England university, albeit with a particularly pretty campus.

It's not until my fifth or sixth time through that I spot it. In the background, another female student barely visible in the rear of a classroom. Livia Samdi. I'm certain of it.

She and Angelique ran away to join a college? No way. I don't believe it for a minute. So what the hell is going on?

I sit back, feeling more lost now than before.

After another minute, I expand my Google search to Gleeson College as a whole. The website, however, mostly seems to repeat the photos from Instagram. I find a page where I can request additional information; I plug in my e-mail, hoping I'll hear back sooner versus later.

Then I get up and pace the entire length of the dining room several times.

In the end, there's only one thing I can think of to do next. I need to speak with Livia's mom, Roseline Samdi. Presumably without getting shot at again, which is easier said than done.

More pacing. Finally, it comes to me. I creep back upstairs and snag my jacket and flip phone. Lotham is snoring away, a soft, rumbling sound at odds with the deep scowl etched into his troubled face. I don't think his dreams are happy ones. One more thing we have in common.

I return downstairs, where I fumble through my jacket pocket till I find what I'm looking for: the phone list from my first AA meeting. Which includes Charlie's number. Six A.M. is definitely early by most night owls' standards. Charlie still picks up almost immediately.

"Who's this?"

"Frankie Elkin."

A pause. "You doing okay, Frankie?"

"I'm not about to take a drink, if that's what you're worried about. But I could use some help."

I explain to him about the discovery of Livia Samdi's body, coupled with the revelation that she has an older brother.

"I don't know the family well enough to know anything about that," Charlie says.

"I understand. I want to meet with Roseline. But last time I went to the house . . . Let's just say I like my head bullet-free."

"So what do you want from me?"

"Do you think you could reach out? AA to AA? Maybe get her to meet you somewhere. Say that little diner where you took me. I need to get her on neutral ground."

"I don't know if she'd listen."

"But you could try. Tell her you have information. About her daughter. But for her ears only. Which is true. I do have information for her ears only."

Charlie is silent for a long time. "I'll try," he says at last. "But no promises."

"Thank you, Charlie. And just . . . Well, I need to speak to her as soon as possible. Angelique Badeau's life is at stake."

"You remember what I said before? Plenty of folks don't like trouble. Especially some white woman barging in when she's not welcome and not wanted."

"Story of my life, big guy." Pause, then I say more softly, "I want to bring Angelique home. I want to get this right. I *need* to get this right."

"'God grant me the serenity to accept the things I cannot change,'" Charlie intones.

"I know."

"I'll see what I can do. But my guess is that family doesn't rise before noon, so it'll be a few hours."

"Thank you, Charlie."

He disconnects. I close up my phone. Noon gives me a solid five hours to do something. Next logical line of questioning? I mull the matter over while I climb back up the stairs. I open my door, then halt in my tracks.

Lotham's eyes are open and fully alert. He's not moving, though. Possibly because Piper is also awake and now perched on top of the bed, glaring at him.

"Help," he says as I enter my apartment.

"Is the big bad boxer scared of a little kitty?"

"Help," he says again.

But I don't move closer. I still have blood on my arm from last night. "I looked up Gleeson College. One of the pictures shows Livia Samdi in the background. I'm sure of it."

"What?" Lotham is startled enough to twist toward me. Piper immediately growls. He returns to his frozen state. I kind of like this game. And the view's not bad at all. Lotham, in a tight-fitting tank, is one good-looking man.

"Hang on, I'll find some food to distract her. Be right back."

"You're leaving me alone with her?"

"You have a gun."

"I'm not shooting a cat!"

"Good. Because I'm pretty sure she'll pull a *Pet Sematary* and come back even scarier."

I retreat downstairs, where I find a small container marked "Piper" in Viv's refrigerator. I dish out a few pieces of something that smells plenty foul and carry it back to my apartment. Piper is still on Lotham watch. Lotham still hasn't moved a muscle.

I set the dish on the floor. Minutes pass. Then with a final twitch of her tail, Piper leaps gracefully from the bed and pads over to the peace offering. She gives me a narrow look, then gulps down the pieces of chicken liver in two bites before retreating once more under the bed.

"It is now safe to move about the cabin," I inform Lotham. "Just don't step too close to the mattress. She likes to go for the heels."

"Great." Lotham sits all the way up, looking discombobulated, though whether that's from his long night, too little sleep, or a homicidal wake-up call, it's hard to be sure.

"I gotta go to work," he says.

Makes sense. I move to the end of the mattress, where I manage to climb up with a lunging step designed to avoid raking claws. I cross my legs, eye my evening's catch. I like the detective. I think he likes me. But I'm still not sure if I want to tell him about my plans regarding Roseline Samdi. In my experience, men tend to be over-protective, especially law enforcement types. Then I tend to get cranky, if not downright rebellious.

I should learn from my mistakes, but again, one of those things that's easier said than done.

"Who's Paul?" Lotham asks.

"Don't you have a murder to investigate?"

"I can spare five minutes."

"Too bad. The story takes at least thirty."

"Former lover, boyfriend, husband?"

"I've never been married."

He nods, that tells him enough. "How long were you together?"

"Nine months. Maybe a year. Depends how you want to count things."

"The infamous 'we can't even agree on our first date'?"

"Something like that. We met twelve years ago. He helped me get sober the first time around. He believed in me, when I needed someone to have more faith and perseverance than I did."

"And now?"

"Turned out 'normal' life wasn't for me. Not to mention he didn't approve of my new hobby. He thought I was being obsessive and self-destructive, substituting one addiction for another. It happens."

"He's an alcoholic."

"No. Just a man with a savior complex."

"So he helped you get sober—"

"I got myself sober, thank you very much."

"Touché. But you meet. First him helping, then it becoming more, until you get too interested in playing detective—"

"Are you trying to die this morning?"

"I had a rough night."

"Me, too, buddy. You want answers, ask some honest questions."

Lotham is silent for a while. His breathing has accelerated. Mine, too.

"Where is Paul now?"

"We parted ways ten years ago."

"Are you still in touch?"

"I dial his number on occasion."

"And he takes your call?"

"No. His widow does."

Lotham doesn't speak anymore. Neither do I.

"I'm sorry," he says at last.

"Nothing to do with you."

"Still . . ."

"Like you said, you have a murder investigation. And I have work to do, as well."

"Bartending tonight?"

"Shift starts at three."

"Until then?"

"Don't worry. I'll do my best not to get shot at or chased by anyone who looks like a mall-walking gangbanger."

"A girl has been murdered. Things are getting serious."

"I'm aware."

"You're a civilian—"

"Get out of my bed, Detective. Shower is that way, if you're interested. There's food down the street. As for me, I don't require a babysitter. I have my own life to tend to."

"Is it because Paul died?" Lotham asks me, his voice softer, genuinely curious. "And now you can't trust anyone?"

I lean forward slightly. "Or maybe, because I can't trust anyone, Paul died."

I climb off the bed, turning my back on the detective, and stripping off clothes. He wants to take in the show, that's his problem. I have work to do.

I pull on jeans, find a fresh T-shirt. And maybe, because the universe has its own sense of humor, the one I grab happens to be a faded red shirt with the stick figure of a happy camper standing in front of an old VW bus and distant mountains. *Life Is Good.* Paul gave it to me to celebrate three months sober, when we officially inaugurated our burgeoning relationship by going camping. The cotton is worn with age, a soft caress against my skin.

I don't look at Lotham. I grab my tennis shoes, head for the door. He doesn't call me back. Which is good, as I rat-a-tat down the stairs and into bright daylight.

Sun is still shining. The world still spinning.

And Angelique Badeau is still missing.

I get to work.

CHAPTER 31

I HEAD TO FRANKLIN PARK; it would be faster to take a bus, but after the night's adventures I could use the exercise to settle my churning mind. The park is on the map Charadee from Dunkin' Donuts drew for me the other day—a massive green space just beyond the rec center. The rec center is my next stop, but I doubt Frédéric will be in till late morning. And maybe it's my mood, or maybe it's another sign of my obsession, but I want to see where Livia's body was found.

I agreed with Lotham last night. How terrible to lose a child most of the world never knew was missing. Is that why I do what I do? Because I can't stand the thought of a life not mattering? Of a child being forgotten? Or a person sinking without leaving behind a single ripple in the universe?

I don't know. The vulnerability of Livia Samdi or Angelique Badeau speaks to me. After all, my own ties to this world are delicate at best. Should one of these cases take a wrong turn, that speeding bullet finally catch up with me . . . I don't know that there would even be a funeral. Maybe I'll just be gone. Which is both terrifying and comforting.

The walk is longer than I expected. A solid hour up a broad avenue. The weather is mild, the sun having traded in its summer warmth for fall chill. But the exercise refreshes me, helps clear my head and makes me glad I headed outdoors.

I come to the zoo first. It's small but charming, a classic city setup. This early it's still closed, but I spy a few women with young children prowling the fenced perimeter. No doubt they've been up since the crack of dawn and are already desperate for distraction.

I find a path and walk, though given the massive size of the park, wandering around aimlessly is probably not my best strategy. I decide to stick close to the main road that winds through the green space. I've played this game before, and the sad reality is that a human corpse can be carried only so far. Ergo, any body dump is going to be near a major thoroughfare.

Sure enough, fifteen minutes later I come across the first police cruiser, parked alongside the road to ward off looky-loos. Deeper into the park, near a copse of trees, I can just make out a sliver of yellow among the leaves. Crime scene tape. I have arrived.

I make a left turn, cresting a small rise. From this angle, I can peer down at the secured area. Another uniformed officer is pacing the perimeter, around and around. Poor officer has probably been here most of the night and is now doing his best to stay awake.

I can't see much. A few trees, a smattering of thick green bushes. I should've asked Lotham more questions. Was the body found laid out peacefully? Hands crossed over chest? Or just tossed to the ground? I'm no expert on murder, but I've been around enough investigations to know there's a difference. One being more personal, tinged with regret, colored by remorse. Say, what might happen if a family member had been forced to take dramatic action versus a third party who'd grown impatient with a terrified teen.

Livia's nails were chewed down to the nub, Lotham had said. A clear sign of stress.

I continue my study, and within minutes, I know what I need to know. There are plenty of other places to dump a body in this city. Dumpsters, back alleyways, abandoned buildings. But this placement: beautiful, serene, private.

The kind of person who would bring Livia's body here is the kind of someone who cared.

Livia's mysterious older brother? Or perhaps her other brother, drug-dealing J.J.? What about Angelique herself? Had she been forced to participate in this atrocity? Again, control 101. Establish fear and intimidation through death and destruction of the people your subject cares about most.

The pieces of this case swirl around me. Two girls with promising futures. At least one scam involving fake IDs. Coupled with a second scam involving a scenic university in Western Mass. Except what did that mean? Because both Livia and Angelique were pictured at the college, yet I didn't believe for a minute they'd run away to join some college under fake names.

I stand on the pathway. I can hear birds chirping, feel a soft breeze on my face. It is peaceful. It is beautiful.

I gaze down again where a girl's body was abandoned just last night. Livia Samdi deserved so much better. She deserved being found alive. She deserved growing up, discovering her own unique self. She deserved a life.

I feel now, more than ever, the weight of my own failure.

So many missing persons cases. And yet none I've brought home alive.

"I'm sorry," I whisper to Livia Samdi. Then I stand quietly and just be. Weigh the magnitude of my regrets. Resolve to do better, because that's the best any of us can do.

Then, ten, fifteen, twenty minutes later, I head back down the path, keeping away from the police, to the entrance of the park. Ten A.M. I already know where I'm headed next. Hopefully Frédéric will now be at work at the rec center.

Only one way to find out.

I HAVE TO walk all the way around the rec center building again. It's very quiet here, and with the outdoor fields and courts, it reminds me of the hushed beauty of Franklin Park. Is that significant? My mood has gone dark. Even with the sun on my face, I'm thinking of dead girls, and personal failures and memories that won't help me now.

Focus. I round the giant metal structure, finding the back doors unlocked and stepping gratefully inside. Once more the space is hushed and quiet. Lights out in the long corridor with pools of deeper dark marking the abutting classrooms and gym area. Such a huge space. Filled with plenty of nooks and crannies for Marjolie to sneak off with her boyfriend DommyJ. Not to mention shadowy corners perfect for drug exchanges, fake ID sales, and . . . ?

I have that tremor again. I don't know what's wrong with me. Starting my day with a handsome man who asks too many personal questions? Visiting a crime scene? I'm a mess of nerves. I don't like this building anymore. In its own way, it's also a crime scene. Where Angelique stood up to a bully with the help of her new friend. Where Livia Samdi thought her life was finally looking up. Where some summer programming happened to be going on in the background, but that had nothing on the real drama taking place among the teen participants. If these walls could talk . . .

I find my way to Frédéric's office on my first try. In my jumpy state, I'm walking softly, as if I don't want the ghosts of teenagers past to find me. As a result, when I rap lightly on the partially opened door, Frédéric startles, knocks a pile of papers off his desk, and whacks his computer monitor.

"Sorry." Not the most auspicious start to a conversation.

"How did you get in here?" he asks sharply.

"The back door was open."

"Mmm." He seems to collect himself. "I try to keep it locked when I'm alone in the building."

So I'm not the only one spooked by all this empty, lurking space.

"I just had a few more questions," I start.

Frédéric nods, bending down to collect his fallen papers. "You are looking for Angelique Badeau," he says, in his beautiful French-laced English. "I remember. Any word from the girl?"

"No. But after my conversation with you, we were able to connect Angelique with Livia Samdi. They were friends."

He nods, straightening his long, lean form, but the statement doesn't seem to mean much to him.

"Livia Samdi also disappeared. Eight months ago. This morning, the police found her body in Franklin Park."

Now Frédéric swallows hard. It's difficult to read his face. Stoic, resigned. As a man who works with at-risk kids in an inner-city neighborhood, he's probably had this conversation before. Does it make it easier to take?

"I am very sorry," he says at last. Then, more tentatively . . . "Overdose?"

"She was murdered." I deliver the words bluntly, and am rewarded by a ripple of emotion across his smooth dark features. Then he subsides once more to stoic acceptance.

"You believe Livia's death and Angelique's disappearance are related? That is why you have returned?"

"Yes."

"Why?"

"They met here. Became friends here. During the summer program."

Frédéric offers a shrug. "Are you sure they met here? Many of our kids already know each other. This neighborhood isn't that big."

"They met here. What can you tell me about DommyJ?"

The abrupt change in topic catches him off guard the second time. His face goes flat. Instinctive defense mechanism. As in he knows plenty about DommyJ, and is already mentally sorting out what he should and should not reveal. Question is, because he needs to protect himself and the program, or because he's afraid of DommyJ?

"What do you want to know?" he asks at last. Excellent strategy. When in doubt, answer a question with a question.

"I hear he deals in fake licenses."

"The subject came to our attention," Frédéric allows at last, steepling his fingers in front of him. "There was an incident, toward the end of the program. Angelique was involved. She was angry with DommyJ for selling an ID to her friend. But not that he shouldn't have coerced her friend into doing something illegal. Rather, the quality of the forgery was so poor, he should be ashamed of himself. She claimed he owed her friend a refund. Naturally, Dommy disagreed. I walked out in time to break up the altercation and order the three teens to my office. Upon further questioning, however, all parties involved denied there was a problem. You know how it is. My staff and I kept an eye out, but we never saw any more signs of trouble. Then the program was over, and the kids moved on."

"Do a lot of your charges buy fake IDs?"

"I have no idea."

"Come on. You work with teenagers. Surely you must have some sense of the demand?"

"Not really. The amount of illegal goods and services these kids can already get on any street corner, from drugs to guns to phones . . . This whole area is a black-market economy. You don't need valid ID for those kinds of transactions."

He raises a good point. Marjolie had wanted her ID to keep up with her club-hopping boyfriend. So there were some things the local dealer couldn't supply. But apparently, not much.

"What would've happened if you'd caught DommyJ selling fake IDs?"

"We would've kicked him out of the program. Zero-tolerance policy, remember?"

"Like you did with Livia Samdi's older brother?"

"J.J. Samdi? Yes, there were issues. He was banned from the rec center after a volunteer caught him selling drugs. The police were informed, though I don't know what became of the matter. We do not hold the sins of the brother against the sister, however. Livia Samdi remained welcome."

"Very enlightened of you."

Frédéric simply waits.

"Did you ever interact with J.J.?"

"Yes. As part of the after-school programming. We open up the courts for basketball, other sports, while offering mentoring opportunities, tutoring instructors, and special classes in art, video design, computer programming. Our mission is to keep these kids off the street. We must help them make good decisions, as they are growing up surrounded by bad ones."

"I have a friend who says he helps out with the mentoring. Charlie."

"Ah yes, Charlie. The kids, particularly the boys, like him very much. He is one of them. A survivor. When he talks, even our tougher teens will listen. And every now and then, it is enough to make a difference."

"J.J. wasn't the every now and then."

"No. Sadly."

"But Livia?"

"I didn't know her well enough. She was a gifted artist, as I said. But very quiet. She did our after-school programming, too. She worked with one of our teachers in one of the trade school courses."

Trade school catches my attention. "You have teachers come help out?"

"Of course."

"What about computer design classes? Say, taught by a Mr. Riddenscail?"

"Absolutely. He is very good. One of our few white teachers. The kids don't make it easy on him, but he is tougher than he looks. Has been working our after-school program for years."

"Were he and Livia close?" I ask immediately.

"She took one of his classes."

"And you have computers here?"

"A dozen. We got them through a special grant."

"What about a 3D printer?"

"Yes." He regards me curiously. "Through the same grant."

"Did Mr. Riddenscail write that grant?"

Frédéric sits up straighter. "As a matter of fact . . . Wait, I don't understand."

But I'm already moving. I need to reach Lotham. Demand that he get a warrant and return here immediately.

"I'll be back," I inform Frédéric.

"Wait," he says again.

But I don't. My sense of urgency has taken over. I must move, I must act. Livia is dead, Angelique may be next. The rec center, computers, 3D printers, forgeries. It all ties together. I feel like I'm on the edge of watching the pieces click into place. If I'm not already too late.

I nearly run down the long shadowy corridor. I bolt out the doors, back into the blinding sun, whipping out my cell phone to call Lotham.

And run smack into J.J. Samdi.

"Lady, I'm gonna fucking kill you."

CHAPTER 32

I DON'T HAVE MY WHISTLE in my pocket, or my tactical clips in my hair. I'd left my apartment in too much of a huff. I glance at my cell phone, move my thumb to hit emergency. But J.J. is one step ahead of me, knocking it out of my hand.

"Don't move a muscle." He pulls back the flap of his unbuttoned shirt enough for me to see the black butt of the pistol he has shoved into the waistband of his jeans. An intimidating sight, but a dumb move. He'll be lucky if he doesn't blow off his own balls.

We are twenty feet outside the rec center doors but out of sight of the street and, given how deep in the building is Frederic's office, light-years away from the closest known human. That leaves me and my charming personality versus a homicidal drug dealer.

I tell myself I've faced worse.

That might be a lie.

"Is the safety on or off?" I ask J.J.

The question catches him off guard. Score one for me.

"I would have the safety on. I mean, don't you have valuable body parts currently in the line of fire? Knee. Thigh. Or if you fumble getting it out, penis."

I like saying the word *penis* in front of boys. It never fails to fluster them.

"Stop talking!"

"I'm not saying it's common to shoot off a penis," I continue now. "But after seeing it once, it's not the kind of thing you forget. So really, I'm thinking of your own well-being." My voice drops. "Don't you think your mother has lost enough for one day?"

My quiet words hit him harder than my smartass comments. He recoils and the look on his face . . .

He's not just a homicidal brother. He's a grieving one.

"Stay away from my family. My mother doesn't need you or your fucking gorilla."

I take it Charlie's outreach didn't go as planned. I don't blame him. The situation had been dicey from the start, with Roseline Samdi in a very dark place, and that was before she'd learned her daughter was murdered.

"Did you shoot at me the other day, Johnson—"

"J.J.!"

"Are you the one who chased me out of your house?"

He regards me belligerently. His silence makes me believe he didn't do it. But there's a vein thrumming in his sweat-dotted brow and I swear the coils of ink snaking up his arms and around his throat are nearly vibrating with agitation. He's on something. His dark eyes are too dilated, his fingers twitchy. He's high, he's angry, and he hurts. A very dangerous combination.

I know. I've been there myself.

"Who is your older brother?" I ask.

"I don't have no older brother."

"Livia did. At least she told people she did. An older tall, skinny guy partial to gold chains and tracksuits. Very early two thousands. I've seen him myself."

"Son of a bitch."

"So you know him?"

"He's not our brother. I mean, he's a half brother. From some asshole my mom was with years ago. Damn fool went to prison. For all I know, he died there."

"You have a half brother who's been in prison?"

"Deke got sent up for armed robbery. He's ten years before my time. Fucking loser."

J.J. spits the words, his rage now directed at this half brother and less at me. J.J.'s still twitching more than I'd like, though. And his fingers keep plucking at his open blue plaid shirt, as if feeling for the comforting weight of his piece. He's geared himself up for battle. An armed druggie looking for a fight.

A half sibling who's spent quality time in prison. That would explain the outdated fashion sense. "Why is Deke a fucking loser?"

"Broke my mom's heart. She needed him to help out. Put food on the table, hold down the fort. I was just a kid at the time, but even I got that. Instead, he took off. Next thing we hear, he's busted for holding up a gas station. Good riddance, I think. But my mama cried every night. She didn't need that kind of shit."

"Versus *your* kind of shit?" I can't help but ask.

His response is immediate and defensive. "I do what I gotta do. It keeps a roof over our heads."

"And Livia?"

"What 'bout Livia? She's not into this shit. She's going to school. She's good, goddammit. She was good!"

J.J. whips out his gun. His cheeks are wet, his pain a feral beast I can practically watch claw at his throat. I once hurt that much, too. I know exactly how it feels. It allows me to take one step closer, then another, till we are nearly chest to chest.

He is so much bigger than me. All muscle and sinew, rage and grief. The gun is down at his side, but it would be very easy for him to raise it between us. Fire at me. Blow away himself. One last giant *fuck you* to a world that's done him wrong.

I don't move. I don't speak. I keep my gaze steady on his face, willing some of my calm into his trembling form.

"Angelique and your sister were friends. Close friends. Did you know that?"

He practically snarls at me. "No way!"

"Yes. They met here, during the summer program. Something happened. It scared your sister. And Angelique stepped up to help her. She disappeared that day, dressed in your sister's clothes. Posing as Livia."

J.J. shakes his head. His eyes are still wild. I can watch his erratic pulse throbbing at the base of his throat. "My sister didn't have friends. She was quiet. Kept to herself."

"Angelique was posing as her," I repeat.

"Why would my sister keep something like that a secret?"

"I don't know, J.J. Why would she?"

I can see the answer on his stricken face. Because it would've been one more thing for her to lose, in a house filled with a stoned brother and a drunk mother. In a house where she'd probably learned years ago to walk softly and never call undo attention to herself.

"Fuck!" J.J. explodes, waving his pistol, vibrating in place. He's going to hurt himself. Or me. Or all of the above. Later, he might regret it, but now, caught in waves of unbearable rage and unending grief . . .

Instead of shrinking away, I get right up into his foam-flecked face.

"Your sister's dead," I yell at him. "And someone's gotta pay, right? That's how it works. She's dead and some bastard did it and he needs to hurt! He needs to feel this pain. He needs to burn in agony, scream in terror, cower in fear. All of it. Over and over again. Till he feels exactly as terrible and awful as you do right now. I understand, J.J. I want that, too."

I have his full attention. It wasn't really that hard. I just had to tell him the words that ten years ago I most wanted to hear.

I grip his left shoulder. "Help me, help her. Can you do that, J.J.? Can you pull yourself together long enough to avenge your sister?"

"Is it Deke? He's out? He did this?"

J.J. moves to step away. I fist his shirt in my hand and hold on tight. "Fake IDs. What does your sister know about fake IDs?"

"What the hell—"

"Focus, J.J. Focus. Look at me. Listen. There was this kid here two summers ago who was selling really shitty fake IDs. Piss-poor quality. And your sister and Angelique embarrassed him."

"DommyJ."

"There you go. Did you ever see him around your home? Your sister mention his name?"

"Nah. But some of the guys talked about it. They said she got him good. And yeah, shitty fakes. I don't even see the purpose."

"Your sister knew exactly what was wrong with them. In detail. Why did your sister know so much about fake licenses?"

"I dunno. She's smart like that. She's always copying things and doing stuff on the school computer. She's gonna get out of this place, you know. First member of the family to make good." He catches himself. The use of the present tense. The statement of a dream that is now past.

The trembling starts again. I smooth my hand on his shoulder, rubbing slightly to soothe.

"Could DommyJ have hurt your sister in retaliation for her shaming him?"

"DommyJ's nothin' but a wannabe. Why do you think his fakes were so bad? He doesn't have the juice to be anything but a poser."

"Okay. So DommyJ isn't the badass he pretends to be. What about Deke? He was spotted hanging out around the rec center that summer, watching Livia. Maybe also talking to her?"

"She never said—"

"DommyJ appeared scared of him. So did Livia. Why would they be scared of him?"

J.J. looks down, issues a long, shaking sigh. Some of the tension is finally draining out of him. Less adrenaline, more rational thinking. "If Deke's out . . . He's got real connections. From his own days, plus serving time. Around here, you gotta respect that. If he showed up at my front door, I'd have to let him in. I wouldn't want to, but I'd have to."

"But he didn't show up? Didn't contact your mother? At least not that you're aware of?"

"I don't think she'd have anything to do with him. Especially not with Livia in the house. He's a cold motherfucker. Everyone knows that."

"Your mother said your house wasn't safe for girls. Was it Deke she was talking about?"

J.J. doesn't answer right away. But there's a look in his eyes. It wasn't the half brother Roseline Samdi was referring to. It was J.J. and his cronies, and he knows it.

"Would Deke know about making forgeries? Licenses, money, green cards, anything?" I force J.J. to focus on me again. I need him thinking. Angelique Badeau needs him thinking.

"I heard rumors," J.J. says at last. "Deke with some real OGs, courtesy of his dear old dad. They wanted to go upmarket. None of this drug shit. They wanted to be, like, crime bosses or something. Huge scores, major paydays. Word on the street was that they were in talks with some other gang. Gonna buy their way in. That's what the robberies were about. Proving themselves."

"And this other gang dealt in forgeries?"

"I dunno. Umm, coupla years after Deke left, I found some money. In a shoebox, back of the closet. Piles of hundreds. My lucky day, I thought. I started spending them left and right. Money, rent, you name it."

Drugs.

"Next thing I know, some dude is screaming at me I paid him in fakes. I had no idea what the hell he was talking about. I managed to talk my way out of it, but after that, I hid the rest. Didn't want to stir up more trouble."

"Your mother always live at that house? Even with your half brother, Deke?"

"We haven't gone anywhere."

"Meaning the fake bills, they could've been Deke's, part of his new criminal enterprise?"

"Coulda. I was just a kid."

But I'm already nodding. The counterfeit hundreds had to be the older half brother's stash. It was the only thing that made sense. Part of a larger operation he'd started, only to get busted and sent to prison. He must not have told anyone about it, hence the bills were all but forgotten before J.J. stumbled upon them. Years later, Livia probably did the same.

Except maybe she'd recognized the bills as counterfeit from the start. Either way, she knew enough not to tell her brother J.J. Instead, she smuggled them out of the house, giving them to her new friend, Angelique, for safekeeping.

And became inspired as well? Fake hundreds, fake licenses. Maybe she'd decided to take a crack at it with her own design skills and new and improved computer technology. That part I don't completely understand yet. More importantly, how did Deke fit into that scenario? Because clearly, he was out of prison and tracking his baby half sister. He approached her? She approached him?

"Was Livia ever close to your half brother?" I ask now.

J.J. shakes his head. "She was three when he took off."

"Did he seem partial to her? Like protective or anything?"

"Hell if I know. That's too long ago."

I nod, decide to come at it from a different direction. "What about school? Did your sister ever mention one of her teachers, Mr. Riddenscail?"

"Nah."

"He also worked at the rec center. Part of the after-school programming?"

"How many times can I say, I don't know!"

"It's okay, J.J. I understand. You had your life, and your sister had hers. And part of your life was to get her out of here. Part of your life was to ensure she could do better."

He doesn't answer, but his silence tells me enough.

"Your sister met her teacher, Mr. Riddenscail, here." I gesture to the rec center behind us. "Your sister also met your older half brother, Deke, on this property. Why, J.J.? I need to know why."

But J.J. can't answer the question. I can see it in the growing wildness around his eyes. He loved his sister, but he hadn't spent time with her. He didn't know her as well as I needed him to know her right now.

Had anyone?

"I fucking hate you," J.J. whispers.

"I understand," I assure him softly. "Some days, I hate me, too.

But I'm going to find out who killed your sister, and you're going to help me. Because she deserved better, right? Because . . . She was Livia Samdi. Bright and clever and alive. And the world should mourn her. All of us should know your pain. She is worth it."

He nods miserably.

"I need you to tell me where I can find Deke."

"Oh, I'll find him—"

"No, no, no. We need him alive. I have questions only he can answer. For your sister's sake, no killing your half brother. Promise me, J.J."

"Livia's dead," he says. And I can tell from the look on his face that it's the first time he's spoken the words out loud. The permanence of them is like a knife, slashing across his face. What it leaves behind . . . Even I have to look away.

I smooth my hand one last time across J.J.'s shoulder, then pull back. I'm sorry for his loss. All these years later, I'm sorry for my loss, too.

"Your sister loved Angelique Badeau. Whatever happened this past year, they were in it together. I know it. We find Angelique, we discover who killed your sister. We do right by both of them. Okay? So Deke. Where can I find him?"

J.J. doesn't answer right away. Finally, he takes a deep breath. Straightens up. Returns the gun to the waistband of his jeans.

He picks up my phone from where it dropped on the ground, flipping it open. His fingers fly across the tiny keys. Then he folds it closed, hands it back to me.

"Don't worry," he says. "When the time comes, I'll find you."

CHAPTER 33

I FEEL LIKE I HAVE my breathing relatively under control by the time I dial Lotham, but I must not be as good as I think because in a matter of seconds:

"What's wrong? Where are you? Is it the guy in the tracksuit?"

"The guy in the tracksuit has a name. Deke. He's Livia and Johnson Samdi's older half brother."

"What?"

"I ran into J.J."

"*What?*"

"This would go faster if you'd stop interrupting."

"Are you okay? Tell me that much."

"I'm fine. I visited the rec center. Now I'm walking home having made some progress." I'm not walking home, but I don't feel like telling Lotham that particular detail. "From the top?"

"Christ," Lotham says. He sounds exhausted. "From the top."

"Roseline Samdi has an older son named Deke by another man. Apparently, Deke has been in prison for armed robbery, but he's clearly out now, and he's the one who was watching Livia at the rec center."

"Why?"

"I don't know. According to J.J., his own mother would have nothing to do with Deke, he's such a cold bastard. But get this. Shortly after Deke went to prison, young J.J. stumbled upon a shoe box filled with counterfeit hundreds. He was working his way through spending them all when he got caught passing forgeries. After that, he tucked the rest away, where I'm guessing Livia discovered them years later."

"Older brother Deke had a stash of counterfeit hundreds?"

"Apparently he was an aspirational criminal. Wanted to get into the big leagues. Armed robbery was a means to buy his way into another, larger criminal enterprise that offered better career advancement."

Lotham doesn't talk right away. It's a lot to take in, so I don't blame him.

"You think Deke knew his half siblings were peddling his pre-prison counterfeit stash?"

"I don't know. Deke is clearly out now and had some kind of interaction with Livia. Livia had clearly discovered the counterfeit bills and passed them along to Angelique. Which leaves us with? Half brother and sister comparing notes on forgeries, bigger criminal enterprises, future career opportunities? Hell if I know. But Marjolie links Livia to Deke, and according to J.J., anything involving Deke is bad news."

"You got a last name?" Lotham asks.

"I didn't think to ask that," I admit.

"Can't be too hard to track down. One paroled armed robber named Deke. Vice or gang taskforce probably has him on file."

"But wait, there's more."

Another silence. This one radiates tension. As if Lotham is angry at me. Which gets me huffy, because what does he have to be pissed off about? I'm the one doing all the work here.

"Go ahead," he says at last, and there's definitely a cool edge to his voice. Big bad Boston cop frustrated that the civilian is making all the cool discoveries? Fuck him, I think. But my feelings are hurt.

"I went to the rec center," I hear myself say, "to talk with the director again. Turns out, in addition to the summer program, the center offers after-school activities. Including a class in computer design taught by none other than Mr. Riddenscail. Who wrote a grant gifting the center with twelve computers and one 3D printer."

Lotham manages not to exclaim *what* this time, but I can tell he's thinking it.

"Livia Samdi was in that class," he states.

"Yep."

"Angelique?"

"I didn't ask. Livia's attendance is grounds enough for a warrant, right? I mean, she goes missing, then turns up dead. Surely some judge somewhere will grant you access to the rec center's computers."

"I think I can manage that much."

"Don't hurt anything." Now I'm the edgy one.

"I looked up Paul," Lotham says abruptly. "I found the case, Frankie. I know what happened."

I don't say anything. It's not a question and doesn't deserve an answer. Besides, it's none of his business. It's no one's business but mine and Paul's. And yet all these years later, ten long years later, I can feel my throat closing up and my eyes starting to sting.

I think of J.J. and his feral grief. I know exactly how he feels.

"What are you doing?" Lotham asks me quietly. "Between you and me, Frankie. What are you doing here?"

"Finding Angelique Badeau."

"It won't change anything."

"I'm not an idiot."

"And if you get yourself killed in the process? Is that what you want? You don't have the courage to do it yourself, so you'll just keeping chasing this madness till someone does it for you?"

"Fuck you." But there's no heat behind the words. He's not saying anything I haven't wondered myself. "Don't you have a murder to investigate?"

"As I believe you told me once, I can multitask."

"Then what do you have to show for the morning, because I just gave you plenty."

"I have bags of trace evidence and piles of security feeds to watch. I can tell you a plain white van pulled into Franklin Park shortly after midnight. I know the license plate was smeared with mud to obscure the numbers. I can tell you the driver's face is hard to make out, but height and profile is about right to be a tall, skinny Black male. I can also tell you, there was a passenger in the van. She was wearing a ball cap."

"Deke and Angelique," I murmur. But then I catch myself. "Except it can't be Deke, because he was standing outside my window last night."

"According to the time stamp on the video . . . You're probably right, it's not Deke."

Which leaves me as confused as Lotham feels. Clearly there were other players involved, who'd kidnapped Angelique and Livia, who most likely took turns watching over the girls. But again, who and why? What the hell had Angelique and Livia gotten themselves into that involved both of them missing for nearly a year, not to mention a college in Western Mass?

"I have to go," I tell Lotham.

"I need to know you're being careful, Frankie. No chasing down this Deke. Meeting with J.J. Samdi was risky enough."

"I'm not looking for Deke," I say, thinking, no need. J.J.'s got it covered.

"Will you please talk to me?"

"No. This is my life, my choices. Manage your own."

I click off the phone. I honestly don't want to hear it. I'm well aware of my strengths, and I'm well aware of my weaknesses. And I've designed a lifestyle that fits both accordingly.

Right now, that lifestyle involves locating Angelique Badeau.

I don't have a time machine. There's nothing I can do that will ever change what happened ten years ago. No amount of handwashing that erases the blood, no amount of repenting that eases the guilt. I screwed up. Paul died. It is both that simple and that haunting.

And now? Now my life is about helping others, serving victims.

I already failed Livia Samdi. Meaning now, more than ever, I need to get this right.

Angelique Badeau, here I come.

I TAKE A taxi to Livia's school. I don't have the time or energy to figure out the maze of buses it takes to get from here to there. Class is in session when I talk my way through the front doors and head to Mr. Riddenscail's room. I let myself in, standing in the back. He's not lecturing, but drifting from workstation to workstation, checking each student's designs, offering comments here and there. He spots me immediately, pausing as he inspects a male student's drawing on the computer monitor. His guilty conscience? Does he already know why I'm here or at least suspect he couldn't get away with it forever?

I'm not the police, but I don't need to be. I want answers. After that, Lotham can have at him.

I wait. Riddenscail continues to focus on his class. Twelve computers, I note now. The same number as at the rec center. This is where it started, I think. Whatever it is that got Livia and Angelique in so much trouble. The idea to design their own fake IDs? If a jerk like DommyJ could do it, why not them? Livia would be the design team, Angelique marketing. Both had the brains to think bigger, better. Livia would knock off near-perfect fakes. Angelique would sell them. Given the number of underage college kids in Boston looking to join Marjolie's club-hopping and pub-crawling ways . . . That would certainly explain the amount of cash in Angelique's lamp, while Livia would've contributed the counterfeit hundreds from her own household.

Had they thought if they mixed the fake Franklins with real bills it would improve their chances of being able to spend the money?

Which is where I started to get lost again. Why the college pics? No way two teenagers ran off to attend a college under an alias. Let alone, why would Angelique have dressed up as Livia to do so, and why would Livia appear so terrified?

Then there was Livia's meeting with her long-lost half brother. Not to mention Livia's body, discovered just this morning, laid out in a tranquil park environment . . .

Running out of time. Livia dead, Angelique soon to follow. What happened, what happened, what happened?

I had so many questions for Mr. Riddenscail. And no more patience for lies.

A bell finally rings. The students rise, pack up their stuff. Several of them eye me curiously. Mr. Riddenscail and I are the only white people in the room. Maybe they think I'm his girlfriend or an acquaintance coming to meet him. No one asks. The kids simply shuffle out the door, some already deep in conversation as they head to the next classroom.

No kids file in to take their place. I must've caught Mr. Riddenscail on a break.

He's already moved to the front of the room, where he's pecking away at his keyboard. Lotham should get a warrant for that computer. He probably will. He's thorough that way. Looking up Paul . . .

I order myself to focus.

"I assume you have more questions about Livia?" Riddenscail says at last. "Or would you like to learn more about 3D printers, the AutoCAD platform, design basics?"

"I've come from the rec center," I say, watching him closely for his response.

He taps a few more keys, then glances up. He regards me patiently, as if waiting for me to say more.

"I know about the grant. The computers and 3D printer you got for the after-school program. The class you taught there that also included Livia Samdi."

He continues to stare at me blankly.

"Why didn't you tell us that earlier?"

"Honestly? I didn't think of it. You were asking questions about Livia in this class, so that's what I focused on."

"You made it sound like you didn't really know her. Yet you had her for multiple classes at multiple locations. That doesn't sound like a distant relationship to me."

"Actually, I told you I'd pushed her to sign up for a spring competition. That's what she was working on at the rec center. Preparation. That location was more convenient for her, as it was walking distance from her house. Plus, she needed my help to figure out some of the newer tricks involving the software. So when I was running the after-school program at the rec center, it made more sense for her to join me there. I said she was gifted and I was trying to get her to come out of her shell. I'm sorry if I missed some of the details."

"Livia Samdi is dead."

Now I get a response. His face goes pale. He sits down heavily in his desk chair.

"When?" he asks softly.

"They found her body this morning." I peer at him closely. But I don't see any evidence of guilt. Just shock, and maybe even grief.

He swallows hard. "What happened?"

"Someone strangled her, then dumped her body in Franklin Park."

"Oh my God. That poor girl." He trembles slightly, wipes at his eyes.

"What was she doing here? What had she gotten herself into? It's time to talk, Riddenscail. Before you find yourself hauled in on murder charges. What the hell did you have her doing?"

"I have no idea what you're talking about. And I certainly didn't kill anyone. She had such promise. I was sure she was going to get out, go off to college. I already hoped . . ."

He shudders again, swipes his eyes with the back of his hand. If I didn't know any better, I would say the man is crying.

Maybe I don't know any better. I finally move away from the door and approach. "Look at me."

Riddenscail drops his hand. His cheeks are wet with tears. He looks devastated.

"Don't you think this is a bit much for a student you claim you didn't even know?"

"I know enough. I saw enough. What, you think I'm doing this

job for the great pay?" He waves his hand around the tired classroom, with its beat-up linoleum floor and stained drop ceiling. "I
show up each day for kids like Livia. The ones who sit in front of
those computers, and for the first time in their lives can see their
own futures. The software clicks for them, 3D design makes sense.
And just like that, they have college potential and job opportunities
and an entirely new track to follow. Those kids make everything
else worth it. Those kids are why people like me become teachers in
the first place."

I continue to regard him suspiciously, but I'm finding less and
less justification. So far, this conversation isn't going anything like
I'd thought.

"Could Livia have forged a driver's license? Did she understand
design and computers that well?"

Riddenscail stares at me. Abruptly, he reaches into his pocket.
I'm just stiffening in alarm when he withdraws a small key, inserts
it into the lock on his desk drawer, and opens it. He pulls out his
wallet, from which he takes his driver's license. For inspection, I
realize. Because how many of us truly pay attention to such things.

"You were asking about forgeries and stamps earlier. Could
Livia forge something. But I thought you were looking at currency."

"We're now thinking fake IDs."

He nods slowly, turns his own Massachusetts driver's license
over in his hand. "The background, definitely easy. I bet you can
find a template online. The hologram, that's specialized technology,
ink. I don't think she could do that. Certainly, I don't know how."

"She faked it with brighter ink. Not perfect, but close enough
for say, getting into a bar."

"Given that, yeah, Livia could design and print out a license.
Especially if the standard is merely close enough. But I never saw
her working on anything like that here. Not that she'd need the

AutoCAD. This is way simpler than 3D design. But she would need a computer and a very high-quality printer for the specialty inks."

"You have that kind of printer here?"

"Yes. But I don't have fancy ink cartridges. The basic ones are expensive enough."

"Detective Lotham will be here soon with a warrant. And given that printers store information in their cache, you might as well tell me now."

Riddenscail shakes his head. "I have nothing to tell. If Livia was counterfeiting licenses, it wasn't on my watch and it wasn't here. I haven't seen her since January. So warrant away. For that matter, this school is covered in cameras. Check them, too. Livia hasn't been here. If she had . . . I would've tried to get her back into school. I would've tried to connect with her, find out what made her go away. I would've—"

His voice breaks. He rubs his eyes again.

I want to say something, press the advantage, but I've got nothing. Abruptly, I feel stupid, standing in front of a classroom, making a grown man cry.

"Did you ever see Livia with a tall, skinny guy, prone to retro fashion statements?"

Mr. Riddenscail looks right at me. "Older guy? Definitely. At the rec center. He met up with her several times when she was done. I assumed he was her father, come to walk her home. I thought it was sweet."

"He wasn't her father," I inform him, "but her recently paroled half brother. If you see him again, please contact the police immediately."

"Okay." Mr. Riddenscail's voice has dropped again, clearly getting overwhelmed.

"Have you ever heard of Gleeson College?" I press him, trying desperately to gain some shred of data from this conversation. "It's located in Western Mass."

"No. But then, I can't even begin to list all the colleges in Boston."

"Can I show you something? On your computer. It'll only take a minute."

He nods, pushing back from his desk as I take over the keyboard. I load up the website for Gleeson College, scrolling through till I find the picture with Livia in the background. Then I gesture for Riddenscail to join me.

"That certainly looks like Livia. On a college website. Huh." He frowns, grabbing the mouse and scrolling down the page to view more photos. Then he clicks on various options from the drop-down menu, surfing the site, with its photo after photo of laughing, happy kids sitting before rolling green hills. "Hang on. I may have something for you. I swear I've seen this before . . ."

More internet navigation. Riddenscail flies across the screen, clearly a guy comfortable with technology. He opens and closes a series of pages in rapid succession. I barely have time to note the names of colleges before he's moved on, one after another after another.

Then: "Got it." He steps back, indicating for me to move in closer. I study the screen, then frown at him. "You have the website open in two different windows."

"Look at the title bar."

I read the headings. Gleeson College, says one. Lannister College, says the other. The photos are the same. Smiling kids in classrooms. Laughing kids hanging out in front of rolling green hills. They aren't similar; they're identical.

"Give me a sec." Riddenscail grabs the keyboard, his fingers flying. He's back on the page for Gleeson, clicking on links at the bottom. Again, too fast for me to follow.

"Okay, you need a computer forensic specialist to be sure, but this website for Gleeson, it's months old. As in, this whole college magically sprang to life over the summer. With most of these photos lifted from other colleges' websites. At least the outside shots and pictures of buildings. And I'm going to guess from several different schools, now that I'm studying it more."

"I don't get it."

"Let me put it this way. I don't know if Livia was faking licenses, but to judge by this website, she definitely faked a school. Though why you'd invent an entire college . . ." Riddenscail shakes his head at me. "Your guess is as good as mine."

CHAPTER 34

EXIT LIVIA'S SCHOOL FEELING befuddled and overwhelmed. I need to get back to Stoney's for my work shift. I need to call Lotham and let him know about Gleeson College. I need . . . magic answers, the secrets of the universe, an X that marks the spot. I rub my forehead, squinting against the bright sun as I pull my phone out of my pocket.

I'd just flipped it open when it starts ringing. I answer it in surprise. "Hello?"

"This is Emmanuel. They say the police found a girl's body. In Franklin Park. Is it . . ."

"Oh, honey. It's *not* Angelique. I'm so sorry, Emmanuel. You didn't need to be worried. If it were Angelique, your family would be the first notified, not the morning news."

Emmanuel doesn't speak right away. I can hear his breathing, hard and ragged. He must've been terrified. And why the hell hadn't Lotham or Officer O'Shaughnessy contacted Guerline and her nephew?

"What . . . what about the other girl?" Emmanuel murmurs. "LiLi's secret friend?"

I wince. I'd hoped he wouldn't connect those dots. I'm not sure how much I should say without his aunt present. But my general policy is to start with the truth.

"The body was identified as Livia Samdi."

Loud swallow. "How was she killed?"

"The police are still investigating."

"And LiLi? Have there been any more sightings? Now, with her friend dead . . ." His voice edges toward fresh panic.

"No new sightings. But that's good, Emmanuel. It means she's alive. We're going to find her."

Long pause. Then, very softly: "I'm scared."

"I'm scared, too."

"You said you found people. Why can't you find her? Why can't anyone find LiLi?"

I give him a moment to deal with his grief. Of course he's frustrated and terrified. I'm the professional, and I feel the same way myself. So I treat Emmanuel how I would like to be treated. I give him something to do.

"Emmanuel, have you ever heard of Gleeson College?"

"No." Shuddery sigh. He's regaining control, caught off guard by my question. Which is exactly what I wanted.

"It appears Livia or your sister created a website for a fake college. Can you think of any reason why? The website is new, as in from this summer. I'm guessing you'll be able to determine that much. Most of it appears to be derived from stock photos copied from other, existing universities."

"I . . . I don't know why anyone would do that. Gleeson C? I'll look it up."

Perfect project for the internet junkie and a legitimate task. Our assumption had been that Angelique and Livia had been kept alive for their skills. Though forging a college had never entered our thoughts. And still confused me. But still. The college was a forgery, as Riddenscail had revealed. Completed this summer. With Livia now dead just months later. Because that had been the task and it had been completed? Though again, what could be so special about a college website?

I momentarily change gears. "What about the name *Deke*? Or, have you seen a tall skinny guy in a tracksuit and gold chains hanging around your house?"

"No, no. I don't know any Deke. Is he another new friend of my sister's?"

"He's a person of interest in the investigation," I say, sounding so much like a cop I'm worried Lotham has contaminated me.

"A suspect?" Now Emmanuel is excited.

"Not necessarily. But close. We're making progress. I promise, Emmanuel. There is nothing more important to me right now than your sister. Me, Detective Lotham, Officer O'Shaughnessy, we are on this. Full time, all the time, completely obsessed. Now, shouldn't you be in school?"

"I was. But then I heard the news. And I couldn't . . . I just couldn't. I am outside now. There's a no-cell-phones policy in the classrooms." Emmanuel pauses. "I found something."

"With the fake license? You decoded the number?" My turn for excitement.

"I can't figure out the license number. It is something, but I'm not sure what. I have a friend with a computer program for algorithms. I'm taking it to him. But the other things, my mother's birthday, the year of Haiti's independence. LiLi misses my mom."

I nod into the phone. He had mentioned this before.

"So . . . I got down my mother's picture. And I opened it up."

I don't have the heart to tell him I already tried that trick.

"There's a piece of paper in the back. With a note from LiLi and a drawing from me. It is our offering to our *manman*. But this time, when I unfolded it, another slip of paper fell out."

Now he has my attention. I'd just noted the sweet picture, never realizing it was on a folded scrap of paper. I'd been focused on locating evidence of more obvious crimes.

"It's a receipt to an electronics store. Written across the top is a number. A phone number, in LiLi's handwriting."

"Emmanuel, do you have the receipt on you?"

"Yes."

"Look at it. What did she purchase?"

"I already saw. A Tracfone."

And just like that, I'm beyond excited. "Emmanuel, this is perfect! We know your sister had been using a burner phone, correct?"

"Yes."

"But the police haven't been able to do anything without a phone number. There's nothing to trace, track, et cetera."

"You can trace a Tracfone?"

"If it has GPS technology, yes you can. And these days, most of them do. It also has to be on at the moment of tracking."

Emmanuel is getting it now. "The police, they could ping this number? Locate my sister? Just like that?"

"Assuming she has the phone on her." I hesitate, just now seeing the flaw in my plan. "Which . . . may be a long shot. I'm assuming she bought the phone last fall?"

"August thirty-first."

"I would guess it's the one she used to communicate with Livia. Once Angelique disappeared, I don't know if she would've kept the phone." If she would've been allowed it, assuming she was being held against her will.

"Oh." Emmanuel's voice grows small. He's a smart kid. He already understands what I'm not saying. What kind of kidnapper lets his victim keep her cell phone?

"But." I do my best to rally. "There's other information the police should be able to access, including previous calls, copies of texts, saved voice mails. There's no telling how much we'll learn from those alone. Including exactly what Angelique and Livia were up to."

"Livia is dead," Emmanuel says. His voice has definitely changed. He sounds flat, almost grim. Like a thirty-year-old man, versus a teen. "If she's been killed . . ."

"We're going to find your sister, Emmanuel. And you finding this receipt, that's huge. Your sister's talking, but you're the one hearing. You get her messages." My voice grows thick, despite myself. "You're doing right by her, Emmanuel. I can't . . ." My voice trails off. I have no words to tell him the power of this bond. I just hope he understands. Whatever happens next, it's not his fault. It's on me. And Detective Lotham. And neither one of us wants that kind of regret.

Though I can already picture Livia's brother J.J. The kind of grief and rage that had the tattoos crawling across his skin. I would like to say we will do better, but fifteen dead bodies later, I don't know. And it haunts me. Every case, every discovery, Lani Whitehorse's body at the bottom of her local lake, it all haunts me.

I force myself to speak: "I need you to contact Officer O'Shaughnessy. Let him know about the receipt. The police need it immediately."

"I have it in a plastic bag," Emmanuel says.

Which makes me smile. His very own evidence bag. He has been paying attention.

"Gleeson College," I remind him, glancing at my watch. I need to get moving.

"I'll look it up," he promises.

"The site includes a photo with your sister, as well as one with Livia. Just so you know."

"I'm good with websites. I should be able to learn more, especially if it's new, and copied from other sites."

"Thank you, Emmanuel. And just . . . keep an eye out. Okay? For your sister, for anything out of the ordinary."

"I'm spending the afternoon at my friend's."

"Good. Sounds like a plan."

Emmanuel ends the call, I remain standing on the corner, phone still in hand. I'm exhausted, I realize now. And overwhelmed, but also overstimulated. Hyperaware. Which makes me feel it. That itch between the shoulder blades. Someone is watching me. I turn in place, not caring if I'm being obvious. I have to know. I want to see him.

But I just spot random pedestrians walking down the street. One guy here. Two women there. It's quiet this time of day. A little too late for lunch, a little too early to be headed home.

One last look, then I start walking to the larger boulevard. I'm going to have to flag down a taxi, burn through more precious dollars. But I'm running out of time.

Angelique's running out of time.

I dial up Lotham and prepare for his next lecture.

I COME FLYING into work right at three P.M., after having just enough time to dart upstairs, wash my hands and face, and clip back my hair. Perfectly ready. Not late at all. I hit the tables, grabbing chairs, flipping them to the floor. Spray, wipe, spray, wipe. Then behind the bar, drying trays of clean glasses, stacking them up. To the kitchen. Lemons, limes, and cutting board. Slice, peel, slice, peel. Garnish tray filled. Countertop sparkling. Peanut bowls filled, ketchup bottles topped off. Beer kegs properly pressurized.

Ten minutes left, I attack the shelves of booze, pulling down each bottle, furiously wiping everything, then lining the bottles back up in perfect order. I scrub down the edge of the shelves, touch up the mirrored backdrop.

When I turn around, Stoney is standing there, staring at me.

"Rough day?" he asks.

"My head hurts."

"Heard they found a girl's body."

"Livia Samdi. The other missing girl." I falter, my hands falling to the countertop. "She was murdered."

Stoney waits.

"I've been trying so hard to figure out the missing pieces, to reconstruct the trail that will lead us to both Livia and Angelique. But I didn't make it in time. Once again, I'm too late." I hate the raw edge to my voice, but I can't stop it. These cases shouldn't be personal to me. But they are. That's the thing I can't help, and Paul couldn't understand.

Stoney waits.

"I just . . . I want to get it right," I confess in a rush. "I want to be the one who brings home the missing loved one. I want to be there for the parade of hugs and sheer relief. Fourteen cases later, I *need* to get it right."

"Angelique Badeau is still alive," Stoney states.

"As far as we know."

"Then you still got a job to do." Stoney holds up his key ring.

I get his drift. Working out there, working in here. Livia is gone.

But Angelique still needs me. Charlie would approve of this strategy. Focus on the souls you can still save.

Not on the pieces of yourself you lost along the way.

I unlock the front door and get to it. Happy hour starts off too slow for my jangly nerves. I refill peanut bowls the second they're down a nut, top off water glasses after the first sip. Given how many of my customers didn't even ask for water, I earn plenty of strange looks. But I have to keep moving. To stand still is to think. To think is to descend once more into the abyss. Fake IDs, fake colleges, one dead girl. And one caring younger brother desperate to see his sister again.

Lotham hadn't been in a chatty mood when I'd called him. He'd been as confused as I was to learn that Gleeson C wasn't a real college. Intrigued by the possibilities of the Tracfone receipt and phone number Emmanuel had discovered. And definitely mum on the subject of Deke's last name, which I was already guessing wasn't Samdi.

Lotham had been denied the warrant for the rec center's computer, he'd volunteered grumpily. Not enough probable cause that the computers were connected to Livia's murder, given her body had been found nine months after she'd last visited the place. He should be able to get a warrant for Angelique's missing Tracfone, however, and yeah, they could absolutely try pinging it, let alone the data dump of text messages, incoming calls, et cetera. At this point, we could use a lucky break.

I'd ended the call with Lotham with the same tension we'd had at the beginning. Maybe Livia's murder had taken its toll on both of us. Maybe we had taken a toll on us.

Shortly after six P.M., a familiar form walks through the door and I exhale a giant sigh of heartfelt relief. Charlie ambles up to the bar and takes a seat. I already have a glass of water waiting for him. "Coffee, food, nonalcoholic beer?"

"Viv working?"

"Yes, sir."

"Then I'll take a burger. Tell her it's for me." The man definitely has a twinkle in his eye. And I bet when I mention his name, Viv will have that same sparkle. Have to hand it to the woman, she has good taste in men.

I head to the kitchen to place the order. Sure enough, Viv positively preens. "You tell Charlie I got him covered."

"Aren't you married?"

"To the best man in the world, absolutely, honey. But it never hurts to look. YOLO, baby."

"I have no idea what that means."

"Don't I know it. Speaking of which, where's your handsome hunk this evening?"

"Probably sitting at his desk sulking. Apparently, he likes his strong, independent women less strong and less independent. Men." I shrug.

"He'll come around, sweet cheeks. The good ones always do."

"Ah, but being the strong independent type, I'm not sitting around waiting for the phone to ring."

"And more power to you. You give Charlie a hug for me. That man has the best arms."

I don't want to know how she knows that. I return to the bar with a cup of fresh coffee for Charlie, then check in with a couple of customers. Next lull, I plant myself across from him, arms folded, ears waiting.

"Sorry about Mrs. Samdi," Charlie says. "I stopped by in person. Her son didn't take it so well."

"It's okay. In a weird way, it worked out. J.J. tracked me down himself, told me some interesting stories of an older half brother named Deke, who apparently had connections in the counterfeiting world as well as a penchant for armed robbery."

"Deke Alarie? You serious?"

"That's his full name? And I'm being completely serious. Now fess up. What should I know?"

"Alarie's a big name back in the day. French for 'all power' and, boy, did he live up to it. Cold bastard. If he decided he wanted what you had, or you were a threat to what he had . . ." Charlie shook his head. "Kind of guy who'd sell out his own mother to get ahead, that's for sure. Maybe he did."

"I imagine he had some equally cold associates?"

"Deke ran with a serious-shit kind of crowd. Kind of men you should have your detective friend look into. Not for you, little lady. Not for you." Charlie's deep voice is so serious, I'm almost tempted to listen. "Last I heard, Deke Alarie had just started some new business partnership, but then he got sent away for armed robbery, and that was that."

"What did you hear about him and counterfeit bills?"

"Nothing. But if there was a gangster interested in getting involved in something that sophisticated . . . Yeah, Deke Alarie, I could see it."

"So maybe his new business partners hooked him up?"

"Even gangsters have dreams, you know."

I roll my eyes.

He gives me a wink. Then his expression sobers. "Any news on Angelique Badeau?"

"Nothing yet. With Livia murdered . . . I don't know. Something's clearly changed and it can't bode well for Angelique." I lean closer. "We're pretty sure Livia and Angelique were selling fake IDs. Except, I can't figure out how that would lead to kidnapping. Like you and I talked about, sure, there's money in fakes, but these aren't top-dollar forgeries."

"DIY enterprise."

"Exactly. So how did they get from *that* to being abducted? Holding two teenagers against their will . . . That's high-risk stuff, and complicated logistics. Gotta involve more than a few people, meaning also a larger-scale enterprise. No longer DIY."

"More like a gang?"

"Yeah. Which made me think of Livia's brother J.J., except based on his reaction to his sister's death, no way. Which leaves us with half brother Deke, plus a few of his associates."

Charlie nods slowly. "Sounds about right."

"But doing what, Charlie? Fake drinking IDs can't be *that* big money. Like you said, fake passports, identity packages, hell, work visas, that all makes sense. But how do you get from good-enough driver's licenses to that level of expertise?"

Charlie frowns, taps his coffee mug, frowns again. Viv rings from the kitchen. I head off to fetch Charlie's burger, then get busy settling bills, refreshing drinks.

By the time I return, Charlie has an idea. "You need an expert."

"Expert what?"

"Forger. Someone who can walk you through the logistics. That's how you catch a criminal, right? What do they need? What are the issues? That kind of thing. Think like a forger."

"I met with Livia's AutoCAD teacher. He said the licenses would involve a computer and specialty printer, plus some expensive inks. Didn't sound that complicated, or as if it would require tons of space." I pause, consider. "Though definitely they have to be working out of somewhere. Maybe the same place the girls have been kept?" I have another thought. "Probably someplace local, as Angelique's been spotted walking around Mattapan. Here's the other thing: The girls had created a website for a college that doesn't exist. And they'd gone into great detail. Photos of a campus, course offerings, a message from the president. The whole nine yards."

Charlie takes a bite of his burger, chews thoughtfully. "Why a fake college?"

"That's the question. From forged IDs to a fake college. I'm lost."

More chewing, swallowing. I spy a customer trying to grab my attention. I get back to work. Charlie is finishing off his burger by the time I return. I pour him more water.

"There was this thing," he starts. "Five, six years ago. Guy invented a company. Used it to issue work visas."

"You mean his company manufactured forged visas?"

"Nah, his fake company produced paperwork that real people could use to apply for real visas. Guy got greedy, though. Soon enough, the powers that be got wise to a small firm needing hundreds of engineers. Especially when none of the foreigners applying for work had an engineering degree. Good while it lasted, though."

I lean closer. "So, not forged visas, which is nearly impossible, but creating supporting documents from a nonexistent entity to apply for real visas." I remember what Emmanuel had said about his sister, her drive to take additional courses online so that she could graduate from high school early and get into college as soon as possible. Which would earn her a student visa and secure her place in this country.

"Charlie, what about student visas? A fake college, to issue fake student visas?"

"Could be."

"Wouldn't someone notice? Aren't there checks and balances for that kind of thing?"

Charlie shrugs. "Fake company eventually got shut down, but not before earning millions. System's only as good as the time and energy the bureaucrats have to police it. If a cursory check shows that company or that college exists, who really has time to dig deeper? Not to mention, I hear rumors of kids entering with genuine J-1s from genuine schools. Once they're in the country, however, who pays attention to where they go and what they do?"

"But their visas expire."

"Which is an issue if they leave and reenter the country. But what if they stick around—say, with a new driver's license?"

I get goose bumps then. What would be worth more money than fake IDs? What would be worth kidnapping two enterprising teen girls and holding them hostage? How about setting up a system to generate real student visas? I can even see Angelique's personal interest in taking on such a project, given her immigration status, and her brother's. Maybe that had made it sound like a good idea . . . before it wasn't.

Had Livia involved Deke on her own, or had he approached her? I'm not sure it mattered. Deke, with his criminal partnerships, must've taken over the enterprise and run with it. Forcing his half sister and Angelique to work for them. Given the girls' aptitudes in computer programming and design, this little enterprise could've gone on and on, growing in scope and size. From a fake college for student visas to a fake corporation for work visas, such as Charlie described. That revenue potential would be through the roof. Definitely worth the risk of holding two girls captive.

Except Livia was now dead.

Because having produced the templates, she wasn't needed anymore? Or the stress of the situation had made her too unreliable? And what did her death mean for Angelique? Poor, problem-solving Angelique, desperately leaving us breadcrumbs, doing everything in her power to lead us to them.

Then late last night, climbing into a van to help dispose of her friend's body.

Knowing none of her plans had been good enough.

Knowing she would be next.

"Thank you, Charlie." I glance at my watch. Eight P.M. Way too early to be cutting out of work. But I don't have a choice. There's no way I can stand here, slinging drinks. Not with so much at stake. I need to move. I need to do. I hope Stoney will understand.

I untie the apron from around my waist. Charlie stands up at the bar.

"Where are you headed?" he asks.

"I don't know." Maybe the BPD field office to have it out with Lotham. Or . . . "I'm going to head to the rec center."

"This time of night?"

"It all started there. And all roads keep leading back there. I can't put my finger on it, but that's the place to be."

"Then I'm coming with you."

I don't argue. A hulking bodyguard is not a bad idea at all. Which leaves me one last task. I bolt back to Stoney's office, where he's pecking away at his ancient computer.

"Bye," he says, without looking up.

"I have a lead."

"Bye."

"I'll be back, I'm so sorry."

Stoney finally glances at me. "Go," he says.

So I do, Charlie in tow. We've barely stepped outside the bar when my phone rings. It's Emmanuel and the boy sounds hysterical.

CHAPTER 35

"LILI," EMMANUEL IS GASPING. "SHE just called. I heard scream-ing. She was screaming. 'No, no, no.' Then, 'Sorry, sorry, sorry.' But not to me, like she was talking to someone else. I think she had the phone tucked away, where they couldn't see it. But then there was this huge *boom*. I didn't understand. I started yelling her name. She came back, speaking right to me. She said, 'I love you.' Then the phone went dead. What is happening? Frankie, *what is happening?*"

"Did you try calling back?"

"I couldn't. The number is blocked."

"What about the cell number you found on the receipt?"

"Nothing. I don't think it's turned on."

"Okay, we're headed toward you right now. Give me ten min-utes, I'll be there."

"Where is my sister!"

"I'm working on it. I swear to you—"

"*You are lying!* You don't know anything. You're lying!"

"Emmanuel! Listen to me! Your sister needs you. The license number code. Think. Where are you with the license code?"

"All I got was another string of numbers. Maybe a code within a code? I'm still working on it."

"Give me what you got, right now."

He starts rattling off numbers. I repeat each one out loud. Charlie reaches into his massive coat, pulls out a pen, and writes the string of numbers across the palm of his hand, as if we'd been working together for years.

"Stay where you are," I order Emmanuel. "Keep your phone on. If she calls again, do everything you can to keep the connection, okay? Maybe the police can trace it. I'll call Detective Lotham, right now."

I hang up with Emmanuel, dial Lotham. Charlie doesn't say a word, just keeps on trucking beside me as I strike a furious pace toward the Badeaus' apartment.

Lotham doesn't answer till the fourth ring. "Not now—"

"Emmanuel just called me. LiLi phoned him five minutes ago. Screaming for help, call disconnected, number's blocked. He can't call back."

"Shit."

"Charlie and I are headed there right now."

"No! I'm sending uniforms. Go home. Right now, Frankie. I mean it."

"Not to sound childish, but you are not the boss of me."

"Goddammit!" Deep breath. He's clearly struggling for control, but I could give a flying fuck. This is my case, and I'm not backing off.

"Frankie, I'm outside the Samdi residence. He's dead."

I falter, miss a step, glancing up at Charlie. "Who's dead?"

"J.J. Samdi. Gunned down. Probably in the last thirty minutes."

"The website," I whisper.

"What the fuck, Frankie?"

"That was the last project. The final piece of the puzzle. They needed the girls to finish the virtual college so they could graduate from fake IDs to fake documents for real student visas. Now that everything is in place and online, they're cleaning up shop. Deke Alarie is cleaning up shop."

"Go home."

"Angelique's family could be in danger as well."

"Which is why officers are on the way."

"Good, we'll meet them there."

I disconnect the call, turn to Charlie, who's clearly heard every word.

"How do you feel about running?" I ask him.

"Knees don't love it, but given the circumstances . . ."

We both take off down the sidewalk.

WE HIT THE final block where Emmanuel and his aunt live and I register two things at once. The sound of distant sirens. And the wailing of a nearby woman.

"They took him," Guerline screams the second she sees me. "They took Emmanuel!"

"Who, where?"

"Some man. I came downstairs to fetch Emmanuel. This white van pulled up in the middle of the street and a man jumped out. He had a gun. He pointed it at Emmanuel and told him to get in before anyone got hurt. I tried to grab Emmanuel's arm. I tried to stop him. But then the man . . . He leapt up the steps and smashed Emmanuel over the head with his gun. My boy . . . He collapsed. And blood, so much blood. I started screaming at him to stop, but the man just looked at me. Then he put Emmanuel on his shoulder and threw him into the van.

"As it drove away . . ." Her voice broke, dropped. "I heard a gunshot. I saw it . . . a flash through the side window. They shot Emmanuel. My baby. Oh my God, what have they done?"

I grab Guerline's arm as she starts to collapse. "Did the man say anything?" I demand, doing my best to anchor both of us.

"No."

"What did he look like?"

"Tall. Skinny. His hair was all these tiny braids tied back. And he was wearing gold chains."

"Deke Alarie." I exhale.

"Ma'am." Charlie's turn. "The van, which way did it go?"

Guerline points down the block. I can hear the police sirens, finally drawing closer.

"Emmanuel's cell phone, did he have it on him?"

"He dropped it. When the man hit him."

"Damn." Because the phone would've given us a way to track him. Which no doubt Deke also knew. "Mrs. Violette, can I enter your apartment? Emmanuel was working on decoding a cipher we believe Angelique may have left for us. I need his notes."

Guerline appears too shocked to answer. I leave her with Charlie's comforting bulk while I pound upstairs and burst into the apartment. There, the open laptop on the kitchen table, surrounded by piles of paper. I don't bother to look. Laptop, loose papers, I grab it all, shoving it into a rough pile. I spot a dark blue backpack propped on the floor against the wall. Probably also Emmanuel's. I dump everything inside, slinging the pack over my shoulder.

A squeal of tires outside, two patrol cars screeching to a halt. I

hear Guerline wind up again, along with Charlie's soothing under-
tones. Then Officer O'Shaughnessy's unmistakable voice, demanding to know what's happened.

I exit the apartment, pausing on the second-floor landing. If I go
downstairs right now, Officer O'Shaughnessy is going to demand
my version of events as well. He may also recognize Emmanuel's
backpack and force me to hand it over.

Time. I feel it. The drumbeat that's been chasing me since early
this morning. Right now right now right now. Everything is happening *right now.*

If I go downstairs, submit myself to police questioning like a
good girl? There will be no right now. There will be talking and
explaining, followed by outrage and heated exchanges. Then heaven
help me if Lotham arrives and we have to start the conversation all
over again.

In the end, it's not much of a decision at all. Angelique. I am here
to find Angelique. To save a girl.

To redeem a sin I can never change.

And maybe to chase a bullet I dodged ten years ago.

I turn left, down the end of the hall to the fire escape. Then, I
vanish into the dark.

I HIT THE bottom of the fire escape. I drop onto a patch of dirt, exit
the rickety chain-link fence behind the triple-decker, and pray I
don't get shot by a paranoid neighbor. I've landed in a narrow alley
running behind the row of town houses. I need light and a secure
space where I can quickly sort my way through Emmanuel's notes
to find the decoded numbers he'd rattled off by phone. First question, do I head left or right?

I strike out right. Then promptly hear a noise behind me.

I whirl instantly, hands up in a pugilistic stance. I only know what I learned during self-defense at the Y. I refuse to be an easy mark, though. Bad guys want me, they're gonna have to work for it.

No forms materialize in the dark. Instead I hear the sounds again. A low moan, a hissing sigh. The clatter of someone trying to walk but doing a poor job of it.

I slip into the darkness rimming the edge of the alley and creep toward the sound. What I discover leaves me shocked beyond words.

Deke Alarie, leaning heavily against a lowered fire escape, arm gripping his side. I don't have to look closer to see he's been grievously wounded, his shirt covered in blood. So he was the one shot in the van. Not Emmanuel. But Deke.

He goes to take a staggering step forward, only to collapse.

"Whoa, whoa, whoa. Hang on." Smart or not, I sprint to his side. His breathing is shallow. In the reflected light of a distant streetlamp, I can see sweat dotting his brow.

The sight threatens to send me spiraling, to another time, another place, another man on the ground, bleeding out.

Deke grabs my shoulder, gripping painfully. I wince, grateful for the distraction, as he tries to use me as a human crutch. Unfortunately, he's too big and I'm too little. Both of us go careening to the ground. He grunts painfully. I scramble to get my feet back beneath me, assume the offensive.

"Gun," I demand. "Where's the gun?"

"Don't . . . have . . ."

"Who the hell shot Emmanuel? Where's Angelique?" Fired up on adrenaline, I lean over him and scream my questions into his face.

"I'm sorry," he whispers. His eyes are closed. His skin graying.

Another time, another place. Me, rocking back on forth on my heels. *"No, no, no. Stay with me. Please, Paul, stay with me stay with me stay with me. I need you."*

"Your family's dead, you know that, right? Your half brother, your half sister. Both of them. Murdered."

He shakes his head, drawing another painful, rattling breath. "No one was supposed to . . . get hurt."

"What a bunch of horseshit. Where's Angelique?"

I try to step back, but he grabs my ankle. I glance around. There's no one in this alley. Just him and me. Just me and a dying man.

Paul, on the ground, his head on my lap, while his hands grip his stomach, trying to keep his insides from leaking out. "Well, that didn't go as planned."

Me, screaming. Screaming, screaming, screaming.

Paul. "Shhh. It'll be okay. I love you."

Me, screaming some more.

"I didn't want them hurt," Deke is rasping out now. "No need. This is . . . supposed to be . . . upmarket stuff . . . Just wanted to see my family again. Mom wouldn't take my calls . . . Johnson hated . . . me. Found Livia. Little Livia. She said hey. We started talking."

I close my eyes. "You poor stupid son of bitch."

"Yeah."

I think he's smiling. It's hard to tell as he coughs and blood sprays from his mouth. He's not going to make it. I know the signs too well. Deke Alarie, my lead candidate for all things evil, is about to die.

I take a seat beside him. I smooth back the fuzz on his forehead. He is both sweaty and cold to the touch. It won't be long now. We both know it.

Paul: "Promise me you won't blame yourself for this. Promise me you won't use it as a reason to drink. Come on, Frankie. Promise me!"

"I liked Livia," Deke murmurs now. "So fucking smart. Was I ever that smart?" A bloody smile. "She got all bent out of shape over fake licenses . . . bad merchandise. I told her she should fix it. She could do better. I could get her the equipment. I could get her whatever she wanted."

"You set her up to manufacture fake IDs."

"Rough start . . . these new state licenses. Not as easy as they look."

I nod, stroking his damp cheek. His eyes are closed. His breathing rougher.

Paul: "I'm glad you called tonight, Frankie."

Me, crying hysterically.

"I'm happy you still trusted me that much."

"Livia brought in a friend. After school. Worked on it together. Got to a point . . . Product wasn't half bad. I brought the fakes to my suppliers . . . went into business. But soon . . . not enough. These guys, real counterfeiting pros . . . wanted Real IDs. Something bigger, better."

Deke coughs wetly. More blood, dribbling from the corners of his mouth.

Paul: "I'm thirsty. So thirsty. Do you have any water, Frankie? Can you get me some water?"

"What happened, Deke?" I stroke his cheek.

"They demanded a meeting . . . with my source. But Livia, too scared. Angelique showed up in her place. She had . . . a new plan . . . not Real ID. Couldn't"—he breaks off, coughing again—"be done. Visas. Student visas."

"Angelique figured out," I provide for him, "that forging a visa would be just as difficult as a Real ID. However, she could create an entire fictional college that would issue the application documents needed for a real visa."

Short nod.

"Why a college for student visas, versus green cards?"

"Student visas . . . less scrutiny. And so many colleges. Easier place . . . to start. Plus, Angelique's idea. She wanted. For herself. Her brother."

"So this was the initial offer. Get these documents right and not only make huge sums of money now but set the stage for larger money later. Except they didn't let Angelique come home from that initial meeting, though, did they?" This much Lotham and I had already figured out. "Angelique's grand idea put more at stake. So big bad associate guys decided to protect their investment by keeping her. Which also provided leverage to force Livia to engage."

Faint nod. Deke's breathing is ragged. I can hear the beginnings of a rattle.

Paul: *"Hold my hand, Frankie? Please. Just hold my hand."*

Me: *"I'm sorry, I'm sorry, I'm sorry."*

"I know. And I love you anyway. I've always loved you anyway."

"But progress wasn't happening fast enough?" I push now. "So they grabbed Livia anyway. Forced her and Angelique to work day and night?"

"Livia wasn't doing . . . so good. The pressure . . . They got nervous. Worried she'd tell. Took her, too. Stuck 'em both in an abandoned building. One leaves . . . The other suffers . . . Couple of guys standing watch. I tried . . . when I could. Give them some breathing room. Let Angelique out . . . but she had to come back. She always came back."

"For Livia," I supply.

"She . . . she loves Livia."

So he knew, then. How much Angelique and Livia meant to each other.

"What happened?" I asked, stroking his cheek. Not much longer now.

"I thought I could keep Livia and Angel safe. I thought . . ."

"You could control the situation?"

"Couldn't. Everything harder than it looked. Guys, panicking. Girls, freaking out. Month . . . into month . . . into month. Took so long. Livia . . . poor Livia. Then you came. Rocking the boat. So I tried to . . . scare you off. Stop questions."

"You shot at me, outside J.J. and Roseline Samdi's house."

"Thought better . . . if you gone."

"But I didn't leave," I murmur. "And it didn't get better."

"Angelique thought, if they cooperated, everything'd be . . . okay. She got college website, registry documents . . . done. Had our first trial."

"And it worked, didn't it?" I fill in for him. "Heaven help you all. Angelique's master plan succeeded, meaning suddenly, they didn't need any of you anymore. Not Livia, not Angelique, not even you?"

"I tried to warn Livia . . . wanted to get her out. But . . . caught us. He killed her. Right in front of me. What happens if you try to run."

"You got away. You came to Stoney's bar. I saw you, outside my window."

"Wanted to talk to you . . . But then . . . saw the cop arrive. Didn't know who I could trust."

"Where is Angelique, Deke? Tell me. I'll protect her for you. I'll save her, and I'll be sure she knows it was because of you."

Deke's breathing is definitely ragged now. Suddenly, his body convulses. He winces, grabs his stomach, then heaves sideways just in time to vomit up blood.

"Please, Paul, just hang in there. Help is coming. Paul, Paul. Please God. Paul!"

"Housecleaning now," Deke whispers. "No loose ends. I gave Angelique my phone. Told her to warn her brother. They knew . . . about her messages to him. But her call . . . not in time. They grabbed him. Threw him . . . in the van. I went for the gun. Enough . . . is enough."

And there it is, the final death rattle I know all too well.

Me, clutching Paul's hand. Keening, keening, keening.

Sirens in the background, still way too far away. They won't be able to save him. No one can save him.

Paul, eyes fluttering open. "You are so beautiful. First time I saw you . . . I knew you were the one. So many, I tried to fix. But you . . . You healed me. I love you, Amy. Forever and always. I love you, for loving me."

Me, keening, keening, keening.

As her name goes on and on. Amy Amy Amy. The woman he truly loved. The woman who loved him.

The woman I could never be.

There are no sirens now. No final declarations of love. A long, shuddery sigh.

"Livia," he whispers.

Then I watch the life expel out of Deke Alarie. I feel his hand go limp in mine.

I bend over long enough to close his eyelids. I brush a soft kiss over his forehead. I thank him for trying to save Emmanuel and Angelique. I bless him for having the fortitude to tell me what I need to know.

Where I must go next.

When I finally rise to standing, I'm coated in blood and tears. And once more, that night, so long ago.

"*I love you, Amy . . .*"

I accept the pain as my due.

Then I grab Emmanuel's backpack and I start to run. There's not much time anymore. But finally, I know exactly where to find Angelique, as well as her brother.

I know how to get this one right.

CHAPTER 36

DIAL 911 AS I race toward the wide boulevard, then track north. I rant about a gunshot victim in a back alley. I tell the confused dispatch operator it's Deke Alarie and he's already dead and Officer O'Shaughnessy is in the vicinity and please let him know. And P.S., please tell a guy named Charlie that I'm sorry. Then I hang up before the operator can ask me any more questions.

Next I call Lotham's cell. He answers instantly this time, already on high alert.

"Where are you?"

"They have Angelique and Emmanuel. Deke tried to stop them. He's dead." I tell him where I'm going, then warn, "Lights off, sirens quiet. If they know the police are there . . ."

Lotham doesn't require further explanation. I think of his broad face, his mangled ear. I think he's a good man, an excellent detective, and if anyone can get this done . . . I think, if I get shot next, he's the one I would like to hold my hand.

He's not speaking. I hear his thoughts instead. His quiet desperation for me to go home, be safe. His relentless need to save Angelique, to protect me.

But maybe I am growing on him, because he doesn't say the words out loud anymore. He doesn't tell me to do things we both know I won't do. I hang up the phone. I keep running.

Toward where it all began two summers ago. Where it will end tonight.

The rec center.

And its kindly director, Frédéric Lagudu.

I COME UPON the van first. It is parked out front, the back doors slung open, the inside empty. I don't dare use my pocket flashlight to examine it more closely. I sniff instead, catching the unmistakable scent of blood. From Deke, before they dumped him? Or am I already too late?

I refuse to believe that Emmanuel is dead, if only because I can't bear the thought. All of my other cases, I've pursued my target from a distance, never having met the missing person in question. But Emmanuel, I've talked to him, comforted him. He's just a boy. He doesn't deserve this.

I creep my way around the giant metal building. I don't see any trace of lights or detect any sounds of activity. But I know how immense the building is. Plenty of internal classrooms and smaller storage spaces that aren't noticeable from the outside. What was it Mr. Riddenscail said? The operation could be as simple as a single computer and printer. Wouldn't require much square footage at all.

Did that mean Livia and Angelique had been there every time I'd visited? And Frédéric, holed up in his office bright and early each morning, hadn't been the diligent savior of at-risk teens I'd thought him to be?

In hindsight, the description of the driver who'd dumped Livia's body, a tall, thin Black man, fit Frédéric as well as Deke; I'd simply never connected those dots before. Combine that with Deke's comment that "they" had seen me talking to J.J.—that conversation had taken place outside the rec center. Again, all roads leading back to this one enormous building. Where Livia and Angelique had first met. Where someone in Frédéric's position would have plenty of opportunity to scope out their talent. He'd probably been recruiting local kids for various enterprises for years. Well over a decade, if Deke knew him from his days before prison. So many things that now made sense, if only I'd paid attention sooner.

Now, I try to remember the name of the shorter, muscular man who'd been in the building the first time I'd visited. Dutch? Something like that. According to Deke, there were multiple other players. Certainly Dutch would make for excellent hired muscle. Though there could be criminal partners I'd never met before. One, two, half a dozen?

I still don't know what I don't know.

Which doesn't stop me from creeping around to the rear entrance, slowly cracking open the heavy glass door.

I pause, listening intently. No alarms sound, no bodies materialize on the other side. I slide myself through, halting again to get my bearings.

I can just make out a light down the long corridor, near Frédéric's office. Which presents me with my first obstacle. Discovered in that corridor, I'll be a sitting duck. And these guys have real guns they're not afraid to use. Unlike me, who is the proud owner of a red rape whistle.

I take a steadying breath and do what I do best. Think like a reprobate. Seventeen-year-old me, desperate for a drink, confronted with the challenge of sneaking down a long, dark hallway unseen in order to score a bottle of booze, what would I do?

And just like that, it comes to me.

I dart sideways, hitting the checkout desk for outdoor equipment. Behind it, I feel around in the dark, making out the locked cabinets holding sporting goods. A touch to my hair, and I have my tactical hair clip in hand. Time to test it out.

It takes me a couple of tries—being in the dark doesn't help—but then, with a click, the lock gives, the broad doors open up. I stick the hair clip back in my hair. Best four bucks I've ever spent.

Then I resume feeling around in the dark, identifying the texture of a basketball, the shape of a soccer ball, then baseball bats, mitts, balls.

I start with a baseball. Standing behind the desk, I wind up, then hurl it for all I'm worth at the glass doors. Nothing shatters, but there is a distinct clang as it ricochets off the metal doorframe, then careens around the space. I wait, poised and alert. When nothing happens, I follow with a basketball, then a soccer ball. More rattles and clangs.

Finally, from the end of the hallway. "Who's there?"

In response, I bounce a basketball down the corridor.

"What the hell?"

I pound another basketball, followed by a second, third, fourth, fifth. Then, before I can think, before the person can think, I grab a bat and give chase, darting down the hall behind half a dozen bouncing balls and relying on them to mask my footsteps.

It's Dutch. He has just enough time to look up. To register my form materializing out of the dark. His hand fumbles belatedly at his side.

Then I nail him in the middle with a baseball bat. As he folds over, I swing at the back of his head. I hold nothing back. He collapses and there's blood. A lot of blood. Maybe I've killed him. In my adrenaline-fueled state, I have no idea.

I pause long enough to fumble around the body. I discover a radio clipped to his waist, as well as a handgun tucked in the back of his jeans. I help myself to both. Then I strip his sweatshirt half off his head and tie it up behind him, restricting his arms. Just in case he isn't dead.

I check the gun long enough to flip the safety off. I'm no good with firearms. Guns are loud and violent. They take me back to places I don't want to go and memories I don't want to experience. However, this is no time to be squeamish.

Next, I check the radio. I turn the volume down, then flick it on. As I slowly turn it up, I hear a voice. Frédéric's.

"Dutch, do you copy? Over."

I think about it for a second, then start clicking. SOS. Over and over again. Let's see what Frédéric does with that. I drag Dutch's incredibly heavy body over to an open classroom, leaving just his feet visible.

Then I find the darkened doorway directly across from it and melt into the shadows.

A full minute passes. I know because I count off the seconds, trying to steady my breathing.

A figure appears. From this distance, I can't be sure who. But as it draws closer, I can tell it's not tall enough to be Frédéric. Henchman number two, I decide. I don't recognize the approximate size and shape as someone I've met before, but it hardly matters.

Have baseball bat, will travel.

"Dutch?" the voice whispers. I resume my mental counting. Not yet, not yet . . .

"Dutch! What the hell?"

Feet spotted. Henchman number two racing toward his fallen comrade.

Not yet . . .

Now. I spring out the instant the man passes my doorway. A low swing of the bat, directly at the back of the knees and henchman number two is down.

He rolls over surprisingly quick. I have an image of a gun lifting. Hear the crack of it firing. Singe of heat, stinging pain. I swing the bat again and the gun goes flying. I smack the man over and over. Targeting arms, shoulders, chest. I'm breathing hard, a blur of fear and rage.

At the last moment, I halt myself, registering that the evil henchman is no longer moving but groaning low and bubbly. I've broken his ribs, I'm sure of it. I have an instant of guilt. Then I remember Livia's dumped body, Deke's dying form, and I'm over it.

I search around in the dark again. Find the fallen gun and toss it across the hall into the second classroom. Another radio is clipped around the man's waist. I take it out. Then, I am once more on the hunt.

THE DARK HALLWAY is quiet as I creep down it. I'm shaking head to toe. More bad guys? Dozens of them? I have no way of knowing. I'm trying to think of what I learned from Deke. A counterfeiting operation for student visas. Requiring one mastermind, followed by enough men to kidnap two teenage girls and force them into servitude. That shouldn't require too many bodies. I think. I hope.

All criminal enterprises have the incentive to run lean. Fewer people for splitting the profits. Again, I think. I hope.

Assuming Deke was one of the minions, plus Dutch, and broken ribs guy, the operation is now down three. Can't be that many more to go.

I think. I hope.

Up ahead. I see a light. I hear a voice. It's not a man's voice, though, but a girl's.

"Quick," she says urgently. "Wake up. Please, Emmanuel. Please!"

And just like that, I'm staring at Angelique Badeau inside a lit room. Her hair is pulled back tight—the image from her Tamara Levesque license. She wears jeans and sweatshirt, but she is covered in smears of red. Blood. From the van, I think. From the kidnapping of her brother.

Which brings me to Emmanuel, whose bound form lies prostrate on the ground. He doesn't seem to be moving.

I'm too late.

"Please," Angelique hisses again. She kneels at her brother's side, shaking him hard. She is trembling, gaze darting around the classroom. I note several computers and what appears to be a pretty impressive printer. The heart of the operations, I think. But I don't have to time to consider the matter.

Angelique is clearly on high alert. Because of the commotion I've made, or because she knows she and her brother still aren't safe?

I want to say her name. I want to march in the room and declare, "My name is Frankie Elkin and I hereby rescue you."

Except I'm terribly aware that a key individual is missing. Frédéric Lagudu, the center's executive director and the voice I heard on the radio. So where the hell is he?

Angelique darts behind her brother, plucking at the knots on his wrists. And several things happen at once.

She looks up, spots me.

I hold a finger to my lips, gesturing for her to be silent as I heft up my bat.

She shakes her head frantically.

And I'm tackled from behind, the baseball bat flying from my grasp.

"You stupid bitch!"

I barely get my arms out in time to break my fall, then Frédéric is upon me, pressing down against my back, pinning me into place. His hand tangles into my hair, jerking my head back.

I buck helplessly, but I can't get him off. He's too heavy, and with my arms trapped beneath me, I can't reach the gun at my waist, nor the bat rolling across the floor. He slams my face against the floor.

I hear a crack, my nose bursting into a bloody mess, my forehead ringing in stunning pain. Then he yanks up my head again, preparing for the second blow as my eyes water and my mouth fills with blood. He's going to kill me. I am dying.

Not a bullet after all. How interesting.

"No, no, no!"

I hear Angelique's voice. Then sense her running approach. *Save yourself*, I want to yell at her, but I can't manage the words.

She barrels into my attacker, the weight lifting from my back as Frédéric topples to the side.

I roll away, staggering to my feet, trying desperately to get my bearings. The bat—where is it? Or the gun? It must've fallen from my waist because now I can't find it.

"I hate you!" Angelique is scrabbling with Frédéric. He's bigger, stronger. But she's incensed, smacking at his head and face. An older sister, desperate to save her brother. A girlfriend, mourning her partner's murder.

It's not enough. With a twist of his arm, Frédéric throws her off.

"Goddammit."

"Angelique!" I cry.

She barely gets her hands up before Frédéric socks her in the face, followed by a quick jab to her kidneys. She doubles over in pain, while I continue frantically searching the floor. Bat. Gun. Bat. Gun. My head is ringing, my vision blurred.

A fresh sound. Emmanuel, now awake. Emmanuel, still bound hand and foot, desperately trying to inchworm his way to his sister's side.

"Angelique!" he screams.

Frédéric wallops her again and again.

"No," I say helplessly, still staggering about.

Frédéric materializes before me. And now he's the one with the gun. Sighting me, then Angelique's weeping form, then Emmanuel's bound figure.

It's over. I can see it on his face. Simply a matter of whom to shoot first.

"Me," I hear myself say. "Shoot me. The kids are no threat to you."

"You bitch. You shouldn't have come back here."

"The police are on their way. Run now, while you have the chance. I'll lie. Leave Angelique and Emmanuel alone, and I'll send the police in the opposite direction. I promise."

"It doesn't matter."

"It does. Deke told us everything, about the website, the fake student visas, Livia's murder. It's over now. Take your profits and get out."

"I still have my prize." Frédéric grabs Angelique by the arm, forcing her to stand. She gasps in pain. Her face is bloody, but in her eyes I see a fierce light of determination, or maybe it's simply hatred for this man. It doesn't matter, I'll take either, as I finally spy the bat. Two feet behind her to the left. Too far for me to reach, but maybe not for her. If I can just distract Frédéric, buy Angelique a moment of time.

My gaze, darting to the bat, back to her, the bat. Her eyes widen slightly. I think she understands. I remember what Emmanuel said: His sister doesn't dream, she plans. And I think that I'm very sorry I'll never get to meet this amazing young woman, because there's only one way I can think to grab Frédéric's attention, and it doesn't end so well for me.

Emmanuel, whimpering from the floor. Angelique, tensing in anticipation.

Frédéric, raising his gun.

And me . . .

I'm back in a liquor store, ten years ago. A young kid, sweating in desperation and shaking with withdrawal, waving a pistol all about. "Give me your money! All of it, now!"

Except I don't have any money. I just spent the last of it on a bottle of vodka, right before I broke and called Paul and begged him, all these months later, to come save me from myself. Now the store clerk is wide-eyed and anxious.

Only Paul is calm, as he steps forward, raises his arms in a placating motion. "Easy now. No need for anyone to get hurt."

Did the kid mean to pull the trigger? Or did it just happen? All these years later, I still don't know. I just remember the sound of the gunshot. The look of horror on the kid's face. And the look of surprise on Paul's as he sank down, down, down.

The kid fled out the door.

And Paul . . .

Paul.

Now, I keep my eyes open. I want to see it coming. I want to watch death finally find me.

As I look Frédéric right in the eye, and charge forward. A split second where I register the shock in his face. He isn't expecting it. He jerks the trigger wildly, releasing Angelique as he braces for contact.

She rolls to the side. *Please grab the bat*, I think—as I register pain, so much fucking pain. I drop, rolling across the floor, keep rolling.

Bang, bang, bang.

Screaming. Angelique's, my own, Emmanuel's.

Followed by a new booming voice. "Stop! Police! Lower your weapon!"

Lotham explodes into the classroom, leading with his pistol.

Frédéric pivots wildly, caught off guard by this fresh threat. Angelique appears behind him, bat raised high.

"LiLi," Emmanuel cries.

"Police!" Lotham shouts again.

Paul is down. Paul is bleeding.

No, it's me now. I am down, I am bleeding.

Angelique swings the bat. She connects with the side of his head, but not quite hard enough. Frédéric turns, gun still in hand . . .

And Lotham takes him out. *Bang, bang, bang.*

Angelique drops the bat. "Emmanuel! Please help my brother."

"LiLi! Are you okay? LiLi!"

More pounding footsteps. Cops pouring into the room, flooding down the hall. I should say something, I should move. But I can't seem to get to my feet. I can't seem to find my voice. An unbelievable pressure is building in my chest.

Then Lotham is kneeling over me.

"Hold on there, Frankie. Just hold on. I got you."

"Angelique," I whisper. "Emmanuel."

"You did it, Frankie. You found her. You rescued both of them. They're safe."

"Paul," I say.

"He'd be very proud of you."

I start to cry then. Blood and tears. Past and present. Old wounds and fresh scars.

"I got you, Frankie. I got you," Lotham reassures me.

And I believe him.

CHAPTER 37

'M IN THE HOSPITAL FOR a matter of days. I don't remember much.
A blur of pain as I fight the doctor's orders for morphine, screaming that I'm an addict. Lotham might be there. Or maybe it's Charlie, Viv, Stoney. At one point, I'm convinced even Piper has paid a
visit.

I don't have insurance, which means once the bullet is removed
from my left shoulder and the wound patched on my right arm, I'm
back out the door. This time it's Lotham who definitely does the
honors of picking me up, driving me back to Stoney's and leading
me upstairs.

I sleep. I dream. Of Paul, of Angelique. Of Deke dying in my
arms. Of Livia chasing me through a park: *What about me, what
about me?*

When I wake up, I don't have an answer, so I sleep again.

In one of my more lucid moments, I learn that Frédéric, Dutch,
and some guy named Holden have all been arrested. Dutch survived
my encounter with him. Holden is still in the hospital, recovering

from broken ribs, a broken jaw, and a ruptured spleen. I'm told he'll live. I think I'm grateful, but I can't be sure.

Apparently, Frédéric had gotten into the drug business nearly twenty years ago. He'd used his position at the rec center to meet and recruit other lower-level dealers, before going upmarket with the purchase of hundreds of thousands of dollars in counterfeit currency.

He'd initially been amused by Deke's idea to enter the fake license market. But once he'd realized Livia's and Angelique's full potential, he'd quickly gotten on board. Then Angelique's fateful idea to set up a sham college for issuing real student visas . . . As I'd suspected, the revenue potential was too good to pass up. If he had to kidnap two girls, so be it.

He'd stashed the girls at an abandoned town house just around the corner from the rec center, with Deke, Holden, and Dutch serving as rotating guards. Livia and Angelique would work at night, and sleep during the day, lowering their profile.

Most of the time, the girls were confined to the town house, utilizing a couple of computers Frédéric had brought over for them. But every so often, they'd journey to the rec center after dark to print out new and improved versions of the driver's licenses. Deke assisted with local sales, while Dutch handled online marketing. The license business hadn't been bad but, given the not-quite-Grade-A quality of the forgeries, still limited. Merely a convenient cash flow vehicle while the girls worked toward the larger goal of perfecting a sham college.

Unfortunately, Livia had slowly but surely deteriorated under the constant pressure. Angelique's initial kidnapping had stressed her out. By the time Deke grabbed her as well, under Frédéric's orders but also because Deke genuinely thought he could control the situation better if he had the girls together, Livia was a constant bundle of nerves. Angelique had done her best to run interference and buy them time. Especially once she'd realized Deke had a soft spot for his sister.

Unfortunately, Frédéric wasn't the sentimental type. Once Gleeson C was perfected and the first round of student visa paperwork issued, he considered the girl to be little more than a liability. He took care of Livia first. But as Angelique and Deke quickly realized, she wouldn't be the last. Frédéric, ordering Holden to shoot J.J., kidnap Emmanuel, then kill Deke when he tried to intervene . . .

On and on until there was no one left.

Sixth day, or maybe seventh, I manage to get out of bed long enough to shower, force down some soup. Afterward I stare at my reflection in the mirror. My drawn face, my heavily bandaged shoulder. I look like shit. And I feel like . . . ?

I can't decide. I found Angelique Badeau. I brought home a missing girl. It's not that I expected to feel like a superhero, but I did hope to maybe feel like a better person.

Mostly, I feel the same I always did.

I go back to bed. When I wake up again, Stoney is standing in my apartment.

"You really are a lousy employee."

"Yep."

Piper appears from beneath the bed, winds around Stoney's ankles. Purrs. Traitorous bitch.

"But you're not bad at the missing persons thing," Stoney says.

I give him a weak thumbs-up.

"You got visitors."

Then he's gone, and Guerline is standing in my kitchen, Angelique to one side, Emmanuel to the other. My breath hitches. I feel a stab of pain in my shoulder, as I drag myself up to sitting, but I don't wince. I don't want to scare them away.

Emmanuel has dark bruises fading on the right side of his face, remnants of his kidnapping. He also has purple smudges beneath his dark eyes, remnants of recent nightmares. In comparison, Angelique appears relatively unscathed, just some scabbing along one cheek. She stands very still, however. A traumatized girl holding on tight. A survivor, alone in a crowded room.

I wonder which is worse for her, the painful memories or the unrelenting guilt? I want to tell her I know exactly how she feels, but I doubt she would believe me. She's not there yet in her own healing. She's merely the teenager who went missing, and I'm merely the woman who finally found her.

I have no idea how our relationship develops from here. It's never come up before.

I offer a tentative smile.

"Thank you," Guerline says.

"Emmanuel and Angelique deserve the credit. Without Angelique's messages and Emmanuel's determination, we wouldn't be here."

"I'm sorry you got shot," Angelique states.

"Totally worth it."

"Do you . . . Can I . . ." Angelique begins. She doesn't seem to know quite what to say, but I think I understand.

"Can we have a moment?" I ask Guerline and Emmanuel.

Both hesitate. Having gotten Angelique back, they clearly don't want her out of their sight. But after another second, Guerline concedes with a nod. Emmanuel follows her out.

Alone, Angelique appears even more uncomfortable. I finally pat the side of the bed. "Sit. It's okay."

She complies, but again, holds herself rigid.

"It will get better," I tell her. "Not today, not tomorrow, but eventually."

"It's all my fault."

"No, it isn't. But I understand it feels that way. I lost someone I love. It's been ten years. I still blame myself."

She regards me solemnly. "I loved Livia. When she first came to me about the fake IDs, I told her it was too risky. But she wanted to make me happy. And she'd started meeting her older brother. Deke. I didn't think he was good for her. But he was her brother, and family is family." Angelique shrugs.

Given her closeness with her brother, Emmanuel, I could see her not wanting to take such an opportunity away from Livia.

"But Deke's friends . . . They kept wanting more. So we would work harder. But nothing seemed enough. Deke tried to tell us it would be okay. Just do this, do that, it would all be fine. But I knew. I suspected . . .

"By the time Deke said his friend wanted to meet face to face with Livia, we were both nervous. Livia didn't think she could do it. I told her I would go in her place. I thought I could protect her. I even had a plan—I had found online articles about groups that had set up fake universities for issuing student visas. They made millions and millions. Even ICE set up a fake university to trap foreign students looking for visas. I thought such a sophisticated operation would placate Frédéric. He would leave us to work on some mysterious website. We could forget about the fake licenses, which were much more difficult to perfect than we'd thought, and Livia could stop being so stressed out. I assumed I was doing something good. Instead, I made everything worse."

I understand. The lure of so much money had caused Frédéric to become even more intense, leading to the eventual abduction of both girls.

"You can't go backward," I advise Angelique, "so consider this: If you can't save the people you already lost, maybe you can save someone else instead. Become a doctor. Build a life. Livia, Deke, they would've wanted that for you."

She looks down at her hands.

"I was with Deke when he died. He tried. For you and Livia. He loved his sister, and genuinely regretted what happened to you. In the end, this was more his fault than either of yours."

"Deke tried to help," she says, still looking down at her lap. I'm assuming she means her and Livia's relationship. "The night, when Frédéric strangled Livia . . . He would've killed me next, but Deke stopped him. I was still useful, he argued. The student visas had been my idea, yes? He also convinced Frédéric to drive Livia's body to Franklin Park. He said it would distract the police and be safer than having the cops discover her body near the rec center. But really, Deke couldn't bear the thought of Livia being dumped in some alley. I couldn't either."

"I'm sorry."

"Holden shot him in the van. Emmanuel saw. Deke . . . He wasn't a good man, he made many mistakes, especially with his sister, but I'm sorry he's dead."

I'm not sure what to say. I'm getting tired, the ache in my shoulder deeper. Finally: "You're a survivor, Angelique. You're strong, resilient. Don't forget that. If you hadn't risked posting the essay, dropping the fake license, appearing in public, we wouldn't have found you. We wouldn't have been able to save you or your brother."

It's not gratitude I see reflected in her eyes, however, but guilt. She wasn't trying to save herself. She'd been trying to save Livia. And her girlfriend's death was now her burden to bear.

"It will get better," I repeat, though I can already tell she doesn't believe me. She's not ready to forgive herself yet. Maybe she never will. I understand that, too.

Angelique stands up, gives me a final, solemn nod, then departs. I manage some water, more of what I'm assuming is Viv's home-made soup. I brush my teeth, comb my hair, refresh my bandage. The bullet graze on my right arm is already significantly healed. Which leaves only the recently stitched hole in my shoulder. That will definitely leave a scar. I can picture myself fingering it at night, reminding myself that once, I was successful. Once, I got it right.

Do I feel like a different person yet?

I keep waiting, but no such luck. I remain Frankie Elkin. Alcoholic. Ex-lover. Lost soul.

I retreat to the mattress, taking with me my brown leather messenger bag. I pull out two manila files, pore through the contents till my eyes grow heavy. When I wake up again my room is dark and a shadow looms beside my bed.

"Shhh," Lotham says as he climbs onto the mattress beside me. "Just rest." Then he gathers me up against him, and I feel the heat of his body. I drift off to the steady rhythm of his breathing. Later, when I wake up crying, he wipes away my tears with his fingers and then with his lips and I turn myself fully against him. I move urgently and demandingly until he finally gives up and gives in. Then we are skin to skin, gentle but rough, soft but demanding, and it is better than any drop of booze.

Afterward, I finally sleep deep and hard and when I wake up to find him gone, that's okay, too. It makes it easier for what I have to do next.

I pick up my phone and dial. First time I've ever called in daylight. I'm not even sure she'll pick up. Then:

"Frankie, please—"

"I found a missing girl. Her name is Angelique Badeau. She's sixteen. I brought her home alive."

A pause. "That's . . . that's good. Paul would like that. But you don't need me to tell you that, Frankie. And all these years later, please, can you just stop calling? It hurts."

"He died saying he loved you. He said . . . So many he tried to fix. But you healed him. You were the great love of his life."

A much longer pause now. Maybe she's crying. I know I am. I've never told her this before. I should've. But I just couldn't. I needed, selfishly, for Paul to be about me. I needed, terribly, to keep his last moments as mine.

"Thank you," Amy says at last. I can hear her drawing a shuddery breath.

"I'll stop calling. I'm sorry. I don't know why . . ."

But I do, and she does, too. Because she is all I have left of him. Just like I am her sole connection to his memory.

"Well, maybe every now and then," she allows.

"Are you happy?" I ask her, genuinely curious.

"I have a new husband, a baby girl. Life moves on, Frankie. But thank you for calling. Thank you for telling me that."

"Good-bye, Amy."

"Good-bye, Frankie."

I set down the phone. I take a deep breath. And then I'm ready. Not new and improved, but maybe the old model is better than I thought. Final shower, fresh change of clothes, then I find Stoney downstairs in his office.

He doesn't have to ask to know. "That's it, then? Back on the road?"

I nod.

"You can keep the apartment till the end of the month. Longer, if you want to return to work."

I nod.

"Bet there's more cases around here. Maybe people will even come to you, as word gets out." He studies me. I love the lines of his face, a man who's known heartache but also hope.

"Thank you," I tell him, and for both of us, it's enough.

I return upstairs and pack. Five shirts, three pairs of pants, same threadbare underwear I still haven't gotten around to replacing.

I pause long enough to write a note. Lotham will be angry, but he won't be surprised.

He is who he is. And I am who I am.

My name is Frankie Elkin and finding missing people is what I do. When the police have given up, when the public no longer remembers, when the media has never bothered to care, I start looking.

Now, I take my suitcase. Head downstairs.

And then, I disappear.

AUTHOR'S NOTE AND ACKNOWLEDGMENTS

This entire novel started with an online article from BBC, regarding Lissa Yellowbird-Chase, an everyday person who also searches for missing persons. From that news brief, I discovered an entire world of amateurs who seek to make a difference by working missing persons cold cases. What I gleaned: Especially in situations where technology has failed, the right person asking the right questions can make all the difference. That total strangers care that much for the missing among us, I found powerful—though also heartbreaking. So this book is for the dedicated, whether they're amateur detectives, professional pilots, registered dog handlers, et cetera, who give their time for another family's closure. I am totally inspired by you.

In the nuts-and-bolts department, several others made a difference. First off, Mary Nèe-Loftus, who brought the world of Mattapan—not to mention the school system of Boston—to life. Thank you, also, Betsy Eliot, for introducing me to Mary.

Also, for my dear friend Margie Aitkenhead. When I said, hey, I need to walk the streets of a tough neighborhood in Boston, she never hesitated to say yes. Also, the locals went out of their way to assist our efforts—and the food was beyond amazing. I reference several Mattapan landmarks in this novel, from Le Foyer to Simco's; you should visit and eat at both. Haitian meat pies are my new favorite food, and I can't wait to eat more.

I'm also indebted to Superintendent-in-Chief Dan Linskey, Ret., Boston Police Department, who walked me through all the resources the BPD have at their disposal. Let me just say, disappearing a person in this day and age of traffic cams and LPR is extremely complicated. And I'm extremely impressed by all the resources a major city police force has to bring to bear.

I'm also indebted to my daughter, who—having eavesdropped on my conversation with Linskey—informed me that I asked all the wrong questions. She then proceeded to tell me all the resources available to any halfway intelligent teenager for shielding communications from nosy parents. As a mother, I wasn't sure whether to be impressed or appalled. I went with impressed because it allows me to sleep better at night. Maybe.

Which brings me to Lt. Peter T. Eakley, Ret., Millburn New Jersey Police, who walked me through fake IDs, forged visas, and all sorts of fun. I took some liberties in this novel, as there's a fine line between entertaining readers and instructing aspiring forgers.

Also, please bear in mind this is a work of fiction and all mistakes are mine and mine alone. The real world is quite complicated, so thank goodness for fictional escape.

People who want to die: You know who you are. Congratulations to the winners of the Kill a Friend, Maim a Buddy Sweepstake, as well as its international counterpart, Kill a Friend, Maim a Mate. First up, Lupe Giron, who won the right to kill off her friend, Peggy Struzeski Griffith, whom she described as a "slightly crazy, bookloving blonde." I approve of all slightly crazy, book-loving people, but per the terms of the contest, Peggy still had to die. Hope you enjoyed! Next, congratulations to Gwynne Andal, self-described proud Filipina and oldest of three kids, for earning the right to kill off herself. I'm sure this wasn't as gruesome as you wanted, but I hope it's still fun. For other aspiring winners of fictional death, the contest is back up and running at LisaGardner.com. It's never too late to enter, and do encourage family and friends to nominate you, as well. Dying in a novel is a surprisingly enthusiastic and competitive sweepstakes.

Also, here is to the real-life Piper, an extraordinary rescue cat who now enjoys a pampered life with my wonderful neighbors Pam and Glenda, while hissing at me every time I walk into the room. I tried cat treats, then catnip. Literary immortality is all I got left. If only cats could read.

As always, my love to my family, friends, and fellow authors who kept me sane for the writing of this novel. Given that most of this happened during the pandemic, focus was hard to find, and support most appreciated. For those who follow me on social media, you understand hiking is my salvation (and my preferred method of brainstorming), so thank you to Michelle Capozzoli and Larissa Taylor for keeping me on trail and deep in homicidal thought.

For my readers out there: Love, gratitude, and best wishes for health and happiness. Thank you for your support. I've lived my entire life captivated by the power of story. Thank you for sharing that journey with me.

WANT TO KNOW WHAT HAPPENS
TO FRANKIE NEXT?

TURN OVER FOR A SNEAK PEEK

ONE STEP TOO FAR

OUT JANUARY 2022

CHAPTER 1

The first three men came stumbling into town shortly after ten A.M., babbling of dark shapes and eerie screams and their missing buddy Scott and their other buddy Tim, who set out from their campsite before dawn to get help.

"Bear, bear, bear," first guy moaned.

"Mountain lion!" second guy insisted.

Third guy vomited.

Maybe, maybe not, Marge Santi thought, as she side-stepped the spew of liquid. Marge situated the young men in a corner booth of her diner, then got on the phone and summoned Nemeth. To be polite, Marge also contacted Sheriff Jim Kelley, likeable guy, respected by the locals, but an officer with a whole county to tend and the drive to prove it. For immediate action, Nemeth it was.

Nemeth, former legend from U.S. Fish and Wildlife and now a local guide, knew what he was doing. First, he plied the three men with coffee. To judge by the rank odor of fear and booze leaking out of their pores, they didn't need anything else. Two cups later, he had most of the story.

Five guys had set out into the woods for a bachelor party weekend. All friends since college, all with some experience camping, though the trio agreed future groom, Tim, was The Man. Had been back-country hiking with his father since he was six. He was the reason they were camping. The other four wouldn't have minded a golf weekend or quality time at a casino or resort. But for Tim, the woods were his happy place, so into the mountains they'd gone. Fully equipped with packs, tents, sleeping bags, two-burner propane camp stove, cans of beans and franks and yeah, as much beer and Maker's Mark as five fit young men could carry. Which was to say, a lot. But they weren't total idiots. Again, Tim knew his shit and oversaw their packing himself.

They'd hiked seven miles yesterday, looking for the perfect camping spot in one of the deep canyons, near a broad river. Once they found it, they'd unloaded packs, pitched tents, and popped open the first six-pack, leaving the other four to chill in the ice-cold water.

Dusk came fast this time of year. But all was good. They built up a fire, roasted hot dogs, and ate baked beans straight out of the can. Many fart jokes ensued.

More beer, followed by whiskey chasers. How much booze can five young, healthy men drink? Plenty. But no place to be, no cars to drive, no nagging cell phones to answer given the lack of reception.

Just them and the starlit sky. They killed off the first bottle of Maker's Mark, started on the second. Tim sat next to the fire and scratched away on a piece of paper. Working on his wedding vows, writing a letter to his beloved? They teased, but he refused to fess up.

Hour grew late. How late, no one knew, and it hardly mattered. They finally turned in for the night, two men in two tents, Tim, the future groom, in a single shell all by himself. One of his last nights on earth sleeping alone. Should enjoy it while he could, they joked.

Then . . .

A sharp, keening wail. Crashing in the trees around them.

"Grizzly," Neil said now, sitting in the diner.

"Mountain lion," Josh insisted.

Miggy, short for Miguel, crawled out of the booth and vomited some more.

Maybe, maybe not, Nemeth thought. Marge got a mop.

At the camp, the men had burst from their tents, flashlights bobbing, nerves strung tight, trying to pinpoint the source of the disturbance. Build up the fire, Tim demanded. Make noise of their own. Double-check the food stash they'd strung up in the trees away from their campsite.

Which is why it took a few minutes, maybe as long as five or ten, before they realized their party of five had become four. Where the hell was Scott?

Miggy had been sharing his tent and Miggy had no idea.

"No . . . fucking idea," Miggy clarified for Nemeth, in between bouts of dry heaving.

Tim, future groom, got serious. Scott could've wandered off to pee. Scott could've just plain wandered off, drunk and disoriented. But given the cold temps, dangerous terrain and carnivorous local wildlife, they needed to find him.

Arranging their group into two pairs, Tim directed the first duo to start searching north of the campfire, while the other would cover the woods to the south. Whoever found Scott first would blow their emergency signal whistle.

Except they didn't find him. Up and down the water, bushwhacking deeper and deeper into the forest. No Scott. But they did find trampled brush. Broken limbs. Possibly blood.

"Grizzly bear," Neil moaned.

"Mountain lion," Josh ventured.

"Fuck me," Miggy whispered.

That Nemeth agreed with.

Four A.M., the fall air brutally crisp, the clear night relentlessly dark, Tim made the decision: they needed help, and given the total lack of cell reception, hiking back out was the only way to get it. As the most experienced—and sober—member of their party, he grabbed his pack, clicked on his trusty headlamp and set out to civilization.

Neil, Josh, and Miggy huddled around the fire for another three hours, pounding water and working themselves into a terrified frenzy. First glimpse of daylight, they refilled their canteens and hit the trail. Left everything behind. Tents, sleeping bags, food. Young men, fit and now semi-sober, they were on a mission to get the hell out of there as fast as humanly possible.

Still tough going. They half ran, half stumbled their way up and down steep terrain, clambering over boulders, careening through brush, splashing across streams. Till they came to the trailhead and their rented ATVs. All five of them. Shouldn't there be only four?

Which is when they started to get worried about Tim.

ATVs to town. Town to diner. And now . . . help. Nemeth. Sheriff. Cavalry. Hunters with big guns. Any kind of assistance, all kinds of assistance. Help.

First things first, Nemeth unfolded a topographical map. Had the men walk him through their journey. They knew their trail, could guess where along the river they'd camped. Nemeth ran his finger along various geological features, thinking, thinking, thinking. Marge worked the phone, brewed more coffee.

Being a mountain town, they had a local team of fifteen volunteer search and rescuers. Given the circumstances, however, this would be all hands on deck. Neighbors contacted neighbors, people started pouring in, and Nemeth did what he did best: organized the efforts.

First up, hasty team. He wanted his best searchers dispersed along key perimeter areas circling the PLS—Point Last Seen—of their two missing hikers. Fortunately, the same location applied to both missing men, their camp. Working some math—the average distance a person could travel an hour in that terrain—Nemeth drew a massive ring around the site. Hasty teams would hike, ATV, horseback into various points along this ring, then work in toward the epicenter, conducting a down and dirty search of the trail and surrounding areas as they went. Look for the men, but also look for signs of human passage, in case that provided additional data on where Tim the experienced hiker and Scott the drunk buddy could have gone.

Ramsey, a town of four thousand situated at the edge of the Popo Agie Wilderness, was filled with experienced outdoorspeople. The mountains were both a lifestyle and a professional calling. Nemeth was a veteran general working with expert foot soldiers.

Which made it very hard for the family to accept what happened next. The first eight hours of the search turned up Scott, wandering blindly along the rocky banks of the river. Still clad in his long underwear, face covered in scratches, fingernails caked with dirt. Clearly disoriented and shell-shocked.

"Grizzly," Neil whispered.

"Mountain lion," Josh repeated.

"Shit . . ." Miggy moaned.

Even sobered up, Scott couldn't provide any details about where he'd been or what he'd done. He remembered drinking with his buddies around the campfire and teasing Tim for working on his wedding vows. Scott went to bed and . . . Daylight. Cold. So cold. Wandering in nothing but his stockinged feet, till he found his way back to the river and followed it. Eventually, people appeared and a shrill whistle blew and now he was here and hey, where was Tim anyway?

Timothy O'Day. Thirty-three years old, first member of his family to go to college, graduating from Oregon State University with a degree in mechanical engineering. Described by his family and friends as a regular MacGyver. Engaged to be married to Latisha Gibbons, whom he'd met three years ago through his college buddy, Neil. Latisha hailed from Atlanta, worked in marketing and spent her weekends in a state of perpetual motion, hiking, biking, skiing, every bit as crazy as her future husband.

Everyone said they looked beautiful together. The ultimate modern-day L.L.Bean couple. They'd buy a house, adopt a lab, and produce two point two gorgeous dark-haired children to chase along trails, down mountains, across streams.

Theirs was to be a wonderful, magnificent life lived out loud.

Until hours stretched into days stretched into weeks.

Tim's family arrived on site. His father, Martin, driving from Oregon to Wyoming with his mountaineering equipment piled in the back. Martin was a lean, nut-brown professional carpenter and experienced outdoorsman ready to take up the charge. In contrast, Tim's mother,

Patrice, appeared nearly translucent, a pale shadow of a woman. Cancer survivor, the locals learned. Fifteen years ago, multiple bouts, barely made it.

Marge made it her mission to serve the woman coffee above board, and administer a little medicinal assistance on the down low.

Martin conferred with Nemeth, as well as Sheriff Kelley, who'd taken charge of the search efforts. In the beginning, Martin would nod, approve, express his gratitude. By day five, he questioned and stewed. Day seven he headed into the woods himself, snarling under his breath when both Nemeth and Sheriff Kelley tried to hold him back.

The hasty teams stopped being hasty. Search efforts slowed, grew more methodical, no longer hoping for an easy victory, but now settling in to scour the wilderness foot by foot, trail by trail, grid by grid. Choppers scanned with infrared. Air-scenting dogs tracked areas of interest. Couple of psychics called in with hot tips, most involving flowing rivers or dark caves.

More volunteers showed up. The National Guard arrived to assist. Until twenty-three long, arduous, exhausting days later, as the temperatures plummeted and snow blanketed the upper elevations . . .

The searchers faded back into their real lives. The canine teams went home. The choppers were redirected to new missions. And only family and friends remained.

Martin O'Day fought the good fight the longest. He had a lifetime of experience and the advantage of being the one who'd trained his son. He headed back into the mountains, expedition after expedition, while Patrice held press conferences with her future daughter-in-law by her side. Twin advertisements for grief and desperation. The college friends—Neil, Josh, Miggy and Scott—did their best to assist, while having to accommodate the demands of jobs, family, obligations of their own.

Martin O'Day searched for his son. Then he searched for signs of his son. And then, he searched for his son's body.

"Grizzly bear," Neil whispered.

"Mountain lion," Josh argued.

"Goddammit," Miggy said.

As for the real answer, the woods never said. As seasons turned into years and Timothy O'Day became one more missing hiker, vanished without a trace.

*

Here are things most folks don't know: At least sixteen hundred people, if not many times that number, remain missing on national public lands. Hikers, day trippers, children on family camping trips. One moment they are with us, the next they're gone.

There's no national database to track such cases. No centralized training for search and rescue—or, in many cases, even clear jurisdictional lines to identify who's in charge of such operations. There's also little in the way of designated funding. A large-scale search effort can cost upwards of three hundred thousand dollars a day. For many county sheriffs, that's their annual budget.

Meaning when the volunteers go away, so do rescue efforts. Leaving behind a family with little hope and no closure. Most will continue on their own for as long as they can. Some, such as Martin O'Day, continue the hunt every year, assisted by friends, funded by online campaigns and advised by various experts.

According to the article I'm reading in a local paper, Martin's been at it for five years. This August will be his final attempt. His wife Patrice is now dying from the same cancer that tried to kill her before. She wants to see her son one last time. She wants her body to be buried next to his.

I sit in a diner not so dissimilar to the one Tim O'Day's hiking buddies must've rushed into the morning after. I've spent the past twelve hours on a bus, and am now catching my breath, somewhere west of Cheyenne and south of Jackson, Wyoming. I don't particularly know, and I'm enjoying a sense of freedom—life on the road—as I read the article again, then again. Something about the story has sunk into my skin, refusing to let go.

My name is Frankie Elkin and finding missing people is what I do. When the police have given up, when the public no longer remembers, when the media has never bothered to care, I start looking. For no money, no recognition, and most of the time, no help.

I have no professional training. I'm not a former detective or a registered PI or ex-anything special. I'm only me. An average, middle-aged white woman, short on belongings, long on regret. I tried real life once. There was a house, a job, even a man who loved me enough to hold my hand as I fought my way sober.

In the end, the walls closed in, the relentless sameness drowned me. And the man who loved me . . .

One day, a woman in my AA meeting talked about her daughter who'd disappeared and the police's total lack of interest in searching for a young woman with a troubled past. I became intrigued, started asking questions, and the next thing I knew, I'd found the daughter. Unfortunately, the daughter's fucked-up boyfriend chose to blow off her head and abandon her body in a crack house rather than let her go. But it got me going. And despite the fact the case didn't have a happy ending, or maybe because of that, one search became another which became another.

Ten years later, this is now my life. I travel from place to place, armed with only my good intentions. Currently, I've been traveling by bus to Idaho to take up the case of Eugene Santiago, an eight-year-old boy now missing sixteen months. I read about Eugene's disappearance in one of the various online cold-case forums I frequent. Something about his soulful dark eyes, his very serious smile. I don't always know why I choose the cases I do. There are so many of them out there. But I spot a headline, I read an article and then, I just know.

Kind of like now, I think, setting down the local paper. I haven't done a woodland search in forever. Mostly I work small rural communities or dense urban neighborhoods. I gravitate more toward kids than adults, minorities more than Caucasians. But my mission is to help the underserved, and as the families of those sixteen hundred people vanished in public parks will tell you, they are so underserved.

Mostly, I keep thinking of Timothy O'Day's mother, who just wants to be buried next to her son.

Eugene Santiago has been missing for nearly a year and a half. A few more weeks won't make a difference. And while there may be no chance of finding Tim O'Day alive, I know from experience that finally bringing home a body can still make a difference.

I pick up the bus schedule, and plot my new destination.

ONE STEP TOO FAR

COMING JANUARY 2022

PRE-ORDER YOUR COPY NOW

Keep in touch
with
Lisa

WWW.   lisagardner.com

 @lisagardnerbks

 @LisaGardnerbks

ABOUT THE AUTHOR

Lisa Gardner started her writing career aged seventeen. Having caught her hair on fire working in food service, crafting a novel seemed like a safer bet. A mere ten years later she became an overnight success with the publication of her first thriller *The Perfect Husband*.

Now an internationally bestselling author and winner of the International Thriller Writers Award for best suspense novel. Lisa lives in the mountains of New Hampshire with her family.

When not glued to her computer, she can be found hiking in the mountains with her dogs and/or researching new and interesting ways to get away with murder.